# HISTORY'S ANGEL

# HISTORY'S ANGEL

*A novel*

*Anjum Hasan*

BLOOMSBURY

NEW YORK · LONDON · OXFORD · NEW DELHI · SYDNEY

BLOOMSBURY PUBLISHING
Bloomsbury Publishing Inc.
1385 Broadway, New York, NY 10018, USA

BLOOMSBURY, BLOOMSBURY PUBLISHING, and the Diana logo are trademarks of
Bloomsbury Publishing Plc

First published in 2023 in Great Britain
First published in the United States 2023

ISBN: HB: 978-1-63973-040-7; eBook: 978-1-63973-041-4

Library of Congress Cataloging-in-Publication Data is available.

2 4 6 8 10 9 7 5 3 1

Typeset by Integra Software Services Pvt. Ltd.

To find out more about our authors and books visit
www.bloomsbury.com and sign up for our newsletters.

Bloomsbury books may be purchased for business or promotional use.
For information on bulk purchases please contact Macmillan Corporate
and Premium Sales Department at specialmarkets@macmillan.com.

For my father

# ONE

Someone's remembered the living.

Alif turns a corner and sees sliced bread soaked with milk laid out in earthenware platters. Sleek crows swoop down for the offerings, lifting the sodden pieces jerkily as if unsure of their marvellous luck, flapping back when a stray dog comes to lick at the sop, while large red ants march in file, working on the sticky splashes that dot the pavement. The sight of these bowls of food put out under the last summer blossoms of a gulmohar tree for any creature in need makes Alif feel he has been transported to some earlier, reputedly more enlightened, stage of civilisation.

His ruminations are interrupted by a message from his wife.

*U hd promise to cum home erly. Dont eat too much and dont forget.*

She speaks in Hindustani but writes always in this impatiently compressed English.

*All right Tahi,* Alif replies.

*U hv to help me with my asgment on sales strategising, rmber?*

He has forgotten, if he ever knew, what this is all about but he makes, as always, an effort to say something conciliatory, assure her he'll be home right after lunch, his words pointedly spelt out correctly and punctuated right. An unnecessarily decorous reply for she comes back with only a string of those cutesy plastic symbols that have come to stand in for emotion – among them joined palms, a livid red heart, a golden smiley.

He tries to recover the thread of his thoughts. Perhaps this was how it felt to walk the streets in the third or fourth century before the common era, he thinks – even as a vilely large Scorpio honks in his face – when, under the influence of the gentle creeds of Buddhism and Jainism, emperors patronised dispensaries for sick animals or, very much later, during the proud and pompous reign of the leading Mughals, several of whom when not hunting were animal lovers too, commissioning paintings in which the predator and the prey, the lion and the lamb, were often pictured together in metaphorical harmony. And then came the British who, dispensing with such kindly fancies for relations between ruler and ruled, set about administering with the sword and decimating wildlife with the gun.

Alif is something of a historian and if there's one thing to be said about history it's that there's too much of it; he is but a struggling apprentice, trying always to sound the past's unfathomed depths. Every free moment he subjects to a historical test. This is now but how was it back then? Or that was then but how does it matter now?

He has just left the company of the Maharishi, his former teacher at university who, some twenty-five years previously taught him that the past always seems simple from a distance, that we subdue it with stuff like rise and decline, conquest and submission, golden ages and dark ones, but that in fact it is full of inexhaustibly interesting mysteries. Alif drops by to see him once in a while, and today, sitting on worn concrete benches at an outdoor canteen in the university's north campus, drinking over-boiled tea out of paper cups, hearing students tease and chaff each other in a vociferous mix of Hindi and English, the two men occupied themselves with deeper themes. Alif was reflecting on the medieval Delhi Sultanate – an outcome of the eastward expansion of that powerful Muslim caliphate, the Abbasids, a thousand years ago. The hardy, once nomadic Turkish slaves who accompanied these sultans sometimes took over and became, in India, sultans themselves. Their roots, pointed out Maharishi, were in the Central Asian steppes. And almost two millennia before that, from near about those regions, the Aryans arrived, forerunners of today's Hindus. Two eventually different peoples with perhaps a common origin.

Maharishi chuckled and Alif understood the piquancy of what he was getting at – what every historian worth his salt knew.

'Hindus and Muslims,' said the professor, smiling as if these were upstart species that had been spawned but yesterday. 'Forever conjoined and sometimes at war.'

Alif wondered if the conceit was to blame – that imposing idea of a country as a pre-existent something which other people settle, invade, mix into, enrich or impoverish.

'Perhaps if we stopped believing so fanatically in these entities,' he said, 'and came to realise they're practical necessities, not timeless ideals.'

The Maharishi perked up at Alif's donnish tone and asked how his research was going. This research is a putative thing at best; his interests are many and his attention is liable to be diverted. He's started and stopped several projects over the years, unable to find the one he would like to take up to the exclusion of everything else. Even so, something's always compelling him. For the last few months he has been trying to collect his thoughts on what is known as the Delhi Renaissance, those all-too-short decades in the first half of the nineteenth century when the citizens of the city took to the study of modern astronomy, geography and mathematics in the newly opened Delhi College, when fatwas were passed sanctioning Western education provided it did not conflict with religious ideals, when translations were undertaken into Urdu of Western texts, and when, the frictions notwithstanding, Hindus and Muslims in Delhi often saw eye to eye. There was something hopeful about that time of determined self-improvement under the protection of what came to be called the 'English peace' and it has been the subject of Alif's sustained if often haphazard reading.

He told his teacher that what most attracted him was the tenor of that time, that atmosphere of hope, that idiom of progress. Just then a beefy student in a saggy kurta and a militantly neat crew cut, who'd been sitting with his tea quietly to one side, appearing to be lost in idle thought, walked past them and turning to the Maharishi said softly, 'Your time is up.'

He strolled away, empty hands swinging by his side.

Maharishi looked at his watch and then confusedly at the boy's back.

'Did you hear that?' Alif asked.

'He asked me the time but didn't stay to get it.'

'No, he said, *your time is up.*'

'I thought it was "What time is it?" reminding me of the class I have to take.'

Alif looked at the figure who had by then slipped out of the tall gate at the entrance, and he noticed the graceful, knobbed, arrow-shaped finials that topped it, which stirred something in him, a memory of his own cheerfully foolish days drifting about this campus, trying to drink, along with the undrinkable chai, as deeply as he could of the Pierian spring, imagining his future as somehow bound up with this: history's endless byways. But this student, if he was a student – what could he be drinking of?

'Do you think he meant…?' Alif asked hesitantly. The boy had clearly been following their conversation.

'It's happened before,' said Maharishi. 'They never know what time it is.'

He was unperturbed, continued discussing it all – Turks and Aryans, breakaway slave dynasties and over-extended caliphates, Muslim conservatism and Muslim progressivism. Then he took off for his class, a sparse man with thin hair, bus-windshield-shaped spectacles and a much-washed shirt, a sparse man and a modest one, the Maharishi. As he now drifts away from the campus on this raspingly dry July morning, Alif worries that his teacher is becoming a voice in the wilderness. But a voice in the wilderness is still a voice, however feeble.

A man is selling colourful, outsized teddy bears flopped in a row on the pavement, trying to interest passing motorists but not Alif because he is walking and so can't matter. Those hues, not mere pinks and oranges but fuchsia and tangerine, are so shockingly vivid against the air's usual muted murk they look almost malevolent. Alif feels something of a shiver despite his sweating and thinks of Siberia, the Siberia that each of us children of the twentieth century carries an imprint of, that wasteland to which you are ever in danger of being sent not for your sins but because you must be rendered a voice in the wilderness.

His own voice seems sometimes to be dying on him. At school the previous day he has taught a class on countries old and new and that grand mess, that mottled dawn, of 1947, and felt the thirty children of Class Nine consider him with all the large-eyed yearning of the deeply disinterested. Nations, he thinks, and feels again the same doubt he had been trying to get across to his own teacher.

And then he hears a passing girl loudly tell her companion, 'Raat ko mooli ke parathe banaye thay' and a little further down on Malkaganj Road a shopkeeper screams hoarsely from behind his counter at his slouch-shouldered assistant holding a tatty broom in his hand, telling him he is a motherfucker for whom motherfucker is too forgiving a name, and Alif is in Delhi again, a city made so insistently, so noisily, of now. The past is a minor chimera – all that's here is some bread and milk probably gone sour by now in the day's heat and in the face of the day's contingencies. More real than the histories of a thousand kings is that girl's precise voice discussing her cooking of the previous night, certain her flimsy moment in time is the only one there is. She is right, too, except that Alif could never command that tone, throatily fill the morning with it. All he can do is walk and he wants to walk despite the assaults of summer; strolling like this, on this wide street in this part of North Delhi where few are likely to know him, he can be anonymous and, so, himself. Walking, he is just a clean-shaven man with grey at the temples, in new leather shoes and a slightly worn backpack: a middle-class nobody.

He's heading to his parents and cannot walk all the way to Jamia Nagar; he'll have to get on the metro soon. His mother will have cooked and now be pacing through the flat waiting for him, and his father will have, first thing in the morning, fussily purchased choice cuts of meat (and overseen their carving or mincing), the season's plumpest fruit and a box of sweets, while their long-time retainer in his pyjamas loose at the knees – hallmark of kneeling five times a day – will be flicking a duster at the arms of the living-room sofa, laying the dining table, stacking up the scattered books and magazines and sundry papers his father collects — all in honour of Alif's weekly visit.

Tahira is not with him on this filial sojourn. She used to dress for these occasions in her prettiest salwar-kameezes when they were first married, giving off, by the time they reached his parents' gate, a mixed scent of exertion and Charlie that made Alif want to kiss her, his elfish wife, in the newish but already grubby lift up to his parents' fourth floor, and she would not protest as she normally did in the face of these open-air overtures, returning the kisses as if emboldened by the proximity to her in-laws, knowing she would have to effect demureness the minute the door opened. Gradually the cherry satin and pista silk disappeared as did the damp eroticism of the perfume. She'd pull on whatever old thing was at hand and the weekly drive was spent trying to restrain the jack-in-the box Salim who knew from the age of eighteen months what paradisiacal pampering awaited him at his grandparents, what monuments made of crackling jalebis and what sticky visions formed of melting Cadburys bars.

And then, as Tahira started to lose her obligatory shyness, Salim lost his passion for sweetness. They all became more familiar with and less excited by each other, that is to say they became family. In recent years Alif has had to eat his biryani always anxious that his wife and his father might approach rudeness over that burning topic, the only one they ever discuss — Muslims. It's always Muslims they talk about — people who are them but also not them, a body of sufferers out there regarding whose suffering these two have come up with completely different diagnoses. Alif had tried gently putting across to Tahira that she leave his father alone and limit her chatting to his mother, but this attempt, like all others to domesticate his wife, backfired.

Nowadays Alif breathes easier when he's at his parents for Tahira is busy applying herself to an MBA and her weekends are given over to that which makes the world go round, or so say Dale Carnegie and Steven Covey. Business Communication, Financial Accounting, Salesforce Management, Digital Marketing, Social Media Management. Alif spies the headers in passing and marvels at her tenacity. His wife works long hours as a store manager at a

Karol Bagh supermarket and Saturday used to be her weekly day off, the one morning she didn't have to put on her pinstriped trousers, her carefully delineated kajal and discreet lipstick, her eyes not aglint with the foxiness of someone with more to sell than there are people to buy, her features on a break from that mature, that middle-aged attractiveness that can produce in Alif a churn of tremulous awe when she bursts through the front door every evening, tearing off her headscarf, shaking out her long curls, calling on Allah to save her from perfidy.

Three quarters of an hour later, he rings the doorbell and his mother opens promptly, asking as usual, 'And why couldn't Tahira come with you?'

His wife hasn't accompanied him for months but still his mother enquires and Alif replies, 'She's gone for class.' If she were to ask him the same question a little later in the afternoon he might say, 'She's resting, she had a hard week.' He feels no compulsion to present a convincing excuse for he's aware his mother is happier to see him without her and yet unhappy in some way about this happiness.

Alif unzips his backpack and hands his mother yet another of those minor gifts he brings her – this time a set of four glinting knives in four sizes with grass-green handles. Tahira gets such stuff on employee discounts – Chinese-made gewgaws that cost almost nothing and inevitably make Alif consider Marx's theory of surplus labour. What worth the work of human hands when the price of all these teddy bears and tin-openers and T-shirts is unlikely to cover even a day's sustenance for their makers? Nevertheless, he will pick out something, one of Tahira's sad takeaways from consumer heaven, to carry with him.

His mother hands the package to Ahmad – who stands there salaaming unsmilingly at Alif, the eternal duster tucked under his arm – and she asks then about Salim. For him, Alif cannot answer. Their fourteen-year-old is sometimes glad to come along on these visits but at other times, immersed in his labyrinthine laptop, behaves as if he can't be bothered. Alif misses his son's child-hood – the pleasingly inarticulate toddler with something sugary always dribbling from his mouth, or the consistent and consistently

9

cheerful six- or seven-year-old, as against this moody half-adult who never seems to know his own mind. On the other hand, Salim is now able to discourse on things – social media influencers and lifestyle hacks – and just the popular phrases issuing from the son's mouth impress the father, no matter how well he knows these fashions are schlock. The boy's authoritative tone is something to Alif who in his own adolescence was good at nothing except the historical lives over-colourfully portrayed in the *Amar Chitra Katha* comics he collected or Tintin's adventures in various wonderlands.

Alif's father strolls into the living room, smelling of the cigarette he has no doubt been contemplatively smoking on the balcony, and casts an affectionate eye over his son but says nothing, while his mother brings him a bowl of shelled pomegranate from the fridge. Alif must undertake the rituals – wash his face and hands, sit down with his folks, pick at the fruit, report on what has taken place in his life since he saw them last – not much, really – and only then will they speak of themselves. They spend much of their time inside this small flat but, circumscribed as it is, more seems to happen to them than him. Perhaps it is just their gift for narrative, which he lacks. Well into his middle forties and he still does not quite feel at the centre of his story but his parents, despite retire- ment, old age, imperfect health, historical burdens, the bloodiness of the times, continue to be wonderfully full of themselves.

'Imtiaz has three children and a fourth is on the way,' says his mother and it is no use Alif asking who Imtiaz is. Or Sara. Or Zoya. These names are just names that flit in and out of his mother's stories – the women she meets at the local health centre run by a madrasa where she volunteers three times a week.

'Her youngest is sick. She was born sick. And when Imtiaz was pregnant with her, the husband got TB ...' And so on. Alif already knows the outlines of the tragedy but listens to it again only because his mother has the patience to tell it again, and to talk to these stricken girls, try to educate them despite their decrepitude and their diffidence.

'They could have delivered a brood before learning there is something called nutrition. Or be grandmothers before noticing they have wombs,' says his mother.

Alif's father clears his throat and delivers to them without sentiment the statistics. 'One quarter of the world's hungry live in India and more than a third of the country's children are stunted from malnutrition.'

Moved by something – it must be hope – his mother looks astonished at this information.

'God help us,' she says as if she means it and then she goes back to Imtiaz. 'But there is such a charm to her. She will smile even when there is nothing to smile about. Her abaya is always clean though she ploughs through the dust of Batla House to come to the clinic with two of her little ones hanging onto her. She complains about nothing.'

'She ought to be angry,' says Alif suddenly, speaking perhaps in Tahira's voice. 'This goodness of angels will come to naught.'

'Eat up,' says his mother and Alif obediently chomps on a spoonful of the chilled fruit, even if that gentle command is touched with a stab of irony. His father and his mother sometimes treat him like a child, out of love of course, but they also treat him like a man who has not done enough to earn the respect due to a man and is therefore still a child. And so he can do nothing but revert to childlikeness on these occasions – it is better than trying to assert himself and be reminded of his failures, the primary one being his lifelong failure to assert himself.

'If she were angry,' continues his mother, 'her mother-in-law would slit her throat, her husband would have to take sides and the already screaming kids scream louder. She may not have enough to feed her children but she has God-given endurance. I only hope she doesn't die in childbirth this time, she is as thin as my little finger and as easily bent.'

Alif wants to tell his mother that her efforts amount to nothing. Some medicines, some supplements, some advice, some charity – it might incrementally improve Imtiaz's lot but what, really, is her life worth? Why must she live like this at all – denuded by deliveries, knocked around by relatives, cowed down by religion? When will the revolution come, thinks Alif, to free Imtiaz? But he knows not to say the question out loud; he knows revolutions have come and gone and Imtiaz remains.

'Please,' he can't help telling his mother. 'She must be able, first of all, to ask herself — what is it to be human?'

'Death in childbirth...' begins Alif's father but he seems to have forgotten the relevant figures; instead he gets up, switches on the old television set, finds it unresponsive, bangs on it a few times and then returns, seemingly satisfied, to his seat.

So this is you in your time, Alif thinks as he, not without a twinge, studies his parents — Mahtab and Shagufta — sitting side by side on their bulbous sofa, framed by a wall hung with some drawings of them made by their grandchildren — Alif's sister's twins — a gargoyle-like pair with electrified hair, Mahtab with swollen head and pinched body, Shagufta vice versa. Next to it a prayer mat of crimson velvet, which a relative had brought from Mecca and which was deemed too beautiful to pray on and so put on display, but which is now too frayed and faded to pray on, the white minarets and domes of the mosque in its weave turned grey, just like the grey of the wall behind it, just like this whole crowded two-room apartment, about which there is something insistently grey. It was built only a couple of decades ago but is grey. Everything seems to have attracted and then internalised the outside greyness — the sofa has a bottle-green print but looks grey, the glass-walled cabinet on which the dead TV stands is stuffed with the useless, greying remnants of Alif and Samara's childhood: geometry boxes and sticker collections, report cards and illustrated readers, while the grey ceiling fans laboriously churn the grey air, contributing to the greyness. Yet the aged two who sit day after day in this consuming drabness have not yet been done in by it. How has this come to be? Perhaps because they were born in the 1940s and grew up in that other country, the one freedom had birthed, in which every forward step, however faltering, seemed like a victory. He knows that in the early adult lives of both his parents there has been struggle, which makes them sympathetic to Imtiaz.

Shagufta slices a handful of almonds as she continues to cluck over the poor but winsome girl, while Mahtab tries to interest his son in what he's been reading, an article about some bureaucrat or other who took on the corrupt system and is still alive — not yet secretly poisoned or knifed in the dark. This is the only sort

of literature that excites him now that he has left the police –
stories about upright public servants, people who act in keeping
with the original meaning of that word, servants. Alif browses
the magazine; the piece is written, he notices, in the most excitable prose. Then he tries to direct his parents' attention to the
shoes he neglected to take off at the door – two-toned, pointed
Oxfords decorated with shapely arcs of perforated detail. They
are the most expensive shoes he has ever bought in his life and
every few minutes his eyes stray to them in silent admiration.
In buying these he has finally, belatedly, given in to the present
century and its powerful insistence on indulgence. They feel like
an altered destiny; in them he might do something joyfully reck-
less though they're pinching him a little at the moment.

His father acknowledges the shoes with a grunt and Alif gives
them news of his cousin Farouk from whose new shoe shop out
in Vasant Kunj he bought them.

'Business is slow, he said. Not everyone who crowds these malls,
he is discovering, is actually there to buy things. But he was happy.'

'Farouk is always happy,' says his mother complacently.

'There were no customers so we could sit down and talk.
But after ten minutes I felt there was nothing left to say. It's just
Farouk and his shoes. What do I care about which home-grown
companies are making a killing by bringing in European design-
ers and which have fallen by the wayside because they think
Indian tastes are still stuck in the 90s?'

'He is a man of the world,' says Shagufta.

Alif knows that there is in this some criticism aimed at him.
But hers is so slight an innuendo, so mild a rebuke that again it is
almost love. She has long forgiven Alif his lack of what she calls
duniyadari – worldliness – but this does not mean she will not
hint at it whenever she gets the chance.

'I spent too much,' says Alif waving his feet, watching them as
if they're possessed of a life of their own. 'He insisted on giving
me a discount but he's also the one who talked me into buying
this very pair.'

'Farouk is always happy,' repeats his mother and Alif knows this
is a familial trait: Shagufta's easy smile and winning disposition,

her younger sister's tendency to go through life giggling and chortling, and this aunt's son Farouk, with his unkillable optimism. Mahtab's side of the family, all those relatives mostly scattered across various dead-end towns not far from Delhi, are a more sombre lot, and he, the eldest of three siblings, has something of this gravity too. Happiness, he says now, sounding almost poetic, can be bought for the price of a pair of shoes. If Mahtab's nephew Mir were here, he would offer something more profound. Mir is not a poet but in his constant and ardent invocation of poetry, perhaps more than one. He can always produce a couplet or two to animate the theme under discussion.

'The TV's gone,' says Mahtab. 'I've been asking Ahmad to get someone to fix it.'

He speaks with a low-key exactness no matter what he is saying; life is rife with disasters but they tend to be equal in his eyes.

'Can't he fix it himself?' asks Alif. 'He's always handled electrical repairs.'

'Two days ago the picture was jumping and then it became a single line and now the line's gone too. Nothing, just darkness. I had wanted to watch that cooking programme last night.'

Shagufta sniggers. He who has over a lifetime hardly stepped into the kitchen, and would not know what to do with a chopping board or even a tea kettle, now finds entertainment in watching people perfect their tiramisu and bouillabaisse. It is not as if he wants to eat these things or even learn to pronounce their names. No, he just enjoys, when the news gets too much for him, switching to the channels where all suspense and all valour has to do with making an artfully arranged plate of food.

'There's no point expecting anything from Ahmad,' she says. 'These days he does only what he wants, no more, no less. Ask his wife.'

She is beginning to sound testy. Alif knows he ought to behave better, see if he can assist with anything around the house, but he is always made lazy by his parents' solicitousness and besides he's besotted with his shoes which he can't help studying again for their shape and their shimmer. Then he checks his phone but nothing more from Tahira and he tries to hold at bay, because it's difficult to untangle, the thought that he misses her messages when they don't come and finds them onerous when they do. As for Ahmad, he is prone to moods and perhaps going through an extended one at the moment; he is a pained and long-suffering man, a soft-spoken, perpetually doleful man, who looks well past sixty but is just about forty.

Mahtab doesn't answer his wife directly.

'I stepped into a few electronics stores the other day and spoke to a few fellows. But they don't seem to be making this model any more.'

Alif looks at his father, then at the weathered, bulky TV which has sat there probably since the turn of the millennium.

'Of course we don't really need a new one, ours has some years in it yet. But why stop making a perfectly good thing?'

Alif tries to explain the breathless advancement of technology and the capitalist logic of insistent newness, though Tahira would have done it better.

'Son, I understand the world has changed,' says Mahtab. 'But how quickly can we, with our bad knees and our weak hearts, change with it?'

And again he sounds like a poet. It's because of the language, thinks Alif – the Urdu that is his father's tongue, while Alif, who went to an Urdu school till he was ten, dived into English as soon as he encountered it and is still submerged there. But he recognises Urdu all too well: it is the means through which, forget everyday nuisances, even doomsday can be rendered beautiful.

When they move to the table for lunch, Alif murmurs about the excess. The feast being laid out is not his parents' typical fare; they eat plain rice and shorba most days but Shagufta insists on outdoing herself for him. Ahmad serves them, shuffling in and out of the kitchen with the tureens, saying nothing.

Mahtab had once found Ahmad begging outside a neighbourhood mosque, the outstretched palm a part-time cover for a hustler in his late teens, and he'd surprised the boy by proffering some notes instead of the usual coins. Ahmad was emboldened to ask if he could come back home with him. He was open to doing any work gratis if given food and a place to stay. The family took him in and he became an odd, but over the decades indispensable, combination of servant, companion and son.

Alif avoids the man's eye. Ahmad has begun to bore him somewhat – the permanently sad eyes under the white skullcap, the set jaw, the tribulations.

'You eat, Ahmad,' Shagufta tells him as he comes in with a bowl of black jamuns. 'Don't wait for us to finish.'

Ahmad says, 'Since Alif bhai is here I wanted to discuss my future plans.'

Alif is gorging on the food – all those generous cuts of mutton glistening with fat, fragrant mouthfuls of rice, the pile of delicately browned shaami kebabs placed by his mother within easy reach of him, and now this unstoppable greed for the raisin-centred sweets, purple-black like the colour of the fruit from which they take their name. He grew up gawky and it's only in recent years that he has come to feel in his body like a man, the sense of finally tuning in, recognising how much and how little this flesh can do. The sum of it falls short still; with Tahira in bed there's often something left unproven. He would turn up all the stones if he knew which bend of the river to find them in but it's starting to seem a little late in the day.

He pushes away his empty plate for Ahmad to clear and says to him earnestly, 'We must have a long talk one of these days.'

'We will have a talk,' says Ahmad, making no attempt to conceal his mockery. 'One of these days. Some Saturday when Alif bhai has time. But which Saturday will that be? He's such an awfully busy man.'

Shagufta clicks her tongue in irritation and Alif says, 'It's just that Tahira has her exam coming up and needs my help ... and of late Salim has been fooling around with his studies too.'

Ahmad piles up the used dishes on the table as Alif, having quickly popped two jamuns in his mouth, reaches for a third. There will be time enough to deal with this fellow, he thinks. The man is muttering as he returns to the kitchen, the same unsubtle stuff about Alif having no concern for him or even for his own parents.

16

'Of course he's is a busy man,' says Shagufta to Ahmad's back. 'He is a historian.'

She doesn't mind riling Alif herself but if Ahmad makes any moves to she will rise at once to her son's defence. In another age Ahmad's peeve might have been taken for a sign of godliness, reflects Alif. He could well have acquired a reputation as a mystic – not the handful of Sufis whose names are world-famous and sacred to this day but all those many other unnamed local antisocials who once drifted around settlements of Muslims everywhere in the land, pronouncing eccentric truths, living steeped in their own filth and coming across like the dregs of humanity yet able to see into the divided hearts of respectable men. But those divine madmen of old seem to have vanished and this Ahmad is a family chap – his erratic behaviour has a constrained, homebound quality to it. Since his seven-year-old son died the previous year, he's become even surlier.

Mahtab has long stopped eating and now leaves the table. He's spent decades out there, in the world of hard knocks and hard facts, and Alif is still trying to get used to his father's new-fangled cosiness – his interest in cooking shows and the prices of home products. He is rifling through a pile of newspaper cuttings, no doubt eager to share with Alif some other report on some other lotus untouched by the mud of Indian reality – a fearless cop or a single-mindedly efficient councillor.

Alif hurries to join his mother on the divan where she has gone to study videos on her phone featuring the cute antics of her daughter's children or peruse her own set of magazines with reports on the highly public private lives of shiny-faced film-stars or weight-loss regimens she will never follow. He is his mother's son much more than his father's and vaguely discusses Salim's development with her partly because she is keen on her grandson and wants to know, and partly because in this way he can forestall further discussion with his father on these legends of society or, even worse, the politics of the day. Alif, made sanguine by history, rarely bothers with the news. Better to eat and drink, feel lime paste and catechu from the folded paan his mother has handed him searing his tongue or the friendly bite of a new shoe, and think with fierce conviction: *this* is my life.

'You don't have to take Ahmad seriously, he keeps talking his rubbish,' she says after they've finished with Salim. 'And when he's angry he hits Zainab with whatever's at hand. The last time I called he'd thrown a clothes iron at her that was still cooling. He could have seriously burnt her but she managed to get away.'

Alif is revolted. 'Why don't you talk to him?'

'You think I don't? You talk to him. He'll more likely listen to you. Make some time for him. Counsel him. Request him to calm down.'

Alif agrees readily though the thought makes him sleepy.

Shagufta is pleased and then goes away, absorbed again in one of her innumerable daily chores. Mahtab says something; Alif with one of his ears pressed against a cushion on the divan where he is sprawled from the exhaustion of over-eating, can tell from the muffled intonation of his father's voice that he is reading out for his son some lines of vital importance from the scrap he's been saving. Ahmad is washing dishes in the kitchen and something shatters abruptly: a ceramic plate or a glass jug.

But the noise only sends the prostrate man deeper into slumber, his hands clasped before him as if beseeching the world to leave him alone.

*

Alif is telling his class of nine-year-olds about Prithviraj Chauhan, the valorous ruler of Delhi who lost his kingdom eight hundred years ago. But first there was romance. He was a hero, says the poet who recounted his story. He swept into the neighbouring kingdom of Kannauj on his horse and swept away its princess Sanyogita who'd been secretly in love with him from afar. Her father was royally peeved but the couple got away, speedily disappearing into the horizon.

The class would be quite glad to close with this happily ever after. They like the tale, which is what it is – the spirited horse, its dashing rider, the bold and beautiful princess, her displeased parent. But then comes the darker chapter, more bald fact than ballad. A year previously Prithviraj had defeated Mohammad Ghuri, the Afghan who was already in Punjab and greedy for more of India. In 1192, Ghuri returns with a bigger army and it is Prithviraj's turn to be routed, for the friend who had helped him earlier is now none other than his father-in-law; miffed over the stealing of Sanyogita, he will not come to his aid. Delhi falls out of the hands of the Chauhans and into the hands of the Afghans. Over the next twenty years they will rapidly expand from there.

*Sir, why is he called Ghuri? Is it because he rode a ghora? Sir, why did he kill Prithviraj when Prithviraj did not kill him? Sir, what happened to Sanyogita, did she stay at home only? Sir, my sister's name is also Sanyogita but she never stays at home. Sir, can we go to see Afghanistan? Sir, sir, sir...*

He speaks into the eager cacophony of their questions, trying to drive home the difference between history and story. In the poem by Chand Bardai that celebrates Prithviraj, he is captured by the Afghan but manages to put him down with the sure shot of a single arrow. In the textbooks, it is the other way around – the invader trumps the local. Each account must be seen for what it is. And then there are recensions and elucidations, alternative tellings and subsequent retellings, new evidence and changed perspectives – none of which is kiddie fare. Already, now that the storytelling is over, the more listless among them having taken to doodling monsters and fairies, arm-wrestling, braid-yanking, whispering twaddle.

As Alif tries, half-heartedly and therefore ineffectively, to rein them in, he is musing on medieval Kannauj, populated with temples and monasteries till those earlier invaders, the Turks, broke it up and then the Afghans went on to wipe it out. He considers the king of that preceding pack, Mahmud of Ghazni, and the poet he grudgingly patronised, Firdausi, author of that epic in praise of kings, *Shah-Namah*, for whose composition it is said Mahmud paid the poet just a few paltry dinars; this so insulted Firdausi that he went to the hamam and then bought a draught of beer, dividing his kingly fee between the hamam attendant and the beer seller. And then there's Chand Bardai, composer of Prithviraj's story, who in the manner of other subcontinental poets put himself in the narrative even if he was, quite possibly, writing a century or several centuries after the saga being described. In his version of events, it is he, court poet to Prithviraj, who travels to Ghur where the king has been imprisoned by the Afghan and devises a ploy to save him from the ghastly Ghuri. The poet as both creator and character – not unlike Ved Vyasa, progenitor of the Mahabharata as well as begetter of its main characters.

But how to get this across to his students – that kings and battles are not all, are nothing in fact without the imagination in which they survive, by which they are coloured? *Impossible!* Alif wraps up his exposition, tells the class to get their things together, refill their water bottles, form a queue in the corridor. And then to the wordless envy of younger children watching from the open doors of the other classrooms, they climb into the waiting bus and escape school. He herds his flock outdoors now and then, shows them a relic or two, anything they can size up and freely touch, anything to prove to them that history is not a gag he springs on them every day with the connivance of their unenticing schoolbooks.

On the bus the children are frantic with excitement over nothing, while Alif is still lost in his reverie, thinking of that hunger for heroes that defines our vision of history – the past is nothing if not held up by proudly moustached men on horses, god-like men, even as the gods themselves are, given their grace and fallibility and moustaches, men-like. Ram Rajya. What are its hallmarks? Moderns like Gandhi and Tagore imagined it as a state of enlightened self-rule: tamping down one's ego so as to make space for the other, living in the perfect harmony of mutual regard. But that's not how most people see it, even today. We are still desperate for saviours and our stories are still swollen with the exaggerations that make some men impossibly broad-chested and lion-hearted and the rest just men.

Then he rouses himself and calls his wife on her lunch break.

'We're passing by the Supreme Court,' he tells her. 'What would you say to that?'

'I wouldn't want to live there, I'd have to walk hours just to get a potato.'

She tells him about her day so far – the small upsets and minor victories in the mini-empire she helms, one she loves for its order and rules, an exemplary system always in danger of being compromised – a bottle of shampoo in the wrong place, a carton of curd long outdated, a return not entered in the inventory, a cashier dawdling at the till, a cleaner cutting corners. She's a pro at this, she's done it for more than a decade, starting out at the till herself, no whiff of management mania about her then, just a humble bachelor's degree in that – to Alif – much more expansive word, commerce. The everyday commerce of life. Tahira had caught a colleague pilfering and reported it speedily to the store owner, the genially overweight Ghai, who laughingly fired the boy for what turned out to be the long-running theft of perhaps the humblest thing in the establishment, paper bags stuffed with sona masoori rice and masoor daal. Also laughingly, Ghai sahib had promoted Tahira to supervisor as reward and later, when he saw she was more driven than everyone else, ever alert to slip-ups on the part of her colleagues, to general store manager. He's out in Shahdara running a bigger supermarket he started with the profits from this one and Tahira is boss here.

Curiously, it was the promotion that did it: brought on the feeling that she was too good for the place and it was time to move. Alif admires her ambition even if he cannot, given his natural slothfulness, emulate it; he is happy about her rise to the very top of Tip Top supermarket though he does wonder now and then about that disgraced boy and the relatives or friends whose starvation he had for a while, till Tahira put an end to it, mitigated with stolen rice and daal. She never talks about him, instead keeps repeating that she has run out of possibilities for self-advancement in Tip Top; she longs for something fancier, a glittering mall in Greater Kailash or Saket where she can call the shots – or maybe Vasant Kunj, she says, where Farouk is, immersed in the expensive beauty of his shoes.

'People can't even do simple division in their heads any more,' she announces happily and then not so happily tells him the billing software's caught a bug and she's had a futile day so far, chasing technicians. She knows it's only a tiny edge she has over the others – the band of underpaid, semi-educated, gormless girls and boys she lords over, none committed to Tip Top, none really wanting to spend all their years deferring to the sleek and ghee-coloured, the fat and intricately coiffured housewives of Karol Bagh who have made a life out of fussing over the daily shopping.

'We're passing by India Gate,' says Alif.

'Sad waste of space, don't you think? Lakhs of us crammed into Old Delhi and that vast arch leading to nothing and all those lawns of grass where nothing happens when they could be filled with castles in the air.'

She and Alif live in a seventeenth-century, fort-centred town, some bits of it going a couple of centuries further back, a small town within what later became the colossal city of Delhi. It goes by many names – Shahjahanabad, after the emperor who built it; Hazrat Dilli, Delhi the Revered; over time, Old Delhi or Purani Dilli; or simply Fasil Bandh Sheher, the Walled City. Once all the world's cities were walled till the nature of the possible threats against them became more diffuse and could not be withstood by mere bastions; yet this walled city remains even though most of its walls and most of its fourteen gates have gone.

They are hemmed in by Daryaganj. On the river landings south of the fort, boats carrying merchandise up the Yamuna used to be unloaded four or five hundred years ago, and the mart that sprang up alongside in that era when the watercourse was closer by came to be named thus – Daryaganj, the market by the river. Tahira grew up not far from where they live, in a family home almost a hundred years old, while Alif and his family settled in the area when he was fifteen. All these decades later he's still here – in the upper floor of an apartment by the crossroads named after the Mughal military general and poet Bairam Khan, deep in one of Old Delhi's old tangle of lanes. He should have moved out when they married but instead his father sold a pocket of land he had back in the village to buy the place in Jamia Nagar, and the natal family went off to live there. Alif has come to be proud of his insistent immobility. Tahira, mean-while, is fed up of history and starting to dream of dream homes.

'We're passing the Oberoi,' Alif tells his wife.

'I don't know about the Oberoi,' she says, though she has driven past dozens of times. 'I have nothing to do with the Oberoi. What would you say to Faridabad?'

She tells Alif what he has been hearing about for some time now: Gurgaon is too far, South Delhi off limits, Ghaziabad too arriviste for her tastes. Faridabad might have something to offer. Alif agrees at once even though Faridabad means nothing to him; yet another of those words he hears as if from far away. And yet because she has spoken them they acquire something: a womanly resonance, a wifely claim. He tells her this – that he would go and stay with her even on the moon though he is perfectly happy where he is.

'That is what you are,' she says. 'Made useless by your contradictions.'

He laughs it off and she concedes then to laugh with him before that usual quick intake of breath at the minutes gone by, that stress of hers that he can feel burning down the line.

*Sir, my stomach is paining, Azam hit me. Sir, by mistake – the driver braked suddenly and my hand jumped like this. Sir, can I vomit from the window? Sir, Bijoy and Ishrat are sitting together, and boys and girls must not sit together. Sir, I want to change seats and be with my best friend Aakash. Sir, can you give me your phone just once? I must call my mother and tell her about Prithviraj Chauhan. Sir, where are we going?*

Alif ought to be taking them to Qila Lal Kot, the fort of the Chauhans, but there is little of it left to see. 'Humayun's Tomb,' he says.

He explains that Humayun, emperor of Hindustan, is not quite the same thing as local king Prithviraj, that they are jumping a good four hundred years, that Delhi is mostly flat and so everything seems to exist on the same level but actually there are layers and layers: some visible to the naked eye, others apt to be seen by that of the mind should one try.

'Tombs were very dear to the Muslim rulers of this land,' he says once they have spilled out of the bus and he's managed to quieten them down. 'They often had their own tombs built before they died. And they obsessively created lavish tombs in the memory of those they loved.'

'Like the Taj Mahal?' says one bright child, an awkwardly tall girl called Aditi, her braces and glasses giving her a confined look, yet her always lively eyes suggesting she is struggling to break out of all that glass and metal.

Alif is glad; perhaps his history teaching has found its mark after all. The class spontaneously applauds Aditi.

'Remember that what you're going to see was not built in a day nor by a handful of people. Many old-time monuments would take years if not decades to raise. In some cases, the personage would pass away before he could complete what he had started. Purana Qila is an example. And Qutub Minar. What you have here also took its time...'

'Sir, we have not seen Purana Qila. Nor Qutub Minar,' says Afzal firmly, in a manner suggesting that if they have not seen them they don't exist. This pleases Alif too, the boy's confidence in the importance of seeing.

'But history is not only three-dimensional buildings,' Alif cautions as he leads them through the entrance. 'It can also throw up one-dimensional ghosts. You could keep your ears and eyes open for those...' If you weren't so busy bashing each other up, he adds in an undertone to himself.

'What did you say, sir?' asks the ever-alert Aditi.

'Bathrooms. If you need them they're that way.'

They walk through the second, more imposing archway suitably awed and then gasp, as they should, when they see outlined against the stark summer sky and on the far side of the landscaped garden of water, grass and trees, the most beautiful building in all of Delhi – dusky pink, off-white and gold.

Akbar, thinks Alif, addressing the sixteenth-century emperor, son of Humayun, you and your mother made sure we would, even if only for a moment, even despite ourselves, blink before this grandiosity and acknowledge your unremarkable father's existence, this domed extravagance of sandstone and marble, there for no purpose other than to describe beauty. And here again that ancient mix – Central Asian and Indian. It appears to be not merely from another time but a different dimension altogether, out of place in the often smoggy, often small-hearted city. He takes every new batch of middle-schoolers to see the tomb and has not lost the flair yet of himself seeing this old thing afresh.

One child has been straggling and Alif waits for him. Ankit, when he comes through the gateway and is faced with the thing, cries in exaggerated disappointment, 'It's a mosque!'

'Not quite,' says Alif. 'But tombs and mosques often go together. Over on that side is an older, smaller tomb with a mosque beside it. Want to see?'

'But you said we're going to Hanuman's tomb.'

'I said no such thing, Ankit.'

They are walking down a path laid out between perfect squares of hedged-in grass interspersed with runnels of water, still pools and fountains. Alif thinks of the British-made lawns around India Gate that Tahira just dismissed and recalls that the grass here is a later, colonial brainwave. Mughal gardens featured flowerbeds, fruit trees, cypresses and murmuring water; grass was useless in the Indian climate — it drank water and provided neither scent nor shade.

Everywhere visitors are immersed in taking photographs of themselves against the monument, roused by the sight of it to obsessive selfie-clicking rather than deterred by its grandeur.

'Hanuman,' says Ankit obstinately. 'The Hanuman temple.'

Alif stops to look at him but he doesn't appear to be joking. 'I'll take you all to a temple next time. For now, look at this. Perfect symmetry. You understand? If you walk slowly around it, you'd see it's exactly the same from every side.'

But the thing has no effect on the boy — the extraordinary tidiness of the proportions through which they have been brought together, these cusped arches, light-filtering jaalis, soaring canopies.

Alif tries another tack. 'Do you know that other than Humayun a hundred and fifty nobles lie buried here? But not the man who had it built, Akbar. Where do you think he is?'

'You go pray here, sir. But not me.'

He is the chief whip of the distracted and the distracters, those Alif has the hardest time pulling in however delectable the historical nugget he offers.

'What does it matter where you pray and where I pray?' says Alif, trying to keep his voice level. 'I'm just the fellow who comes in to teach you history. That subject you rarely have anything to say about – your hand never goes up in class.' And that's because you have rubbish about temples and mosques filling your empty head, he thinks.

Then he looks at this undeniably charming child, the delicate brown of his skin and the eyes always mobile with mischief, and relents, putting his arm around Ankit's shoulder, 'Chalo beta, there's lots to see here.'

The boy immediately stiffens and pulls away, in his face, Alif is alarmed to see, something like disgust. He flees and then, turning around, makes a short run, shoulders flexing, fist balling, right arm making a complete rotation to sling at the tomb an imaginary hand grenade or cricket ball.

'Get away from me, you idiot,' yells Alif, and Ankit, grinning, takes off to join the others on the plinth, as high as a double-storeyed building, which holds some of the tomb's many crypts. The children absorb the monument, trailing their fingers on the warm sandstone, peering dutifully at the intricate decorations on the ceiling of the high dome, pausing at Humayun's cenotaph, asking questions and not always waiting for answers. *He must have been so fat to need a big fat tomb? Did people come in BMWs to see it or bullock carts? Children went to school in those days and learnt history? Where is the shop to get a Coke?*

Once they are done Alif sits them down on the lawns, looks at their faces flushed from novelty, tiredness and sunshine, and feels a need to tear them away from historic time, give them a glimpse of the eternal. This building, however everlasting it might seem, however celestial its elegance, is not created for eternity because nothing is created for eternity.

He recites to them from memory bits of a poem by Safdar Hashmi. Akbar declares he is the emperor of all the world. It's all his – every blade of grass, every honey bee, every tower and minaret, every wall and door, every chip of stone, every everything. He stumbles on a sadhu asleep on the threshold of his palace and orders him to get off his property. The sadhu asks – who lived here before you? My father, says Akbar. And before your father and grandfather? And before that? And if this whole procession of emperors is gone and if they, like you, ruled the earth and owned it, why didn't they take it with them? In truth, says the sage, this is only a serai in which we, all travellers, pause for a while. *Ya toh duniya sab ki hai, ya nahi kisi ki bhai,* instructs the sadhu. The world either belongs to everyone or is no one's. Akbar is silenced. He understands.

A favoured metaphor with the poets, of course. Omar Khayyam was already on to it: that battered serai, with alternating night and day for a doorway, in which sultan after sultan stayed an hour or two and then went his way.

'The might of emperors,' he says. 'That we acknowledge. But this poem also reminds us that however done-up your tomb, the size of your grave is the same as the next person's. Questions?'

It is only when they are ready to leave, lining up and counting themselves, that Alif notices they are one child short. The students look around, not sure who it is but he realises at once: Ankit. He does not recall seeing him after their little tiff.

'Where is he?' he asks the class but they don't know. The boy has a friend, Utsav, but Utsav is absent today. Did Ankit run away when Alif's face was turned, return to the bus, given his declared disinterest in what he called a mosque? He sends two boys to check, but Ankit isn't there. Alif calls school but he's not back either. He approaches the staff at the ticket counter. A couple emerge from the booth, in chalk-blue uniforms that look unconvincing, the epaulettes slack on their thin shoulders, each with a toy-like walkie-talkie in their hands. The lady surprises Alif by being efficient, asking straightaway where the boy was seen last and what he looks like. Alif scans the faces of his kids and points at a child whose height and features come closest to Ankit's. The couple and Alif fan out to search and the children wait in a huddle on the grass.

Twenty minutes later, they have combed through all of it – the three other, smaller tombs on the grounds, the dusty interiors of the two mosques, the open grounds. They have climbed back onto Humayun's tomb and scanned the whole thirty acres but nowhere spotted a stray nine-year-old in a red checked shirt and dark shorts. Alif rejoins his students with his heart beginning to hammer and his phone ringing with queries from school to which they were expected to return half an hour ago.

'One of the kids has run off somewhere,' Alif tells the principal's secretary, Jha.

The new principal, Mrs Rawat, then phones in person, asks for details, demands to speak to the teacher with Alif and Alif must reluctantly admit that he's on his own; he's been flouting the rules for years because the earlier principal didn't mind, she let him take these liberties.

Rawat keeps asking Alif how he could take off without her permission and unaccompanied. And then Jha comes on the line to echo, viciously, that Principal Madam is very angry, exactly how could Alif have taken off without her permission?

*Please God*, breathes Alif softly to himself.

The children have theories of their own.

*The ghost took him, the one Alif Sir said lives here. He saw Humayun King and he fainted. But there is no such things as ghosts. Ankit no, he hates history, so he just went off home. He went to the mall to play go-karting. But he has no money, he said his father slaps him if he asks. He went into the crypt and died.*

The security folk say they have informed the police who are on their way. 'What happened?' asks the woman whose name tag identifies her as Anita Kumari. 'Did he get into a fight? Children this age sometimes storm off if they're angry.'

'He didn't fight with anyone,' snaps Alif, taking a deep breath and exhaling a prayer. He looks at the tomb – the cold, classical perfection of it – and he is afraid. He can see the back of Ankit's head as he jauntily sprinted off, seemingly unaffected by his scolding. Was I harsh with him? If he has slipped out – onto the busy Mathura Road – and if he keeps asking for the way to Daryaganj he might just land up at school eventually, after a couple of hours of walking. Like Anita Kumari, Alif has known children to walk away in protest, without the faintest sense of direction or destination. A nursery-goer from school once wandered as far as the Red Fort. He was found and returned by a peanut vendor who recognised the uniform. When asked where exactly he'd thought he was going, he said confidently, 'To Delhi.'

Two constables arrive from the nearby Nizamuddin police station. Alif is a policeman's son but he's never been sure of the right manner to adopt with cops, the style that will communicate, without him having to spell it out, that he is blameless as well as, given his parentage, almost one of them. His friendly, perhaps too eager salaam-ailekum is ignored and his thinly disguised panic does not seem to move them. They merely ask for an account of what happened, tell him he is to blame for imagining he can manage alone with so many children in this open a space. He must come to the station with them and file a complaint.

'I can't leave my students, I'm going nowhere till the child is found.'

'Without a complaint we can't help,' says one.

'That's all right, then. I'll manage on my own.'

'But a child has disappeared, we can't let it be. You have to be questioned,' says the other.

'Why don't you help me look for him instead?' Alif asks as calmly as he can.

'The school authorities, the parents, will ask us what we did and if we say we let you off the hook there'll be trouble for us,' says the other cop.

'There wouldn't be trouble for anyone if we just found the boy.'

He looks at the class, emptying the last of the water from their bottles over each other's heads or trying, with bent arms locked over throats, to strangle each other. He herds them to the bus; when he turns back the cops are waiting for him. So he has to go across to the station, sit down with them, answer irrelevant questions, fill in forms, try to recall if there are any Hanuman temples nearby which the child might have sneaked off to. They finally let him go but they don't return to the tomb, instead dismissing him by saying he can report to them if the child isn't found.

Alif rushes back; Anita Kumari is still pacing about with her walkie-talkie and agrees with him about the uselessness of cops. She's the only one concerned; her male colleague returned long ago to the ticket counter to resume the faffing Alif interrupted. She speaks into her device, tells him they're still looking. Alif circles it yet again, all that unrelenting, painstakingly chiselled stone, and tries not to consider the more extreme possibilities. Do kidnappers really hang around on these premises? Has the child walked out and been run over?

He is at the front-facing, western wall of the tomb and almost turning the corner to the southern one when he sees the fellow. He's just standing there in one of those high bays, his body in the shadows of the late afternoon sun, not doing anything in particular.

'Ankit Kumar,' shouts Alif and sees his face is morose and mud-streaked. He runs out from his useless hiding place. Alif resists the temptation to smooth back the hair from his sweaty forehead, hug him in weepy relief.

'Where were you?'

The arched bays – seventeen on every side of the plinth, and one each on the four chamfered corners – have a locked wooden door on ground level that leads to the crypts, and above, much too high to look through, a simple stone lattice. One could not conceal even a pin in this bare space so how have Alif and the others missed him?

'I climbed a tree,' says Ankit, gleeful now. 'I could see you all searching for me. Everyone with serious faces except Afzal. He was laughing even though I was lost.' He had hoisted himself into the leafy branches of one of the large mango trees on the south side where there are fewer visitors and a boy might scramble up a trunk without being noticed.

'Then I came down and hid there. That aunty with her radio walked by so many times but didn't see me!'

He is bubbling with triumph and Alif, having loved him for a moment, almost clasped him to his breast like an overwrought mother, is annoyed with him all over again.

'Do you realise I had to answer to them at the police station. And the principal has done nothing but scold.'

Pushpa Rawat is already somewhat suspicious of Alif and his insistence on dragging historical references into every conversation. And now this. But Ankit is unrepentant; he smirks and says nothing. He has abrasions on his knees and thighs, his water bottle seems to be missing, his shirt hangs outside his shorts.

Alif presents him thus to Anita Kumari, has to prompt Ankit to thank her.

In the auto-rickshaw back he is unusually quiet till he finally squeaks, 'Sir, sir,' and Alif knows from the tone that remorse is brimming over, that he is going to beg him not to tell Rawat or his parents how he absconded, that he is sure to never behave this stupidly again.

Alif prepares to be indulgent; Ankit looks properly chastised, shrunk into a corner of the seat.

'What is it?'

'Are you a dirty Musalla?'

Alif, before he can parse this, finds his hand reaching out to Ankit's ear, the soft and easily mashable ear of a child. He twists it with moderate force while giving Ankit a friendly, enquiring look.

'What did you just say?'

'Don't touch me,' cries the boy, in tears at once. Alif doesn't really want to yank off the worthless ear but continues squashing it to make a point. Then he sees the rickshaw driver leering at him from the rear-view mirror and dancing on a string before it is a little orange-snouted and pinkly muscular Hanuman doll.

'I hate you,' says Ankit, still crying, and what outrages Alif is not this but, crystal clear behind the tears, again, that hint of derisive laughter. He presses his hands between his knees. Beauty be damned, beauty won't save us, he thinks. As the great philosopher said, there is no document of civilisation which is not at the same time a document of barbarism.

*

Ganesh flings his phone on the table in a way that makes Alif suspect he is already fed up of it, though two months ago, when brand new, it so compelled him that he felt it worthy of a human pronoun. She's exactly what I've been waiting for all my life, he'd tenderly proclaimed. As for Alif, he has yet again misplaced his much humbler device and is making do with a specimen Tahira discarded, something from the era, very recent and already prehistoric, when phones were just phones.

'So you hardly go online and you don't know what your son, who's online all the time, might be up to. Do you have any idea what interests a teenager?' asks Ganesh. 'Look in on him once in a while, yaar. Don't neglect your fatherly duties just because you can't tell the difference between a motherboard and an ironing board.'

Alif says, 'Tahira watches him like a hawk, so I don't need to. We just chat.'

'What about?'

Alif clears his throat, sips his drink and chews on a leg of chicken. 'He is teaching me about the world these days. Which start-ups make money. How champion league football is organised. What the South Delhi restaurants cost. I am teaching him about the world as it used to be. Not that I can claim to have succeeded there… yet. He can't see a practical use for history and he is a child of a practical age.'

'Where is he heading, this baccha?' asks Ganesh suspiciously. 'Does he have a girlfriend?'

Alif shrugs because he doesn't really know. 'Wherever he's heading, he doesn't want us to buy him the world or even burn our savings to educate him. He understands money, he says.'

'He's right,' admits Ganesh. 'The way it works now is you do a short-term course online, you get hired for some years. Your skillset gets obsolete. You get fired or downgraded. You study again so as to move up the ladder or switch tracks completely.'

'Tahira knows all about it. Even if I don't.'

His wife is taking classes in some place out in Pitampura whose degree is not cheap but the only one they could afford. Alif tries his best to help with her course work but he is too taken with the fundamentals and only ends up hindering. Uneasy, each time they sit down with her books, at how oblivious they seem of the dark roots of capitalism, he asks the wrong questions which she fends off with gossip about her robotic, if not moronic, lecturers and with pictures she shows him of the glass-and-chrome facade hiding the empty library shelves, the abandoned canteen, the broken toilets. So ponderously silly it would be to say to this, brilliant in her own way, wife: resist becoming a tool of the ruling classes. When *this* is her resistance – sales strategising. So Alif stops, then starts, then gives up altogether.

Meanwhile, Tahira, as soon as she is home, composes herself as if to pray, then opens her homework and starts to whisper a litany of business-like and business-related facts to herself. Sometimes she will break off to actually pray, but hurriedly and without the same intensity. All the same pray she must, if for no other reason than habit, if for no other reason than that her God may just have a hand in the workings of the brave new world in which she so longs to succeed. And she has the history of the religion to back her, for was not the Prophet himself a merchant, and hadn't traders done the work, along with kings and Sufis, of disseminating Islam in this land and, much later, in the nineteenth century, didn't puritan reformists of the religion, some fomenting armed rebellion against the British, rely on the age-old trade networks between India and Central Asia to further their cause even as they bought weapons from European arms-dealers? The business and the faith, the bread and the butter…

'That's the thing,' Ganesh is saying. 'The world changes, you try to change with it. Do you know what the half-life of a skill is today? Max five years. The twenty-five-year-olds in my company know more about all this new shit – ethical hacking – than I will ever do, and in five years they'll be overtaken. As for me…' He looks deep into his glass before taking a draught. 'Do you know how much a single minute of downtime can cost a company?'

He mentions a figure of several thousand dollars which Alif gasps at, then promptly forgets. 'I think our very conception of time has changed,' he says, speaking over the group of Sadar Bazaar businessmen doubling up drunkenly at the next table, their talk peppered with that profuse invective sans which no spirited Hindi male exchange is possible. 'When we were Salim's age the horizon was out there, solid but distant, like that space mission of the 1980s, remember? We, that is the common people then, had little stake in the future. But for a teenager now the future is already here.'

Ganesh shrugs. 'Last week they fired a dozen customer care folks. Why? Because they've got someone to develop a chatbot-based app that can take care of customer queries. The sister-fucking future's here and do you know what it looks like? An hourglass.'

He explains the image. The specialised jobs that earn the most money are at the top. This is where the big thinkers are lodged – those who can design the systems, make the apps, break down the data, crunch the numbers.

'You and I,' he tells Alif, 'and all those others with average skills are in this constricted middle that's getting further squeezed every day. It's a wonder we can still sit here breathing. And down below are the millions of losers who just push the buttons, real or supposed, crank the handles, keep the lines running, the services operational, the mills grinding, the goods delivered.'

Alif is touched that Ganesh has put them in the same neck of the bottle, considering he earns three times Alif's schoolteacher salary.

'Do you think Tahira's clued into this hourglass business? She has dreams of sending the child abroad.'

'No course, however deep, however foreign, can teach you even half of what you need to learn to stay on top. My boss, who knows a thing or two about foresight, says that in a decade from now the ideal employee will not be the one who pulls in the most business. The ideal employee will be a self-learning machine.'

'Tahira…' says Alif, then stops himself, aware he should think for himself and speak for himself, yet unable when it comes to these pressing temporal themes to do either, knowing that he will lose interest well before he is done with the sweating, icy glass of whiskey and soda before him.

'What?'

'I took the children to Humayun's Tomb,' he says. He tries to evoke for Ganesh the astonishment of seeing it, even though he has seen it so many times before. As has, on Alif's insistence, Ganesh.

He listens, then says, 'You know what? That was technology. They're the ones who had it, making impossibly grand things like that. Is this technology, this phone, these apps, this ugly furniture, these buildings, this city? Logon ko chutiya bananey ka tareeqa hai, bas.'

Alif agrees. The Mughals were one up on them. Their monuments are still around hundreds of years on to dazzle but will anything from this time and place survive that long to impress the descendants of today's superfluous men? And *ought* any of this shit to last?

'Someone should come and wipe us out,' suggests Ganesh. Of all the history lessons Alif has given him over the years he tends to remember only the destructive bits: how Alexander overran Persia, how the White Huns knocked down Taxila, the Muslim iconoclasts went on rampage in India, the Mongols destroyed Baghdad, the British wiped out so many landmarks of Old Delhi.

'Of course, there will be pain, there will be horror, but maybe after all that, something nice might happen,' says Ganesh.

Alif himself can despair of Delhi but it is a warm, intimate sort of despair because he doesn't really know of a substitute to it and cannot imagine an improvement on it. He has never lived anywhere else; neither has his friend.

All the same, Ganesh can't stand long-winded laments. It is in the present that he prefers to live, armed to the hilt with lustrous gadgets that he is always in a flurry of replacing with, in salesman-speak, 'latest models'. And there is something in this instrumentalism that has always sobered Alif. He uses it as a measure of the airy nothingness that fills his own head. The more Ganesh hauls him up for understanding little, the more Alif knows that the little he understands amounts to even less. But half an hour and a second peg of whiskey on, Ganesh is less assertive and talking about his father.

'People keep advising me to take him to a doctor but I feel I should take him to Lahore.'

'Does he say anything?' asks Alif, thinking of his own father's moodiness.

'Not to me and not to Mummy either. She has her own theories. That he is going back there in his mind – to Lahore. It's strange. I don't ever remember him talking about childhood and nonsense like that. He said what was necessary to say to keep the wheels turning – and he never spent an extra minute at the gurudwara or even when we visited my uncles. Do your dua salaams, quickly knock your head on the ground, get back to business. And now this silence, it's a daily headache for me trying to imagine what's going on. But she's sure what it is. The names of distant relatives, she tells me, gossip about the neighbours, the pets he had – it's all coming back. And I'll be sitting in the same room, at the same table, but he's not looking at me, and for her he'll only let out a word or two if she keeps at it. He's just not talking to us, he is talking' – he pauses as if this were a realisation that had just dawned on him – 'only to himself.'

'Maybe if he met other people who had the same stories…' says Alif. 'This city… so many people now on their last legs, and all they're doing is thinking. They're the last generation alive with those memories and it's all starting to evaporate…'

As always a vision is forming in his mind; a historical canvas takes shape made of the various ifs and buts, the missed chances and divided loyalties, the pride and intransigence, that led to Partition. To Alif all these decades later it is still a shocking and not yet completely acknowledged sadness. We did it to ourselves, he thinks. For the years that led to the tragedy were also the years that gave us a voice. And what did we demand as soon as we could speak? Separation.

Ganesh is barking down the phone, some work issue that has caused him to scrunch his face and hunch his shoulders, fingers tapping anxiously on the table's edge, one leg thrust out and shivering violently, a picture of unconscious aversion. So this is what they look like, those suffocated by the hourglass, Alif thinks, and tries to straighten his own far from upright posture.

When Ganesh is done trying to sort the problem by seeking to kill the messenger, Alif informs him, 'For the whole first half of the twentieth century we had a chance to turn our back on those who talked in communal terms and we didn't.'

But Ganesh does not, in his own words, give a flying fuck about Partition, even if he is in some ways a product of it, whereas it can still agitate Alif to the point of tears, and he is not sure then if he really is a historian. Historians don't cry.

'Will you come with us if we go to Lahore?'

'Yes, of course,' says Alif promptly, though not entirely sincerely. They often move in these same loops over and around these familiar nodes, the narrow but riveting subject matter of their lives: Ganesh and Alif, as well as Ganesh's parents, Mr and Mrs Khanna, easy-going landlords, they, too, comforting in their predictability – the parathas she never fails to send her tenants on the weekend, complete with homemade butter and home-made pickle, the newspaper the old man comes to borrow some mornings, standing there on their landing to discuss its contents even before he has read it.

Ganesh and Alif were born about the same time and since high school have been in the same building – upstairs and downstairs – and perhaps that is why they can do this now: indulge in sodden repetition a couple of times a month in this packed bar called Bright & Blue where the lights are always blue, the whiskey cheaper than anywhere in nearby Connaught Place, the snacks just about passable.

Mr Khanna has had a grouse with his son. What started as an annoyance was finessed, over the years, into a corrosive acidu-lousness. The rift has its origins in Ganesh's doing nothing about the fact that his wife, Sahana, decamped. She went away in a huff to live with her parents and it's been eight years. Alif is not even sure Ganesh cares any more about why his wife was upset. It had something to do with her wanting to go back to her modelling job. She had represented, pre-marriage, one of those stunning but chaste-looking housewives with the high-necked sari blouse and the airtight bun and the blood-red bindi who urge the usage of powdered masalas and mosquito repellent and bathroom tiles on the watchers of tediously long-running TV soaps. Ganesh's parents were reluctant to let their daughter-in-law be the reason for anyone's interest in any of these things, Ganesh took up position on the fence, and before the matter could be resolved Sahana had stormed out. Ganesh didn't think he was obliged to do anything. She would cool down and come back. But she had cooled down to an unexpected degree and the thaw was still awaited.

Ganesh was insouciant about the separation but had over time developed a certain callousness of character. He'd become impatient with his colleagues, always short with the great army of those who waited on him – shopkeepers, car-washers, maidservants, delivery boys – and abusive towards any fellow motorist who veered too close to him on the battlefield that is Delhi's roads. Women he treated with a strange mix of contempt and want. He appeared to still love his friends, or need them, but his father was really the only person who could move him with his rage and his sorrow.

Mr Khanna blamed his son only incrementally less than he blamed his daughter-in-law, though with the passing years it had become hard to decipher, through his growing silences, where his disappointments had taken him. He would still go, at eighty years of age, to his shop, Classic Touch, on Nai Sarak, open it up and stay there till afternoon though few customers strayed in. That older dress culture of 'suiting and shirting'; the polyester blends in busy prints and the heavy bales of worsted in serious colours – charcoal, navy, olive, tan; the catalogues with side-burned men in daggered collars and short waistcoats and flared trousers – all that paraphernalia that had seemed so indispensable to male elegance when Alif and Ganesh were growing up had in the new century been edged out by readymade clothes and casual dressing. Which meant that Khanna Uncle sat behind the counter largely unoccupied day after day, sorting through his grievances and nursing his woes, or maybe retreating into that twilight where even these things no longer matter.

'It's time you made some move,' says Alif, strange advice from one who believed, above all else, in staying put. He knows Mrs Khanna's arthritis is too severe for her to do anything more than hobble cheerfully around the house, chanting her Gurbani and cooking ghee-drenched meals thrice a day for her husband and son. She'd long ago made peace with the fact that she might not ever see Sahana again, and she wanted Ganesh to remarry. He seemed to acquiesce – divorces are raining down all around us, he would say, and who really cares any more about holding on to one person or making a monument out of one passing pain. But then, like Sahana, he decided to be mulish about the whole thing. He goes out with women now and then through the licentious dating apps but snarls at the mention of love. Yet he still imagines, Alif knows, that Sahana might turn up some day. Through all that bitterness this one innocent hope.

'I'll try and talk to him though he'll resist leaving the shop, even for a week.'

'His assistant should be able to handle things.'

'Yes that Gujral fellow knows better than him the ins and outs of the whole business. He's been there forever. And in any case what's the use of that ancient stock and the dusty shelves and those cockroach-filled, suited-booted, balding dummies and that stupid name. What classic fucking touch? We should really let it go.' This has long been part of Ganesh's plan — to dispense with both old shop and old house, to leave the old town altogether and move to a more respectable address. But sold as he is on this ambition and easy as it is for him to afford it, he does not dare bring it up with his increasingly fragile father.

'It gives Uncle something to do — wake up and get dressed to go there every day, boss over Gujral, attend to customers if they happen to come... I'd say, let him hold on to it.' Alif likes to think of the old man as an uncle even though he is his landlord. And he hopes Ganesh's ambition never comes to pass despite his complaining every day about having to walk a block to his car which is too big to be parked in the narrow lane by their house.

'But you know he's depressed — not talking, barely eating. What if he broke down on the journey? Maybe I should really take him to some dimagh ka doctor first,' says Ganesh, as he orders more alcohol and more meat, and then starts on the unheard of capabilities of the sleekest phone soon to hit the market. 'I know you think you've seen it all before but just take a look at this,' he says, trying to interest Alif in a promotional video.

'Make sure all this stuff you keep buying doesn't become a noose around your neck,' cautions Alif.

'Abey oh Sufi bhai, taana mat maar. We all choose our own nooses. I can curse my work but I still love the money I earn from it,' declares Ganesh loudly, spelling out what he doesn't need to spell out, comforting himself for his crassness or taking comfort in his crassness. And it's true. He likes dressing up every morning in clothes of pristine fashionableness; he likes the embossed smoothness of the visiting card that reiterates he is employed by this or that American company; he likes looking around in the traffic jams on his way to Gurgaon and knowing he comes across as top of the line even if he might fall off that line tomorrow.

The owner of Bright & Blue, ruddy-cheeked and cheery Sardarji, arrives at their table to ask them if all is well. His whiskers look blue in the blue light of the restaurant, like the colour of Mandrake the Magician's hair in the comics Alif adored as a child, and his turban today, as it is on most other days, is of an electrifyingly matching shade, thus completing his embodiment of the restaurant's name.

'The tandoori chicken is fine,' says Alif, in order to point out, obliquely, that it's not always so well done, while Ganesh squeezes the man's hand, jokes with him – because there are none – about the unusually high percentage of women in the bar tonight, asks him where he stashes his black money, and tells him he is the loveliest sardar in all of North Delhi.

'Ab tu bata,' Ganesh says to Alif after Sardarji has guffawed and retreated. He has noticed, finally, a disquiet on Alif's face that even the coloured lights cannot conceal.

'Tell me.'

'I was told off by the new principal.'

'Is she hot? Is she married?'

'One kid wandered off at the tomb and there was some panic but we found him. The news got out so Rawat decided it's my fault. Because I didn't have another teacher with me, because I do these outings on my own.'

He neglects to mention the aftermath – the low charge and the twisted ear. He is trying to wish that part away.

'But you take these kids out regularly. Nothing's ever happened.'

Alif nods. 'I've been in that bloody place for twenty years. What does Pushpa Rawat know? She came just a year ago from some posh school in Shimla but she can't spell the word historical.'

'Stand up to her, yaar. Suppress your brains for once and bring out your muscles.'

'She can't touch me, I've been there too long. But she's starting to divide the staff, I can see that. The younger ones love her because she is full of new schemes: daft stuff about developing classroom etiquette and ramping up parent-teacher meetings. The older ones know things are perfectly fine as they are.'

'Just shut her up. Use your fancy English if you can't raise your voice. You won't raise your voice, that I know.'

'I could, I could,' says Alif nervously. 'If things came to that.'

Ganesh looks at him with undisguised pity and says, 'You're too smart to be in schoolteaching.'

'No, but a good number among my newer colleagues are too stupid to be in schoolteaching.'

Alif has always wanted to teach children. There was no calamity behind it, no stumbling block that sent him hurtling down this particular path, the way his wife often implied, as did his brother-in-law, the bossy paediatrician his sister had married and moved to Kanpur with. His classmates from university thought likewise. His parents were mildly disappointed in him. None of these people had made a dramatic success of their lives, yet schoolteaching was seen as a categorical failure. Only Ganesh could on occasion be sympathetic.

'Not that I am in a field filled with the nation's brains,' he says, and then, suddenly, 'Do you remember Prerna Mittal?'

Alif gulps his whiskey like water and nods slowly.

'She's the only one who used to think me great. I was doing just a little better than her and this convinced her that I was some kind of genius. No one, before or since, has really ever credited me with that kind of intelligence.' Ganesh is silent for some moments and then wistful. 'Feels so long ago, yaar.'

He and Prerna had had a thing for each other in the final year of college, and Ganesh had started taking Alif along to her house in Rajendra Nagar. He was too shy to see her on his own but not so shy as to resist flirting aggressively with her in company, while she was taken by how he always winged it and yet did well; she wanted him to share with her the shortcuts to success.

Prerna's father was in agricultural science – and also a poet. In contrast to the functional living room in Alif's home, Prerna's had shelves of books – novels and essay collections and slim volumes of verse. There were paintings on the walls of bleak cityscapes and contorted sculptures on side tables that appeared to present difficult riddles. On the second or third visit Alif learnt that Prerna had had an easel set up in her room since she was little. She was taking an engineering degree but really wanted to be an artist.

She and Ganesh would sit around satirising their college teachers, falling over with childish laughter, but when she sobered up it was Alif she'd address. He would watch the incessant movement of her lush mouth and want to eat it but ate instead the masses of blubbery pakoras Prerna's mother always made them, after which she'd plant herself in a corner of the room by the squat, toady brown phone, get started with some friend or relative, going on about illnesses unapparent in her face or movements, these rambling calls obviously her way of keeping an eye on her daughter.

On one of these visits Prerna happened to be alone at home. She and Ganesh were joking about college as usual, teasing each other about the crushes – real or made up – the other had on various classmates. Prerna attacked him in protest every time he brought up a new name to link with hers, pummelling his arms and chest and he, in turn, started tugging playfully at her chunni.

'Get this man out of my house,' she ordered Alif breathlessly. She turned to him when he didn't reply, broke off to get him a Hindi magazine, its pages open to a couple of poems with short lines. *Khule gagan ki chhat, dar darwaaze zameen ke, kabhi gunguta lehron ke sung, kabhi aankhein vrashti se nam: ek mazdoor.* He tried to make sense of the images, something about the son of the soil with the sky for his roof and so on, but the sentiment, like the art in the room, like the girl before him, like his own emotions lately, confused him.

His two friends had, meanwhile, decided to arm wrestle each other and when Prerna proved the easy victor, Ganesh slapped her face so hard the sound sliced through the room. Holding her cheek, Prerna sat cowed, her neck sunk low, body turned away. Ganesh apologised, declared he was an asshole, that he didn't expect to lose to her, and she still said nothing, so he moved closer, tried to soothe the livid skin with his fingers. Dramatically, her face transforming instantly from tearful woundedness to manic joy, she pulled hard at Ganesh's hand and bit so she drew a maroon trickle.

Alif just sat there watching this ridiculous scene, unable to move or speak, his mouth dry, feeling detached from himself, somehow inside their bodies rather than his own, his whole being vibrating to a tune he had never heard before, a crude thrashing rhythm, the new sound of blood inflamed by desire. He tried to look away, focus again on the magazine in his hand, the poems whose author, he realised, was Mr Mittal, the decor in the room, the sheer curtain at the door behind which Prerna's mother might reappear at any moment.

Ganesh sucked at the wound and appealed to Alif, as Prerna, hysterical, giggling, took up a seat in the furthrest corner of the room. Just hold her down, will you, he said with feral roughness and Alif swore at his friend so Ganesh did it himself, yanking at her hair so hard she screamed. Alif tore himself away, buying a packet of cigarettes from a paanwari at the corner and smoking as he walked for more than an hour, all the way to Daryaganj – angry, embarrassed, unfulfilled. He never saw her again and he knew from what Ganesh did not say later, because he was reluctant forever afterwards to talk about her, what happened in that room. Alif has spent years trying to imagine the exact proportions of fear and excitement in Prerna in the face of the animal her goofy friend had become, the exact moment at which she went from teenage adoration to womanly shame. He shared her secret and that made him, because he could not have her, hang on to the next best thing: Ganesh. They were all three somehow joined sordidly in this – Ganesh's numb indifference, Alif's day-dreaming, her disappearance.

And now, Ganesh says, a good two decades down, he had in a bored moment sought her out on Facebook and she'd responded. She was married, two kids, had worked in a construction company, currently stayed at home. Ganesh suggested they meet and she had agreed.

'Marvellous, no?' says Ganesh laughing. 'If she wants to see me, how can I deny myself the pleasure?'

'What, exactly, is the point?' Alif asks, addressing his surprisingly already empty glass.

He does not want to think of that afternoon, has almost succeeded in blanking it out, and can no longer relive the hunger that made him yearn, over painful months, for Prerna Mittal. He could see that Ganesh was worried for a short while, maybe anticipating an angry phone call, men from her family at their door, even a police complaint. But she had dropped out of his life. So why meet him now, wonders Alif. Murky possibilities start to take shape in the dim blue light of the bar.

'She's a friend of mine. I want to see how she's turned out all these years on,' says Ganesh to Alif's question.

And what do I want, thinks Alif. The couple of whiskeys have sharpened his self-awareness, clarified him to himself as they always do. *Nothing.* Happiness, at this point in his life, means status quo. But he knows the laws of history and how they ensure only one thing, change. He shuts his eyes, a spontaneous prayer on his lips, but he's not sure what he should be pleading for – his own small life to remain untouched by the larger shadiness or the world to redeem itself even if this means some definite action on his part, a clear stepping out of line.

'Ganesh,' he says, wanting to stamp out the image of Prerna. 'Forget that. You have to get Sahana back.'

'Every second week we sit here and we drink and after drinking you drift back every time to the same gandu idea.'

Alif does often counter Ganesh's bellyaching about Sahana by saying he'd be better served by calling her and trying to make amends. He has never idealised marriage and knows his own is far from perfect but he cannot think what or who might tame Ganesh except his wife. And today his suggestion has more urgency; he must lead his friend away from Prerna and this irresponsible dredging up of the past.

'That's because you've become a gandu and only she can save you.'

'She should be the one...' mutters Ganesh.

'Give up that petty line. Call her. Call her now.'

They look at each other and then at the sleek rectangle of the phone on the damp table between them, and as Alif steps out for a smoke, Ganesh shakes his head and picks her up.

TWO

Alif is back to his half-attentive rows of Class Four, dulled by the midday heat and the inexorability of history. The walls are bare except for a faded conviction from Tagore in a child's shaky cursive on pink chart paper: *The highest education is that which does not merely give us information but makes our life in harmony with all existence.* Other than that just two blurred fans, hairy black with dust, and two small barred windows looking down on the empty yard.

It seems like a long time ago that Prithviraj Chauhan flew away on his snowy steed with the ecstatic Sanyogita. There is another horse rider charging out of the horizon now, and she is being pursued by an army of typically driven Englishmen. Queen of a small kingdom called Jhansi, which the Brits laid claim to four years previously, she is now bent on wresting it back from them. Lakshmi Bai, the Rani of Jhansi, is only one of the several hundred warriors joined in sudden and ferocious battle, and she will go down fighting. But she is young, does not seem afraid, and her battle cry is freedom and not just the restoration of Jhansi.

'Sir, can we go now and see her tomb?' asks Afzal.

Alif starts to explain about burial grounds and funeral pyres, tombs and samadhis, how the gallant, sword-bearing queen died a soldier's death and, according to the storytellers if not the historians, an ascetic hurriedly cremated her so the English wouldn't get to her body.

'Ankit broke my elbow,' squeals a girl.

Once he has established that the elbow in question has been pinched rather than snapped, Alif wearily faces his back-row bête noire again.

'Good afternoon, Ankit. How are you today?'

The boy appears triumphant, perhaps glad that his wilful disappearance the other day put his teacher in more than a spot of trouble. Alif feels his annoyance rising, then remembers the devilish look in the boy's face when he mishandled him, and he makes sure to be polite.

'The Rani of Jhansi, Ankit. A war, Ankit, a nineteenth-century war that was fought in Delhi and in towns not far from here. There is a memorial to the fighters nearby. Want to go and see it?'

'No,' says Ankit without rising from his seat which he must, as per the new principal's new rules, when addressing a teacher. 'Sir,' he adds grumpily.

Alif is stumped and a gentle babble rises from the class.

'All right, forget her for the moment. Go back to last week's class. What did we discuss?'

'Europeans,' says someone.

'Vasco da Gama came on a ship,' pipes up a bright spark.

'It's Ankit I'm asking.'

'No, it was Alexander the Great with his army,' says another voice.

'I don't know, sir, I wasn't listening,' says Ankit and Alif sees that his suspicion is not unfounded, the boy has acquired a new impudence, more brazen than his previous.

'Give me a name. Or one date. Anything at all.'

'That foreign uncle, East India Company, sir,' comes the answer from elsewhere, 'who came to visit the Great Mughal.'

'Ankit, stand up,' says Alif icily, and his voice passes like a tremor through the restless bodies of his students and stills them. They are waiting for him now, all aware that Ankit has committed some special wrong and they find themselves guilty by extension, just in the way that if one child breaks into giggles, the whole class will catch on to it, and if one child wants to go to the toilet then this will produce a sudden epidemic of swollen bladders. But if they behave like a herd, Alif also knows that they're not all alike, that the quick mind behind Aditi's myopic squint has little in common with Ankit's thick-headedness, or that Afzal and Dilip may be friends and yet one has perspective, can put the Rani of Jhansi against Humayun and see what emerges, while the other is utterly immune to connections historical or otherwise, starts each day on a clean slate, succumbing all over again to the juvenile junk food and the puerile computer games that make him overweight and dull. If Alif loves these kids it is because he knows they are, with their flashes of distinctiveness, not just kids.

'Ankit,' he says, trying again to be kinder. 'Leave last week. Let's return to the Mughals. Or the Mahabharata. Or the mummies of ancient Egypt. Anything! Open your mouth and give us a sentence on the subject of history.'

The class looks to him and the leer is slowly effaced.

'It's all...' he starts reluctantly.

Alif stares at him blankly.

'It's all...'

Alif raises his eyebrows. Ankit's expression is verging on troubled and his classmates are beginning to titter. They see now that Alif is affecting a mock horror, more sarcasm than anger.

'It's all lies,' whimpers Ankit.

'What is?' asks Alif.

'My father said Musalmans lie. They go on haj every year but they never open the doors to the Ka'bah, why?'

'But the Ka'bah is just an empty cube, child.'

'They never open the doors because inside is actually a Hanuman temple.'

A great laugh rises in Alif but the child is defiant again and then the adult is, for a moment, afraid. He has remembered the idols they once worshipped there, those old precursors of the Muslims, and a cold thought grips him: whatever might happen if they came back to life? Ankit can't know this but there is something Ankit does seem to know.

'What are you talking...' he starts, then seeing that the class can't follow the debate, just gives up, shaking his head. 'Okay, so I'm a liar, then. We're all liars. That's the only thing you can come up with? Is that *all*?' And now he is infuriated again and no longer cares to sound reasonable. 'Go ask your father that.'

'My father said he will put a complaint to the principal that you boxed my ears,' blurts Ankit. The class looks to Alif for a reaction to this allegation. He turns his back to them and starts scribbling on the blackboard the names of the leading participants of the 1857 War of Independence. He remembers Ankit's hateful words, the obviously adult bile he was repeating, and he dreads having to deal with the loathsome dad.

'You were going to murder me,' wails Ankit but Alif keeps writing.

*What came over me?* He's never laid a hand on anyone before. As a child he formed his letters beautifully and rarely tried to get the better of his teachers, thus avoiding the common fate at the slovenly Urdu school, which was to have the wooden ruler come down forcefully on one's outstretched palm, and to become smilingly hardened to it the harder it came down. When he was a little older, his father moved him out to an English institution where teachers did not cane students, though bruises and blood came with factions the boys formed and broke up. Alif managed to remain oblivious to it; he had discovered anthologies of historical fiction in the library and would have the hardbacks wedged between his knees during lessons, responding to class war by keeping his head down. As an adult he has gone out of his way to ignore provocations, to cross the road when a fight is brewing, to smile wanly or shrug dismissively when an insult is meted out, and to most definitely try and avoid crossing Tahira. And so his is, incredibly, a whole four-decade-plus life spent in Delhi without stepping on anyone's toes, or not stepping hard enough to be treated to much more than a screaming 'maderchod' or a jeering 'ulloo ke pathey' or an almost affectionate 'abey gadhey'.

And now he has hurt a child. He wants to somehow get across to Ankit, and the rest of the class, that he didn't really mean it but he finds, at the same time, that it's a struggle to maintain sympathy. He's taking it personally, these insults to religion and history; he wonders if religion and history will repay him for his efforts and if so what form the recompense might take. Or is it just that he's a poor fool unable to keep even a nine-year-old punk in line and history has nothing to do with it whatsoever?

He'd never have made a college lecturer but is schoolteaching proving beyond him too?

'If your father has all the truths then he can come here and take over the class, tell him that.'

He is trying what's not a habit with him, brusqueness, and that usually shuts up a child but again, glancing at Ankit, the unsettling feeling that the contest is equal: not student and pupil but man to man. The barb doesn't even nick him, he's lapsed back into sullenness, and Alif lets him be as he returns to the gruesome fallout of that doomed war and the sad fate of the last emperor of the realm, whose palace is just around the corner. He tries evoking the grandeur of the thing for them and promises them a trip soon to its modern and much-reduced version. But he no longer has even that precious half of their interest; they are clearly dying to get to the bottom of what happened for they know corporal punishment is a no-no.

After the class, Alif throws himself in his corner of the staffroom, his battered wicker armchair wedged between the water dispenser and an open shelf crammed with props, curtains and decorations used in the school's most recent play; the printed backdrop was for some reason later installed on a wall here so that teachers must now face daily the exhortation to *Pledge together for a New India – Clean India, Poverty Free India, Corruption Free India, Terrorism Free India, Communalism Free India, Casteism Free India.* There seems to be nothing they've missed – except ordinary decency.

*Shoes*, he is thinking. His own are hurting him and in fact it was something of a trial to get out in them today though he's still adamant that this is a small price to pay for style. But it's what the Rani of Jhansi's brought to mind – shoes. An old account he once read by an English writer who went to see her some years before the war; she wanted him to intercede on her behalf with the usurpers of her kingdom. She had never received a European before and the court had just one request: could he please take his shoes off before admittance. The writer was in a quandary; he had refused to see the emperor of India because of this shoe business. He can keep his hat on, he is told, but *that*, he explains to his hosts, is rude in civilised European society.

Relenting eventually, he is let in, and in stockinged feet, with hat on, which is a pain because the punkah cannot cool his temples, he converses for several hours with the queen from one side of the purdah separating them.

The meeting had no momentous outcome and yet it makes Alif breathe easier. A tiny interchange, a gesture of civility on one side, a polite request for an exception on the other. Not the sort of stuff of which history is made and yet the sort of stuff which complicates history and makes it interesting. The Maharishi's insistence on the necessary strangeness of the past has for Alif tended to take the form of this – a weakness for that enlivening anecdote or detail which can lead to no thesis, fill out no book, and which yet makes the centuries accessible, human, bearable.

Lost in these thoughts, Alif pays no attention to the peon Ramu, the tubercular and always cheery old Ramu who knows well each teacher's personality and preferences and has promptly brought Alif his cup of coffee. He loves to buttonhole Alif because Alif is the only person who will lend him half an ear, allow him to tell his side of the story, for he has been here for ages too – he, too, has seen empires rise and fall if only within the narrow confines of this school.

Alif likewise, after a lukewarm hello, ignores the couple of younger colleagues who are gossiping about their day while marking notebooks. To them Alif is one of the ancients. They are blithe women, full of a half-baked zeal about Education rather than an interest in education, easy for Rawat to co-opt. They are still recovering from an encounter the previous week with a giraffe-tall former beauty queen and an apparently world-famous dancer, both ex-students come to inaugurate the school's Sports Day and hand out aphorisms about healthy minds in healthy bodies. He could hardly turn to these teachers and say he does not know what to do with Ankit. Miss Moloy – ageing and experienced, talkative and frank, explainer of the most difficult maths problems to the most recalcitrant child, speaker of the most orotund English sentences – is his only remaining friend among the staff but she's on holiday.

As he's downing his coffee, trying to work up energy to go across to the principal, tell her Ankit needs to be tackled, Ramu looks in again to inform Alif that Mrs Rawat herself wants to see him at once. Her smile when he enters her office is patently false and short-lived. Alif is obliged to smile back.

She hems and haws to begin with – inviting Alif to share her joy at the success of Sports Day and her excitement at what's up next – the once annual but now biannual play. Following from her project of bringing on a new India, Rawat has discovered another field that urgently requires her attention – the degraded environment. She is gearing up for an extravaganza on the theme of devastated nature and on every wall of her office are posters featuring glaringly over-exposed photos and large-fonted legends: *Nature's Fury*, *Why Man Should Revere Nature*, *Musings in the Lap of Nature*, and *Nature Never Did Betray the One Who Loved Her*.

Alif makes polite noises while taking it all in, glancing too at the glitter on her fingernails and wondering if the lady herself has ever really dirtied her hands with nature. Mrs Rawat asks if he would like to help with one particular segment of the play: teaching the chorus a Sanskrit song about nature's maternal qualities. Him being a historian and all that, he should be able to dig out the appropriately Vedic-sounding verses. Alif apologises at once, says he cannot sing and knows no songs.

'Please don't joke, Alif Sir,' she says. 'We are depending on you.' And then she gives him a breakdown of the planned performance, the bandits dressed in black who will represent the evil excess of carbon we produce that has messed up the ozone layer, and the angels dressed in white to stand in for all the innocent ice-caps that are melting because of our wrongdoings. And so on.

'Sounds nice,' says Alif, trying to make his voice sound, if not nice, then at least neutral. 'And before I forget, wanted to let you know that Ankit of Class Four-C –'

She interrupts him swiftly. 'Ankit came in just now, crying. He must have said something very, very naughty for you to scold him yet again?'

So he's beaten him to it! Alif looks at her square, heavily powdered face, the lips painted a sticky maroon, and he wonders if he will ever be able to penetrate this armour and have a genuine conversation with her. He misses Mrs Pant, a rational woman free of make-up who had occupied this chair when Alif joined the school and been ensconced in it for many years prior too, directing the development of this little place, extending the buildings, enriching the facilities, urging on the students, fraternising with the teachers, but doing it all with a certain good-natured unobtrusiveness. She would have left it to Alif and Ankit to sort out their minor altercation and got on with more important things. But this new lady makes everything her business so Alif has to describe the exchange in the classroom and the child's implicit belief that history is bunk. She's not impressed, and her question to Alif is probably only in order to make a show of fairness and disguise the fact that she's actually on the other side – the side of the doubters of history.

'Mr Alif Mohammad,' she says. She has been fiddling with her keyboard and now gives him a stern look. 'What exactly happened at Humayun's Tomb? All we knew is that you put the children in danger by taking them out on your own, that one child disappeared and we had to keep everyone calm till he was found. But now I hear Ankit was lost because you insulted his Hanuman, left him behind and went around with the others. And then on the way back you attacked him, threatened to throw him out of the rickshaw...'

The facts are fast losing their relevance. Alif explains how the kid deliberately mistook the tomb for a mosque, how he decided to dislike it without really even looking at it, and then ran away and hid himself.

'I pulled his ear, I admit,' he says. 'Shouldn't have done that,' he adds with a weak smile. 'Won't happen again.'

'And you threatened to kill him, sir?'

'Of course not, no such thing.'

'It's against the rules in this school, sir. Touching a child.'

Alif wishes she would cut out that condescending 'sir'. He does not want to repeat what Ankit said to him, he just cannot bring this into every discussion, this damned disjunction: Hindu–Muslim, Muslim–Hindu. All that matters is explaining the child's corruption and owning up to his mistake.

'He was harassing me,' says Alif. 'Then he took off to spite me and I had to deal with the cops who also harassed me. Harassment, you see.'

'And why could you not discuss this with me? Instead of creating trauma in him? I had to send him to the sick room to lie down. He's a tough kid, a sportsman. Not one to break down so easily. Children need to be handled with care, you know, sir.'

*Chup bey*, Alif thinks with sudden vehemence, but he's not about to say it out loud. He never messes with authority, however annoying the colour of their nail polish.

'Yes, of course. But Ankit is blasphemous. He condemns history. That's the only serious thing that happened. It's his father who's behind it.'

'You are into history and so on but I have heard that you don't teach it in the proper way. One day you are telling the children about Gandhi-Nehru, the next day you have jumped to Harappa-Mohenjo-daro, third day you are onto Golconda-Bijapur. What is this system? Why don't you follow the order of the textbook? You are confusing them.'

'I want to surprise them. Pulling things out of the pages of history, showing it to them not as something that had to happen but... contingent. Do you know, madam, when an event becomes historical, by which I mean of historical value? When we are able to remind ourselves of its *unexpectedness*.' He all but knocks on the table for emphasis. 'The usual way of teaching history – cramming their tender heads with dates and chronologies and processions of facts – won't do. Why try and get them to remember things if you can't first teach them why those things matter?'

He waits for her to ask the inevitable question, why do they matter? but she sighs, pretending to be weary of such nuances.

'And when the exams come? They don't seem to be doing any better than kids from other schools only because their teacher is jumbling up the whole story.'

'I would like them to see that India is not any one thing, with any one obvious destiny.'

'India?' asks Mrs Rawat, with the sudden alertness of one who counts herself among the nation's guardians.

Alif nods vigorously. 'All these millennia of cross-connections, all these cultures and religions mingling...'

'I do not think, sir, that you should bring religion into this school.'

Alif is stunned.

'Where you took them the other day is a...'

Just a silly tomb, he wants to cry. 'That is a grand piece of architectural history. I would not reduce it to the religion of those who built it.'

'They are children,' she insists, fake smile back in place. 'And to children the only thing that matters, in my view, is a positive message. Who are the heroes from our past? Can we please turn the spotlight on them? Why do you think I am always planning these activities to teach them about the country's greatness — our leaders, our languages, our festivals, our environmental resources?' She gestures at the posters illustrating nature's wrath and nature's bounty.

Alif tries to think of a positive message, cannot come up with one.

'You understand?'

'I'd like to take them to Red Fort next month — we've just read about 1857. And Class Seven must see Raj Ghat or they will scarce believe that such a one as Gandhi ever in flesh and blood walked upon this earth. I called Miss Moloy last night. She said she'd be glad to go with us when she's back.'

'No sir, no sir,' says Mrs Rawat. 'No more of that. Ankit says his father wants to pull him out and put him in a better school because of your so very violent behaviour. And think of what will happen then to the name of our institution? I must call this man and pacify him, ask him to forgive us, tell him that we have cancelled all these outings forever.'

'But madam, but madam, what about the heroes of our history...?'

She holds up one warning finger. 'Concentrate on the text.'

All the scores of arguments he can think of for why a past made of just words will bore his students to death die in his mouth in the face of this threatening figure, a parent on the verge of ruining a school's reputation. Alif can do nothing but briskly nod acceptance and beat a quick retreat. As he stands in the lobby, unsure, a random insight passes through his head and cheers him even though it would have had no effect on Rawat or on anyone else he knows. Prithviraj and Shah Jahan mean more or less the same thing...

He is done with teaching for the day but no staff are permitted to leave until school's out. Alif looks at the open doors on the far side of the lobby and then at the hefty black newly installed gizmo on one wall – a biometric machine to track the teachers' goings and comings. There is no one around and he takes his chance, ignoring the thing. Passing by the sentry box at the end of the driveway, he must explain to the ever nosy guard that his wife has suddenly taken ill.

He walks to the Chandni Chowk metro station and when he gets to Nehru Place takes the elevator to one of the ritzy new cafes. It is full of moneyed kids eating red velvets and blueberry muffins whom he cannot help staring at as he tries to make sense of the menu: the languorous beauty of the girls, their thigh- and cleavage-disclosing summer dresses, their thin bodies so impressively uniform, like a collection of buffed mannequins supine on the couches, trying to impress their egos on each other when they are all really one ego, one voice, one desire barely concealed by slinky cotton. The boys are all too tall and have stylised beards, toadstool haircuts, gruff accents, broad shoulders, skinny-fit trousers, and Alif writes them off, the South Delhi brats, the Daddy's boys.

He tries to follow the chatter.

*Meri cousin bhi London mein dentist hai.*

*Fuck that fucking baseball game was so fucking lit.*

*Abu Dhabi kithe hai?*

*Shaadi hui nahi, divorce pehle.*

He has never been here before; he doesn't really care for these glittering mirages unless Tahira insists. With Ganesh it is Bright & Blue or one of the grubby eateries in their own mohalla if they want their fill of hot rotis and kebabs. But Ganesh has fixed on this place today because he wants to impress Prerna Mittal. The other night in the bar he had picked up his phone and called not his estranged wife, as Alif was urging him to do, but Prerna. He'd told her that both of them – Alif and he – could not wait to see her.

'Why me?' demanded Alif, trying to be heard in the increasingly shouty 10 p.m. atmosphere of the bar after Ganesh hung up.

'What's the harm in having a coffee?' asked Ganesh lazily. 'She seems to have a lot of time.' But Alif didn't really trust the person Ganesh became around a woman. He was avaricious for females but also always eager to prove their dispensability.

Alif hopes the meeting will be as superficial as possible, that they will marvel over overpriced coffee at the changes time has wrought, and then go their separate ways, Ganesh's curiosity sated. Or perhaps she has a score to settle. She'll arrive smiling and mislead them with her friendliness, after which a gallery of men will slowly, Hindi-movie style, reveal themselves and threateningly encircle the two friends – one guilty and the other just slightly less so. From there the script can only play out in one direction but Alif imagines the denouement as a farce.

He has no idea how to face this long-forgotten woman. How much of the past does she want to consider? Should he try to atone? Should he affect amnesia? Should he say nothing just like that distant day when he said nothing and vanished from the scene. He continues studying the needlessly elaborate menu – he still has twenty minutes to kill – and tries to take stock of his own development. Has he changed at all from the boy who followed Ganesh to Rajendra Nagar and who is still hanging on to Ganesh? He thinks of character, that always elusive goal which, one comes to realise by middle-age, cannot be a goal at all because one has it or one doesn't. Putting himself against Firdausi who laughed at the sultan for his paltry fee, and Prithviraj Chauhan who daringly made off with a woman, and Rani of Jhansi who held out so staunchly against the stronger foe, Alif can't help feeling that he lacks character.

And yet however many times since that afternoon he has pictured himself backing away from her door, smoking, shivering, sick with desire, he cannot see himself acting in any other way.

★

Alif is deep into his self-examination when his phone rings. He sees the name 'Abba' and braces himself for a report on the accomplishments of yet another real-life superhero or on the doings of Alif's niece and nephew, now seven, whose exploits their grandparents take a keen interest in from a distance.

'School done?' asks Mahtab.

'About to leave,' mumbles Alif, glancing at his watch. His father, with a cop's precision, has given him fifteen minutes and called at the dot of a quarter to three.

'Would you have the time to go with me to Mehrauli?'

'Not just this instant, but…'

'I could go on my own, of course.' His way of saying, I wouldn't mind if you came with me.

'Is Phuphi all right?' asks Alif.

'That's just what it is. She isn't.'

Mahtab's sister, Amina, lives in Mehrauli and has been unwell. Mahtab gives his son the details, which are sketchy. It could be the start of something serious or it could be a passing ailment. She isn't coming clean with her brother but she seems to need his help. They discuss her difficult situation – practically on her own, her relatives from her husband's side all dead or married into families outside Delhi. They wonder if it would not be a bad idea at this stage for Mahtab and Amina's youngest brother, who is also alone back in the village, to move in and look after his sister. But this brother is a muezzin at the local mosque and takes his duties very seriously. Why shout out to God when you could instead offer solace to people, Alif asks himself but not his father.

'He knows the situation. He can see. But he hasn't offered himself.'

'If you ask him, he'll agree,' urges Alif.

Mahtab is the only one who has had a government job among his extended family and they all, even the muezzin, tend to defer to him.

'Accha, let me see,' he says. He was never a big talker but now, in just this simple desire to chat, Alif senses something of an old man's vulnerability.

'I'll call Phuphi soon as I reach home. And what else? Is Ahmad behaving himself?' he asks. Ahmad who broke some crockery the other day, perhaps in silent protest. He'd seemed greatly pissed off about something.

'Yesterday I went out to get my boots fixed. There's a new mosque coming up near the police station. I saw him hanging around there,' says Mahtab. 'This is the second time I've spotted him. Why, when he has our mosque to go to, when he's been known there since childhood? Of course this one is much showier, you should see the tilework they're doing on it and the double-double minars. Seems to be Wahabi-Salafi money behind it.'

'What's he after?'

'Various stupid ideas. He wants to pull out his boy from nursery and send him to the madrasa,' says Mahtab. Ahmad has been threatening this since the older one died, as if punishing himself in some way for the accident. He was punching above his weight, imagining his son might become an English-speaking someone, and it would be far more to Allah's liking that the child make do with a religious education: these are some of his repeated arguments, reports Mahtab. In his voice Alif hears the heated attachment to the subject of Ahmad. This is what his world has shrunk to in retirement, while as a policeman he was used to keeping an eye on a town full of Ahmads.

'Oh let him be, Abba,' says Alif. 'Has he fixed the TV?'

'No, no,' says Mahtab. 'No TV. He's after higher things.'

'Don't worry, then. I'll get it done. On the weekend.'

Here he is in a cappuccino-scented, hipster-favoured lap of luxury while his father cannot watch even a snatch of cricket or cooking to while away the time. Alif feels guilty, then the guilt passes.

'Till then I can read,' says Mahtab. 'Or try to forget.'

'Forget what?'

There is a moment of silence and then he says, 'It doesn't matter. You go on home. And call her.'

Alif is partly relieved. It has always been awkward for him to talk of anything but the day-to-day with his father, a distant father, for Mahtab was posted in one or another town of Uttar Pradesh, appearing suddenly at home in that peaked cap with the silver badge Alif always itched to tug off, a short furlough, and then taking off again to attend to the bad guys. The result of these sudden encounters, stolen glimpses and long absences is that Alif feels he only partly knows him, cannot be sure what dreams or opposite of dreams he has. And yet in essence it is very clear to Alif who he is – a Hindi. The poet Mohammad Iqbal's famous nightingales singing in the rose-filled arbours of Hindustan, *Hindi hain ham/vatan hai Hindustan hamara*. Every schoolchild knows that. Or do they? Alif cannot recall when he last heard it sung at morning assembly. In fact, he's been skipping assembly lately. Could they have really stopped invoking that old ideal and he hasn't noticed? What are they worshipping instead? Fat-bosomed, pink-cheeked Mother India, or rather, Mother Bharat, in a tinsel crown and a voluminous, filigree-edged sari, looking a little too sexy to embody a national ideal? He decides he needs to check out the new standards under General Rawat.

In any case there are only a handful of them left, these Hindis, some men and women from his parents' generation, shuffling about in their retirement, baffled by the times – not innocent of the divisions between the Hindis, because those have always been there, but unable to understand how these divisions came to count for so much. What stirred the blood at one time was the idea that they might join hands – the Hindis. That was once the dream of Hindustan but Hindustan was being dismantled now, Bharat was taking its place, and his father has to find ways of burying his disappointment.

It is only when the woman who's occupied the couch facing his looks around her, fixing her sunglasses on her head, that Alif realises she is not sitting there for want of space in the cafe nor has she mistaken him for her date. It's her, Prerna Mittal, the dirty secret from the past. She motions for him to continue his phone talk, orders something from the attentively bending waiter, and sits back without self-consciousness, as though she knows this place, or she knows what this is going to be like.

Alif is thrown.

'Abba,' he says softly. 'I'll call you tomorrow. And let me speak to Ahmad when I come that side. Find out what exactly he is up to.'

The swinging ponytail, the loopy earrings, the chubby chin, the honest, open, almost naively silly face, the giggly style – all gone. Alif is disconcerted, wonders if he should say that there's been a misunderstanding, he is actually someone else. But Ganesh will burst upon them any moment and besides she's clearly recognised him.

'And when should we go to Phuphi's?'

Where has he seen her before, this transformed thing Prerna's become? Alif cannot recall but is certain he knows her, this woman, in her simple kameez and ruffled hair.

'I haven't been to Mehrauli,' Alif adds. 'Not since Nani died.'

She is, he realises then with some elation, an Indian woman. Not the servility of the bowed and sari-covered head, nor Mother Bharat radiating ruddy-cheeked virtue, nor any of these new creations around them in the cafe, these perfumed, pouting babes who demand yet rebuff attention, and not even Tahira whose straight-backed, steely conviction Alif once admired but now finds difficult to measure up to – none of these. Perhaps it's in a Premchand story or a Satyajit Ray film that she exists – that combination of something new and something ineffably old, the poise, he can't help thinking, that is historical.

She is smiling knowingly at him and Alif is at a total loss for words. Mahtab repeats his claim that he can get to Mehrauli on his own and Alif realises his father has mistaken his vagueness for hesitancy, and finds he cannot undo that impression now. He tries, all the same, to reassure him, and hangs up.

'How have you been, Prerna Mittal?' Alif then asks, a little too heartily to cover up his dread that, for all these ruminations about her, he may not have anything to say to her at all.

But before she can reply, Ganesh is calling Alif and Ganesh is saying that Alif needs to hang on to Prerna for him because he is stuck in a pointless and pointlessly long meeting which will take some time to wrap up. And after that the obstacle race of the traffic from Gurgaon.

64

Alif finds himself trying to find out why Prerna had wanted to see them. He'd like to give her a window she can jump out of but she just sidesteps the veiled questions and asks him about Ganesh – and then himself. She seems to have no obvious game plan, not even the idea of extracting an apology. But just when he is advising himself to relax, glad to recount to her the exchange with his father and his concern, because he feels she will understand, that the Hindis are in danger of extinction, she is all at once talking about what followed from that afternoon.

'I stuck to my room and my sketch pad. Grosz. *Grosz.* I spent days just copying his faces. Those faces, Alif. Just everywhere. Don't tell me that was Germany, don't say it was a hundred years ago. I traced every pimple in every dirty face and I knew, I knew, I *knew.* I would never be an artist. He squeezed the life out of my fingers, that horrible man. To grip the pencil and draw – an over-fed jowl, a hollow eye, a bald head. Do you know what that takes?'

Alif has no idea which man she means, and her own face has grown warm with the telling.

'I hope your family…' he says.

'Don't ask me how my mother guessed. After two days of me cringing at the table, pretending to eat, she was on to it. And the first thing she whispered to me was, Don't tell your father.'

'So then you let out everything?'

'She didn't want to know everything. Especially not how I felt – how I made myself not mind because I was sure he would come back. I waited for him,' she says without guile, and then without remonstrance adds, 'but he never took my calls and he never came back.'

Alif recalls himself and Ganesh over the slow months that followed. He thought of nothing but her – and of himself in relation to her with a despicable, desperate longing – but then the year passed, he entered university, he met people who had read much more than *Reader's Digest* adaptations, and she became a shadow, and then a smidgen, and then nothing at all. And now seeing in her eyes that the reverse is not true, that in her case this has been a defining pain, Alif is belatedly shocked – at his own eventual indifference. As for Ganesh, who had shut out Alif whenever he tried to speak about Prerna, declaring the less said about that the better, all Alif can tell himself now with regard to the man is just this: the less said the better.

'What did you do?' he stammers.

'Nothing,' she answers, calm again. 'Except try and resist my mother's pity. She stopped going on about her own imagined illnesses. She stopped always taking my brother's part. She would take me to Karol Bagh to buy me stonewash jeans, give me the better pieces of chicken to eat. She started scanning the matrimonial columns. You know the sort of thing our parents do when they can't get across to their children. Because they don't have the language. No words,' she says, smiling sadly.

Her brother, Alif is thinking with unease. He recalls him being mentioned but has never met him – a child who was not in the picture then. How much does he know?

'And your father...'

'Never found out.'

'Did you ever consider revenge?'

She smiles again – at his stupidity. 'After I finally accepted that the phone wasn't going to ring, that Ganesh was chucking out the letters I'd been posting, that I didn't have it in me to go across to Daryaganj, just turn up at his door, I gave up. Grosz murdered me. I would take very long detours to stay out of the path of trouble. I would cry sometimes and be afraid of myself because there wasn't any reason. Then I got married. He's a nice man,' she says casually, as if talking about a random acquaintance. 'And then there are children. Children, no, they change everything.'

He recalls his mother describing a girl who visited the clinic, a suffering woman who always smiled. There is more than toleration in this, perhaps there is even wisdom.

'Why...' he begins, still worried, still wanting her to explain this meeting, considering her equanimity now, her obvious detachment from the whole fiasco, and especially from Ganesh. But it would be so rude, so instead he says stiffly, 'I am sorry to hear you gave up your art.'

She is stirring sugar into her tea and seems to be in no hurry to answer. If everything is already in the past, her endless pause seems to suggest, and there is nothing left to come, then one has all the time in the world to parse actions and their consequences, choices and their outcomes.

'I was obviously never going to get anywhere with it,' she says. 'Just something I got hung up on because of my father. The books he bought me from the Daryaganj pavements. The great and terrible twentieth century he and his friends talked about. The art he would take me to see – Sunday trips on his scooter to the National Gallery or Lalit Kala. My mother had no interest and my brother was the eternal baby Krishna with his dyed feathers and his flute, the wooden bansuri he was always charming all our relatives with. He was a timeless being – or at least my mother saw it that way. So I was my father's companion.'

'What does your brother do now?'

'He's operations manager at a dry fruit company,' she says laughing. 'Mewa.' Alif too finds this hilarious – the coming down to earth of baby Krishna.

'I had no real talent. I wanted to be a painter but all one must want is to be *in* the world and I couldn't. You see the difference?'

Alif is reminded of an artwork he'd noticed on the wall of their living room – an unbeautiful view, bare terraces with concrete joists and rusting rebar poking out of them, one of which had skewered a fat black crow. The harshness of that painting, but more than that its ordinariness, had bewildered him. He'd connected it to Prerna's talk about her ambitions and felt then that she knew something about the world he didn't. She understood art and how it might even incorporate ugliness. She read literature while he was happy with Alexander the Great or even Mohammad bin Tughlak. Her father published incomprehensible poems in serious-looking magazines with dull covers while his father was not into poetry – in any language – nor would he have dreamt of taking his son to the National Gallery on his scooter.

'Was he disappointed?' Alif asks her.

'My father? No, he knew what I was. Because he'd understood it in himself first, even before he started writing. That he wasn't really a poet. The point is that the world needs people like him too – people who don't have the fire but who recognise it, flirt with it, make space for it, idolise it. It was just me who wanted more without realising...'

A sudden silence overtakes her again and Alif is afraid she might be crying. But her eyes when she focuses them on him show no hint of anything as revealing as tears.

'And then?'

She takes a deep breath. 'And then what had to happen happened and I saw that I was nothing. I became as humbly ugly as a little fly. Forget painting, I didn't even dare pick up a book for fear that it would lure me with some attractive untruth, make me believe I mattered more than I did. I would watch the worse kind of TV for hours. And then put on my hat and go work at my site engineer job.'

Alif is fascinated, as much at the tone of her voice as at the idea that they – he and Ganesh, or at least Ganesh – could have so drastically influenced the course of a person's life. Is this the lesson she has come here to teach them – that something did happen, that people can be hurt, that human beings are defenceless and human destiny therefore pliable? He checks his phone: Ganesh's update is that he is just starting out and Alif is glad because he wants a little more time with Prerna. Everything she has told him so far has been an accounting in the past tense and he is waiting for her to return to the present, which she does eventually. This present takes the form of that apparently nice husband who happens to be a devout follower of a local and not yet so famous god-man.

'He's an eccentric,' she says.

'The guru or your husband?'

'My husband is not eccentric at all. He is a very rational man who has very convincing arguments to support every irrational belief of his.'

'You think this irrational? Gurus, teachers...'

'What can one say, really, about people's need for certainty? They will look for it everywhere and they will take it in whatever strange form they find it. Jagan's younger brother lost a leg in a bomb blast. You remember those terrorist attacks of 2005?'

Alif nods. 'All over the city. One of them just a few metres away from the bar where Ganesh and I...'

Then he swallows his words.

'Some fifty, sixty people died, many more were injured. He kept saying he was lucky but the fact is nothing was the same for the family after that. And they were all believers, of course – Jagan, his parents, his brother. But after this they took to it very seriously. They started to spend a lot of time and money and emotion on this one thing.'

Alif cannot remember who was behind the blasts or even what they were meant to convey. He looks at her face, trying to find some grief there to commiserate with, some wound he can recognise. But she's just a woman drinking her ginger tea, talking with what could seem, from a distance, and in fact appears even up close, to be mild cynicism.

She tells him more about this brother-in-law. He was a young man with ideas, even ideals, and had started the first natural ice-cream parlour in Sarojini Nagar. Her husband, Jagan, was just all right – a low-profile chartered accountant, someone not going to, someone who did not want to, make a mark on the world, not even through trying to earn more money than was strictly necessary, not even through investing in natural ice cream, although his brother had offered him a share. Whereas this brother had an appetite for business. Then he was crippled and started visiting Babaji. And the whole family followed suit.

'You too?'

She considers him with her cool eyes, this woman who is a Hindi, who has stepped out of some precious novel or film and is as startlingly real as a figment of the imagination. No, she says, she doesn't follow the god-man. 'I stay at home. Not because I have a better philosophy than Babaji to offer. He seems clever enough. But if those old things I once believed in – poetry, art – could not help then what hope do Babaji and his cryptic statements have? They don't like it but I keep myself away from all that.'

Alif is strangely relieved.

'Has Ganesh changed?' she asks. 'You clearly haven't.'

And this unsettles him again, this way she has of honing in on a point before he can anticipate it.

'Some things have taken place in his life, he'll tell you himself.'

'Where is he?' she asks. And for the first time something like agitation flits across her face.

Ganesh has evaporated somewhere between his meeting and the traffic. His messages to Alif have been getting briefer and angrier. Alif is apologetic, says something to Prerna about the three of them meeting some other evening when Ganesh is free, though he is not sure now if he can deal with his uncouth friend leering at this unexpected woman.

'What's he making these days?'

Alif has to explain that her former tormentor is not some spirited engineer with the light of progress shining in his eyes, out on the tarmac every day directing the material advancement of the nation – all he is making, if he is making anything, is money. Ganesh's engineering degree was not in computer science but with dogged swotting he was able to complete various courses bearing baffling acronyms, and so build a career as a systems administrator. Prerna understands better than Alif what that is.

'A company's IT set-up,' she says. 'He's in charge. And the more a company depends on those systems, the higher paid and more demanding his job.' She seems approving, if not impressed. Alif doesn't tell her that Ganesh has over the years quit three companies, this is his fourth. And while all the jumps have been made in search of greener pastures, the green has not always had the desired lushness. Some of those moves have been miscalculations.

*Fuck this city* was Ganesh's penultimate message. Now he sends a final one: *She's all yours*.

*

There's never been room for a desk of his own so Alif sits at the dining table pushed up against a wall and good for only three, the red chilli pickle and amla murabba splotches from the sporadically cleaned, tacky, plastic, sunflower-motif tablemats seeping into his paperback. He is trying to read a history of the poets but keeps skidding on the figurative politesse of the language – *Jab Lucknow mein adabi sargarmia badhi to Dilli ka bazaar sard ho gaya…*

*Chiragh ki lau madham ho gayi … Phir bahar aayi … Urdu zubaan ko
char chand lag rahe thay …*

One of Tahira's college texts that he is dipping into for no
reason he can think of except love – for her and for this literature. But the prose shuts him out; he gives up and looks at his
Madonna with child. There they are with their feet up, thick
as thieves on the worn cane settee with cushions spread flat
from years of sitting, the covers of fraying chintz with silvery
lozenges turned to sepia. Son reads out to mother some bit of
the out there he has called up on his phone in a couple of swift
swipes, some worldly wisdom that sounds to Alif as insipid as the
account in his own book is overwrought.

He has to lean into the table to look at them, past the fridge
that implies a division in the tight room, its off-white door plastered with cut-outs of cars and motorbikes and jet planes from
Salim's long-abandoned cut-out phase. Mother's diminutive
frame dwarfed by lanky son's, looking, from where Alif is, like
his wily younger sister, questioning every single thing he says,
not pointed criticism, more amused disbelief. 'Huh?' she answers
every time he delivers another leaden sentence and then she
echoes it as rhetorical question; only when Salim insists that it
is so does she accede – okay, okay, maybe it is – and scribbles in
her notebook.

'Tahi, what does "gulzar naseem" mean?' Alif asks, though he
knows.

'Nice breeze in the rose garden,' she says without taking her
eyes off her note-making.

'What does "tassavvuf ki batein" mean?'

'Mystical matters, Sufi talk.' The same swift reply, the effortless
conversancy with the language that Alif envies.

And Salim takes over. Alif is aware, yet feels it every time as
keenly, that the boy is more his mother's son than his father's.
He tries to recall what the great thinkers of the subcontinent
have had to say on the native bond between mothers and sons.
It occurs to him that all the ones he knows are men. Maybe he
should be looking to the women. He looks to the woman and,
suddenly remembering, asks, 'What happened to the assignment?'

71

'Sallu wrote it,' says Tahira, her nickname for her boy which Alif has never been able to mouth.

'I completely forgot…'

'I didn't write it. I helped you find the sources,' says Salim.

'And this week's? If you need me, I'm around today.'

She looks at her husband and then at her son, head held back assertively, puckish smile saying she's not all serious. Which one will she choose? There was never any doubt which one. What does Alif know about corporate social responsibility and how to bring the darned thing to life with contemporary examples? They're smart, these two. They have built a raft out of such devilish fictions to stay afloat in the barbaric present. And his own raft? Just these two. Only you, he wants, but cannot bring himself, to say. He tries returning to his chutney-smelling book.

'It's okay,' Tahira says, seeing his face. 'This is the last one and then I'm done for life.'

'What does –'

'You know, baba, you've just forgotten,' she cuts in.

'Tell me anyway.'

So she listens and then explains: finding words that were the most obviously appropriate as well as the most richly charged was the key to the style of the poet he is reading about.

And therein the crux of this poetry. Alif is glad to hear it said in Tahi's voice and glad, too, that she is soon finished with these day-in, day-out studies of hers. He goes in to change into one of his three good shirts – today's choice a cambric of heavenly blue. His no longer entirely new but still radically stylish shoes are, he's been finally forced to admit, killing him. They are too narrow for his broad feet or too hard for his soft soles or just made to look at but eminently unsuited to wearing. He has them back in their box in his backpack and steps out gingerly in a pair of Salim's old sneakers on his ruined and blistered feet. He must return to consult with his cousin regarding the fate of these shoes as well as his own – for so much of the recent joy in his life has been linked with them.

Farouk is a highly affable man, a father of three, by all standards prosperous, who looks in on Alif's parents from time to time, bringing news of relatives from Alif's mother's side, most of them in minor professions, trying to keep their heads low, their children educated, their bills paid, their piety intact.

'Alif bhai, you look well. You have never looked better,' he declares as soon as the man walks in. His optimism is a beacon too powerful to ignore and so Alif reciprocates though he is, apart from the blisters, feeling bilious. For the first time in his working life, he does not feel like returning to school to face his unsympathetic boss. Farouk turns his attention to a customer, convinces her that the sandals she has chosen are the absolute best for her but if she should settle on another design those will be, unquestionably, as befitting.

Just a fortnight ago Alif was here and had found himself taken with the elegance of Farouk's shoes, taken as well with the ingeniousness of their display in the spacious store. Farouk had, with consummate salesman shtick, pointed out each individually: the aluminium slatwall panels from which shoes hung, the wooden pop-up display stands in which shoes nestled, the fibre racks in which shoes sat.

Alif is usually shod from a cramped place in Chandni Chowk whose owner he's known since childhood but whose stock has lately been shrinking and prospects dipping with people preferring more and more to take elevators up and down malls instead of trawling through markets like that one. And then Alif, doughty patron of the old world, betrayed Chandni Chowk too by giving in to his cousin's demands that he come and visit. Now he wonders if this is rather telling – the pain in his feet, the disquiet in his soul.

As Farouk tries to please the undecided woman, Alif thinks of the fact that his cousin is not making as much money as he'd like to. It's partly overkill. He has forked out big cash in fitting out a new store and is paying a king's ransom in monthly rent, so it follows that he might just sink. But there is also the larger uncertainty Farouk rarely speaks about, the one that in recent years has made risk-taking riskier.

On the small television in a niche near the cash counter something disagreeable is unfolding. Alif is sitting too far to be able

73

to tell, just from the shots of the weeping women, the poker-faced police officer making his statement to the camera, the mugshot of the dead man, and the screaming reporter, whether an untouchable has been murdered for being an untouchable, a Muslim lynched for being a Muslim, a Naxalite shot for being a Naxalite, a Kashmiri liquidated for being a Kashmiri, a journalist assassinated for asking questions or a farmer dead from suicidal despair. Doubtless one or another of these. But it doesn't affect the atmosphere of this place: the well-dressed salesmen who assist Farouk, the bouquet of room freshener and new leather, the strategic lighting that picks out all the many women's shoes, as distinctive and lovely as human faces, and then all the many men's shoes that had so recently inspired in Alif an illusion of grandeur.

Farouk is finally able send off his hard-to-please customer with two pairs instead of one – the simple consumer solution to the problem of choice – and he sits down with Alif and calls for tea. Alif tells him about his troubles, though he stops short of displaying his wounds. Farouk considers the issue silently as if it were a complex, scientific one.

'You're walking too much,' he says finally. 'Look at these heels, they're already wearing out and it's just been, what, a few days?'

'But I only strolled about in North Campus once. Other than that the usual – to school and back. Rushing between classes. Going out in the evenings sometimes to sit in Jama Masjid.'

'Then you should have told me you want lace-up boots. Good for hiking. I have three kinds, all super comfortable.'

'Hiking?' asks Alif, trying not to show his surprise or point out to his cousin that the shoes he lived in all his adult life from that hole in the wall used to stand him in good stead whether he walked, stood still or ran.

'Bhai, these are the very classiest. They are meant for those who move around in cars and sit with ankles crossed in office chairs.'

'Why did you tell me, then, that I should get them and nothing else?'

'Because I thought you're headed somewhere. I mean in life,' he adds, smiling with great warmth to show he's only joking.

'You know very well I'm hardly heading anywhere. And a new pair of shoes is not going to make me.' A lie because he had actually started to believe himself a changed man in these beauties. He eyes them regretfully.

'Fine, fine,' says Farouk, suddenly a little gruff. 'Return these, take something else.'

Alif tells his cousin that he is too kind and considers, softened by his generosity, to also tell him about the trouble at school. He knows Farouk would console. But no, he doesn't really want to reveal that he is on the back foot in every department of life. He mustn't seem so little in control of his show relative to Farouk, who, when not busy shopkeeping, is driving his children to and from a flurry of life-enhancing activities – tuition, horse riding, Korani taleem. Every summer, they holiday abroad or travel to visit relatives in Bangalore and Bombay and Hyderabad. Farouk is a family man who wishes to be nothing but a family man.

In some respects – the beard, the easy laugh, the unflappability – he reminds Alif of his dead grandfather, the man who'd stood in for Mahtab while the latter roved from posting to posting. Alif and his sister's early childhood was spent with their mother and her parents in Islam Colony in Mehrauli, within view of the looming red and buff sandstone pillar of the medieval Qutub Minar. Perhaps something of Mehrauli's old collection of tombs and minarets, mosques and shrines touched Alif's imagination and led him from comic-book history to a deeper consideration of it. He would try and interest his cousin in these matters, but Farouk, the son of Shagufta's sister who lived next door, felt nothing for the ancient stones of Mehrauli. He would rather sit with the women in the kitchen and partake of the chopping, the peeling and, when he was allowed it, the stirring as well as the gossip.

He was the first person in the family to acquire a mobile phone and has ever since used it to talk without seeming to pause for breath. He has enormous social zeal and even his being a businessman is essentially a way, or so it seems to Alif, to be engaged with people, keep tabs on the ins and outs of human

affairs, try to play a useful role in the lives of the dozens of relatives, friends, acquaintances, staff and business contacts he has.
Alif is sure that should he ever be in serious trouble, Farouk will
be the first one he'll turn to.

'And how did Tahira's exam go?'

'Next week. And then we'll have a new hurdle to cross. I
know what she'll be on to soon. In fact, she's already on to it.'

'She is studying, she is working full-time, masha Allah. We
admire her. My begum says Tahira aapa is her role model and I
can do nothing but smile because begum will not lift a finger if
she can help it. She is lazy but we're not complaining.'

The Hindi word he uses – aalsi – has a sensuous indolence to
it that somehow fits Alif's cousin-in-law perfectly. She is a plump
and long-lashed beauty who, every time Alif meets her, seems
to have spread out further, as if settling ever more comfortably
into life, yielding, with ever greater pounds of flesh, to Farouk's
loving pampering.

'Tahira wants to move,' says Alif with his usual anxiety. 'As
soon as she has her degree she wants a modern flat.'

'I can get you a good place, a brand-new place,' says Farouk as he
directs one of his assistants to attend to a customer; the customer
soon has an arc of gorgeous shoes spread out at her tattooed feet
and an increasingly discontented expression on her face.

Farouk himself lives in a swanky apartment in Mayur Vihar
but he has property here and there, and now reveals he's
bought another place, in Jamia Nagar, not too far from where
Alif's parents live. 'Just go with me. Don't pay broker commis-
sions, don't pay exorbitant advances, don't pay unreasonable
rents.'

But Tahira does not want to live there, the unspoken worry
being the closeness to Mahtab and Shagufta, the spoken one that
living in a ghetto is a moral failing.

'I'm not sure,' murmurs Alif.

'Have you seen what these new apartments are like?'

'It's more about her wishes actually,' says Alif. So Farouk pulls
out his phone and calls her then and there. Tahira has always
liked Alif's cousin; perhaps she even wishes, tacitly, that Alif was

more like him – that neat division, that clever balancing between matters sacred and worldly. Farouk unleashes his sales talk on her but is suitably vague about where exactly the place is; in ten minutes Tahira has agreed to have a look and a foray is planned following her exam.

Alif confesses that he wouldn't mind staying put. But this Farouk will not entertain: the idea that one could, despite a fondness for walking about, hold inertness dear.

'You have to move,' he declares. 'Look at where we were and where we have arrived.' And then he begins reliving the old days as usual – their dear grandmother, how she could transform stale rotis and a sprinkling of sugar and ghee into rich malida or a taste-less and shapeless gourd into gooey squares of barfi; the detailed motifs on the winter sweaters she knitted them; the fervent prayers she whispered for them – urging them away from wrong-doing with her tawbah, tawbah and her Allah, Maulah, begging God for three things in the main: that her grandsons become like the angels, creations of light; that they get to lord it over the jinns, clever creatures of fire who can take human form; and that they stay safe from the devil Iblis, who when he tempts is that fallen angel, satanic shaitaan. For Nani, Qayamat – Judgement Day – was never far and she never stinted in her description of the hellfire, jahannam, in which the condemned would burn.

The child Alif developed an early sensitivity to this whole scenario. Perhaps because he liked to experiment with small transgressions in order to get his Nani's attention – pointing to a bearded man in a picture book and saying, that's Allah, or calling out to her in tears during namaz, only to be told when she broke off her prayer: tell me a story.

Nani was dead against figurative art; she believed that on Judgement Day all those presumptuous creators of the human image would be asked by God to breathe life into them and then there'd be hell to pay. And as for those who interrupted the namaz of their elders … But eventually she'd hand over that story, that hug, that extra portion of dinner he wanted. Even so, Alif clearly saw himself on the side of the sinners, though he could never imagine the experience of burning in hell as anything other than an especially hot day in a generally hot Delhi summer, he still himself, still six or eight or whatever age he was then rather than someone who had lived the full span of his life. He'd lie indoors under the creaking old fans of their Mehrauli home, bare-chested, in shorts, stirring only when he heard the sweet chimes of the handheld bell of the kulfi-seller, old Ajmal, and not having to answer for once Ajmal's question of whether he wanted pista or badaam, since these were special circumstances that called for eating all the kulfi one could so as to fend off the heat of hell. And so those little earthen tubs of both pista and badaam, and each many times over, rather than the ration of one per weekend.

As an adult he traced the overlaps among Jewish, Christian and Islamic eschatology and learnt that hell *was* an actual place – not the ravages of a Delhi summer but a valley near Jerusalem called Ge Hinnom, the valley of Hinnom, which was named 'Gehenna' in New Testament Greek from which the Arabic word 'jahannam' comes. And his seeing himself as an ice-cream guzzling child in that livid hell was not entirely off the mark either, because in this valley children had in the pre-Christian era been burned as sacrifices by both the Ammonites and the Israelites. Today he looks at pictures of Gehenna online and thinks of his grandmother who died in her sleep, almost smiling, certain of her own place in heaven but having left unsolved for Alif the question of whether there existed divine intercession or there did not. Did repenting sinners stand a chance on Judgement Day? The orthodox doctrines leant towards a negative answer, he found. The notion, derived perhaps from the Christian idea of redemption, did exist in Islam, but if God were to start handing out reprieves to anyone and everyone, the promise of rewards to the good and punishment to the bad would go for a toss, believed the ulema. So no, most probably no forgiveness, though what harm can there be in trying, considering that his grandmother herself was always so ready to let him off, her favourite grandchild? And if forgiveness is one of the attributes that secures you a heavenly seat, then why could God himself not be forgiving?

That, then, had been their grandmother's love and as for their grandfather's it took the form of a spiritual calm as he sat behind the counter of his shop of spices and grains on Zafar Mahal Road, in the pristine whites that he washed and ironed himself, his lips moving as he told the beads of the jade rosary always in his hand. For if Nani was all exhortation and encouragement, then Nana was all restraint and humility. He would chat a little with his old-time customers who came to share their news with him as they bought monthly supplies of daals and rice; sacks of wheat flour; canisters of mustard oil; small brown paper bags of whole spices, transparent unmarked packages of ground spices; bricks of Vim and cartons of Surf, their bills made out on long thin strips of paper as sinuous as snakes. Alif loved the mixed smells of the shop – detergent, dalda and dalchini – and his grandfather's cross-legged presence on a takht before the glass-walled counter in whose shelves were visible rows of only the humblest biscuits – Parle-G, Thin Arrowroot, Milk Bikis – and on top of which, partly obscuring Nana's face, were tall jars with homemade hardboiled sweets in a handful of colours – some shaped like orange flakes and others like green limes. Nana did not believe in keeping up with the times but the times were amply evident in other grocery stores nearby – all the novel delights of the 1980s that lured Alif and Farouk to them – Rasna orange juice powder, 007 bubblegum, Maggi noodles, Cadbury's Gems, Licia macaroni rice, Amul chocolates in six flavours: milk, crisp, bitter, coffee, orange, and fruit and nut.

Growing up on his grandmother's stories, Alif saw how his grandfather was the kind of person those tales idealised. The Koran says everything has been created according to its own measure, taught his Nani. And human beings are the noblest of God's creations, all else is subservient to them. But they can be frail and fallible, their greatest sin being their tendency to believe they are a law unto themselves. If everything in nature is made to a purpose, then the purpose of man is this: submission. Nana enacted this submission every day – by his scrupulousness in business affairs, his dislike of ostentation, his ability to sit silently

79

for hours fingering his tabiz, his cautioning Alif and Farouk when they got too loud, too petulant, too excited, greedy or ambitious. It did not matter to him that they were both just about average students as long as they stayed out of trouble. Alif was growing into a bookworm as his cousin leaned towards business. Farouk would save his pocket money and, away from his grandfather's watchful eye, loan it out at considerable interest to his older cousins in the area. He had an arithmetical mind and put it to use early, dropping out of college and starting a shop for ladies' wedding garments in Mehrauli and then developing sidelines gradually. By then their Nana was dead, the family home divided, and Alif and his family had moved out to Daryaganj.

So here he is today, and even though his looks and mannerisms are Nana's, he is actually nothing like him. He has none of Nana's modesty but what he took from them both was faith – that hard and glittery-as-diamond faith in the holiest of holies and the glory of his name. What Alif took from them was romance – the extraordinary vigour of the past, the thrilling possibility of its being as real as the present. So now, as middle-aged men, Farouk is more into religion than stories, and Alif is more into stories than religion.

Once they are done lamenting the deaths of their beloved grandparents, Farouk asks after Mahtab and Shagufta though he has just been to see them a few days ago.

'Abba doesn't really know what to do with himself in his retirement,' says Alif, then recalls something his father said the other day on the phone. *I can try to forget.* He realises, with a lurch, that this is not the first time he's heard him let slip something along these lines – the need for erasure. He wonders if his cousin, always privy to the hidden intricacies of his relatives' lives, has noticed this too.

'He wondered how long you were going to sustain school-teaching. I told him you were writing a book and bound to earn name-fame any day now,' says Farouk. 'I've been hearing about your book for ages but your Abba didn't seem to know anything about it.'

'Abba doesn't read books of the sort I want to write,' says Alif, somewhat self-consciously flexing his bare toes.

Farouk accepts this line unquestioningly. 'But how's it going?'

'Oh, I'm still on it.'

'Will you make good cash?'

Alif shrugs. 'It's not about money.'

'So, then…?'

Alif shrugs again so Farouk moves on to what's always closest to his heart – his children. His son has been riding since he was six and wants to be a jockey. His daughter is also a rider but she is utterly torn now, in her early teens, between architecture and fashion modelling.

'I should not be saying it, I should not be saying it,' declares Farouk but then says it anyway. 'I am proud of them. Subhan Allah, they are turning out very capable.'

And then this road too, like all roads, leads to money.

'Alif bhai, I am thinking of the Gulf. I never wanted to be one of those men – one knows so many – who leave their families, build them houses and load them with gold, but are not there to hold their hands when they need them.'

'True, true,' says Alif. 'What a shame to do that.'

'But I'm considering it now,' says Farouk quickly. Alif looks at him and sees, despite all the good humour, the subtle glint of anxiety that Farouk generally keeps well concealed.

'I know some people in Dubai working in the restaurant business. They say they can find a managerial opening for me. All I need is someone reliable to handle things here…'

Alif looks away from that insistent gaze and examines, with silent and forced detachment, all the shoes Farouk's assistants have started bringing forth for him. He ignores anything even remotely handsome. That original mistake – that stab at connoisseurship when one does not deserve it, has not earned it – will not be repeated. Comfort must override style; style must be sacrificed altogether at the altar of comfort.

'The United Arab Emirates is an empty place,' Alif instructs his cousin. 'Just a desert land built on oil and tourism.'

'But when have you been there?' says Farouk.

'One doesn't have to go to a place to know it,' says Alif. 'You will be unhappy.'

'What is happiness, bhai? I would be so relieved to recover a percentage of what I've put into this place. Give my children all they want. It's just about a few years – three or four. They are grown up now and can do without me for a while. They need my money more than me.'

This sounds like a terrible fate. Alif hopes there will never come a day when he is compelled to say the same of Salim. But he cannot advise Farouk to dismiss the demands of his family for his own Tahi is making demands on him. Besides, in Farouk's case it is not just wife and kids – there are the ageing parents without pensions he must provide for, the sundry relatives he supports in various ways, the Muslim causes he donates to, and the poor who must be regularly fed as per the injunctions of Islam.

Alif caresses an informal and modest pair of footwear. If the first set was sublimity itself, these are merely good-looking.

'Alif bhai, please keep it in mind. I would trust your recommendations. Someone who can handle the cash here, oversee the orders, keep an eye on my boys. I was even thinking of you.'

Alif is so surprised he almost drops the shoes. Me, a shoe seller?

'I know you love your schoolteaching but you've done it forever. And you'll earn more here.'

Alif finds he is unable to reply and just then a puffed-up youth walks in and spends long minutes trying out the many sneakers, chukkas, brogues, loafers, espadrilles – all the names that Farouk has been throwing around. He seems to want something not yet imagined by man. So his cousin sees in Alif a fellow not much different from himself; he believes they are interchangeable or, at least, that all jobs are interchangeable. How different can it be – the business of shoes from the business of history?

'The Emirates have a lot of petrol but it will run out in this century,' he warns Farouk. 'Where then will be their riches?'

'I am not planning to live there for a hundred years,' says Farouk, amused.

'Just giving you the historical perspective.'

'But half the population over there are Indians and Pakistanis. I'll feel at home.'

Alif takes up his chosen pair, puts them on sadly, walks about as if stepping on thin ice, and cannot find any fault in them.

'Will you think about it?' Farouk pleads.

Alif gazes at the TV — again that sobbing woman and the portrait of that violently extinguished man. Sickening repetition, time moving in circles. He knows what the great philosopher believed — history not as a great, undistinguished mass of data, history as that image of the past that suddenly flashes up and must be seized at a moment of danger. Give me, all you long indifferent centuries, that augury that will anchor me in the present. He looks at his newly shod feet and he just wants to go home.

'Tahira's exam. We'll see you after that,' he tells his cousin. They say their salaams, embrace and then Alif rushes out, feeling decidedly short of breath in the gilded, too-bright and too-chilly air of that mall. As he is pressed between the bodies of men on the metro ride home he is thinking not of Tahira's exam but of Prerna's face. And the inflection in her voice when she said, *people want certainty, they will take it wherever they find it.* He should have asked her then what she wanted and he should have stayed for an answer.

# THREE

As Alif sits relaxed in his Saturday afternoon pose before his parents – trying again to lend half an ear to his mother's stories about Imtiaz, or maybe it's Sara or Zoya – he can hear Ahmad on the balcony, hammering at something, his expression no doubt grim. Alif has never been sure if life threw Ahmad challenge upon challenge to match that shrunken face and bony torso, or if his body and features had slowly altered with each new hardship.

'What's he making?' he asks his father.

'The question to ask is, what's he breaking?' answers Mahtab.

And with this couplet Ahmad is, more or less, summed up. Though he and Shagufta have relied on him for years, Mahtab has lately begun to insinuate that the man is not much good at anything and therefore not much good for anything. Mahtab has a policeman's disdain for everyone who fails to seize the day, take the bull by the horns, measure up.

A superfluous man. The thought faintly bothers Alif for he once felt a solidarity with Ahmad and was grateful to him. He'd been abandoned as an infant, then adopted by a certain Mustafa who ran a fruit juice stall near the Fakr-ul Masjid in Kashmiri Gate. The first seven years of his life seemed to have been tolerable ones. Mustafa shared his food and his philosophy of praying earnestly and working diligently with the child, sent him to the madrasa and kept him out of trouble. Then he died and Ahmad was washing dishes in a Paharganj dhaba by the time he was ten, following which it was one odd job after the other, and one foot always on the street – unloading crates of vegetables in the Azadpur Sabzi Mandi, selling drinking water on the platforms of the New Delhi railway station, sitting in a hovel somewhere making sham shampoos and pretend lotions to fill in jars and bottles bearing counterfeit labels of leading brands. By fifteen he was a bellboy in a shady hotel fronting a shadier massage parlour run by a man who apparently had three wives – either a fact he boasted about or a rumour he denied. The rooms on the top floor were reserved for girls brought in batches from Nepal and the north-eastern states, some routed to brothels in Goa, others to fancier brothels in Dubai. Ahmad's task was to unlock the doors on the top floor, give the girls meals twice a day, pretend to not see the men having their way with them. Then the hotel was busted and he'd been subjected to the third degree in the lock-up because he was clearly underage and they didn't even have a strong enough case to send him to the remand home. He appealed to God all through that time, having understood that 'massage parlour' was a euphemism for hell, and hell came in levels, that set-up having been pretty high up in the hierarchy.

His foster father, Mustafa, had told him that when he spotted him as a baby, crawling unattended in a corner of the mosque, he'd been wearing a locket with a picture of Meher Baba on it. But this intriguing twentieth-century Sufi, who had followers both in Hollywood and rural India, would not go on to determine the direction of Ahmad's life. The boy was sworn to Allah with that name Mustafa gave him when he took him in, and nothing, it seemed, could puncture his faith. Allah had got him out of lock-up and Allah had put him back on the street and Allah had brought him under Mahtab and Shagufta's protective care. They saw to it that he learnt to read and write, and eventually arranged for his marriage to the daughter of their tailor. He'd moved out and rented a small place in High Tension Lane, the name suggesting lately a sick irony since it was a live wire looping out of the towering pylon on the lane that had killed Ahmad's child as he played on the roof of their building, one constructed, like many others in the neighbourhood, danger-ously close to those low-hanging cables.

Ahmad's latest obsession, reports Shagufta, is pilgrimage.

'He wants a loan to go to Mecca and won't take no for an answer,' she says.

'God helps those who help themselves,' offers Mahtab.

Alif is silent, thinking of how Ahmad and he were friends once, back in the days when the boy had just joined the household and the family was trying to make place for him, figure out which of his many versatile skills – fruit-juice making, speedy vegetable chopping, auto-rickshaw repair, mountainous dish-washing, coolie work, basic carpentry – they could find a use for. Alif was still living with his parents, still content in a way that he would learn later, after he was married to Tahira who enlightened him on this point, is not really contentment but a mere absence of ambition. The two men, one a teenager always eager to please, the other just starting to get used to the gravity of earning an income, the 8 to 2 working life, would go out for the still innocent and lovelorn Hindi movies of the mid-1990s. Ahmad was at this stage, having survived the streets and found a home, full of a renewed faith in God. He would tell Alif the story, or the many stories, of his life so far and Alif, in turn, shared some of the old forgotten, far-off things that constituted the discipline of history, discovering that Ahmad did not really know what history was. The Prophet Mohammad could have made the flight from Mecca to Medina yesterday or a million years ago and it'd make no difference to Ahmad. What mattered to him was the fact of the Prophet's presence, both mistily remote in time but also alarmingly close to him.

Alif is mildly nostalgic about those outings, that easy male bond, but once he settled into a new life with Tahira, he was unable to summon again the boyish zeal that had made him try and trick Ahmad into tasting a mouthful of beer, or chortle with him at the barely comic scenes in those films. He goes out with Tahira and Salim to the movies in some too-expensive multiplex and afterwards they go eat a too-expensive meal and the end result is never satisfaction but stupefaction. When he wants to drink, he and Ganesh head to Bright & Blue, or they buy two quarts of inexpensive whiskey wrapped in half sheets of newspaper and drink it with plain water in Ganesh's bedroom when his father is out or in Ganesh's car if his father is in. Just two middle-aged men with grey in their hair, subdued before their fathers. Neither would dream of holding a glass of alcohol in the presence of the elders. And neither will reflect on this shyness while they drink out of sight. They are perhaps the last ones – after them no more of this decorum, this camouflaging, this gentle deceit. And who's to say it's been a bad thing? Who's to say that bringing every one of our predilections out into the harsh light of day makes them easier to live with?

Shagufta says she has nothing against the haj. There are no hajees in her family but there is every reason to respect them – those people who, having visited the sites of the Prophet's journey, become touched with a reciprocal saintliness.

'We don't have surplus cash to throw on his whims,' says Mahtab, and Shagufta tells Alif – he had no idea or maybe he has forgotten – that they'd been funding Ahmad's now-deceased boy's education and will do what they can for the younger one, though Ahmad is being obstinate. He wants the money for himself.

'I have half a mind,' says Shagufta, 'if he goes on like this, to open a bank account for his wife and give it all to her instead, the little we can afford.' And then she starts off again on the girl's appalling domestic situation. Shagufta herself could have been Zainab, thinks Alif, or she could have been any of the under-nourished and ill-educated women she counsels at the health centre. She's only at one remove from them. Her shopkeeper father, who was always far from well-off, let her take a paramedic's degree, her husband let her keep her job, and Alif and his sister grew up with a mother who spent her days at the none-too-clean lab in a local hospital, examining blood and urine samples, and filing reports by hand. That's where she developed it, that knowing, matronly attitude to people that has come to define her.

Ahmad bursts into the room, holding his hammer. 'Since Alif bhai is here I wanted to talk about my plans.'

Mahtab rises from his seat, fiddles with the TV as usual, finds it quite dead as usual, takes up a magazine.

Alif was supposed to organise repairs; instead he suggests they buy a new TV but Mahtab is deaf to this idea. He is not enamoured of the new, he cleaves with tender fanaticism to the old. He still wears shirts with antediluvian prints from middle age and a watch whose dial is yellowed by time, handed down from some equally thrifty ancestor. He has carefully stacked away in the wardrobe files bulging with mysterious papers from his police days which Shagufta periodically threatens to discard, and all around the house lie orderly, assorted piles of the things that Mahtab cannot bear to throw – used envelopes, grocery bills, calendars for years gone by, magazine cuttings in English and scraps of Urdu papers with half-imagined and wholly opinionated news reports in elegantly sloping nastaliq, flyers advertising new playschools and branded apparel stores and neon-lit, air-conditioned restaurants which Mahtab studies with all the seriousness of a discerning patron though he isn't and will never be one.

'If you're thinking of asking him for money put it out of your mind,' says Shagufta swiftly. 'While we're here we are your providers.'

'If Alif bhai was that way inclined he'd come to Saudi with me. Since he's not, he could contribute something towards fulfilling my one desire,' says Ahmad and these words, if spoken with the man's familiar melancholic air, might have stirred Alif. But Ahmad is clearly upset. Is that confidence he once put in God, certain that whatever he ordained was ultimately for the best, turning to a religious aggression?

'I would have come with you, my brother, if you were going to Mecca a hundred and fifty years ago, when the city was one of the intellectual centres of the Ottoman empire…' says Alif. 'Yes,' he continues, ignoring Ahmad's look of puzzlement. 'People didn't always go there just on haj. They went there to discuss and debate the reform of Islam. They came there from India and Indonesia, from Istanbul and Cairo.'

'Are you listening?' says Shagufta sharply to Ahmad who has started drifting towards the kitchen, hammer's head knocking testily into one palm, mumbling something about getting the rotis going.

'They tried to combine the Western scientific outlook and the teachings of the Koran and the Hadith. A lively city and a hospitable one – the caliph would have welcomed us if we came seeking refuge from the British empire, fleeing persecution.'

'The caliph...' starts Ahmad, returning, seizing on that word.

'I have no interest in these latter-day upstarts who style themselves caliphs. And I have no interest in the Saudis who took over Mecca and Medina, and who have forced on us all their version of Islam.'

'So this servant's only dream means nothing to you, then? This servant you call your brother?'

Alif is amazed at the rancour in his voice.

'If you need more money why don't you let your wife work instead of always slapping her around?'

Ahmad grimaces but looks him in the eye.

'I will never send Zainab out. We might be poor but we have our pride.'

There is silence in the apartment after this banal but unexpected statement.

Ahmad returns to his hammering which sounds very much now like destruction rather than construction, while the latter slips out of the house saying he forgot to buy the post-prandial sweets Alif cannot do without, but no doubt also needing to pick up cigarettes. Shagufta has moved to the kitchen and is wreathed in the aromatic fumes of a paste of onions and masalas she is frying.

'Zainab is the sensible one,' she says as Alif joins her. 'She sits at home and helps in her father's business but even that our man has forbidden lately because it means people visit the house and no one is to visit the house; she is not to show herself to anyone. Have you seen her tailoring? She really has the gift. She ought to have her own shop. Meanwhile, our man is bent on going to Mecca-Medina with some big group from the new mosque.'

'He might come back a calmer man,' says Alif.

'He might come back an even worse hothead.'

'What exactly did Abba say when he asked him?'

'Would he ever speak upfront to Abba?' asks Shagufta, stirring the pot with practised vigorousness, then throwing into it a

quartered chicken that lies there pell-mell for a moment looking strangely out of place and then, enfolded rapidly in the gravy,
gives up its animal appearance and becomes just food.

'And your father's becoming harder. He could never stand
nonsense but now he'll snarl at the first sound of a needless
word. He spends so much time out there on the balcony smoking and sighing and breaking his head over I don't know what.'

She turns away from her cooking to present her son with a
saucer of sliced mango from the fridge. He must eat this standing
there before her, and she watches him with that parental affection
whose noble side consists in its making do with so little – just
the pleasure of feeding your children with your own hands, even
if they are already fed, even if they are no longer children, even if
they have existential doubts and moral confusions and don't feel
themselves deserving of such mango-scented love.

Ahmad has always been a little scared of Mahtab, keeping
his eyes downcast and his talk curtailed before the ex-police
inspector; it is usually to Shagufta and to Alif that he brings his
appeals, out of Mahtab's earshot. But is this show of deference
just that now, a show? Is he falling out of love with his bene-
factors in his pursuit of the greater benefactor in the sky? But
of what use such burning faith if it distances you from people?
Alif knows that his parents have always put people before God,
and somehow, without spelling it out, transmitted this belief to
Alif and his sister. How is it that the very same thing – the same
mumbled prayers on the same white sheets, the same incomprehensible Arabic of the same holy book – which led Mahtab
and Shagufta towards steadfast humanism is now leading their
adopted servant-son towards incipient misanthropy? Or is the
impress of religion overrated and are people, even those who
share a common faith, just that – variously and complicatedly
people?

Alif drifts back to the living room. He tinkers with the television cables and, surprisingly, the thing bursts into life with loud,
querulous voices – a studio debate in which people are getting
increasingly red-faced through their make-up. 'What does it
mean, sir, to be a Muslim in contemporary India?' hollers the

anchor at a man with a shapely white beard. But before he can reply, provide a line or two in summation of his existence, someone else cuts in and says, 'Why should Muslims —' But this line of questioning is not fated to find completion either. 'Madam,' shouts a third someone, wagging his finger. 'Muslims need to —' And then the anchor butts in, 'But Muslims are...'

Alif is at once so fatigued by these familiar openings to these pet questions that he cannot even bring himself to turn the damn thing off.

Mahtab, when he returns a few minutes later, grabs the remote, and runs speedily through various snippets of the world, a universe of possibilities delivered in screechy spurts, till they are back at the shouting and the always inconclusive analysis of that truly tiresome subject — the condition of Muslims. 'Namoone sab, sab namoone,' he curses, trawling again till he finds a Pumblechookian man frying an egg. Peace descends on the living room. Shagufta joins them; from the kitchen comes the aroma of meat and spices simmering together and slowly becoming one while the three sit there together receiving instruction in a musical French accent on the right way to break an egg, the ideal temperature under the pan, the requisite amount of butter, how to keep the white tender and get the yellow glazed, and, by implication, how to make an art out of any plain old thing.

When lunch is ready, Alif eats heartily as usual, not needing yet still receiving promptings from his mother to eat more, eat better. His father, on the other hand, forecloses all attempts to be force-fed with that calm but dangerous policeman's look that Alif used to respect as a child.

'You don't eat,' complains Shagufta.

While this is merely a figure of speech, not a statement of fact — a rumour, says Mahtab — it is true that he is thinning, that there is something about these years of his retirement that have reduced him. He eats with careful restraint, as if a few spoons too many of rice or an extra leg of chicken would be a grievous indulgence, enough to undo some internal balance he has been building. And yet the tranquil expression on his face as

94

he watched the Frenchman sample his perfect creation made Shagufta smirk and Alif feel his father is becoming a stranger to him all over again.

Ahmad hangs around, waiting for some command which never comes, periodically returning to the kitchen for some chutney or plate of salad he has missed putting on the table. Noticing his exhaustion, the sweat-slicked face, the greasy T-shirt, the crumpled pyjamas, Alif starts to feel somewhat sorry for him. When he is done eating he delivers his own plate to the kitchen. Ahmad is sitting in a corner, unhappily shovelling folds of gravy-soaked roti into his mouth – the same food that to Alif always tastes of heaven is being eaten by this man as if it were fodder. He looks down at Ahmad and Ahmad looks back at him with those forlorn young old-man eyes.

'Let's go and get a cup of tea when you've finished.'

They head out into the neighbourhood, which is all sooty squalor and haphazard hustle. Two- and three-storeyed homes, some with walls of naked brick, jut out into the street, clunky air-conditioning units strung up outside, clothes drying on the ledges of open windows. Other apartments have balconies given over to the hoardings of local businesses, the most lucrative obviously education – all the many hyperbolic adverts for career counselling 'centres' no more than poky, windowless single rooms wedged between hardware and grocery stores, the 'academies' that are basement coops for school tuition, and the 'international' schools promising an 'Islamic' education alongside a Western one. Leading off from the main road are bylanes darkened by looming apartment blocks, the electricity cables strung between them snarled like clumps of frayed and greyed wool. It's in one of these lanes that Ahmad lives, and Alif glances at him as they walk, sidestepping occasional piles of garbage and coils of shit. Perhaps Ahmad, too, is conscious of the strangeness that Alif feels – their going out together after all these years. He says he wants to take Alif to a local teashop which the Salafis patronise but the last thing Alif will do is hang out with Salafis.

'The tea is awful there. Let's walk for ten minutes, that other place I remember used to be better.'

'They won't eat you up if that is what's worrying you. Aren't they our Muslim brothers too?'

He swats from his perspiring cheeks the sticky flies that are everywhere, while Alif looks at a single vine with a single leaf on it creeping down one stray balustrade, which highlights the absolute absence of greenery everywhere else. Islam, a desert religion, unlike Hinduism which can render anything in the natural world anthropomorphically holy – from a sprig of tulsi to the thunder in the skies to indents on ancient stones. But, eschewing Arab aridity, what well-watered Persian delights the Mughals wrested from this land. Not the faintest ghost of that vernal spirit evident out here. Out here nothing of beauty except the faces of children. Small girls on their way back from school on cycle-rickshaws with their headscarves tight about their ears and low on their foreheads. Alif's mother does not approve of this new sartorial epidemic; she does not understand it.

Shagufta's family is at the low end of middle class or the high end of indigent; her father took over the shop his father used to run and her mother never saw the inside of a schoolroom. Her pride in her lab technician degree is also pride in the social freedom it gave her. Her stay-at-home mother wore saris, rather than the lugubrious Arab dress that Muslim women favour these days, and she would just slip the pallu over her head when there were elders in the room. For Shagufta, who except when in prayer dispensed with all head-covering courtesies once she started working, and who hasn't gone back to them since, this modest uncovering was a significant victory. So this pains and annoys her now – this increasingly compulsory fashion in veiling, ear bandaging, hair concealing, body sheathing.

'Why are we walking?' groans Ahmad.

Alif feels obliged to put as much distance as he can between himself and Ahmad's new friends.

'New shoes,' he says, gesturing at the replacements. 'Need to test them.'

They continue north, Alif noticing better-looking apartments now and then, with neater facades and roomier balconies but still none holding anything alive. He recalls his father telling him about folk hereabouts who can afford luxury cars but have nowhere to park them, much less drive them. In the old days, people had very little money but enough of everything else; now they have too much money but too little of everything else. This is an insight that Mahtab often repeats though he does not say what this other thing is – light, air, a few living leaves, a clean patch of sky?

To their left, on the far side of these lanes, is the long straight line of the miasmic Okhla Canal along which the metro line runs, and beyond the posher neighbourhoods where his cousin Farouk has bought property. On their right, the colony ends with Kalindi Kunj Road and the vast floodplain of the Yamuna, now empty, the river itself barely visible in the summer heat except for a few glittering shards in the far distance. The neighbourhood of Alif's parents is squeezed into a narrow strip of land in between.

'I think these might hold,' Alif says, eventually, of his shoes. And Ahmad hails a rickshaw at once, refusing to take another step in the killing heat.

'Okhla Head,' Alif says to the driver. 'It's hot, I know,' he tells Ahmad, 'but I am still trying, all these years later, to get used to the new soulless, decrepitude of this place as against the old, soulful decrepitude of Daryaganj.'

Ahmad gives him again that half-mystified, half-dismissive look.

A crumb of poetry stirs vaguely in Alif's memory. *Ham rehne wale hain usi ujde dayar ke* – That's the greatly blighted place in which I live. He would have to call Cousin Mir, a poetry-loving relative from his father's side, to ascertain the previous lines.

At Okhla Head, named after the canal's headworks, they find a few benches and tables set out in the mud and open air of a canteen purporting to serve Irani tea. As Alif tastes its refreshingly salty lemon flavour, served in a chipped and veined cup and saucer, Ahmad quickly downs his own sweet tea and talks about the benefits that accrue to the mortal soul from going on pilgrimage to Mecca.

'How expensive is the haj these days?' asks Alif, trying to be friendly.

'It's not yet the season for haj, you must know that. I will go on haj when my son is grown and I am finished with the world, given away what little I have, ready to tie a shroud around my head and join my creator should I die on the pilgrimage. And I hope to die on the pilgrimage.'

'So the other all-season journey, what's it called?' asks Alif, temporarily forgetting.

'The umrah. Allah has been sending me the signs and I know it is time, it is very much time, for me to go on the umrah.'

Alif faintly recalls having imbibed this stuff a long time ago from his grandfather, but his mind, as usual, must have been elsewhere. As it is even now, for instead of paying full attention to Ahmad the present, he is thinking of his namesake, Ahmad of old, Ahmad Sirhindi, the sheikh who died in the early seventeenth century. By that point in history, Indian Sufis had grown increasingly close to Hindu mystics in outlook, believing there was no essential difference between man and God, a view comparable to Advaita. The resistance to this came from Naqshbandiyah, a school of Central Asian mystics. Ahmad Sirhindi, an Indian proponent of their philosophy, was appalled at these syncretic moves and tried to recover Islam from its increasingly local moorings. So that's who Ahmad is named after, a reformist if not a purist.

Alif is partial to the Sufis – those mystic travellers who were as influential as, if not more than, the jihadis, and who converted so many to Islam on the subcontinent, including, he imagines, his own once Hindu ancestors. What paths might Islam have taken in India had this monism – attractive to that most gentle of Mughal princes, Dara Shikoh – been allowed to take its course? Perhaps a third religion, he thinks, had the prince not been beheaded and the orthodoxy re-established. If permitted, this faith would have been about nothing but mad, unbridled love, dismissing all divisions and differences between the worldly and the divine as a daydream.

'Do you remember Sarmad, the famous Armenian Jew turned Delhi Sufi who went about naked and mocked at emperors? You had fallen to your knees and kissed his grave, the one near Jama Masjid.'

Alif does not add, did not add even then, that the man is supposed to have said, in a religious ecstasy, *I am God*.

But no, things did not go in that direction, he reflects, not without regret. Those popular, heterodox tendencies lost appeal even though the Sufis still compel. Nizamuddin Aulia's shrine is always hectic with devotees and Alif plans to take Class Eight there soon; they are old enough now to get into the music and make some sense of the history. Then he remembers with shame that his excursions have been axed and he recalls, too, the heavy hand of the one who axed them. The watchman at school seemed to have bought the story about Alif's wife needing urgent hospitalisation, but it turned out he saw through it and told on him. Rawat had sent Alif a note asking him to explain the one missing entry in the biometric machine – a note! When her office is ten steps away from the staffroom. Alif has not replied but come Monday he will have to work on polishing his excuse. He is sure she couldn't have noticed unless someone prompted her about his decamping.

'When will you listen to me?' asks Ahmad.

'I've been listening,' says Alif at once, even though the man is starting, all over again, to put him off – the pointless beard, the narrow-eyed focus on God.

'Do you remember Babri?' he asks, and his tone is such he could be asking, do you remember Karbala?

'How can I forget?' asks Alif wearily though he doesn't add that in his mind the infamous demolition of that mosque by those bent on political revenge is linked forever with his feverish dreams about Prerna Mittal – all the guilt and covetousness in his own small, uncertain heart rather than the madness out there in the divided world. The bloody December when he was twenty years old, the bloodier spring that followed – none of it made as strong an impression on him as the sound of that girl in splits, followed by the sound of that girl's long silence.

'Babri changed everything. It's true that at the time I didn't think so much about it – what could I, who was just learning to live without hunger, without the smell of a policeman's armpit in my nose every time he raised his lathi on me, without the pain of a rat chewing my toe, what could I have made of Babri? But these days it just doesn't leave me. I dream about it, Alif bhai. I should have been there facing up to those vandals, putting my forehead on the walls of that mosque so that they'd have to kill me first to get it. I should have died.'

Alif is sure there is some clever line of Ghalib's or Sauda's with which to puncture the sententiousness of those dying to be martyrs. He promptly messages Mir to ask and Mir messages back two lovely lines – not by those poets of old but a contemporary called Nida Fazli. *Ghar se masjid hai bahut dur chalo yuun kar lein/ kisi rotey hue bachche ko hasaya jaae.* The mosque's so far away from home, let's instead/ try drawing laughter from a crying child.

'I should have died,' Ahmad is repeating moronically as he weeps.

Alif does not take personally the breaking of temples and the breaking of mosques but seeing Ahmad's tears he realises that after the death of his son he can no longer reach this man. Ahmad has of course cast it as historical suffering – the straight line from the seventh-century tribulations of the Prophet to twentieth-century battle of Babri – but there is nothing theoretical about his pain. Perhaps my child died but consider the suffering of the Prophet in the early days of his preaching and remember how his son-in-law was killed by the armies of that vile Caliph Yazid. That's how he reasons – the larger suffering makes his own bearable and he cries for one so as to salve the other.

Alif offers Mir's couplet to him, hoping these sweet lines will staunch the flow for a moment, but they don't.

'The qaum has lost its way,' he sobs. He does not mean India, this is a larger nation he is talking about, a worldwide one held together by the transcendental bonds of Islam, or a smaller one within India conjoined by those same bonds. 'Why else is it that we couldn't save Babri?'

As Alif's sensible mother would say: Why not consider saving Zoya or Sara instead of saving Babri? But that, too, is not good enough. One must provide for Zoya or Sara, one must find ways for her children to be fed, but how to also create in them the redemptive hungers and the spiritual satisfactions? He glances at the boys and girls sitting at the makeshift tables nearby, eating biryani and flirting shyly with each other, soon to be worn down by humdrum jobs and insufficient incomes, since childhood fulfilling their religious obligations dutifully. He wishes he could ask them, what's the human spirit really meant for? Any ideas, ladies and gentlemen? From the branches of a stunted, leafless tree hang treadless tyres, a display by the car workshop next door, and those swaying rings of wilting rubber somehow put Alif in mind of nooses.

Once Ahmad was willing audience to Alif's discourses on history and politics, cinema and literature, girls and alcohol, but now much of what he wishes to say to Ahmad he must deliver as soliloquies, and there's the rub, that Ahmad's newfound conviction is constricting him. He sends up a silent prayer – *Ya Khuda raham farmah* – as Ahmad gives him no quarter, clutches his arm hard and tells him he ought to have given himself up not just when the mosque came down but with his brothers in the riots the following year, and with his brothers in every riot since then, and with his brothers in every riot before that. He takes up that all-too-familiar tragic litany – the names of the villages and cities and states in which Muslims have been periodically killed over the good part of a century.

'Where was I? Since Allah took Munna, I have struggled with this question, it followed me everywhere. I had no answer, bhai, till I met the imam sahib at the new mosque. Will you come with me some Friday and hear him once? Just hear him once and then I won't ask you a second time if what he says doesn't strike fire in your heart. Are you coming, Alif bhai?'

Alif considers again the face of his former friend, the deep cuts around the eyes incised by the pointed blade of misfortune, the clumps of lifeless grey on the chin, the sunken cheeks which no amount of rich cooking will ever fill out. *Behold the suffering Muslim*, he thinks. Why is it that his faith did not secure him a greater destiny? How did this religion once empower those desert Arabs to expand outwards till, a mere hundred years after the Prophet's death, they were ruling an empire that extended from Spain to India, larger than the Roman one at its zenith? And how did the sanction of this Islam once make the Mughals glow with self-regard and rule, largely, without religious fervour, and why is it that now all it has to show for itself is a defeated man who is not on an inner quest of self-effacement but an impractical one of self-destruction?

Perhaps the glory of the thing in its medieval version, despite its seeming immutability, is that it has in fact been mutable, taking, for strategic reasons, the form of the many vessels into which it's been poured. And now, its power on the wane for several centuries, those who remain as honest examples of the faith are those who know to leave well alone the dream of a worldly jihad or even any idealised qaum – like Alif's Nana who upheld a private faith, or his daughter, Shagufta, who believes that religion is best combined with a microscope in a lab or nutritional science or just simple goodwill.

'The thing is…' says Alif finally. 'I don't find the time to go much these days. To mosques. Or dargahs.'

'And you think nothing will make you change your mind? This imam will. It's listening to him I realised that there is no answer but prayer. Ibadat. Fast every day of Ramzan, each day is an ibadat. Go now on umrah, that is ibadat. If you earn a hundred rupees, give away nine in charity. Why? Ibadat. Nothing matters but all the prayers that you have said and all the prayers that you have said will circle around you and form an unbreakable shield for you on the Day of Judgement.'

He raises his eyes to heaven, muttering under his breath. *Inna lillahi wa inna ilahe rajiuun.* To God we belong and to him we will return. Then he moves on to the business end of religion and presses on Alif a flyer he has taken from his pocket which offers fifteen-day umrah packages for both commoners and kings. The latter can stay at the Hilton; the former cannot, but should presumably be glad to be air-lifted to and fro the holiest of holies for under half a lakh.

'Will you come with me, bhai?' asks Ahmad and Alif is sick of his deafness and tries another excuse. 'Ganesh,' he says.

'The elephant god?'

'Ganesh, my friend Ganesh. His father is ill... might have to go with them both to Pakistan.'

'Pakistan?'

'He was born there and wants to visit one last time. I have already promised, otherwise, I would have...' All this is bad faith. He is not sure it is even possible to get a visa to Lahore. But he feels no qualms countering over-zealous faith with bad faith; he looks past Ahmad at a girl keeping up banter at the next table. He must see Prerna again. Ganesh has been waiting for a report on their afternoon and Alif was eager to give it, but now suddenly, without knowing why, he is embarrassed. He has nothing to hide except that he wants to hide this – the sense of revelation on seeing her. She slipped out of his life like smoke drift and has returned with a full-bloodedness that is making his head spin.

'Alif bhai, how long has this been going on? When was the last time you joined the jammat or fasted?'

'You think with a job like mine it is easy to keep God in mind night and day?' says Alif, suddenly too annoyed to not let his annoyance show. 'You try managing nine-year-olds or keeping fourteen-year-olds engaged.'

Ahmad switches tack. 'Do you remember on your birthday once we had gone for Friday prayers and something made you tell me right after namaz that you tended to think too much, you were always going over all the arguments for and against, and that's why Allah was upset with you, but I, who believed with all my heart, was exactly the kind of person he looked out for.'

Alif does not remember saying any such thing but he nods all the same.

'You're a good person, Ahmad, you don't need to prove it.' He returns the flyer to him and pays for the tea. 'You see, it wasn't always like this,' he says.

'No it wasn't,' says Ahmad, misunderstanding. 'But even if there is God's wrath, there is always God's mercy.'

'I meant that there was a time when He did not ordain everything. Go back to the early centuries after the Prophet's time. What do you find there? Certain interesting figures, certain unusual opinions, that did not recommend leaving everything to prayer. You have a mind, you have free will, you decide. God wants the best for you but it's you who are responsible for your actions.'

He leaves out the historical background, the influence of Hellenistic thought on this particular school, the eventual stamping out of its philosophy in favour of the more orthodox variants.

'Even if there were no God...'

He stops, seeing how piously appalled Ahmad looks and, besides, the other tables are uncomfortably close and it would not do to provoke a riot at Okhla Head.

'Your mullah doesn't know this. And if he knows, he's not about to shout it from the pulpit. The Arabs produced the house of Islam. The Arabs kept the flame of civilisation burning through what were known as the Dark Ages when Europe was slumbering. But your chap, unfortunately, is not made of the same stuff.'

Ahmad has stalked off, muttering the offended *La haul wala quwwat*. Alif catches up with him, briefly embraces his irate brother and then lets him go. As he is heading to the Jamia Nagar metro station, Mir sends him another couplet from the same poem, the poem about living in the damned right here rather than straining for the exalted over there. It's as if both the poet and its sender had read Alif's mind. *Khud-kushi karne ki himmat nahi hoti sab mein/ aur kuchh din abhi auron ko sataya jaae.* Not everyone has the pluck to kill themselves/let's hang on a bit longer to torment everyone else.

★

Miss Moloy, teacher of maths and science, and believer in nothing unless she has sussed it out for herself, had imparted to Alif the first time they met both the general and the special theory of relativity, which he remembers for the idea, intriguing to a historian, that the faster you move through space, the slower you move through time. There is no history in the human sense out there in the universe, in those mysterious realms whose gravitational fields are much stronger than earth's. It's just here, where we can apprehend how things move, change, die that we're taken with movement, change, death.

She has since then always lent him an ear, balancing out the qualified certainty of his history with the practical truths of her science. There were rumours about Miss Moloy: that she'd fallen under the sway of Catholic nuns in Darjeeling and never married, or had divorced early in Calcutta and been in mourning since, or had a succession of men in Delhi and was loose. But she didn't let on anything and Alif never asked; it's enough for him that she is an intriguing figure in contrast to his own rather straitlaced existence. Besides she has no axes to grind; she is one of the few quite objective people he knows.

She is taking a class and Alif waits for her in the staffroom, ignoring everyone else from the sports sir to the pretty Hindi teacher, all of whom have no doubt heard about the principal's breathing down his neck. The note from her having produced no response, she has just sent Alif another, summoning him. He tries to read a chapter on the late Stone Age and fumes silently. Why is she here? Why would anyone leave the mild climes of Shimla and move to debauched Delhi? Maybe she has something to hide. Most everyone has something to hide and if he could find Rawat's Achilles heel, she might become more amenable. A recent addition to the staff, a man called Jha brought in to handle Rawat's letters and circulars, is sitting by himself, engrossed, or appearing to be, in the *Times of India*.

'I have never known my coffee cup to look this clean,' says Alif to no one in particular. 'Where have they gone, those historical stains that distinguished these vessels?' The newspaper stirs, Jha's head pops out, he bares his teeth at Alif and says, 'Ramu does no work. Or rather, he used to do no work. For the first time in his stupid life, Madam Rawat is making him.'

'Ah,' says Alif and returns to his book.

Ten minutes later he announces, again in general, 'Just stepping out to make a call.'

And again the newspaper is lowered and Jha's steady stare follows him out. Alif slips to the front of the school – the narrow gravelled walkway, the beds of paint-box-coloured zinnias and gently nodding cosmoses, the flagpole and the watered lawn on which no one may step except during important flag-raising occasions. He marches on the grass anyway, gazes for too long at Prerna Mittal's number on his mobile as if even those random numerals express something alluring, and considers what he might tell her, how to express his muddled feelings on the phone. He sees the guard peering at him from a hatch in his box and thinks: what am I doing here, walking in the middle of the day in infatuated circles over a woman when my dignity in this institution is on the line? The thought of locking horns with Rawat yet again makes him so desperate he calls Prerna, asks straightaway if he can see her, then obfuscates when she asks why.

'Something I forgot to tell you last time. Nothing important but just wanted to have a word with you at some point.'

'Yes, yes,' she says, and then, without even bringing up Ganesh, 'Come over.'

He can hardly believe it. It was nothing short of a God-sent miracle – Ganesh's endless meeting and Ganesh's deadlocked traffic jam. Alif got to impress her first and she is clearly impressed with Alif, she's recognised that as much as she is no longer a twenty-year-old with a disastrous crush, he is no longer a twenty-year-old with a disastrous crush. She agrees to see him because she has put the past behind her, he can hear it in her collected tone, and he wants to thank her but his own tone, at this point, is dangerously close to blubbering so he ends the call and goes up to the guard.

'What did they ask you about me? Last week? I told you there was a family emergency, I had to run.'

The scowling guard scowls harder. 'No one asked me anything and I told no one anything.'

So it must have been Jha, then, thinks Alif, who'd been watching him from some vantage point, Jha who is not just the madam's secretary and spokesperson but also, it seems, her eyes and ears. Jha is the key. He returns to the staffroom and pre-history, trying to think of ways to get the better of the man. But the newspaper lies in an untidy heap where Jha was sitting and Alif finds himself, instead, taken with the story he's reading. Humans using crude stone tools and then – in a very short time in earthly terms, just a few thousand years – making bricks, shaping pots, weaving cloth. These our innocent origins!

'I hear you displeased one of our precious disciples,' Miss Moloy announces from the door. Hearing the pretend censure in her tone again after the gap of a long week during which time she has been visiting somewhere – some temple town or historical city or seaside village – and seeing that delicate head of bobbed hair and that serene face, Alif feels a surge of weary relief.

'It's all because you weren't here,' he says accusingly.

She puts away her books, sits down with him, listens patiently to his explanation.

'And now,' says Alif, winding up his short tale. 'Ankit has recast a mild tug at the ear as a mission to kill. Rawat wants to talk with me again – I didn't punch in my exit one afternoon last week. She's looking for ways to pull me up.'

Miss Moloy nods sagely. 'I think the best thing would be to go and see him, the child's father, the man who doesn't believe in history. Suggest to Mother Rawat that you'll speak to him yourself rather than her interceding. Say you want to apologise in person.'

Alif is reluctant to meet so depraved a scoundrel but agrees since Miss Moloy's suggesting it and her suggestions are sound. She thinks it will defuse the situation and help him get on with his life, his lessons, maybe even his expeditions.

He nods unhappily. 'How soon they've been forgotten – the high-minded principles and the high-minded principal?'

That gentleman, the founder, had travelled in Europe in the 1930s studying the extant systems of elementary education and returned to set up a model school with just seven children somewhere in the dingy lanes of Old Delhi. There is a photograph of him hanging on the wall of the principal's office, a bony man in a snatch of conversation with Jawaharlal Nehru, the latter caught in one of his ponderously handsome moments. And what has always struck Alif about this photo, about all photos of

that sadly bygone time, is the black-and-white aura of seriousness they give off. The eager educationist in his crumpled kurta
and Gandhi glasses, and Nehru in his simple white achkan, the
classic rose in the buttonhole – how is it possible that their talk
is about anything other than weighty matters? Photos dissemble,
he knows. Those nation builders were not, in fact, the simple and
confident men they seemed to be. They too could be blinded by
adherence to this fantasy – the nation. But they were figures of
dazzling genius compared to the dwarfish Rawats of today, busy
rendering the nation less a fantasy, more a farce.

Alif has been speaking in a dull whisper, his head bent. The
pinhead at the centre of the wall clock seems to look intently at
him, the couple of teachers in the room marking notebooks are
not sitting too far away to hear, and even Ramu who comes and
goes, wheezing and humming – bringing teacups scrubbed to
snowiness, taking away the used ones, putting up yet another of
the principal's stern notices on the board – even friendly Ramu
who usually seems to live in a simple and small universe of his
own creation might not be as otherworldly as he appears.

'She is still new and insecure,' explains Miss Moloy. 'Let her
organise another over-the-top school concert or two, bring
bhajans into the morning assembly, harangue a few students,
boss a few teachers, and then she'll loosen up.'

Jha returns and settles back into that attitude of feigned
absorption and Alif motions quickly to Miss Moloy, clears his
throat and announces, 'You've seen it all before. And now you're
retiring. Leaving me here to bear my own crosses.'

'I'll still be there, in Greater Kailash II. You can come and see
me.'

Alif thinks of how when he joined the school as a twenty-five-
year-old she'd taken him under her wing. They would exchange
beloved books and bits of their lunch boxes, and the idea of
remaining in schoolteaching all his life was partly fostered in
him through an alliance with this kind woman. The prospect
of walking these teeming corridors without her around to lean
on, figuratively speaking, produces in Alif an icy panic he cannot
confess to anyone and only ironically to her.

He tries to forget, asks about her recent adventure. She declares without hesitation that it was the best trip of her life; she has said this before about other holidays, and he reminds her of this iteration, then demands to hear all about it, he who never leaves Delhi. He's always shrunk from travel – all that human effort only to encounter what one already knows – yet is curious about Miss Moloy's insistent roving. She can travel for him for she has none of his reservations. She can sit for days on trains or hours on planes, converse brightly with everyone she meets, walk the night streets of strange cities without fear, read the guidebooks and tick off all the sights and then go on to discover some of her own. This time it is north Kerala she is returning from.

'Oh, the Malabar? They have all come there – the Christians since the time of Jesus, the Muslims since the time of the Prophet, the Jews from two thousand years ago,' intones Alif. 'They say Kerala is separated from India by those mountain ghats and connected to the world by the sea. So the world arrived and made it cosmopolitan.'

Miss Moloy tells him about a man she'd got talking to on the flight who told her his grandfather never forgot how the lower castes had to shout out a warning when they were approaching the uppers so their shadows wouldn't pollute. 'And look at me now,' the man had said. 'I travel the world. But I never forget.'

'Kerala's used to be the most unsociable caste system in the whole country practically.'

'True, true. The European presence didn't affect these rigid ideas of ritual purity. The Christians and Muslims, too, were sucked in. It was only in the early twentieth century that things started to ease up a little,' says Alif.

The newspaper rustles. Jha's penetrating eyes appear above it. He looks as if he's dying to mount a defence of caste but all he says is, 'Yesterday one man threw his wife over their balcony following an argument about how much spice she put in the daal.'

They wait to see if some insight is to follow from this but none does.

'Delhi,' says Miss Moloy and what more is there to say?

'Five floors,' says Jha and returns to his reading.

'Who else did you meet?' asks Alif and Miss Moloy starts to tell him about a Bengali boy who served her a dinner of curried mussels one night, kallumakai, the fruit of the sea. Scores of youth like him from West Bengal have been landing in Kerala to work in the construction business or as waiting staff in the restaurants, fleeing the poverty of their home state.

Alif waves his hand airily.

'But there has always been space for everyone in Kerala. The spices, the ivory and the sandalwood have been attracting people for thousands of years – the Egyptians, Phoenicians, Romans, and then the Arabs and the Chinese. The Arab traders, already doing business there, introduced Islam in the early days of the religion, and the trade picked up, their ships docking at all those famous ports – Cannanore, Calicut, Cochin, Alleppey.'

'And then,' interjects Miss Moloy, 'Vasco da Gama turns up in his admiral attire.'

'Followed by the Dutch. And then the English usurped Malabar in the early 1800s. Dastardly, the Europeans. Taking over by means more foul than fair the oceanic trade routes which for centuries had been open to all.'

Jha pipes up again.

'Yesterday...'

And they have to lend him an ear: '... a woman stabbed thirty-eight times by her Facebook stalker.'

'Delhi,' says Alif but Jha doesn't look entirely happy with this explanation.

Miss Moloy's growing voluble, tells him in some detail about the magnificent old mosques of Malabar – the arched openings to the prayer halls, sloping tiled roofs topped with brass pot finials, not dissimilar to many temples in the region.

'Why is it that the Arabs remained traders here but further north they invaded?' Alif muses.

Miss Moloy doesn't know but describes meeting a latter-day Arab who had lived in Kerala for twenty years; he was the owner of a perfume shop and it being Sunday was spending his afternoon fishing in an estuary in the small town of Mahe. 'Welcome to Kerala, please be my guest,' he'd said, handing her the fishing rod and then launching into a story about some old-time king of the land who had dreamt of a moon split in two, and converted to Islam.

'Yes, yes,' says Alif, with a touch of impatience. 'That's Cheraman Perumal, ancestor of the hereditary rulers of Kozhikode, the Samoothiri.'

'Just yesterday —' says Jha.

'For God's sake,' says Alif. 'We know.'

'You *don't* know this. Yesterday a basketball player, a teenager, kidnapped from a bus stop, raped for hours, dumped back at the same place.'

Silence. And who knows if Jha's expression — because it's still just those egg-yolk eyes on display — is shocked or salacious.

'I have to tell you,' says Miss Moloy and Jha turns to her but it's Kerala she is on, Kerala she is not finished with. This time it is the cleaner at her hotel. Annakutty had spent decades working in one of the many cashew factories of Kollam, the world's cashew-processing capital, but had lost her job with competition coming in from Vietnam where they were mechanising the business. She had pulled off her gloves to show Miss Moloy her blackened fingers — burnt from caustic sap. No one wanted to hire her for housework, she was lucky to find place in the hotel. She knew others who could no longer afford house rents or school fees for their children.

'The world has changed,' explains Alif. 'Merchandise no longer comes in painted, handmade dhows. It comes in containers on freight ships from the factories of China and Bangladesh. The introduction of a machine in Vietnam can change the fate of a woman in Kollam.'

Miss Moloy tells him of the food she has eaten, the subtle biryanis and the unsubtle goat head curry, the rice flour breads and translucent cakes of halwa in different colours, flecked with nuts.

'The food of the Mapillas of Malabar,' declares Alif, though he hasn't as much as sniffed at it, 'is influenced by the Arabs and that of the Syrian Christians by the Dutch.'

'Oh *Alif*,' she exclaims at last, so warmly that Jha finally seems to have found his cue, and throwing down his newspaper, repeats, 'Oh *Alif*.'

'You know everything but taste nothing. You will read up on every last local custom but never experience it for yourself.'

'But you never read the newspaper. Only yesterday...'

Miss Moloy is a small woman but there is something in her bearing that can, when she draws herself up, deter even the fool-hardiest. She turns her gaze on Jha and says without raising her voice a notch, 'All right, enough.'

Jha starts to fold his newspaper with the carefulness of some-one royally miffed.

'We're talking of history here. No more. No more of what happened yesterday.'

'I wasn't going to read about anything dirty,' he says. 'This is history only. An important news. Jagdishji, the member of parlia-ment, has said we have to remove all these bigoted Muslim kings from the children's textbooks. Why are we still reading about these fellows?'

'Oh stuff and nonsense,' says Miss Moloy, while Alif is on nothing if not his own trip. 'After that overbearing Vasco da Gama had killed the Arabs, he insisted a few Hindus come on board his ship so he could study them. That's vanity, I think – to turn up in a place and believe you can straightaway get a hang of the local customs.'

'You have made up your mind. If you travelled it might change.'

Underlying Miss Moloy's empirical outlook is that nothing is set in stone and no precedents pre-empt anything, whereas Alif has little interest in gaining insights through paltry experi-ence; what matters is the substantial meal of historical learning, whether it's put together from grand narratives or the details of everyday life. He would rather read *The Discovery of India* than discover India. He thinks again of its author, Jawaharlal Nehru, who realised at a young age he was foreign to this country or that this country was foreign to him, and so he took to the road. Years spent travelling: aeroplane, train, car; steamer, paddle-boat, canoe;

elephant, camel, horse; bicycle and on foot. And it was partly those journeys that produced in him this compelling idea: that India had been around for so long and was in so many respects unchanged that it was an entity with almost human traits. His tome is full of this – the unconscious mind of India, the travails she has undergone despite which her ancient wisdom survives.

Alif can be cynical about this but he is not out and out a renegade. He finds that those who want to break away tend to recreate the nation's worst aspects in the islands they carve out. He is no believer in revolutions – all the grand ones staged in recent centuries have destroyed their progeny – and so he finds he has little choice but to stay with the moderate hopes and incremental changes that democratic statehood offers till they find a better substitute for it, which no one has so far. Neither is he with those high-flown souls who would do away with countries altogether, those believers in Universal Man and One World, the radiance of the coming dawn which never comes.

It would help of course if the powers that be favoured less misleading metaphors. 'Mother India' – Nehru's wise and long-suffering female land – is a bad idea because from there it is just one step to seeing every criticism of the nation as an insult to the mother. And which Indian worth her or his salt, product of mother cults, schooled in mother apotheosising by at least a century of overwrought cinema, can tolerate that?

And so the argument with Nehru continues – a man for whom Alif feels an uneasy admiration, an ambivalent awe. Yes, your sensibility was unlike any Indian politician's before or since; yes, you went so far as to call yourself a pagan, so strongly did you identify with the soil of this land. But... and this is always the sticking point for Alif, why did you let the Muslims go? Why, when you knew that separation on a religious basis in a popu-lation so mixed was a disastrous idea, when your spirit resisted this medieval crusade in a modern country, when you foresaw that those who were demanding separation would be the great-est sufferers from it, why did you let the Muslims go? All the conversations in his head with Nehru conclude with this deeply pained question: Why Partition?

Miss Moloy, for her part, is a khadi-sari wearing offspring of the Enlightenment, European and Bengali, and an unregenerate Anglophile who insists that the British empire in India did at least as much good as harm – the drain of wealth versus the English language, divide and rule versus industrialised modernity. She believes that the humanist adventure begun with da Vinci declaring *Learn how to see* is not yet over, though Alif doubts, despite Miss Moloy's flair as a teacher, that it will come to fruition in these dusty classrooms in this busy side street of Daryaganj.

'I can't give up, no matter what,' she says thoughtfully. And she seems to be talking about more than her twice-yearly trips to somewhere or other. Perhaps she means that she will keep trying to get Alif off his high horse and on the road; perhaps she means that Rawat and her sidekicks too can be brought around to see the light.

'And in what exactly are you investing hope?' asks Alif, hobbling slowly to the door. In these imperfect feet he must turn again to face the music or find ways to wriggle out of Rawat's long-nailed grasp.

Miss Moloy doesn't answer his question. 'Let the dust settle,' is all she says.

Jha is with General Rawat – Alif didn't notice him leave the staffroom; he seems to be constantly scurrying around, which is perhaps what spies do – and he and the principal are falling about with hilarity. An unseemly sight, somehow. When Alif enters, Jha sobers up but stays put.

'So sorry, so sorry,' begins Alif and starts to invent a deep and painful illness for his wife to explain his recent negligence.

The general is not interested in Tahira's health. 'I sent for you to tell you the school board met recently.'

Alif steels himself against her toothy and dishonest smile. He knows it conceals only bad things. And he is right.

'Mr Jha tells me that in the entire history of the school no teacher has ever attacked a child.'

'How would he know?' asks Alif, genuinely puzzled. 'He joined just this year.'

'I meant this as an observation, Mohammad ji,' says Jha. 'In the records of such a school, a school as illustrious such as this, such a thing could not have happened.'

'That's what,' says Rawat. 'It's never happened.'

'I wasn't going to throw him out of the rickshaw, Mrs Rawat, madam,' says Alif with all the pained politeness he can muster. 'You know what these children can be like sometimes. They need a little shaking up. But please do enquire if I've ever touched any of them before.'

'So at the board meeting, it was decided –'

'It was decided by a majority vote...' chips in Jha.

*No*, thinks Alif. They're going to take away history and give him civics. They're going to take away the whole of Class Four from him just because of that one bloody, irascible kid.

'We decided by a majority vote to suspend you from your job. An investigating committee will be formed to investigate what happened.'

Alif sits back astounded. Then he leans forward and says, 'You see, the thing is that he called me a Muslim.'

'Muslim?' asks Jha. 'What's wrong with that? What are you if not...'

He looks at Rawat and titters.

'He *accused* me,' says Alif but can't bring himself to repeat what the boy said. 'And he insisted on confusing Humayun with Hanuman.'

Mrs Rawat presses her lips to even out her lipstick, sighs with displeasure and says, 'Your suspension is already underway so if you could kindly now leave.'

'Please wait a minute, madam.' Ganesh is always recommending muscle power but Alif, in the face of this officiousness, finds it difficult to even metaphorically ball his fists. He must think of a defence but all he can think of is Vasco da Gama, yet another one of those unstoppable men of character that he is not.

'Wouldn't you have to show me the papers?' is the only thing he manages to come up with.

'Papers?'

'The resolutions passed. The decisions taken. The minutes of the meeting.'

Rawat turns to Jha who nods smoothly.

'We will have them sent to your residence by registered post within seven working days,' he says.

'And for the time being, please do not enter the school premises. You will receive your salary as usual. And the guard is going to be given instructions.'

'You could have asked the children, you could have asked those colleagues who've known me for years, madam,' says Alif pitifully.

'We cannot overlook behaviour that is a threat to the institution. In fact, Mr Jha here said "terminate his services right away". But I felt, let the committee take the suitable action.'

Alif notices that she has stopped addressing him as 'sir'. Or even 'Mr Alif'. In fact, she's stopped addressing him altogether and is now conferring with Jha about something else, that dreadfully didactic play she is obsessed with. 'By 2050 there will be more plastic in the ocean than fish. Now how do we demonstrate this? Mermaids dressed in polythene bags?'

Jha may be a highly effective secret agent but he does not seem to know what mermaids are. Rawat is charmed by his ignorance and starts to explain. For the second time in two weeks, Alif walks out of the principal's office, not sure Miss Moloy's idea of extending an olive branch would have helped, not sure anything can help, feeling defeated and tired. It could be a civilisational exhaustion. Nehru, for all his passion for Mother India, did note in his *Discovery* that she was at a low ebb, wanting very much to go to sleep. Facing General Rawat's call to battle, that's just what Alif would like to do.

★

Tahira's exam results are out and she has 'killed it' says Salim, not bothering to explain when an unlearned Alif asks how and what she has killed. He suggests they have a party. Since it's the month of Ramzan, only an iftar party will do, Tahira says. She's on a day's leave from work to savour her joy, trying to tamp down this joy, insisting that the exam was easy or that it was just an exam, but Alif knows what an MBA will do for that quality she prizes most dearly – self-respect. He has not let on about the recent knocks his own self-respect has taken as he skulks at home, pretending that he's finally on the few months' leave he's so often yearned for to proceed with his research.

Tahira and Salim have heard enough about the winds of change blowing over nineteenth-century Delhi to not want to know more. As for Alif, all he has come up with since he seized on this subject are a series of tantalising 'what ifs'. What if the handful of enlightened writers, educators, philosophers and translators associated with the Delhi College had continued with their educational project, the so-called New Learning – Arabic and Persian literature, English prose and poetry, science and maths, theology and jurisprudence taught in Urdu? What if this chapter had not been cut short by the war of 1857 in which several of those teachers and scholars, seen as godless or Christianised, were killed by the rebels? It is not just the energy and vision of these men that impresses Alif, but also their belief that Hindus and Muslims were inseparable, though some felt the two parties needed the benevolent liberalism of a Queen Victoria to ensure they kept their hands off each other's throats.

The biggest 'what if' in all of this concerns the British. What if the rebels had not succeeded in ousting them? Would this thing have taken on a more robust life? For even though some call it a renaissance, it started with a colonial objective – to render English texts into Urdu. A flowering of prose followed from this and it could have led to what the wise but ultimately tragic men of Delhi College wanted – to be modern without being out-and-out Western. But after 1857 the new educators turned to English and, inexorably, by the early twentieth century modern and Western started to mean one and the same thing.

Right here, not two kilometres from where he lives, is a construction with all the hallmarks of the Mughal – red sandstone, elaborate arched entrances, projecting balconies – which was once a madrasa that housed briefly the cerebral excitements of the Delhi College, and is today a regular school. Alif would

like to take his wife and son to see it, give them a brief, illustrated history lesson: we needn't have turned out this way. It's
worth remembering that other futures were once dreamt for us.

But they won't be impressed. Other than Miss Moloy
perhaps, few people he knows would really care. 'Indians as a
race are indifferent to history,' his teacher Maharishi Jain had
announced on the very first day of class at university and since
then Alif has heard it said repeatedly. We are scrambled in our
heads, we cannot really distinguish external reality from inner
states – the self from the non-self – and so the doings of our
forefathers are not of abiding interest to us and we do not
regard history as the biography of mankind. But others point
out the beauty in this, our feeling for eternity and our ability to
switch effortlessly between timeless and time-bound. What we
lack in objectivity we make up for with imagination, and each
one of our gods comes trailing her or his own many-chaptered
story.

'Who will cook?' Tahira asks Salim. Alif can't cook and Tahira
won't and Salim would like to but doesn't have the wherewithal
yet. They make do with a rather mediocre helper named Priya
whose culinary skills are not party standard. Every weekend Alif's
mother sends back food with Alif which lasts them a couple of
days, thus enabling them to evade Priya's cooking.

Tahira dislikes the assumption that because she is Muslim
and a woman she must be a great cook. Her colleagues at the
supermarket treat her, whenever Eid comes around, as a source
of biryani and kebabs, an expectation that raises her hackles
sky high. 'Is this all we are?' she asks Alif. 'Bawarchis? Poetry-
spouting fools with minced mutton coming out of our ears,
thinking only of Allah and pining only for behesht between
mouthfuls of zafrani pulao?'

Alif overlooks her antipathy to cooking but his mother's
weekly gifts, those plastic boxes heavy with leftovers, also bear
in them the sadness of having a headstrong daughter-in-law. 'It's
not that she doesn't know how much of what to put into what,'
Shagufta repeatedly tells Alif, as if it were news to him. 'It's just
that she's not the sort of person who's interested in these things.'

Salim hands his mother a stack of the flyers he collects for all the meaty eat-in and takeaway places in the neighbourhood.

'It would be bad form to call friends to an iftar and offer them restaurant food,' says Tahira.

'Who's coming?' says Alif.

Salim wants to have his friends over but Tahira thinks the decent thing to do would be to invite the Khannas given their long history of kindness.

'Ganesh will be back home late as usual,' points out Alif. 'Khanna Aunty's arthritis has been acting up so she can't climb the stairs. And as for Khanna Uncle, he doesn't say much these days.'

'We must have a party,' insists Salim. 'Ammi has killed it.'

In the end Alif phones Ganesh and implores him, for Tahira's sake, to get home before sundown. His friend is not in a Faustian mood today though he often is, trying to balance his resentment about work with his love for unbridled prosperity. Today he's just fed up. 'Beta, you're living a lie,' Ganesh says, ready right in the middle of a working day to, however crudely, philosophise. This is a line he can, depending on his mood, aim at Alif's tedious ramblings as much as his own ravaging hungers. For the moment, it's the latter. This is why I like the man. That is if I do like the man, reflects Alif.

'I am at a point in life where pretty much nothing is my own – not my time, not my thoughts, not even my wife, dammit. Yeh capitalism ki maha chutiyapanthi hai ki kya hai ye?'

'Okay, fine. What the capitalists do to you, you do back to them. But then cheer up. It's a good day. Tahi has passed the exam and surely it must rain soon. Are you leaving there by five or are you not? And don't make promises you can't keep. The other day with Prerna...'

He stops. Anything at all he says about Prerna will be insincere and not to talk about Prerna is also insincere – she was Ganesh's friend first and yet his instinct now is to hide her from him. This is so messed up, he thinks. From the next room he can hear his son explaining in mature tones to his mother why he would be better off, as an adult, getting into the food industry for a spell or starting a hair-cutting salon. Not forever, he says. Just to try my hand at business, make some money and figure out next steps. He suggests boldly that he drop out the following the year once he passes his school-leaving exam. Tahira's response is not audible just yet; she probably can't speak for horrified dismay. Because she has done better than her mother she assumes that her child will do better than her, along the conventional axes – acquire more degrees, get better jobs, live in neater houses…

'You can be virtuous,' Ganesh says. 'You do good things, teach history and all that. You are happy your salary is less than peanuts, you are happy your wife drives some centuries-old Maruti and you drive nothing. Do you have any idea how much all your Sufi shit tortures me?'

'I'm not a Sufi, man. I'm not even a Mus—'

'Shh…that imam guy will hear you,' says Ganesh. And it's true that Alif can see, from the open window by which he's standing, the minarets of the small mosque in the square, a loudspeaker hanging lopsidedly from one them. And it's also true that there are several other mosques around and a ten-minute walk away is the great Friday mosque, the Jama Masjid. Breathing this sanctimonious air for so much of his life has somewhat inured Alif to it.

'Okay, so not a Muslim, not even a Sufi, then what are you?'

Alif goes into the living room. 'I'm handing the phone to Tahira.'

Ganesh is charming at once, congratulates her warmly, says he will definitely make it for the party.

'What do you have to say to this?' Tahira asks Alif when she's finished with Ganesh. 'All I want is to send him away to the best business school and he's preparing to wash dishes in a hotel.'

Salim murmurs something about the joys of entrepreneurship. But then seeing how Tahira is ready to dissolve all argument in a burst of tears, he starts backtracking. Alif does nothing to help either him or her. He doesn't mind if his son has no use for classroom learning as long as he is up to scratch with the highlights of history. And if his wife insists that he fulfil her dreams rather cultivate his own, then that too is fine. They can sort out between themselves what the fate of each is to be. Salim reminds a weepy-looking Tahira that she is an MBA in Sales and Marketing and she relents, embraces her son, though not her husband. Some kind of patchy peace is restored and they return to stillness through the hot afternoon in which the smallest movement seems to invite conflagration.

Ganesh manages to materialise by half past six and they all gather downstairs in the Khanna home, at a table piled with far too much to eat; that glut, muses Alif, that is the hallmark of any celebration in our culture. Tahira waits for the announcement from the mosque next door and the others wait with her in honour of her fast, though they are not fasting themselves. When it is time she prays, and Alif, his eyes only half-closed, his prayer only half-true, watches her, the lips moving soundlessly, the communion seemingly unimpeded by their presence. He wonders what it is she is asking for, and he wonders if she will ever come around to his belief that the deepest prayer cannot be petition, only submission. Tahira's prayers are always regular and always hurried, as though she's just doing them to keep her part of a promise made long ago, a pact tiresome to abide by but possibly fatal to renege on.

*God is nearer to man than his jugular vein,* Alif recalls the Koran as saying. He looks at his son, whose eyes are shut tight unlike his father's, and wonders if he too is praying only to please Tahira. And what about you, asks Alif, turning his gaze inward. Have you simplified yourself to the point where you're ready to submit wholly to the will of God? *Not yet, not yet, not yet.* So why expect your wife to? Why cannot her fast, if she so wills it, be less ennobling sacrifice, more bargaining chip? But then how is that different from Faust?

Alif glances at Ganesh who is discreetly messaging on his phone, at Salim whose eyes are now wide open and hungry, at Mr Khanna who is staring at nothing and has said nothing so far, and at Mrs Khanna who is the most beautiful woman he has ever known in his life and, in all likelihood, will ever know. She is a delicate-boned, large-eyed, milk-and-roses-hued, snow-haired china doll; she looks like something precious someone forgot to take with them into some other, more ethereal exist-ence. She has been left behind here, her knees gone, her eyesight fading, her voice thinning, unable to flee this gloomy house. It's twice as large as theirs upstairs and it was allotted to Ganesh's grandfather when the family moved here after Partition, a Muslim-owned house going to a Hindu family and vice versa happening there, on the other side of the new border. Alif is always curious about what they might have left behind but over the years their things and the Khannas have merged somehow so that now the rosewood side tables with curved legs and scal-loped edges, the cabinet with the tall white china teapot and leaning tower of teacups, the half-moons of mullioned yellow glass above the front door belong, in his imagination, to both former owners and present ones. It is all somewhat dispiriting and then there are the low spirits of these two men. Yet even a lifetime of this hasn't dimmed her, and it astonishes Alif, it always does, that father and son can live with a woman this luminous and not light up themselves.

Women are wasted on men, he theorises silently, and this floods his heart with pain and recalls Prerna Mittal's face to him. Of course he has to tell Ganesh about her. And about the unfair suspension from school. He needs to talk to Ganesh.

Tahira has completed her prayer, kissed her palms, and is passing around a dish of dates. She shares her dream with Ganesh – store manager not in the poky neighbourhood supermarket where she presently works but a well-appointed branded outlet situ-ated ideally in an upmarket mall in South Delhi or Gurgaon.

'Business development head. That's what they're called. In charge of employee strength, new stock, inventories, display ...'

Tahira repeats the phrases. She knows them well but is unable to keep the reverence out of her voice. 'Do you think I have a chance?'

She sounds so hopeful, so eager, so resolute that Alif admires and worries; he wishes he could shape the world in a way that it never disappointed Tahira. That's marriage, he thinks. Or that's our marriage. She is always trying to better herself and he is always trying to conceal his failures. For a moment he imagines coming clean – about why he hasn't gone to school. Perhaps she would forgive. But her self-possession makes it hard. Or she might cry and even that is part of her deadly arsenal.

'The thing is…' Ganesh breaks off, clearly trying to find a way to put it gently to her, whatever it is, this bad news from the intrinsically bad dog-eat-dog world. 'Of course. You have this degree, you have a chance at doing better. Higher pay, a nice-sounding designation. Assistant manager, say. But the assistant manager does not manage the whole store the way you do now. That sort of boss man —'

'Or boss woman,' points out Salim.

'That sort of boss woman needs to have been around for a good long while.'

'I know, I started too late,' she says regretfully. 'Till Salim was eight I didn't work, I was already thirty-five when I got into TipTop.'

'It's okay, Ammi,' says Salim, through a mouthful of chicken roll. 'Think of the money.'

'Yes, but for what? To sell underwear. I don't want to deal with customers, I want to sit in the back office and run the place.'

'Two options, then,' says Ganesh. 'Stay where you are because you're fine there. Or take what you get in a bigger place and learn the ropes, watch out for opportunities, keep applying for openings, and brush up your skills. Get another MBA on the side, maybe in brand management.'

'Another MBA?' shrieks Tahira, and Salim says consolingly, 'Brand management, Ammi. Not cyber forensics or space technology.'

Mrs Khanna has produced from somewhere a bowl of greasy gram flour sweets which she presses on her husband, who ignores it, and then hands to Alif.

'Is he okay?' Alif asks Mrs Khanna. He has been hearing from Ganesh about these increasingly tortuous silences but meeting him now, after several months, he is stunned to see how much the man has aged – the frown of deep vertical creases that cannot unfrown itself, the autumnal translucence of the skin on his hands. He no longer drops by upstairs to chat and his hours at the shop too have been shrinking.

'He doesn't talk to the customers any more,' says Mrs Khanna.
'He lets Gujral do it. Gujral can do it.'

'Does he eat?'

Mrs Khanna nods and smiles conspiratorially, pecking at her date like a fragile, fussy bird.

'Only a little in the morning. At night I have to feed him. If I get him hooked on a story and push some daal roti into his mouth, he might eat.'

'What sorts of stories?'

'What sorts of stories do I care for except those about my gurus,' she says happily. 'I've been telling him go visit Panja Sahib. His people used to take him once a year from Lahore when he was a child. You know the shrine of Panja Sahib, which has a handprint of Guru Nanak? Thousands from this side still visit there, even if it's in Pakistan.'

Mr Khanna suddenly raises his head to look at his wife and, miraculously, the creases on his forehead soften.

'No, no. I'm not going anywhere,' he says in a scratchy voice. 'The shop…'

'You visit Panja Sahib and I tell you, you will be well again.'

'I'm no longer of an age to travel. Mama wants me to go because she can't go herself.'

'Let Ganesh get the visa,' she instructs.

Mr Khanna nods weakly in the negative.

'Ganesh will be there to hold you.'

Khanna's resisting this – this offer his son is quietly making, through his mother, to be a crutch, a walking stick, a pillar of support to his father.

'No,' he breathes.

'You've travelled all over North India. You've gone every-where,' says his wife. 'But just return to Panja Sahib once.'

'I made the big journey…' And that short phrase seems to tire him out.

'You did, you did,' says his wife, her slender porcelain neck all atremble, and in this too she is like a bird. 'The big journey. But was that a journey? What kind of journey was that? You were seven years old. Everyone said it's only for a few months – just leave everything and return, we'll keep it safe for you. But you never saw the streets of Lahore again. Your father died saying, I will never see the streets of Lahore again.'

Alif wonders if soon she will be doing all of it – speaking for him as well as to him, feeding herself and feeding him, being very much more than that pillar of support, being the thing that gladly effaces itself in order to give life to someone else.

'Anyway, how could you have gone back when there was nothing left to go back for?' says Mrs Khanna, smiling as though the tale amuses her. Unlike her husband she is not a child of Partition. Being from Amritsar, twin city to Lahore, only fifty-odd kilometres away, which did not go there but stayed here, she has had to leave no home behind, witnessed no killings, lost no relatives.

'Did you ever want to visit?' asks Alif, wanting the man to speak out, wishing he would unburden himself, hoping it is not too late, that he is not already at the point where he can no longer distinguish the burden from himself. 'I mean later when it became possible, when there were buses going across the border?'

'Ab ...' says Mr Khanna but seems unable to attach that word – 'now' – with any others. It hangs in the air and gradually enforces silence in the room. For some time then, just the sound of them eating: this uncharacteristic sundown meal, this moveable feast of iftar, slipping from month to month in the Gregorian calendar and then returning to where it started. Salim has had his way and ordered a gross quantity of meat. Priya contributed heaps of misshapen puris and chickpeas drowned in a lurid red oil slick of a gravy. Alif is worried about school, worn out by the mugginess of the late August heat, distracted by the memory of Prerna's voice, sad for the Khannas, and he has no appetite. Salim ingests food with the alacrity of a vacuum cleaner, Ganesh too eats heartily, Tahira is, of course, starving, but Mr Khanna only drinks tea and Mrs Khanna is asking everyone in turn if she should make them dahi bhallas for she already has some urad daal all soaked and ready. And despite himself, the atmosphere – people sitting together to eat in a twilight togetherness – touches Alif with a sublimated thrill. He can easily slip back to adolescence, those long schooldays filled with the light-headed ecstasy that fasting brings on, and then the solemnity of hushed evenings when his grandmother cooked, his mother and aunt arranged modest portions on everyone's plates, his grandfather prayed over them and finally the first morsel touched their tongues and felt nothing if not holy. Religion is a child's game, thinks Alif. He remembers Ankit, that absurd slur, and he is sorry.

Ganesh is trying to convince Tahira that her son has grasped a fundament of contemporary existence – not study first and work later but study and work together, or alternately, just like she is herself doing.

'Another MBA?' she repeats, still disbelieving. 'Who will give me the money for that?' She looks at Alif who smiles, acts as if he's thinking of something else.

Ganesh gives her his usual spiel about the speed at which the world is moving and how to keep pace with it – the growing nimbleness of the human mind, no longer that plodding instrument of old to be schooled for a set number of years and then let loose to join the workforce. He keeps throwing his father quick glances of yearning as he talks, but is unable to direct any of these insights at him.

Tahira seems humbled by this tirade, and Salim smug. Ganesh breaks off suddenly and snaps at his mother, 'Stop going on about your cooking. Here, give him some fruit to eat.'

And beaming like a royal's favourite attendant, Mrs Khanna puts one black grape after another into her husband's mouth, transfixed by his slow mastication of each as if she were tasting its sweetness instead of him. Then she stands up in stages to go and look for some photographs she wants to show them – a handful of creased and curling black-and-white prints, some no bigger than large postage stamps, and yet within those small white frames large families microscopically captured, whole streetscapes, the vast facades of buildings of historical importance. These are not photos from Mrs Khanna's past but Mr Khanna's, though Alif notices that the old man avoids looking at them as they're passed around.

'The streets of Lahore?' asks Salim and wonders why Mr Khanna's father died without seeing them again.

This starts off Alif, who is appalled that his own son, the offspring of a historian, is blithely ignorant about Partition and its legacy, and he tries to put across to him the tangled history of hate between the two countries; it's a long story before one arrives at the watershed of 1947.

'Salim, please, you can't pretend not to know this. Our fore-fathers left it to us and we in turn – having mended nothing, having generally worsened the situation, taken one step forward and two steps back, or not even sought to mend, just insisted on the two or rather the two hundred steps back – gift it to you, your generation, to make of it what you will.'

'If it happened so long ago how does it matter any more?' says Salim, who has not stopped eating though his chomping has slowed down a bit as he listens with partial interest to his father.

'How does it matter? Can't you see? We separated so as to not kill each other and we then started killing each other in earnest. Or one side wants to decimate the other. It's come to that now. One side wants to finish off the other.'

'That's enough,' says Tahira. Ganesh agrees. He tells Alif to cool down. Him Alif can ignore, for Ganesh has no historical perspective to speak of.

To his wife he says, 'But I've only just started. Give me ten minutes.'

'Ten minutes,' scoffs Tahira. 'Don't bore the child with the politics of it. It's finished and done with and it's what Allah wanted.'

Alif glances, mortified, at Khanna Uncle but he doesn't seem to have registered.

'Tahira begum,' says Alif. 'Must we really bring Allah into this? Your faith is your private thing. What the politicians got hold of and then didn't give up till the new country was made was your identity. They argued for and against two nations on that basis, the rumour that your identity was in peril.'

'You're splitting hairs now. The truth is that it just had to happen. It was destiny.'

'It was a horrendously costly mistake that could have been avoided,' says Alif quietly.

He wants to educate his son, not argue with his wife, but now there is no stopping her and Alif feels compelled to counter her arguments. She reminds him of Muslim anxieties, of Muslim pain. She is an expert on this – historical suffering – and has in her possession a battery of one-line explanations for how they came to find themselves underdogs, theories passed around for generations in her family, drawn from the subcontinent's politics – the tragic mistreatment of the last Mughal emperor by the British or, a century on, the sidelining of Mohammad Ali Jinnah, their spokesperson. She will unleash these on Alif, as she does on his father when they discuss the state of affairs at the dining table, and lunch sours because Mahtab will not be taught politics by a woman, his daughter-in-law at that.

Alif does not take so one-sided a view of things. As he sees it, everyone is to blame. In facing up to Tahira he is doing battle with the fathers of the nation, urging them to understand, compromise, give and take. History as nightmare – reduced to the bickering of a few powerful men. Alif wishes he could not hear them so well, make out their missteps so clearly but this, if anything, is his inheritance, and Salim's too if only he could see.

He would like to share with his son an account of these political blunders: why did Nehru not yield two seats to the Muslim League after the 1937 elections to the provincial legislatures in the United Provinces which the Congress handsomely won? This power-sharing arrangement would have brought the League and Congress closer and perhaps averted the split. And why did Jinnah float the pernicious idea that the Congress was a Hindu party and the League a Muslim one? Why did the Congress insist on a centralised form of government in the 1920s when the Muslim League proposed a more federal structure? On the other hand, why on earth this insistence on Hindu and Muslim at all, why was religion a basis for political identity? The League was to blame; it petitioned the Raj for separate Muslim and Hindu electorates and got them as early as 1909. Or maybe Gandhi was to blame; he propagated Ram Rajya when he knew that metaphor would alienate Muslims. For if Congress really was the secular party why was the possibility, at the eleventh hour, in 1946, of the League forming the government and Jinnah leading the country so distasteful to them? On the other hand, if the League represented Muslims what about the millions of Muslims who continued to live in India after Partition? Who could claim to speak for them? Why did the League not encourage Muslims to throw in their lot with Hindus in order to free themselves of the British? Why didn't they back Gandhi's non-cooperation movement instead of banging on about Khilafat?

Salim is absorbed in one of Ganesh's modern fairy tales: about how a leading digital company fell on hard times and then turned its fortunes around by moving to cloud computing. Tahira is entertaining Khanna Aunty with that account of the petty thief among her colleagues whom she turned in. She likes this story and Khanna Aunty shows no sign of having heard it before though she certainly has.

And so Alif continues arguing with everyone in his head. That crazy misadventure, Khilafat. Tahira is a great admirer of it. The Turks lose the First World War to the British, the caliph is in peril, and Indian Muslims feel one of the cornerstones of their religion, the caliphate, must be defended. And so, ordinary people donating their hard-earned money for the cause, and the flight of some Indian Muslims out of the country in a modern hegira, refusing to kowtow to a power that is antagonistic to Islam.

There are those who would say that the qaum came to be united by a dream in a way it never has been before or since, and that we also joined forces with Gandhi in the bargain. Yes, it was a stirring idea, thinks Alif. Yes, in the nineteenth century it might have made sense to see oneself as everything at once – Indian, Ottoman, Arab, Muslim, subject of the British empire. But in the 1920s the need of the hour was to fight for an independent nation, not romanticise the Islamic past. It was the era of nationhood. We were barking up the wrong tree.

What you call romanticising the past, we call belief. We call faith. We call religion, Tahira would say. But he can't agree. Faith should not mean being blind to the historical moment and its demands. What we should have done, thinks Alif – and he is so anxious to say at least this much out loud to his indifferent companions – is heeded Maulana Azad. The gentle and erudite maulana, the one decent politician. And why should we have listened to him? Jinnah had a larger following because he appealed to the qaum's fears whereas Azad appealed to their humanism and asked that as true devotees of Islam they live together with Hindus. He was a scholar, he had made a thorough study of the Koran and come to this conclusion.

Ganesh has noticed his friend's agitation and says, 'Listen, beta. Our time is coming. For ages it has felt as though the Western civilisation is the only one there is. Why? Because almost everything we used, from a safety pin to a computer, from an aircraft to a sewing machine, from a bottle opener to a matchstick, was invented over there. But not any more. There are no world capitals any longer, you can be sitting anywhere and come up with an idea that will turn the planet upside down.'

'Such as?' asks Alif.

'Listen,' says Ganesh, turning to Salim, superfluously for the boy is already agog. 'These lousy corporations that are already fuc— messing … with our lives want nothing but more control – spy on us through the cameras in our phones, track our daily activities, make the information about our habits the biggest source of wealth in the world. Big data, you know. Like oil in the twentieth century. Or the gold rush in the nineteenth.'

'I know, I know,' says Salim. 'That's where all the investments are going – artificial intelligence, virtual reality, machine learning, smart everything.'

'Exactly, my precious son,' says Ganesh, clapping an exultant hand on the boy's shoulder. 'So do you want to be the sucker who is just fodder for the masters of the universe, the prisoner of his limited choices, the witless and debt-ridden consumer, a mere lemon to be squeezed dry? Or do you want to be on the other side?'

'Just tell me what I need to do to get there,' says Salim.

'Make a sacrifice,' says Alif.

'What?'

'If you're a Muslim you make a sacrifice. You know the story of Abraham, you know the story of Imam Husain, you know –'

'Oh leave him alone. What sacrifices have you made?'

Seeing the unease on Ganesh's face at Tahira's tone of voice, and it takes something to make Ganesh uneasy, Alif relents and goes quiet again. Sacrifice, he thinks. Something done to make amends. A gesture of penitence. How is it that none of those politicians responsible for Partition, except perhaps Gandhi, ever publicly expressed any contrition? How can so many people die and many more be severed from their lives and shunted off to a new country and all of it attributed to the tidal forces of history – destiny, as Tahira calls it?

The idea of a national destiny frightens him. Where does it come from? Perhaps medieval Europe whose historians started to apply to all races the idea, from ancient Virgil's *Aeneid*, of a noble group of people guided by the gods towards a splendid destiny. Or is it an older obsession – as in the long-held belief that the Jewish people are destined to find the Promised Land? And so, likewise, Indian Muslim destiny – to carve out their own country. Nehru spoke of the karma of nations and how two hundred years of colonial rule had conditioned the Indian future. But he was not a fatalist and he was not a sentimentalist, much as he believed in India's ancient soul.

So who's right? And what do people mean when they say history will decide whether we were right or wrong, when they say that human truths don't matter because time will tell. Every day it becomes more obvious to Alif that history has decided but still no one's owning up to it. He feels an urge to return to *Discovery*. He must get Salim to read it as well, but the boy is stuffing the last bit of his third or fourth roll into his mouth and says, 'I have a game to finish,' a conventional excuse whenever he wants to get away, and especially when Alif and Tahira quarrel. There is always some ongoing, some busily lifelike digital saga to return to and lose himself in; he rises abruptly and disappears through the door before anyone can stop him.

His mother looks despondent for a moment and Khanna Aunty, undeterred as always, asks again about the dahi bhallas.

'Yes, yes. I would love to. You make them, because you make them so well, and I'll watch,' says Tahira.

Alif murmurs his thanks and his apologies, rises slowly from the table, anxious to snatch his son back before he is swallowed by those pixelated fantasies.

Mr Khanna speaks. 'Ab …' he declares again, looking up from the pattern of scratches on the old table he's been patiently studying, long after everyone has forgotten that he can talk. 'Ab rehne do.' *Let it be.*

# FOUR

Alif and Salim walk north through the lanes of Tiraha Bairam Khan and emerge before the grand Jama Mosque just as the light is slipping from the sky and coming on in all the many open-mouthed establishments of Urdu Bazaar. A hundred different enactments of daily commerce – sellers of fly-speckled dates heaped in all shades of brown; squawking cages with scrawny chickens and fluff balls of yellow chicks; biryani rice boiling in a huge cauldron of cloudy water and a man testing one grain between two fingertips; another man outside on his haunches contemplatively smoking his hookah; a hopeful woman with nothing but a tiny heap of garlic cloves for sale; men in spotless white presiding over festering goat trotters; a bookshop with signs for sale that all say the same thing in different calligraphed Urdu words, Khushahmdeed, Istiqbaal, Tashrif Layeye – that is, Welcome and Welcome and Welcome; heaped on the pavement an incredibly emaciated beggar with a bald head the size of an infant's, an even more emaciated child asleep on her lap. Her bare limbs are entangled with the baby's and difficult to tell apart. She is nibbling on a samosa from a tinfoil plate, chewing with dazed slowness as if eating too much or too quickly will kill her after years of eating too little. She has received her iftar from the other side of the road where the row of folding tables on which those small plates of snacks and paper cups of juice that were laid out for the poor fasters like her are now being folded up.

A banner strung between electricity poles flaps in the breeze, asking the government to please leave Muslims alone.

A high-windowed, air-conditioned coach full of behatted tourists from foreign lands trundles past them. Salim talks about the nuisance of his physics homework – 'I just don't get the laws of optics but does it matter when I can see?' – and he does not notice these small things because they are ordinary and Alif notices them because they are ordinary and with each passing day made for him more distinct by their lack of distinctiveness. He sees how an ancient-looking rickshaw cyclist is actually very young and a young-looking ittar shop a hundred years old. And he catches, as always, snatches of phrases that reinforce the laughable puniness of this human drama and the gigantic command of him, the only God – *Baki Allah ki marzi... Bismillah kar ke... Masha Allah... Alhamdullilah.*

When they reach it, Alif and Salim settle down on the broad, warm southern steps of the mosque with the others sitting there like them, in individual or joint contemplation, their hunger sated for this day, one eye on tenebrous sky as they talk of how things were when things were better. Behind them – red sandstone, white marble and black marble; grandiose gateways; striped and fluted minarets and beautiful, bulbous domes; vast courtyard edged with colonnaded cloisters; proportion and precision; plainness and ornament; simplicity and beauty – this, the grandest of Mughal mosques, in whose shadow both men have grown up and within sight of which Alif would like to die. What better place – these flagstones pressed by five hundred years' worth of supplicating feet and an equal number of weary foreheads kissing the earth, submitting before the manmade symmetry of the prayer hall in order to believe in a heaven which mirrors it.

*Delhi.* The city on which the apocalypse descends every day and the city where the apocalypse is always awaited. One of those women had looked down on him from that tourist bus and he wondered what she'd seen – a local, touched with local colour, living his local life. She would preserve in some corner of her mind the mosque built by that building-crazy emperor Shah Jahan in the seventeenth century. And with the mosque there is him – the man in the background or foreground, the minor figure, the passing native. He has always been there to accentuate this grandeur by his apparent humbleness – because he mucks about in these mucky lanes, and so is an element of the scene, as timeless as the stones of which the mosque is made.

But that's not who I am, thinks Alif, and there are days when he is so tired of this – eager day-trippers who come and go, or serious flâneurs who take the measure of the old city, painstaking collectors of historical bricks and falling door posts and vaulted arches. He is tired of the trilling of anklets on the dancing girl's feet and the easy rhyming of the cheesy ghazal, he is tired of the saaqi and the filled-to-flowing jaam, the majnoon and the always unreliable jaan-e-jaana, the shamma and the death-seeking parwaana – all those tawdry characters on the lighted stage on which Muslim culture in this country has played out for eight hundred years.

'What did you want to say, Abba?' asks Salim, not happy to be pulled outdoors.

Alif looks at his son and wishes he could kiss him. He has just berated him for his lack of history, and yet he cannot help, every time, overlooking this too – this insouciance, this blatant disregard.

'The time you waste...'

But Salim is past being told off by his father. He can hear the affection in his tone, he sees it in his face, and he seizes on it at once. 'Please Abba,' he says cajolingly. 'Please, I don't want to go back to school after Class Ten. Or Twelve at the most.'

'Ask your mother nicely.'

'She will never agree. But if I stuck on for three more years? Would you support me?'

'And what happens then?'

'Freedom,' says Salim grinning. Why is he named Salim, wonders Alif. Because Salim is my favourite Mughal. But the emperor also became feckless halfway through his career. He handed over the running of his kingdom to Nur Jahan and just hung around drinking and commissioning paintings of whatever caught his fancy. And yet which Mughal loved beauty as much as Salim?

'Freedom,' exclaims Alif. 'You're already free. When I was half your age our Nana, who had been a very tolerant grandfather

137

thus far, decided we – me and Farouk – were verging on spoilt. The sisters, his and mine, would be shaped by the circumstances of their marriage; women have an invisible, or visible, hand pressing down on them, but the boys had been given a long rope, so the boys now needed some reining in. And so he got us to sit down with him every evening to read the Koran. All day trying to dodge the cursing and the caning at the Urdu school and all evening trying to make sense of this new language. And it had been triggered by a small mistake Farouk made.'

'Did he fail?'

'No, he stole some money. That's all. He pinched twenty rupees from the pocket of a rich classmate.'

'Only *twenty*?'

'This was forty years ago, child. I'd never seen Nana so disturbed. He took it to be a fault in his child-rearing. So he made us prisoners of his conscience. Farouk learnt nothing but I struggled seriously with the book. If we drank down all that Arabic we would apparently be better men. I sensed we wouldn't but had to keep up the battle for his sake. I didn't want to let him down and Farouk already had.'

'But I've never seen you read the Koran, not even during Ramzan.'

'I did try, but very soon it struck me that the book contained nothing I didn't know. Nani had been telling us grand tales since we were lisping and crawling and those had already done their work. I was already converted to Allah and I was already sympathetic to his Prophet.'

'So you mean *I* don't have to listen to Ammi going on about sending me to a maulvi?' Salim's face lights up.

'She says it out of habit, she knows there's no point when two maulvis have tried and failed with you.'

'Will you tell her, please? You always look away when she scolds me.'

Alif ignores this home truth. 'What I'm saying is: you don't want school, you won't go to the maulvi, fine. But the thing is that life is not a game, you know, it's not set up just for scoring, winning, getting ahead of, getting the better of...'

Even to his own ears Alif sounds lame. He wants, as always, to talk of what has receded by now to a vague blotch on the horizon, the spirit. How to talk of the spirit to a contemporary teenager? He thinks of the old-time Sanskrit dramatists and their position — that the world was not essentially made for human beings and in acknowledging this lies happiness. And now we cannot think of anything but the opposite: the world is there for the taking.

'Okay, Abba, you can teach me,' says Salim, agreeable to anything that will let him off the hook. 'You're a good teacher, also,' he adds casually.

Alif has to stop and swallow hard for fear that love will break his voice.

'And when was the last time you paid attention to anything I said?' he asks, trying to match his son's offhand tone.

'Oh but now I will. If you back my plan of dumping school then I promise to do nothing but listen to you.'

'So the nawab sahib is going to actually sit down with me, put away that laptop, hide his phone...'

'Let's say for half an hour every evening?'

'History class?'

Salim nods, bright-eyed. 'But you have to get Ammi to promise first.'

'You really believe that, what you just said about my teaching?' asks Alif shyly.

'Sure, Abba,' says Salim. His attention has been caught by a tour guide lounging nearby who's telling his companion about his day, how he took a group of sun-burnished tourists to see the mosque, how he'd instructed them on its history simply by asking them — Taj Mahal? It's the only thing they've heard of, these Europeans, he says. And so they like this place because it was built by the same man.

'But the new principal doesn't think so at all,' exclaims Alif, miserable at once. 'She had the nerve to suspend me, Salim.'

Alif gives him the whole story and Salim thinks he should have whacked Ankit really hard on the head rather than just tentatively twisted his ear. If the child was properly afraid of him, he wouldn't have told on him. 'Like, you know, Madhav Sir in our school. He scares us. He can't beat but makes fun of everyone in front of everyone else. Me he calls a hairy caterpillar – because of my eyebrows. Sometimes it's creepy caterpillar. Sometimes it's just Creepy.'

Salim could have been at Alif's school and ended up one of his wards but Tahira had decided to put him in a more expensive place much further away where the teachers speak a clipped English unmixed with the Hindi that most of Alif's colleagues favour, and the students sound to Alif, on the rare occasions that he visits, as American as chewing gum. Salim knits those bushy specimens at his father and his father, who has previously heard about and already dismissed the brutish Madhav, as well as the ignorant Madhav who doesn't seem to know that the right term would be 'beetle-browed', says, 'I'm going to write this man a letter.'

'No, no, no,' pleads Salim. And then with an adult air. 'It'll only make it worse.'

'And you don't tell Ammi about my mess. Or anyone else. I called Maharishi Jain. Turns out he knows Shukla ji, who is president of the school board. So he can fix things and, Allah be praised, I'll be back at work. How soon is the question.'

The Maharishi had been sympathetic. Alif knew that he and Shukla ji, son of the founder, someone who played a determining role in the institution's affairs, had been classmates. They were taught history by a man called Arnold, whom Maharishi loved to talk about; he spent a good half hour on this Arnold – his love of the Mughals, his idealisation of the Buddhists – and how these preferences had transmitted themselves to him. He assured Alif that Shukla ji too was in his own way a student of history and he would come down, for certain, on Alif's side once the Maharishi had put in a word.

The tour guide is describing now, in a loudly prurient voice, the indecent apparel of European women and how unsuited it is to the sacred sites he takes them to. He doesn't think that in the days of Shah Jahan they'd have been allowed inside the Jama Masjid at all and Salim, who has wandered in the courtyard countless times and who has stood there praying with his father on occasion, looks as if he has heard of Jama Masjid for the first time.

'What you must understand, Salim,' Alif is saying, 'is that I may not have read every bit of the Koran but the Prophet spoke to me. He was human and he suffered like hell. That can't leave one cold. Here is someone who declares all men are brothers under one God: this to a society where it's so far been each man for himself and an eye for an eye. The tribes fell out, clans fell out, kinsmen and neighbours were maltreated, people stole and slandered, killed children, even ate carrion. Do we know all this for a fact? No, but some of it must obviously have been true for Mohammad to try and knock it down at the risk of his life.'

'And he won,' says Salim.

Alif shakes his head helplessly at him.

'So what did Baba say when he came back and found you stressing over Arabic and Urdu?'

'He said nothing as usual and then suddenly announced one day he's putting me in an English school. And that was that. I was thrilled and then horrified, I understood so little. So I started spending all my time reading. But I never got around to thanking him. You and I sitting here, chitchatting about whatever comes to our heads – this sort of thing was never possible with my father.'

'Why?'

'He was always busy. When he wasn't busy he was preparing to be busy. He's not busy any more, he's not even the same man, but it's still hard to say to him – Abba, let's talk now.'

'Why was he crying?'

'Crying? When?'

'Must have been in June when we went there for his birthday. He was on the balcony smoking and thought we'd left. I came back because I'd forgotten to give him that book we'd got him, on the world's great inventors. And I saw it – the wet cheeks. He took the book anyway.'

A queasy tremor: his father might be ill, he needs to do something to help. Just then Alif sees in the distance, striding with great urgency, the imam of the mosque near his house, his loose pyjamas flapping at the ankles like some herald of distress, his mouth already working out unspoken words of warning, his beard drastically long and pointed, his fists clenched at his sides with six decades of religious righteousness and his eyes lit, his eyes taking their fire from that fourteen-hundred-year-old desert of Arabia where it all began, and his eyes uncompromisingly certain that the truth is that distant and that immediate. *Behold the good Muslim,* thinks Alif, and keeps his head low, gesturing to Salim to do likewise. When he steals a glance to check if the coast is clear he spies his cousin and the source of all the meagre poetry in his life – Mir. Mir is about to hail him from a distance so Alif puts his finger to his lips in warning. Mir glances ahead, sees the reddened beard and the skullcap among the crowd of pedestrians and immediately understands, waiting till the man turns off into a side street.

When he gets to them on the steps, Mir announces, as he does each time he sees Alif, '*Ruswaayi se ab bacha lo Alif/ Pateele mein rakh kar ubaalo Alif.*' A poem, naturally, a cryptic one by the poet Adil Mansuri that invokes Alif by name – Save me now from dishonour, Alif/ dunk me in a pot and set me boiling, Alif.

He sits down with them and, switching at once from poetry to politics, says, 'Things are bad. Have you heard the latest?' He works as a senior reporter at an English daily and is always privy to the latest. Mir would have been a vapid materialist were it not for the reams of poetry he knows; on the other hand, spouting only poetry he'd have come across as boringly maudlin. As things stand he represents a fine balance of dream and reality; Alif admires Mir. He does not hide from the world – or from mullahs – as Alif is often compelled to do.

'No, I haven't heard the latest but it will search me out and pin me down all the same,' says Alif, who does his best to avoid the hysteria of the 24-hour news cycle. '*Mushkilen mujh par padi itni ki aasan ho gayi,*' he adds, giving back to Mir a line the man has quoted to him countless times, this world-famous line of Ghalib's or, if not world-famous, then one that ought to be because who else but the master could come up with this simple, almost homey paradox: So much shit hit the fan that it fell down, transformed, as manna from heaven.

'I've been trying to teach good things to this child...'

They both gaze at Salim who looks as impishly implacable as ever.

'What better place, what better place,' murmurs Mir, his eyes scanning the heights of the mosque.

'The high and the low. Shah Jahan kneeling here. And then the son, Aurangzeb, who imprisoned the father, coming here to pray and set upon by the common people. They'd had enough of him, his murders and his cold-hearted orthodoxies. I know what *you'd* say to him if you saw him.'

Mir smiles. '*Lagee hai toh basti ko jal jaane do/magar ho sake to bacha lo Alif.*' Another couplet from the same poem, another grimly playful juxtaposition – The village's on fire so let it burn/ But if you can save it, please save it, Alif.

'A century on, after the war of 1857 which as you know the British won, they seized the mosque along with most of Shahjahanabad. When they returned it to the community it was with a damning set of rules – seditious language must be reported and the occupiers had the right to enter with their shoes on.'

'With their *shoes?*' Even Salim is awed at this travesty.

'And in 1947, three months after Partition...'

Mir nods. 'Maulana Azad. That famous speech.'

'Maulana Azad, who sleeps right there, outside that gate.'

'What did he say?' asks Salim.

Alif and Mir are both silent for a moment, both perhaps thinking of the pain so clearly audible in that grand rebuke made from the pulpit of the mosque by that sad and defeated man: *I told you Partition is a terrible idea. As soon as the two countries came into being they were at each other's throats. These are borders drawn in blood.*

'Basti mein aag lag chuki hai, ab kya hoh sakta hai,' says Mir, emphasising gloomily how the fire now can't be put out.

'He also said to the frightened Muslims gathered here: this country is ours. We could still, if we had the courage, fill in the blank pages of its history. Do you understand?'

But Salim does not understand, he is so young. Or he does not understand because the zeitgeist – in every age an unstoppable force, thinks Alif as he looks into those sweet and restless eyes beneath those, yes, beetling brows – the zeitgeist has entered his son's soul.

'It was a marvellous speech,' says Mir.

'So hard-hitting. *The very word Pakistan is anathema to me*, Azad declared. The Prophet said God made all of earth a masjid. So how can one parcel off some bit of land and declare it godly, pak?'

'Reminds me of Iqbal's lines – *Patthar ki muraton mein samjha hai tu khuda hai/ khak-e-vatan ka mujh ko har zarra devta hai.*'

'Yes, yes,' murmurs Alif. 'Every particle of the nation is holy and so on.'

'But then the maulana excelled in marvellous speeches. Why didn't he try harder when there was time? Why didn't he get the qaum over to his side in those early days when Pakistan was still an alien idea and the majority didn't support it?'

'We didn't listen to him. I must tell you that I have just locked horns with Tahira over this.'

'An argument in the holy month?' asks Mir. 'And she must have been fasting, unlike you.'

'Only after iftar had been eaten did we find we disagreed,' says Alif.

'And now you're trying to get Salim over to your side?'

'Wrong, totally wrong. I was just telling him how the beloved Prophet was ostracised. I was trying to bury all differences in what I consider the simple truths, the strictly undeniable ones.

'What do you make of this?' Mir asks Salim.

'Must I believe in everything Abba says? Or the imam sahib?' asks Salim.

'Believe if you want to believe,' says Alif, irritated. 'Use your mind if you have one. Listen, you either read and hear a few things, the recommended things, and stick with them. Or you read everything and live in enlightened doubt. What do you want to do?'

'Start a professional tour guide company.'

Alif groans. 'This afternoon it was a restaurant. This evening it was cloud computing. Please put some sense into him,' he says to Mir.

'Why a tour guide? Why not a shoe-shiner? Or a pigeon-flyer,' asks Mir.

'Pigeon-flying is not a proper business,' says Salim.

'It's a passion.' Mir tells him about the pigeon-flyers who once thronged the terraces of this town, the few who still do, and how this hobby could make obsessive adolescents out of grown men, whereas he, Salim, seems to be a grown man in the body of an adolescent.

'When I was your age —' starts Mir and Salim interrupts him. 'I hear that every second day from him. And my mother. *When I was your age…*'

Mir smiles and tells him not to take his parents too seriously.

'So what's the latest?' asks Salim. 'You didn't tell.'

Mir's face darkens at once.

'Trouble brewing. It's been in the works for some time and now it's out in the open. That we've become a strange quantity. Us, Muslims.'

'You mean the government's new idea…' asks Alif.

'Yes, that very one. To kick us down to second-class. To ask for proof of blood, not roots in this soil. It isn't enough if you were born here. It isn't enough if your parents were born here. Does it flow in your veins, the mud of the motherland?'

'If it doesn't in mine, I don't know what does.'

'How terrible, this. To take for granted one has in hand the nuts and bolts of it, the skimpy framework that makes one somewhat human, and then to learn – sorry, no. The state guarantees that and the state can take it away.'

'Take away what?' asks Salim impatiently.

'And what will we be without those nuts and bolts?' says Alif, knowing the answer.

'Flesh on the meat market.'

Alif looks away from him towards the unslowable bustle of Urdu Bazaar, the dead or imprisoned animals for sale there. People translated. Parcelled off into skin and bone and hair and muscle and fat and nails. They both know which murderously icy juncture of the twentieth century *that* image comes from.

'The government is trying to send us all to prison,' Mir explains to Salim and Alif frowns. 'Detention centres. So watch out.'

The boy laughs.

'He doesn't believe me,' Mir marvels. 'Once they're done with us, they'll set to work on the other riff-raff. Christians, Sikhs…'

'Bhai, there are more than two hundred million of us. Are you crazy? How many detention centres would that need?'

'Oh my sweet Lord,' says Mir, clutching his heart as though he's in the throes of collapse. 'Oh my master in heaven. Is this what it's come down to? On the steps of the Jama Masjid? Less than a hundred years ago we were writers with pens of fire, we were brilliant socialists – think Faiz, think Manto – dreaming of world revolution. Now all we can come up with is: no concentration camps for us hopefully because they could never fit us all in. Now we write scared books about being mistaken for terrorists and about our children being mocked in school and about…'

His phone is ringing. He looks at the name lighting up his screen and says he has to go.

'You don't know the inside story.' His favourite clincher. And then he's off, chasing some elusive source, some bit of news that is valuable only because it is new, even though by tomorrow or the day after, thinks Alif, it will have gone from gold to dust.

He turns to his son. 'Tell me again, was your Baba really crying?

Salim nods solemnly. 'He tried to hide it when he saw me. He pretended that he had a cold.'

'I've never seen him cry.' Neither has he ever seen him pretend.

'But then he smiled and said, don't ask me anything. I can answer most of your questions but not all of them. He lit another cigarette and said, Khuda tum ko mahfouz rakhe.'

Alif is quiet as the loudspeakers reverberate with the call for the isha prayer; he inhales the curried scents of the dinners being readied in every eatery nearby, soon to be consumed before another cycle of fasting begins.

'You do what you like, Salim. You go into business.'

'Abba!' Salim gushes. 'Shukriya, shukriya. But you know nothing about business. Where will the money come from?' He lets drop a figure.

'That much?' asks Alif, startled. 'For what? That's a good half of my savings!'

Then he thinks with relief of the Maharishi. It was a wise move to call him and get that assurance about his job. He will call him again tomorrow and pursue matters. Gratitude makes him expansive. 'You finish school and then let's see, maybe I can support you some.'

And the reward is his grown-up son, usually abashed even to have his hair tousled in passing, now, with a cry of victory, throwing his arms around Alif on the grand steps of the grand mosque and burying his face in this kind parent's shoulder.

★

Alif is one of those anachronistic souls never entirely at home with the bewitching half-truths and outright lies, the instant gratification and noxious narcissism, the utterly spooky and yet workaday magic of the internet. He is a habitual attracter of devastating viruses and killer spyware to all the computers he's been set up on; somehow he always manages to click on the wrong thing. After the latest machine became too confused and confusing to work on, he gave up and decided for a time to write his thoughts by hand and search for his facts in real books.

Today, sitting in an old library in Old Delhi, he types, on the laptop he has borrowed from his son, a series of questions into the Great Oracle of the search engine. *Is it possible to develop warm feelings towards someone you have met just once? Is it possible to be drawn to an old flame all over again? Should one confide in one's best friend if one is attracted to his former love? Should one allow oneself to fall* ... He is presented with a riot of answers, all seeming to describe people not him and all offering solutions that have likely been created on the couches of American therapists.

One of Alif's librarian acquaintances settles into the chair next to him and Alif hurriedly pulls up the pages he was meant to be studying – on those shining lights of long ago. The man wants to talk, as he always does. His name is Bedil and he has worked here for ages without appearing to have gained much from the old novels that line the walls, the bound volumes of colonial gazetteers stocked on the first floor, bulky archives of newspapers in three languages, the handwritten manuscripts in Urdu and Sanskrit locked away in metal cabinets, the tattered hardbacks left behind by Englishmen and women who visited Delhi in the preceding centuries – all of it swathed in the high volume of dust that is prerequisite for a government-run institution. Bedil likes his job here: to preside over students reading study manuals to crack exams and jobless old men who come for the newspapers and the breeze from the fans. He likes to drink tea all day and wonder lazily, along with his colleagues, if the municipality of Delhi will give them funds for that long-promised renovation or if this hundred-year-old library will fall apart as it has slowly been doing.

Bedil is, in Alif's experience, the most unliterary person ever to grace, or disgrace, a literary establishment. He often wonders what the man's parents were thinking when they gave him that name, for Bedil was a late seventeenth-century master in Persian, a difficult poet and philosopher whom few today would understand and who even in his own age was derided for his obscurity and honoured more in parts of Central Asia than India. This Bedil's get-up has every appearance of good intentions – the stiff-collared shirt, the shining glasses, the smoothed hair. But were Alif to ask him about anything pertaining to the library's collection, as he has so often, Bedil will ponder the matter and then say – that's the one thing I don't know, ye toh mujhe nahi maloom. He says it with such consideration it always seems like an admission of a rare gap in his knowledge when in actual fact this, or that, is not the only thing he doesn't know. In actual fact he knows nothing, except the story behind the library, a story he keeps repeating as if it justified his own existence. Early in the twentieth century, to announce the shifting of the capital of British India from Calcutta to Delhi, the Viceroy was going in regal, elephant-borne procession down Chandni Chowk, a stone's throw away from where Alif and Bedil are sitting, when he was wounded by a bomb hurled at him. After that incident, several flunkies of empire, obsequious Indian rajas and maharajas, noblemen and noblewomen, put money together as a reward for information about the miscreants. Eventually the contributions were used to set up this grand library with its high ceilings, stone floors, wooden spiral staircase, and collection of now old and disused equipment for bookbinding, page cutting and gold letter embossing. Once a tribute to the viceroy, the library was later given the name of the political revolutionary with whom the viceroy's putative assassins had joined forces to hatch a plan for a pan-Indian mutiny of the British Indian army during the First World War. The plan failed and the revolutionary became a Californian professor of philosophy. The would-be killers were hanged in 1915.

'Things are bad,' says Bedil.

'And do I not know that,' snaps Alif.

'Our politicians and legislators, busy with sowing the seeds of discord, have no time for the crumbling walls of this library.'

Alif tries to offer a historical angle.

'What does it do to a revolutionary to name a building or a street after him?'

'Things are bad,' repeats Bedil, nodding glumly, as if Alif's is a trick question best avoided.

'Do you know that the Mutiny Memorial on the Ridge was built by the British to honour their dead after the 1857 war? And in 1972, twenty-five years after Independence – in fact at the same time that this library was renamed – it was converted into a memorial for those who had rebelled *against* the British. It's a natural thing – to want to commemorate our heroes. But does it deflate them? Does it cause them to lose their edge? Does it absolutely invert the whole point of their revolt?'

Bedil sniffs suspiciously and says, 'You have seen the guestbook. You know how since the 1930s – we don't have records from before that – since the 1930s people have appreciated this library and said so. In those days it had glamour because of the viceroy. In these days it is appreciated because of the man who...'

'Yes, yes, but how many even know that man or why he's important?'

'What are you saying?' the librarian exclaims.

'I'm just asking, that's all.'

But Bedil will not be pulled in. He is yet another of those specimens who don't think very highly of history and have no weakness for literature. He does not read Urdu, avoids English and just about manages Hindi. Bedil understands that the books he works among are valuable – but it is their value in the abstract he recognises and respects and it is with this same respect that he attends to Alif, the serious man. Bedil never misses an opportunity to chat with Alif and thus distract him from this seriousness.

'You're busy with your research today,' he says heartily, noticing the laptop. Everyone here knows of Alif's purported research.

'There's a book I need.'

Browsing is not permitted in this unique library so Alif sends off Bedil for it. He returns with it in a few moments – a guide to Delhi published in the early 1940s, liberally perforated with the bites of marauding silverfish. He turns to the introduction and is immediately struck by the remarkable optimism of the tone, an optimism whose obsolescence excites him. *It has been making a splendid progress in its career ever since its re-birth as the Imperial City*, writes the author, the same re-birth, notes Alif, during whose inauguration that viceroy was almost killed. *Let us confidently look forward to a glorious future for the New Capital. Its stirring past, its quiet present and its significant future provides a most interesting and instructive study.* This suffices to make Alif's day; this is all he needs – to consider the words of one so clueless about what is to come and to try and save himself, by keeping a close eye on the past, from similar ignorance.

Bedil lingers by him with his long-emptied cup of tea. He wants, as everybody wants, to talk politics, the last refuge of the mediocre. Alif murmurs polite ayes and nays to Bedil's litany of grievances till he is called away by his boss, the gracious Mrs Punjabi, who is well acquainted with Alif too and always welcomes him gladly to the library but who, unlike Bedil, leaves him alone to read. Alif returns to his problem. Not Delhi but her – Prerna.

Despite not really wanting to go on reading articles on preoccupations such as 'Five Ways to Know You've Met Your Soulmate' and 'Why Online Romances Can End in Tears' Alif is pulled in; three quarters of an hour passes and he is none the wiser. For several days now he has given no time to the questions that ought to occupy him: how did some intellectuals in the era he is studying combine loyalty to Queen Victoria – memorising Tennyson, her favourite poet – with perfect confidence in their own history, that is Indo-Islamic, and their own language, that is Urdu? How was it that the nineteenth century was both remarkable for its progressivism and yet much of the conservatism associated with Islam today had its roots in that time – the harder, Victorian-influenced strictures directed at women, the looking down on devotion to saints and teachers as heresy, the armed rebellions against the British in the name of religion?

Alif finds that he has been staring for minutes together at a wall – a wall of books, but still. Wherever he is, he is just not here and he's not there either – with his unswerving forefathers. He gets up in some haste and slips out, is soon on the metro to Janakpuri, in his bag the crumbling book on the history of Delhi which he has almost inadvertently taken with him. He flips again through the pages describing the seven cities of Delhi, that is, the seven layers of which it is composed, one from the ancient urban civilisation, some four thousand years old, named after the river valley from which it branched out, the Indus Valley, or perhaps, the writer surmises, Delhi is associated with the later era of the Mahabharata. The rest of its history stretches back a thousand years from today. Alif finds on rereading them that the author's proclamations have taken on a different aspect. *Glorious future* is obviously miscalculated but *stirring past* and *quiet present*? Those make sense to him now for they describe Prerna's life. The woman in the panel advertisement recalls her face to him and the melody in sugary Urdu softly seeping out of the earphones of the fellow next to him in the crowded carriage evokes her.

Emerging onto the street, he gives an auto-rickshaw driver her address and finds it odd that the man does not question his motives. What is he doing on this ordinary morning, heading in the direction of a woman who is neither friend nor foe but something worryingly indeterminate in between? He is playing truant and impressed by how easy it is. All around him people pursue serious goals – the beggar dramatically thrusting his deformed arm at him, the stressed techie with his lanyard tucked into his shirt pocket taking a cigarette break, the workman bare-headed under the – for the moment – delightfully mild and forgiving September sun, carefully repainting the faded black-and-white stripes of the road divider. This is how the day is won, by wrestling it to the ground, and on any other morning he too would be taking the 11.30 period with Class Nine, trying to interest them in the making of the Indian Constitution or the unmaking of the British empire in India. And now he is nodding at the security guard to Prerna's building and climbing the two flights of stairs to her floor, noticing how the odour of old cooking oil hangs in the dark stairwell and leftover patches of powdered colours from as far back as Holi stain the landings. Just as he is about to press her doorbell a quarrelling couple spill out from the flat opposite: the Punjabi loudness of their voices is unaffected by his presence, doors slam, rancour spews; heavily perfumed, heaving bodies hog space. Alif shrinks back and tries to smile politely.

Then they hurtle into the elevator and are gone. He withdraws his hand from her doorbell. This was a singularly bad idea, he thinks, standing there undecided and sans purpose when, no doubt drawn by the commotion, she opens the door a cautious crack and smiles at his confusion.

'Late mornings are the emptiest,' she says by way of a hello.

She seems to have recreated her parents' house in this flat, the same dreary yet compelling sorts of paintings on the walls, the bookshelves with their slanting, dishevelled rows, the sturdy well-wornness of the furniture. She says she doesn't quite know, when Alif asks her how she occupies herself, and adds that till the children return from college and school in the late afternoon she is on her own.

He hands her, because he has brought nothing else, the musty book on Delhi. She is taken with the woodcut reproductions in it – of the ramparts of Purana Qila, the outlines of the Red Fort, the Union Jack, the bullock carts, the tramcars.

'Trams,' she exclaims.

'They built a tramline early in the century, connecting Jama Masjid, Chandni Chowk and the railway station with Sabzi Mandi, which was outside the city walls.'

'Charming.'

Alif nods. 'And do you know why it all seems so attractive?'

She doesn't know.

'Because it's from before Partition.'

'So that's why the glorious future.'

'Yes, because lakhs of people hadn't yet been slaughtered and Delhi hadn't been changed forever by the homelessness and the horror of the refugees. But your family...?'

She shakes her head. 'We're from Muzaffarnagar. We had nothing to do with all that. My great-grandfather came to Delhi to work as an income tax officer for the British. They have always been steady people with steady jobs, my father's family. Nothing there – no political leanings, not even during the independence movement. No unhappy marriages. No black sheep. No prodigal children. No whispered secrets.'

'A history of steadiness,' says Alif.

'My father was the only one who wanted something more but even in him the agricultural expert overtook the poet.' She glances at the shelves as if he's embodied in those spines but also undone by them.

'And the women were never allowed much ambition but they didn't have horrible lives, they were treated all right. When I was young I felt sympathy for my mother and aunts and grandmother. And even a great-grandmother; as a child I knew her for a few years too. She had become quite calcified with age by then and everyone asked for her opinion only because it didn't matter, she was just respected for being there and being old. I thought I understood them all because I felt so different from them. But now I've become very much like them. Ghar mein chup chap baith ke roti belna.'

Alif is not convinced. She is not the kind of woman who sits at home rolling rotis. He wants to protest, then notices that faint flicker of amusement. And again the curious feeling settles on

153

him that she is some kind of relic, too subtle to be noticed by the unsubtle age. She does not want to champion any cause, not even her own. She wants to keep her own counsel. But how much loneliness is the price of that? How much bitterness is it obligatory to swallow? How loud is the sound of one's own voice echoing in the daytime dark?

'You looked so much at home in that cafe. At home and yet not too taken with our... er... contemporary beguilements. I started thinking of the old times as usual.'

'Hmm, but we were little more than children then.'

'No, no,' says Alif hastily. 'I meant the long centuries when women in this country didn't have much by way of rights – though it is a fact that in the ancient era they were freer than women in Greece and Rome.'

'Really?'

'They could be councillors, they could act in plays. But then things changed and they became, more or less, the embodiments of chastity, the cornerstone of family life, and the property of their fathers and husbands and sons. It was only during the freedom movement that women of the middle classes started publicly participating...'

'But why should women be the object at all?'

'The object?'

'Of our interest. Why do we always have to harp on women as something apart from the...'

'The common run of humanity?'

'Yes, for good or bad, that's all one is. It tires me – going to all that trouble to suppress women and then going to all that trouble to lift up women.'

Alif was about to launch into Gandhi's views on women and Nehru's views on women along with the highlights of the modern women's movement. She could be right and yet he is unable to think of her as anything but a woman, intrinsically part of the history of womanhood. She has just described the females in her own family and how she was wrong to believe she could outdo them. Is this her grief, then, the impossibility of overcoming one's gender? He tries to change the subject.

'So you gave up your job...?' he asks.

'You think, like everyone else, that I should have made something of my life?'

'Not at all. No, I don't. I mean who am I to...' He is tripping on his words, unable to find convincing or true ones.

'I like the peace,' says Prerna. 'Instead of chattering with a maid, supervising a cook, I've become domestic and talk to myself. If I went to work, I would have to talk with other people. That's a lot of effort too – the trouble of thinking what to say to people that will not ruffle them and yet not bore them.'

'You're talking with me now,' says Alif.

'Yes but you're...' She pauses for a breath. 'You're from back then.'

'Back then,' says Alif, savouring those words, the great pain and the great pleasure of them. 'Back then when I couldn't do what I really should have done.'

She looks confused for a moment.

'Saved you,' he blurts, studying the walls. The paintings are dwarfed by a huge framed portrait of a laughing, bearded man wearing creased robes and rudraksha beads. There is a little shelf below him on which a clutch of incense sticks smoke.

'How could you have saved me?' she says softly.

'This is what I wanted to say, the burden I've carried. That when I had the chance I just didn't...'

And yet it can be read two ways and this too has been part of the burden – that he wishes he had been able to wrest Ganesh away from her instead of running off hiding his lily liver, but he also wishes it was him she had been playing those breathless games with, and him she had been drawing towards and pulling away from. Instead of just discussing, with a twenty-year-old's bombast, literature and art with him.

He is too torn up to finish his sentence and she nods briskly as if to say these things no longer matter, going into the kitchen to make tea. He thinks of what he should say next, stiff again with the shyness that had handicapped him before her threshold. Aapki dehleez par. That exquisite Urdu word, dehleez. How many authors of how many Urdu poems have, going and coming, paused at the beloved's threshold, either hesitating to enter or forswearing entry for all time to come or coming to understand that the dehleez is not a partition between inside and outside but a border between heaven and hell. No literary form in the whole wide world can squeeze as many metaphorical gems out of the dross of everyday words. How did those fellows – mostly men, a handful of women – develop such extraordinary suggestiveness? Was it merely a function of leisure? Did they all have a lot of time – those poets in the courts of the Deccan kingdoms of South India in the sixteenth century who were the first poets in the language and later the famed poets of Delhi and even later, the famed poets of Lucknow, and then once the Mughals had gone to pot, those voices who wrought a golden age? Or was it that kings and emperors often themselves wrote verse, and poetry was a high art, generously patronised even into the twentieth century...

Prerna returns and Alif sits up straight and tries to return to the moment. He could say, I am not really much for talking either. He sees himself as the man at the edge of the crowd, never the centre of attention at a wedding party or a school function or a family gathering. He might buttonhole someone if the mood strikes or in turn allow himself to be harangued by the oldest person in the room, the one with the longest view. But he is never talkative. His wife, on the contrary, thinks he is always talkative. So do his students who would often prefer that he shut up. What does Prerna think? But before he can put the question to her, she asks, 'So are you happy?'

'What a question,' he exclaims. 'In this day and age? I mean, have you heard of the eighteenth century?'

She looks perplexed but he forges on.

'Imagine living in Delhi through that endlessly long time. The Mughals were falling apart – one debauched or savage king after another. Nadir Shah arrived from Persia, laid the city to waste, killed an estimated twenty thousand people, and returned home with the Kohinoor and the Peacock Throne. Less than twenty years later, his successor Ahmad Shah Abdali turns up and again Delhi is destroyed. Other than that, the Marathas attacked, the

Sikhs attacked, the Gujjars attacked. There was infighting among the nobles at the court, riots among the common folk, looting, an earthquake and a famine. And through it all the poets continued to write, though the leading ones had to leave Delhi – there was no support for them here. And all they had to sustain them was their sadness and their irony.'

'Irony?' she asks, as though she's never heard of the word.

'Yes, like you. The way you view life from some distance. What I mean to say is: all one has to do, when the question of happiness arises, is consider the past. Of course, I don't believe, as some asinine optimists do, that everything was worse before and we're only getting better with time, but I don't believe in vice versa either. It's just that the past comforts, it reveals how everything is provisional.'

'I don't think my daughter would get it at all. She is nineteen and consumed with herself, with her imagined shortcomings.'

'My son is all self-belief. He already wants to break out on his own and leave us behind but all the same we couldn't have asked for a more loving child.'

Dear God, so wonderful how we are joined in this, thinks Alif: both of us taciturn ironists, both parents of teenagers, both suffering at the hands of a devil named Ganesh Khanna. He starts to feel an obscure, a muffled joy. She is telling him more about her daughter – how unsure she is, trying always to tear out of her own skin, become more like one or another of her apparently glamorous friends, and constantly failing. Alif thinks of the excitable young people in that cafe and imagines her daughter soon like one of them. He can somehow or the other get across to children but adults of that green age befuddle him. He would not know how to converse with one.

'We are old, old, old,' says Alif. 'We belong to another time.'

'Why do *you* have so much love for that time?' asks Prerna at once. 'Didn't you become the historian you always wanted to be?'

'You know why I do,' he says. Her smile encourages him. 'Why can't we make it happen, those things the learned men say are impossible – turn back the clock, step into the same river twice...'

He wishes he could put it across less euphemistically – the simple fact that he'd loved her once.

'Prerna...'

She looks at him with perfect equanimity but it's difficult for him to say more and he can see from her face that she's not going to help him.

'Look at that photo,' she says.

It's so large, the whites of the man's eyes are visible from this distance and the healthy pink gums revealed by the hearty, perhaps even manic, laugh.

'Babaji, the man my family worships. His word is law. If he asks for money, they give it. If he says, go on a pilgrimage to so-and-so temple, they'll drop everything and take off. They spend every Sunday evening with him, singing and sharing their troubles. He is often very mysterious. He might just blurt out a few words and leave you to make sense of them. He'll crack a joke where none is called for or not speak at all when everyone is eagerly waiting for an answer.'

'And you think he's an impostor.'

She shrugs. 'He could be one of those wise fools our society often makes space for. I met him a couple of times and understood what he's about. I don't need him; it's so childish to pin all your hopes on one person like that.'

Alif recalls something that over-profound man S. Radhakrishnan – philosopher and former president of the country – had once said about those who have experienced God. *Those who know it tell it not, those who tell it know it not.* He shares this with Prerna, the view that the religious geniuses of Hinduism have intuited God's presence and understood that all the doctrines in the world are not enough unless one goes through things oneself.

'Perhaps this baba man acts mysterious because he's trying to get your family to see the same thing.'

'Yes he can be short with them.'

'Maybe he's saying – it would be best if you went home and found God on your own.' Yet another Sufi, he adds to himself.

'But since you insist on coming to me, all I can do is make you run in circles till you understand.'

They laugh and then she says, shaking her head, 'I wish Jagan would see.'

Alif feels again a flush come over him – she has not so much as mentioned Ganesh and just confided to him that her husband is, more or less, an idiot. For all her apparent self-containment she did get around to that phrase, *I wish.*

'Do you quarrel over the Babaji?' asks Alif.

But far too eager, his tone, and she glances at him and then looks away, slowly placing the empty teacups on the tray and taking it away. In an instant she's closed up again, withdrawn to that place where she's spent the last couple of decades, in the heart of a family and yet strangely alone.

When she returns she says, 'Maybe we are all, in different ways, fools.'

Alif wants to startle her with some cleverer insight but the centuries are now rattling in his empty head like dried tamarind seeds. '*Hindi hain ham, vatan hai Hindustan hamara.*' He recites the lines morosely.

'You haven't changed at all. You're still a wasted romantic,' she says brightly as she shows him out and Alif crosses her dehleez without words, going away with nothing except a sliver of incandescent hope, some precious shoots of newborn confidence.

*

Mahtab sits in his flat putting on a pair of scuffed boots from his cop days and discussing the unscrupulousness of rickshaw drivers, the crowdedness of the metro lines and the exorbitance of taxis. Then he and Alif head out to look for suitable conveyance to Mehrauli. Alif's old aunt, Amina Phuphi, lives in this South Delhi neighbourhood, in a colony of poor and half-poor Muslims. She is almost alone now, her husband dead and her three daughters married and gone. She has as companion a distant, widowed relative, somewhat younger than her, who does the housekeeping. Shagufta is fasting and does not accompany her husband and son but is more pleased than them that they are going. 'She keeps phoning,' she tells Alif as he follows his father out. 'Not a week passes without her calling to ask after everyone. But who asks after her?'

Neither father nor son answer; they walk out to the main road, father striding far ahead of son – like the boots, the still swift gait is also a legacy of police life. He does not haggle with the driver he finds, just tells him sharply he is overcharging for the short ride to the station, and gets in. They are soon going past the new mosque, its yet-to-be-painted, soaring minarets a dirty grey but the bare ground outside its prayer hall littered with the footwear of the devout who are inside saying the maghrib namaz. No doubt Ahmad's worn slippers are among them. And he will be back later in the evening for the isha namaz and then even later for the tarawih prayers said only during the month of Ramzan.

Alif glances at his father but he is not speculating about Ahmad; he grasps too hard at the handrail and is focused straight ahead as if he needed to keep an eye on the road for the driver. And yet there is a thinness in his shoulders and a diffuseness to his eyes that stirs in Alif a vague pity – this contrast between his still forceful manner and the evidence of physical decline. Alif has just stoically accepted his mother's congratulations on Tahira's degree and tried to answer her questions about why Salim is nowhere near the top of his class; now he makes an effort to interest his father in the fact that in this city two hundred years ago some people were starting to get excited about the Copernican system of astronomy. Astronomy was not unknown to us, he points out. The older madrasas in Mughal times had it on the syllabus – they had philosophy and maths and grammar too, a complete education. Much before that, in medieval times, scientifically minded Muslim scholars in Baghdad and elsewhere made great advances in every direction, including the invention of the linear astrolabe.

Alif tries to explain and finds himself lost. How exactly did they calculate with this device the position of the stars with respect to the horizon? How did navigators use it to ply the seas? He can't tell for sure but loves the ring of the names of those early inventors as much as he loves the idea of the heliocentric Copernicus. He loves the *idea* of ideas.

'Acchi baat hai,' says Mahtab, being a little patronising in a fatherly way. 'Is that what you are teaching these days?' he asks.

'I am not teaching these days. I am on paid leave for a few months,' says Alif. 'Research,' he adds, sure this is a word that will impress, if not unsettle.

'Research what's happening now,' says Mahtab. 'Those old things have been retold many times. If you want to write a book that will be read, write about this.'

They have stopped at a traffic light and in the rubble under the soaring concrete piles of the metro track is a family of beggars. A child sits on her haunches carefully pounding what looks like ginger and chilli in a little golden brass mortar; next to her a baby sleeps with flies swarming on her face. The girl sees Alif watching and runs to him for money. As he pulls out his wallet, an even smaller child takes up the pestle. The girl puts the coins she's been handed in a patched-up pocket of her dress and then skips back, shoos her sister away and continues pounding with all the seriousness of a busy housewife.

What does Mahtab mean by *this*? He means the larger forces, the deeds and words of those who have power – contemporary politicians, bureaucrats, petty officials – and their effects on me and you. He has no patience with those who waste time crying over spilt milk, such as our failure to win the war of 1857, nor would he be arrested by a small, torn scrap of everyday beauty. But Alif does not want to start Mahtab on the ills of contemporary society so he says nothing and the rest of the trip passes in a not uncomfortable silence.

Arriving, father and son must dodge the crowds surging forward to take in for five minutes, before they lose interest in it, the most beautiful freestanding column of carved stone anywhere in the world, built to induce in the viewer great wonder at the malleability of the material, admiration for the finesse of the sculptors who created it, respect for the might of the sultans who commissioned it and recognition of the power of the verses of the Koran inscribed on it. They go past this medieval monument, the Qutub Minar, and head up a winding street towards a crowded bazaar at an intersection, and then left into one of the side lanes where Amina lives in a stuffy upstairs house, which she nowadays rarely leaves, her bed of the night becoming her divan of the day, and within easy reach a side table holding an impressively large collection of medicines in tablet, capsule and liquid form. The mauve walls have faded to a shabby shade of pink, all of her home that one large room partitioned by two semi-circular arches, a cheap cement throwback to Muslim style; on Amina's side the walls are crowded with flower-bordered, laminated, mounted inscriptions from the Koran while on a shelf a single orange goldfish swims in a small aquarium and keeping it company in the water, memento mori – a tiny skull-headed doll sitting on the seashells and playing a tinier guitar. Seeing his aunt – those brown, kohl-defined eyes still clear despite the patchwork of wrinkles that is her face – makes Alif glad.

She has been forewarned about their arrival by Shagufta, and she cries a little, seeing her brother, but without expressing in words her complaints – about how rarely he comes to visit, how increasingly lonely her life is, how difficult for her to move about with the ailments in her back, her heart, her eyes.

Some of her tears are for Alif too, who is an even rarer visitor. She says she dreamt of him just the other night – he brought her water from the holy spring of Zamzam, water so sweet she felt she would not need to ever drink again. Alif mulls over the symbolism of this dream. He suspects that what Phuphi probably means to say is that she'd love him to visit more often. Or she is sorry she never made it to Mecca and drank in real life from that spring. Or she is on medicines that make her feel thirstier than usual. But she'd never say any of these things up front. Her opinions are always subservient to her beliefs – in dream signs, ghosts, rumours, evil eyes, auspicious days, auspicious dates, and above all the direction provided by Sufis and fakirs. She is a woman with a high-school degree who grew up, like her brother, in the half-modern country of the 1950s and 60s – reading progressive Urdu magazines like *Ismat* and popular ones like *Biswin Sadi*, speaking some English, getting ideas about glamour from the movies, and being a good Muslim. But he graduated and after that took the police exam. She was married at nineteen and moved to the then village of Mehrauli where her husband had a poultry business. Since then she has been in the same place in more senses than one, cleaving closer and closer to her religion.

'Janab kitab likh ne jaa rahein hain,' Mahtab tells his sister, a mild jibe about Alif and his literary project, but also in some underhand way an expression of impatience with his sister's mutterings about visions and dreams. He would rather take stock of her illnesses and hospital visits, find out if she needs new doctors or better treatments, make sure she is not – as she's prone to – scrambling the dosage and timings of her pills.

Amina knows Alif is a would-be historian, and without pausing to ask what's interesting him at the moment, says he ought to write a history of Mehrauli. No one remembers Mehrauli, she laments, as she always does. Visitors just come to glance at the Qutub Minar. What about the rest of it? Amina does have a sense, but a very half-baked one, of the past – she will declare, for instance, that the oldest mosque in the world is four thousand years old. Or that the Taj Mahal is so ethereal it could only have been brought to life by jinns. Or that Elvis Presley, the singer, became a Muslim and thereby proved the superiority of Islam to Christianity, when it was actually Muhammad Ali, the boxer, who did it, more to ally with oppressed fellow black Americans than to please fellow Muslims such as Amina.

Alif knows better than her but, despite the ease with which he drops that word, research, he's sometimes unsure where he's going with it. He thinks of Nietzsche: *We need history, but not the way a spoiled loafer in the garden of knowledge needs it.*

As for Amina, she is full of a botched love for Mehrauli. There are many like her here – wanderers among the ruins of what was once the stronghold of Delhi's first sultans. The grand minar might still be in good shape but other than that there is much broken down here and so many people around who take cover in the gold dust of twilight, feeding off the crumbs of a medieval ancestry. Every shopkeeper, the imam of every mosque, the hanger-on at every dilapidated pavilion or tomb is a historian. Each will lean in and whisper some half-real or wholly imagined secret of the past. Alif never corrects them, nor does he enquire into the sources of their fantasy. He nods and chats, does what he can

163

to encourage them to go on deriving comfort from their dream world, continue loafing in the weedy garden of quasi-invented knowledge. Of course this tenderness he feels for the lost souls of Mehrauli disappears when he is faced with his students; these latter he has tasked himself with trying to save by inculcating in them the axiom that everything is not moods and feelings, passions and prejudices, that facts ought to have a greater claim on us.

But regarding his kinsmen here, the best he can do is to let them be. He remembers some of them from childhood and when he sees them now, older and greyer, he is amazed at the decline, which is also the decline of Mehrauli. The narrow houses of the grimly genteel press closer and closer together, more people crowding in from elsewhere, Bihar and Bengal, Nigeria and Senegal. In the vicinity of the minar are chic restaurants hidden inside walled courtyards and boutiques displaying goods with styles and prices for those who live complacently unreal lives. South of Mehrauli is the scattering of farmhouses where Delhi's wealthy take their leisure. But in between is the old Mehrauli and it's shabbier and more cloistered yet its spirits are the same. Sometimes, when Alif is in a reflective mood, as he is today, sitting there quietly while his father tries to get his aunt to disclose the exact state of her health, he feels that it is no longer possible to make anything beautiful out of this brokenness.

Those farmhouses of today continue a tradition, for Mehrauli has long been associated with country outings and country homes, even as people have lived here continuously for a millennium, its origins evidenced in the scattered stones and leftover walls of the forts that Rajput chieftains raised, the story of whose dashing, horse-borne leader, Prithviraj, Alif had recently managed to interest his students in. And then all the many grand mausoleums and simple tombs of kings and nobles from seven, six, five, four hundred years ago, the graceful pavilions set among vanished gardens and springs and fountains, and scattered among them, reminders of humility and otherworldliness, and yet attracting the liveliest expression of prayer, the greatest devotions – the mosques and the tombs, the thrumming dargahs, of the Sufis.

It turns out Phuphi is not very sick, or not sicker than usual. Once Mahtab has established this he neatly stacks up her copious medical files and hands them back to her, exasperated with her for having made that urgent phone call and frightened him.

She hems and haws, asks since when things have begun to frighten him, tells him she has never seen him look this feeble. 'Nothing the matter with me,' announces Mahtab in his far from feeble voice.

Then she lets on that it was Shagufta who set it up, advised her to call her brother with the excuse of a medical emergency so he would be prompted to go see her since she is herself too worn out to come and see him.

'She told me you haven't been yourself and you know her. She wouldn't say something like that without good reason, she never tells tall tales. She wanted me to find out since to her you will reveal nothing. I said first of all I must send Bano to the dargah to pray for you.'

'I'm smoking more than I used to, that's all,' says Mahtab, and then tells his sister that along with praying for good fortune she ought to tidy up the place: her walls could do with a coat of paint and her skylights could do with a spot of washing. He is no longer querulous, yielding now, half-smiling. Sooner or later he acquires a certain ease with his sister, perhaps for no reason other than the fact that she knew him before he became a cop, and he knew her before she became a devout old woman.

'Something's flitting around in your head, I can see. You're worried about your begum or you're worried about Alif...'

'Oh not me,' says Alif at once. 'I'm beyond help. Those who bother with me will only be knocking their heads on stone.'

'Talk of knocking your head on the tomb of the Khwaja instead. He's the one who always listens. At least he listens to me.' And she instructs them in the greatness of Khwaja Bakhtiyar Kaki, how he is one of the four pillars of Sufism in this country – the others being Nizamuddin Aulia of Delhi, Khwaja Muinuddin Chisti of Ajmer, and Baba Farid of Punjab.

'When did you last put flowers on his tomb?' she asks her nephew and he is contrite, remembering going with this aunt, his mother and grandmother, and the other children in the family to see the Khwaja, the excitement of those weekly Thursday visits, the rose-petal perfume of the flower-heaped cenotaph mingling with the rose-water-and-whole-spices perfume of the biryani served out of massive deghs to all supplicants. The house of his grandparents, his home as a child, is gone, broken up into a number of small matchbox constructions piled atop each other, in which people live their matchbox lives. His grandparents are gone too, buried in the qabristan of the Sohan Burj mosque, and so they mingle with the dust of the early sultans and the later Mughals, all buried hither and thither in Mehrauli.

'Yes, it's been a while, I must bring Salim to get the Khwaja's blessings too,' murmurs Alif.

'You may have forgotten the Khwaja but I make sure that he doesn't forget you,' says Amina tartly, pulling her hijab low on her forehead and shouting out for her companion and cousin thrice removed, Bano, to go out and get some food. Bano appears from her corner on the other side of the arches, a darker, smaller, shrivelled version of Amina, and salaaming to the visitors rushes out in excitement as if it were radiant royalty come to visit, not two mere men. In the night streets of Mehrauli, hands will now be shaping an elastic yeasty dough and slapping one flatbread after the other onto the insides of tandoors improvised from oil drums and aglow with live coals, and then fishing out each puffed-up piece with a hooked rod and flinging it into baskets piled high. Other hands will be laying on embers the skewered, marinated meat, and fanning the flames so that sparks light the faces of the men who crowd around tearing the hot flesh with their fingers and eating soundlessly, quickly, unemotionally. The making and taking of food at the end of another wasted day, and the smell and sight of food in the darkness, will soften and somewhat redeem Mehrauli and make everyone forget the open drains with their fetid sewage and the piles of garbage, the small struggling businesses in dank lanes, the wandering beggar women and their grubby children.

Mahtab is willing to eat a meal but he won't say what's eating him, so Amina returns to the theme of how Mehrauli has been forgotten.

'But we just saw a pair of tourists outside. They might have been French. Or Italian. Water bottle, guidebook, camera, looking browbeaten but still intent on the mysteries of Mehrauli,' says Alif.

Amina, who herself rarely ventures out any more, is delighted to hear there are people who look beyond the manicured setting of the minar.

'Phuphi jaan,' says Alif. 'In the past people knew what to do with the past. Take the Qutub Minar. It was built by four successive sultans, layer added to layer, over three hundred years, and yet it looks like one thing.'

What he wants to convey is his wonder at how these men effected such a strong connection with their predecessors, how they knew that the best way to speak is in the same architectural tongue. Amina nods; but if she understands it is only dimly. She gives Mahtab news about their brother back in the village, the muezzin Bilal, and then produces a small, battered mobile phone from the folds of her robes to call him.

Alif continues the conversation, half with his aunt and half with himself. This sense of tradition abides through the centuries – history is bloodied by wars and muddied by the intermingling of people – but there remains something solid about it; each new feeling or thought, shape or movement, word or colour emerges from what already exists.

And then the modern age dawns, it dawns everywhere sooner or later, and the bonds no longer hold. History starts to break down in the nineteenth century and the twentieth century sends the debris into the trash heap. What causes the rift? How is it impossible now to add another storey to the Qutub Minar without the action seeming like caricature? Progress. A single-minded forward movement, a determined Hegelian thrust that makes any return to the past unthinkable. And so one can only reconstruct history, as the English landed gentry once used to do, strewing their landscape gardens with imitation ruins, so as to savour the past aesthetically. Right here in Mehrauli it is still possible to spot an old-time English official's 'follies', domed stone canopies that mimic the structures from centuries past.

Everywhere he looks, the detritus of history. The only thing that could make the sight bearable is the promise of the eternal to come, that is, God, if one can find him – as Amina seems to have done, as Ahmad seems to have done. And are they the better for it? Does faith ennoble the faithful or does it just make them quixotic? The question confuses Alif and he would like a drink to resolve it. His father does not know – or if he knows does not let on that he knows – about his son's drinking, and while it is not more than an occasional bout with Ganesh, Alif increasingly catches himself feeling that nothing seems quite clear unless dissolved in liquor. And then he finally lets in the thought of Prerna, even though it's Prerna he has been thinking of all along. *Are you happy*, she had asked. And what a lousy, pedantic answer he had come up with when the right one and the true one would have been – Yes, yes, yes. As long as I can sit here with you discoursing on happiness.

Just two meetings, neither long nor intimate, and Alif has at some point, without his noticing, crossed the border between friendly, even amused, affection, and besotted pain. The more he tries to get her out of his head the more firmly she stays lodged there. She'd laughed and been at ease, confided in him about her husband's shortcomings, reminded Alif of their old association and, best of all, seemed to have forgotten about Ganesh. So this is me, he thinks, studying the dust of Mehrauli that coats his no longer new and never really loved shoes. Just as his feet are almost healed his heart is starting to fall apart. He has already sent her two messages, neither of which she's answered yet; he's likely being too craven and must send her a third, more balanced and polite missive, asking if she'd like to come to Purana Qila with him. The thought of wandering among those adorable relics with her makes his head swim and then he is guilty and pings Ganesh to ask him where he's at. Ganesh answers at once to say he is in jahannam and will call soon.

As the siblings talk over each other, unable to agree on who is to take care of Amina should her health worsen, Alif returns for the hundredth time to that innocuous remark Prerna made – *But you are from back then.* All he managed to suggest to her was: So are you. A precious Hindi. But the sad truth is that the poet

Iqbal, who imagined this wonderful creature, this quintessential and civilised north Indian, would go on to repudiate his belief in a nation of Hindis and instead set his sights on a worldwide qaum of Muslims. He would weep – literally and in his poetry – over the lost glories of Islam and urge his brethren to seize the day, become supermen one and all, not unlike those idealised by Nietzsche, but guided always by the, to him, irrefutable laws of the Sharia. And thus it came to be that Hindis fell by the wayside.

*Khak-e-vatan ka mujh ko har zarra devta hai*... Alif thinks of those lines about seeing God in every grain of sand written by the young, the early, the nationalist Iqbal that Cousin Mir had quoted to him the other day. And he puts them alongside Maulana Azad's belief that all the earth is holy – *Allah tala ne tamam zameen ko masjid bana di.* And yet it was Azad who proposed that there was no contradiction between being a devout Muslim and a patriotic Indian, and Iqbal who, despite once singing with such passionate sweetness of that new altar, that naya shivala, where Muslims and Hindus could worship together, eventually went the other way.

The three elderly siblings have chatted for a good twenty minutes and no conclusion is reached on anything but Amina secretes her phone away with a satisfied look. Dinner is served but she does not eat; she has broken her fast earlier in the evening and now watches over father and son, like Shagufta, urging them on if they so much as pause in their chewing, and at the same time holding forth on the situation facing the qaum. 'Things are bad. They are hounding us. They are finding excuses to kill us. They are making us huddle together in the far corners of every town and city. They are not giving us the jobs. They are not giving us the houses. They are not giving us the right of way. But if that is what's bothering you then forget it. Because it is not new.'

She sounds as if she's reading out an overheated editorial from the Urdu newspaper that's lying folded by her side.

'When was any of this new?' asks her brother.

Amina agrees and at once leaps back several hundred years. 'Think of the Paighambar, peace be upon him. At some point his whole clan was boycotted by his tribesmen, the Quraysh. Is that not the same thing?'

'Exactly,' says Alif. 'Those were hard times. There was to be no intermarriage with the other clans, no trade, and the whole lot of them was confined to one quarter of Mecca. Then when the ban was withdrawn he went to the city of Taif to seek refuge but was stoned out of it.'

'All to the good. But all beside the point,' says Mahtab, 'when it comes to standing up to the government. Try standing up to the government on the strength of your faith. You'll be cut down in a day.'

But Amina wants Alif to go on, so he does.

'Eventually the Prophet found some followers and he would wander around Ka'bah during the annual festival. Once a year the tribes took a holiday from murder and pillage, a temporary truce, so they could convene at the Ka'bah, and the Prophet would use the opportunity to preach. But he had a doubting uncle who hovered around so that whenever our messenger of Allah started to try and get his message across, this man would condemn him and people would say, Your own uncle is unconvinced, how can you convert us? Imagine his plight then?'

Amina's eyes light up at her nephew's familiarity with the traditions.

'And think, too, of the suffering of the other prophets,' she intones. 'How Abraham had to abandon his second wife Hajira in the desert with their young child Ismail because his first wife Sarah willed it. How even if it troubled his conscience he left her to the mercy of God.'

'How Moses was chased by the pharaoh as he led his people out of Egypt...' says Alif.

'You two...' says Mahtab. 'You'll soon be giving the Friday sermon at the mosque.'

'Tawbah, tawbah,' says Amina giggling shyly. 'May that never come to pass. But all this is to say, it's God's will. As for you, you've been an *honest* police officer. You've done what you could.'

Mahtab laughs the scary laugh of the irreparably cynical. 'I was never an officer. Just a sub-inspector. You know I retired as an SI. And honest? That's right. In the Indian police, honesty.'

'You did what you could...'

'It's about either pretending or not pretending. You start bravely, from the word go, to imitate your superiors. Or you act like you can't see what's going on till the point, which comes sooner rather than later, when you can no longer be that evil-resistant monkey.'

'I will never forget that one time when you were posted somewhere in western UP...'

Mahtab pushes his plate away. 'This is not really the time and place to talk about that.'

His father, Alif reflects, is in fact one of those Muslim men of action that Iqbal dreamt of. But it is not religion that inspires or once inspired him, it's the example of the modern world: be forward-thinking, make the most of one's opportunities, succeed in an individual capacity. It's unlikely that the sort of thing that stirred Iqbal, say the glorious rise of Islam under the first four caliphs, was on Mahtab's mind during his years as a constable under the UP sun. As far as Alif has been able to gather he was often outdoors, holding up traffic when VIPs were passing through, at the barricades during religious festivals that might turn into riots, scouring slums for rascals wanted for petty crimes, hounding hoarders of grain and pulses and oils meant for public distribution. And then the slow rise through the ranks – head constable, assistant sub-inspector, sub-inspector – and the chance to sit down more often, but also being, at the same time, sat upon more often, for a sub-inspector, Alif knows, is both answerable to his superiors and responsible for keeping the foot soldiers going.

Alif emerges from his reverie to find that his father looks upset and a constrained silence has taken over the room. He recalls what Salim had told him – *Baba was crying* – and he sees in his father's face what he has been trying all these months to turn his own face away from – a sadness no longer possible to disguise. Just a tear or two slipping from those clouded eyes might drown them all.

Alif quickly leaves the room to wash his hands. A recollection is stirring in him, brought on by his father's obvious despair and his aunt's mention of western UP. He is seven or eight, his mother is on leave from work, unwell, lying for days in the contrived dark of a curtained room. Every morning his Nani is on the kitchen floor, grinding poppy seeds to a paste on the pitted stone mortar, stirring the paste into warm milk, and urging the thing on her daughter to settle her nerves. Every evening Nana sits by the sickbed with his rosary, whispering prayers. And Alif, who knows of death theoretically but not what it might mean for someone familiar to die, wonders with more curiosity than fear if his mother is dying. Death impresses itself on him as a manner of being miserable, for it becomes clear over the weeks that this usually blasé woman is worried sick and that it's something to do with his father. Then Mahtab reappears, Shagufta starts to smile again and move around, the household lapses back into its noisy existence, and that hiatus is buried in Alif's memory.

Returning to the living room, he finds Amina saying a prayer for her younger brother. Rather unclear if he feels blessed or not as he repeats the ending 'ameen' with her. Then, talking of some amulet she has for him tucked away somewhere, she tries to get off the low bed on which she is imprisoned and calls to Bano for help. Bano, who has been sitting to one side, nibbling on her dinner, smiling and nodding occasionally but never, in keeping with her subdued status, interjecting, now tells Amina in an unexpectedly peremptory tone, 'Don't you try to move.'

Amina curses her under her breath, tells her to clear the table and bring them some fruit. The fruit in question is two wrinkled apples which Amina starts peeling painstakingly, keeping up a commentary on Mahtab's achievements as a policeman, not to speak of the fact that becoming a policeman has been an achievement in itself.

But Mahtab is quiet and then, suddenly, putting on his boots, his jaw set. A dozen questions crowd Alif's brain but all he does is gesture to Amina and she quickly sends out Bano for a rickshaw. 'Forget it, it's nothing,' declares Mahtab as they are leaving, and his sister says that instead of Bano she will herself, first thing in the morning, head out, her tortuous back notwithstanding, to tie a thread at the Khwaja's shrine for him.

'It's nothing,' he repeats to his son once they are on their way home and Alif is compelled to consider the terrors this empty and insistent nothing might hold.

# FIVE

An elaborate puja is underway in the school auditorium and has transformed it from a place usually riotous with childish energy – the singing voices of five hundred students or the loudly laughing audience for a school play – to a shrunken centre that holds an improvised sanctum. The place is free of children except a few sombre-looking seniors sitting cross-legged on the floor, surrounded by adults familiar and unknown. Alif lurks by the doors, trying to stay out of sight of the principal as per whose decree, delivered to him verbally and by post, he is not to return till the committee has met and taken its decision on his ostensible murder attempt. But this morning he is back at school, just to say hello – and goodbye – to Miss Moloy and have a peek at the assembly, find out whether it is a secular god they are praying to or none at all. This marigold-bedecked occasion, complete with bare-bodied, sacred-thread-wearing purohits, the sweet fumes of a sandalwood fire being fed with brimming measuring spoons of golden ghee, and the old Sanskrit chanting, draws him in. He has never seen anything like it on the premises. Ramu rushes past, he too suddenly important in a crisp kurta, free of his usual sad-sack stubble. And it is not coffee and tea he is delivering today but bunches of bananas, a coconut or two, and even more flowers.

'You missed the beginning,' he says happily when he returns with the emptied basket. 'But the singing is yet to come.'

'Since when has this been going on?' asks Alif.

'Seven in the morning,' says Ramu and disappears, though what Alif meant was – since when has this school started to need the intercession of priests? For a moment he imagines it as a performance modelled on some pull-out from *Amar Chitra Katha*, Mrs Rawat in her extra-shiny silk and her extra-large bindi and her extra-purple lipstick playing the lead part in a masquerade, the scene fuelled by some illusion of ancientness, the holy men solemnly undertaking the rituals to make a sacrifice on behalf of a newly anointed king – or, in this case queen – so as to consecrate a just-conquered queendom. Alif stares fascinated, forgetting to duck, and Rawat looks away from the fire into which, directed by the pundits, she is chucking handfuls of the offerings, and she sees him. He clears out at once but not before noticing the expression on her face. It is touched with the gravitas of prayer. He is used to her fat-cheeked look of cultivated haughtiness and surprised to find her capable of something else altogether – beatitude. It confuses him for a moment, and then comforts him. She must be human after all, he thinks with relief. Not quite the monster I've made her out to be.

'It's a havan to give thanks for the three trophies we won in the interschool taekwondo competition,' explains Miss Moloy when he finds her.

The esteemed principal, Alif recalls, admonished him for bringing religion into the school and what is this now? Culture, she might say. Indian values. Part and parcel of our daily lives.

'But didn't we lose every single game in the interschool kabbadi competition just a couple of months ago?' he asks. 'Why no havan on that occasion to appeal to the gods for a betterment of our kabbadi skills?'

'Parvez, the sports sir, was ticked off then. You win some, you lose some, it's not like passing an exam. I believe,' says Miss Moloy in that always steady voice of hers, 'this is what he tried defending himself with. To which she said that some students had told her they could hear him wheezing when he did laps with them on the sports field, and so perhaps it was time to replace him with a younger, non-wheezy sports sir.'

Alif is truly astonished. 'And now this very Parvez is sitting by Mother Rawat's side, wearing sandalwood paste on his forehead, because we have won? And what's this business about students reporting to her? She's been dividing the staff but is she messing with the kids too?'

'She bossed us around because she was nervous and new. But the children are another matter.'

Alif goes over the scene in the hall again and tells Miss Moloy that he's all for dressed-up fire ceremonies if they have the effect of placating Rawat.

Miss Moloy only laughs. She is from a Brahmo Samaj family, influenced by those Bengali stalwarts who sought to tear away the fussy rites of Hindu practice so as to reveal at the core the exquisite pearl of belief in a singular divine, which is, correspondingly, also an unshakable self-belief.

'If only people would think,' she says. Alif is as always charmed even if not wholly convinced to hear this, her favourite declaration, the schoolteacherly emphasis she puts on that last word. *Think, think, think.* And then, *Look, look, look.*

'Why must you go?' he asks, trying to sound merely peeved, disguise the frantic if not the fearful in his voice. Her final week at school but she seems unfazed and is marking notebooks with the same pursed lips and the same considerate appearance.

'An awkward time,' she sighs without pausing in her scribbling. 'This suspension business is worrying me. I feel ...'

When she looks at him she is troubled.

'You feel like staying on? At least till this saga plays out?'

'I don't think anyone's ever taken such extreme measures. Pure spite on her part. But mixed with something else.'

She doesn't say what this is.

'But I have the Maharishi taking my part,' says Alif and explains about the professor's influence. 'I'll be back in this old chair soon but what about you?'

'Oh, I'll read. Keep a dog. Always wanted one of those big ones, a Dobermann pinscher. I could park him with you when I go travelling?'

'Yes, of course,' says Alif, though he is not sure his wife is in favour of dogs or animals in general. He wants to learn more about how Miss Moloy intends to spend her solitary time, figure out what a quiet woman might do by herself in her semi-old age in an era when the aged are meant to be running marathons and perusing senior citizen matrimonials and embarking on post-retirement careers, anything but surrendering to the grave failing of ageing. Yet as always there appears this veil over her personal life that he dare not breach. He's scared it will dilute their friendship, the bond that has derived all its substance from debate, and highly civilised debate at that. Yet he wishes that he knew something about her – now, when she is on the point of leaving and he might not see her again given that she lives in Greater Kailash and Alif dislikes every bit of Delhi that he is not already, through long association, familiar with. What is it she is protecting by letting on so little, he wonders, as Miss Moloy smiles kindly at a group of teachers who walk in having a lively discussion in Hindi about the job they've been lately tasked with: the forthcoming school concert on the theme of the messed-up environment. They are full of random facts – how much water it takes to bleach a pair of denims and hence denims should be deemed anti-national, how much grassland it takes to rear cattle for meat and dairy and so meat and dairy consumption is out of the question.

Maybe she would say, a person needn't be all autobiography. That's what she has made an example of – living so as to channel the world's collective intelligence rather than living so as to inflict one's personal life, one's linen, clean or dirty, on society. Before he can ask her if she'd accept this assessment, General Rawat storms into the staffroom accompanied by some of the havan-sancti-fied teachers including Sports Sir who wears an expression of embarrassed relief and, bringing up the rear, Ramu, with a tray piled with paper plates holding mounds of halwa. 'Prasad,' he says ecstatically, extending the tray towards Alif first of all.

'Alif Sir,' she says, 'The committee hasn't been able to meet. We are busy with more important things.' She glances at her entourage and they all nod eagerly, including that smilingly oily Jha. 'But this coming week it is on the top of the agenda. Till then I would request you to please don't come to school.'

Alif is distracted by the buttery offering and thinking of the etymology of that word – prasad. Divine grace. If your bhakti is good enough you receive the divine grace and over the centuries the clever ritualists have devised this stand-in for it – food touched by the gods, sanctified. He decides he is not yet worthy of it but, rising to his feet, takes some anyway and Ramu then presses his loaded tray on Miss Moloy.

'Very beautiful, the… err… puja,' Alif says and sees that his conjecture was right, it has softened Rawat. She is still glowing from the heat of the flames, and there are stray petals of marigold scattered on her woolly hair while dabs of kumkum and haldi gleam on her forehead.

Rawat looks bemused, perhaps unsure about the honesty of this praise. Alif doesn't know what to say next but Miss Moloy comes to the rescue – she tells the principal that Alif ought to be given a chance to talk with Ankit's parents. If they agree to let their son carry on in school then there is no reason to keep him suspended.

'Oh that is such a good idea,' says Alif as if he's just heard of it. 'I am sure his father is a reasonable man.' He recalls the foolish remarks Ankit repeated and knows the fellow is far from reasonable. 'I'll explain, madam, that the child was being being troublesome and I responded in haste and all of us need to make some amends. I'll get them to give it in writing that they've put this thing behind them. Will that satisfy you and the committee?

'I'll go with him,' says Miss Moloy. 'I'll try my best to bring them around.'

Jha is going to intervene but then Sports Sir, with whom Alif has never had much to do, pitches in as well and declares this a worthwhile plan. Perhaps he is newly sympathetic to Alif because his own neck was so recently on the line. Rawat looks reluctant but even reluctance on a demeanour such as hers is a great concession.

'I don't know, I haven't met these people. They have not come for any parent-teacher meetings so far since the child joined the school last year. And now, after this incident, why would they come for any parent-teacher meetings?'

'We can do the work then,' says Miss Moloy. 'Of giving them an update on the child's progress.'

'I don't know…' repeats Rawat.

It could be that Miss Moloy's salt-and-pepper-haired authority has caused the principal to lose some of her aplomb. Or maybe it's the Maharishi, he's put in that precious word and the puppets have started to stir on their strings.

'Okay then, you try to discuss with them and kindly report to me,' she says breathlessly and rushes out as hurriedly as she had come. Jha, looking less smiley, follows her.

Alif and Miss Moloy eat their prasad in delight and stop short of giving each other high fives. Ramu is dispatched to tell Ankit to phone his parents; Ankit reports that they are free and willing to meet, so the two start out at once. Alif, feeling magnanimous, seeing victory well within sight, has summoned a taxi to the school gate. He is cheered up by this little expedition with his friend and wants very much to thank her but instead, as usual, starts arguing with her when she upholds again, like some outdated idealist, the value of reason and reason alone.

'It's a double-edged sword, miss, as you know. Your beloved adage, your *think*. Consider the Age of Empire. Wasn't that all about the same things – reason, progress, civilisation? Where did that land us? But I have a theory about what could take the edge off reason without dislodging it.'

'It only works as an absolute and irrefutable principle. As Immanuel Kant said, act only on the basis of that which you can will to be a universal law.'

'Kant,' groans Alif theatrically, that once grand, now dusty old man of the Enlightenment. But Miss Moloy admires Kant, the system builder. She admires all system builders, however flawed their theories, however much history might have proved them contingent.

'Our principal madam would do well to heed Kant, for in acting out of narrow self-interest she is digging her own grave,' she says.

And though it is she who has invoked Kant, it is Alif who appears, to himself at least, the more proficient on this as on so many other subjects and so he explains a few things.

'As you may know,' he begins, with the taxi driver weaving out of the chaos of Daryaganj's main road, 'as you may know,

Kant believed, like a few other philosophers before him, that human beings were made such that selfishness and reason are always clashing in their heads, or in their hearts.'

'And the question was how to reconcile the two,' says Miss Moloy.

'Exactly. His genius was to see that only reason is common to all human beings, whereas self-interest divides us, so the moral law, if it is to be universal, can be based on nothing but reason.'

He has given this talk before but still enjoys it, if only because it elevates him a little. Kant brings a touch of puissance to the far, far-removed reality of their lives, at the moment this reality being the rip-roaring conduit of the Grand Trunk Road and the passing sight of an overloaded lorry with Haryana number plates lying on its side, leaking grease, a humble white Maruti 800 crushed beneath it, and a number of small boys in chappals studying the disaster with the mien of experts.

'But can it be really true that we are inherently this way?' he asks. 'Not everyone demonstrates the same tendencies. Among the Greeks, for instance, there was no conflict between acting for yourself and acting for the world.'

'Perhaps not among older, simpler societies. But think of the industrialised world…'

'That's the Hegelian view,' says Alif. 'That we have been backward and are hurtling towards an ideal society where everyone will do his duty according to his station and thereby act for the common good. It makes me nervous, this idea of progress, this belief in the common good. Hegel makes me nervous.'

'So there is no hope for people like our principal madam?'

'I don't quite buy that proposition – of human beings as only capable of reaching their full potential when they switch on their reason. As effective a force as reason is love. Compare, say, the British overlords to the Mughals. The first believed in duty for duty's sake. Supressing any conflicted feelings, playing by the rules. To them Indians seemed too easily swayed by emotion, they behaved subjectively all the time. They had to be civilised first, taught to use their reason. And is it only a coincidence that they were the means to fattening the empire while the civilising project was underway?'

'But the British were not all bad...'

'Maybe, but I would say that on the whole they failed in India because they tended to lack what the Mughals had – affection for the people. Can one imagine those stiff-backed Viceroys playing Holi with the crowd as Zafar or Akbar used to do? And so when I see this havan I have mixed feelings. It seems out of place and yet if the students are inspired by it and General Rawat humbled by it...'

Miss Moloy is not convinced but they have to suspend their discussion because the driver cannot find the address. It turns out Ankit lives in some rundown colony between the the railway line that heads north to Punjab and the road they're on running in the same direction, in a huddle of stifling-looking houses of undressed brick tucked inside an industrial area which is all rutty roads and sooty air. The houses have no numbers and they have to keep asking pedestrians, shopkeepers and layabouts till they locate the cramped lane overrun with water from a broken tap or burst pipe somewhere and climb the narrow steps to the third floor. An elderly man in clothes he has likely slept in opens the door and does not seem to know who they are.

'But Ankit phoned you. He told you we're on our way,' says Miss Moloy somewhat scoldingly.

The man introduces himself as the boy's grandfather and says Ankit did no such thing. Could he please check with Ankit's parents, she asks. They turn out to be something of a fiction.

'The child lives with me. His parents are in the village. They have two younger ones to handle and no time to bother with the antics of this one. So what has he done this time?' he asks calmly, beckoning them into a room with durries on the floor, a small room holding the mingled smell of turnips stewing and incense sticks moulting. His name is Ram Ganesh Chaturvedi and Alif explains, starting with the Hanuman-Humayun bind, why they are here, a trifle awkwardly because the man, or rather the god, is right there again, a vividly coloured, framed print propped up on a shelf cluttered with digestive suspensions and health tonics, a jar crammed with disused pen and household tools, a frozen alarm clock. The gold of his mace matches the glitter of his crown, and the fabled mountain of life-saving herbs is held aloft in the other hand, its green as compelling as the blue behind it.

Chaturvedi claims to have heard nothing about the matter. The boy has not breathed a word to him.

'Even if he'd told me I might not have given it the time of day. But since you have taken the trouble to come all the way here ...'

'I know you want to put him in a different school...' starts Alif.

'I didn't say that.' The same unruffled air and the same tolerant smile – perhaps the look of an astrologer who has seen through it all and knows all that is to come. For the Hindi-English sign on the door says that's what he is – 'Ram Prasad Chaturvedi, Jyotish Aur Purohit (Numerology & Astrology & Vastu)'.

Alif and Miss Moloy, sitting cross-legged facing their supposed adversary, find they have nothing to say. They had been building up a defence but there is no one to present it to.

Chaturvedi goes in for a moment, perhaps to attend to his overdone turnips, then returns wiping down his hands on the folds of his grey dhoti and settles down again opposite them.

'You see, he's a habitual liar.'

Alif thinks of the parents he has squared off with in meetings over the years, immediately put out at the smallest critique of their offspring. While here is a man who has fathered or grand-fathered a bit of a devil and is happy to acknowledge it. Alif likes him at once. Miss Moloy doesn't quite seem to.

'No child is born lying,' she says.

'A habitual liar,' he repeats as if he hasn't heard. 'And it's hard to know when he's making grand things up and when he is merely embroidering the truth.'

'Then we too have failed there,' says Alif. 'I mean to reform him.'

'You teach?'

'History,' says Alif. He remembers what Ankit said about the Ka'bah. Did he get that piece of travesty from this underfed and stoic-looking old man or did he patch it together from things he's heard elsewhere?

'I didn't know you had twisted his ear. But then as his teacher you can twist his ear all you want. I've been planning to pull him out anyway and tutor him at home. This is the third school. He started with playschool at the age of three and everyone there couldn't wait to be rid of him. Then he was in another place, near here, where he broke a great many windowpanes and stole from a great many lunch boxes. So we were soon done with that.'

Alif can't help chuckling.

'What will you teach him on your own?' asks Miss Moloy.

'Sanskrit. Upanishads. Puranas.'

'What about maths and science, then? And, yes, history?' she asks.

'Nothing doing. He's going nowhere with that.'

'How long has he been with you? This … er … particular character he's developed, could it be because he misses his parents?' asks Alif.

'It could be because he misses his parents,' says Chaturvedi with that same deadly calm, and leans back with nothing on his face – neither annoyance nor sympathy. 'I would have offered you tea but I've run out of sugar. And as for milk…'

'No tea. We're leaving soon,' says Alif. His bottom hurts from resting on the floor, then it strikes him that they probably sleep here, grandfather and grandson, on these very prickly handwoven carpets. On a low stool is an old reading lamp, its enamel coating chipped, its head tied to its body with thick knots of plastic twine. So this is Ankit's study too. And there, on a hanger suspended from the handle of a dirt-brown steel almirah, is a spare set of the boy's school shirt and shorts that someone has carefully washed and ironed: a nice, clean Ankit, standing quietly to one side, listening.

'Have you tried talking with him,' asks Miss Moloy? 'He's old enough now…'

'What can one tell a child? Say sorry? Never do it again? He will laugh at me. He laughs at the neighbours when they come after him with their slippers in their hands. He cries of course. But he's never short of glee. I am allowed to stay on around here only because I've known this place since it was farmland and I've read the palms and drawn up the horoscopes and resolved the vastu issues of three generations.'

He goes in again and returns with two small spotty steel tumblers of water with outcurved rims. Hitching up his dhoti he says, 'The root of the problem lies in what you're teaching him.'

'Whatever else we teach we try to teach values. Reason is the only one really. Rationality,' says Miss Moloy.

'I understand. How else will our children become engineers and doctors and scientists?'

'Reason...' puts in Alif, 'and we try the other thing also. To inculcate some decency.'

*How?* He takes his students on random field trips, Rawat is bent on making parroting patriots out of them.

'That's the problem. My child is clever, it's just that his cleverness is directed at the very worst ideas.'

'And you think you will be able to reform him all by yourself, without a system to back you?' asks Miss Moloy.

'I have a system in mind, it's there in the Upanishads: sravana, manana, dhyana.'

She shakes her head disparagingly but drinks the water.

'Sravana, manana, dhyana,' he instructs. And goes into pandit mode, explicating how you first imbibe the tradition as a student, then you dwell on it and understand it logically, and finally meditate on it and experience the truth first-hand: that there is no outside and inside, good and evil, self and divine. There is only one perfect ultimate all-encompassing consciousness.

'And a nine-year-old will get all this?'

'You start, when you come to live with your guru as a child, by chopping wood for him, sweeping his floor, filling his water pot, listening to his chanting. You are the once-born and only later does it come – the sacred rites, the initiation that will render you twice-born.'

Alif is all ready to give in to this programme of immersion in the subtle and eternal truths – Tat Tvam Asi and so on – and this vision of ancient beauty except that where are those

185

mud-and-thatch dwellings and where are those rows of scrubbed clay pots and where is that one beautiful leaf of the champaka tree swirling down in the breeze of dawn to float in the clear waters of the village pond? He very much doubts that even in the sticks where Ankit's parents are eking out a living there is to be found the ghost of any such haven or any high-minded savant in charge of it. And Chaturvedi himself? Perhaps he could be an effective teacher but Alif does not feel there is anything ennobling in the poverty of these quarters: the room, despite the lateness of the year, so clammy and without a fan, windows blurred with the grit of the air outside, the water they are drinking tasting faintly of rotten foliage.

He puts his glass down and makes to stand up but Miss Moloy seems reluctant to give in. She is telling Chaturvedi that instead of this highfalutin business about the self and the divine what the child needs is added doses of the extra-curricular. He is unresponsive in the classroom but excellent on the playground so if his grandfather could organise cricket coaching for him or swimming lessons…

'I am not suggesting that one sit at home all day in meditation or become an ascetic,' says Chaturvedi. 'The Upanishads also say: *Go out and do good for the world.*'

'There is no going back, Chaturvedi ji,' says Miss Moloy.'

Alif knows what she means because it's he who's emphasised this to her so often. We are products – of the nineteenth century and its economic revolutions and the twentieth century and its political ones.

'I am not going back anywhere,' he says, smiling tolerantly. 'I am only returning to the place where we have always been.'

Alif wonders what he'll tell Rawat. On the good side there are no angry parents to placate but on the bad side the school is going to lose the child anyway. He shifts uncomfortably and starts to wonder if there really is no way to reconcile them – the teachings of the old texts with the compulsions of the modern world. All he can think of is those self-styled gurus of self-help who mine the scriptures for hacks that will let the moneymakers vindicate their greed or Hindu justifications for every modern development since Hinduism went into decline. He starts to feel greatly sorry for the old man and his dream of a return because, like Miss Moloy, he suspects it's doomed. And sorry for Ankit too, who is likewise trapped, whose intelligence is all violence, whose imagination is all lies.

Chaturvedi is describing the boy's latest escapades. He seems to be developing a new hobby – the theft of mobile phones.

'Oh God, find a better way to save him, please,' blurts out Alif.

'You are bothered, I can tell. But I don't think it's my grand-son alone.'

'I'm all right.'

'You came here on official duty but that does not mean there is no deeper purpose in your coming here. Ask me any question you like. The rate is a hundred and one rupees.'

Practised spiel no doubt but still not a hint of insistence in his tone. Something admirably effortless about this man.

'He's always preoccupied, it's his style. And he doesn't believe in astrology,' says Miss Moloy.

Chaturvedi is highly amused. 'That's like saying one does not believe in the moon and the stars, in the planets, in the time of one's birth, in the certainty of one's death... There is something this man wants to know, he is in some kind of trouble.'

This Alif cannot deny but how to put across to their host that the trouble is many-sided, that it involves relationships, work, faith, money, civilisational decay.

'If you will step into my office, we can have a discussion about it,' he says as if Alif had spoken out loud.

'I don't actually...'

'... believe in astrology,' repeats Miss Moloy.

'But just to please this kind gentleman who has let me off the hook,' Alif says, nodding at Miss Moloy apologetically. He is curious about what sort of astrology goes on in here and he needs to get off that floor.

The fore-room aims, even if it fails, at a vedantic spartanness, while the office has been given over to the gods. No windows and the only light is from the bulbs of yellow and red hung above framed and garlanded pictures, colourful oleographs, of

Kali with her tongue rudely out, dancing on the inert Shiva, and the many-armed, wise Saraswati on a pink lotus, and Durga astride her tamed tiger. The mother goddesses, thinks Alif, with fondness. The old mothers, some of whom might even have their roots in cults that existed before the Aryans arrived with their new pantheon and, eventually, their pantheism. But the males are here too, the indispensable males – silvery statuettes of the sedately seated Ganapati, of Rama with Sita, of Hanuman again with his upright tail, all ranged on one side of the low table.

Chaturvedi takes his place on a plastic chair and, assuming an officious air, enquires if Alif has had his horoscope made. Ignoring his evasions, he takes a sheet of paper, asks him to write down his name and date of birth, gets him to lay his palm on the other side, draws an outline of it, and makes certain markings on the figure. Then he hands over some cowrie shells to shake in joined palms, instructing Alif to pray, as he does, to the God of his choice. Alif drops the cowries on the table, Chaturvedi studies them and more scribbling follows. A significant silence then, in which Miss Moloy says to Alif sotto voce that she did not think him capable of this cheap mumbo-jumbo and Alif feels he might laugh and be expelled from that serious room.

Miss Moloy never returns home to Calcutta to be with her siblings and their children for the Durga Puja festival. Her extended family have all, despite their Brahmo roots, gone back to flaunting religiosity. Only she is holding out, spending the holiday holed up in her flat reading someone rigorously scientific as an antidote, Darwin, for instance. She has no interest in devotions of the hands-clasped variety.

'You are a good man,' says the astrologer, finally. 'You mind your business and let others mind theirs. But for the last few months something wicked's afoot. You're just not getting the fruit of your actions. Witchcraft has been done on you, either in your home or place of work.'

'It's true that there have been things going on recently...'

'The only solution is to get someone to do a puja to negate the bad effects of that witchcraft. Otherwise, however hard you try, it'll come to nothing. After the puja has been performed, in a few weeks, all your wishes will be fulfilled.'

There is a heavy volume lying there, bound in red, but Chaturvedi does not consult it. By that is a bottle of mustard oil used to light the fire lamp before the largest icon on the table of some no doubt local goddess, the devi whom this man likely communes with heart to heart as against the more eminent gods all around. She has a red sari, a crown of many tiers, much jewellery, a brightly yellow face, and fat, somewhat unconvincing, seraphic wings of cloth padding overlaid with tinsel.

'I need to think about it,' says Alif but what he's thinking about instead is how the Vedic people had graduated from simple hymns sung for the deities of the natural world to the sophisticated lessons of the Upanishads. And then what? Several millennia of Hinduism and has it come down only to this: some superstitions in a darkened room with a handful of cowrie shells, a profusion of god pictures in bright hues?

'I can come to your abode with all the items required for the puja,' he says, after Alif has paid him his fee. 'Leave it all to me.'

'Sounds excellent,' mumbles Alif. 'I'll let you know.' He glances at Miss Moloy and says, 'It's time I called a cab.'

Chaturvedi is explaining to Miss Moloy the difference between sun signs and moon signs but, aware of her disapproval, has not yet suggested that he diagnose her problems too. He speaks a high-flown Hindi, a Hindi bound to frighten the weak-kneed and the half-educated. Alif does not know anyone who speaks better English than Miss Moloy and yet here perhaps she has met her match, for her Hindi is everyday while Chaturvedi's, when he needs to make a point, is scholarly, that is, Sanskritic. Alif wants in some way to come to his friend's aid just as she came to his a few hours ago in suggesting this meeting. Instead he starts to contemplate the source of Chaturvedi's convictions.

How is it that this man speaks of the ancient texts – and knows of their principal teaching, namely that divinity is within you, should you have the wherewithal to notice it, that everything is at root one substance and there is really no anthropomorphic god handing out judgements – and yet he is clearly committed to the gods of later Hinduism? A wise one then, who has understood that clients need to be shown into a room featuring deities they know and love, while the deeper truths he reserves for himself. He has to make a living, after all.

The tough cheerfulness of his manner reminds Alif of Ramu, the school peon. Impossible to imagine the personalities of either man without the culture that produced them – Krishna's cosmic song and dance, the parables of the Puranas, the sometimes terrifying mothers who express love through rage. But Ramu would not be allowed access to the teachings of the old scriptures. Their authors roundly declare it's not for everyone, that it requires long apprenticeship by a young Brahmin to a Brahmin teacher. Ramu's grandson, Arun, is a student of Alif's and Miss Moloy's; he will not spend his life behind the tea tray but will he be permitted into the fold? And the fact that he can take his place with the other students, does that follow from the loosening of the laws of Hinduism or is it because of the modernity that Miss Moloy always defends, that she is defending even now.

He finally cuts into their tussle, explains that more than a countervailing puja he needs Chaturvedi ji to help him.

'My job, you see, is threatened because I lost my temper with your grandson. And my job is all I have.'

'I saw it in the cowries,' says Chaturvedi.

'Then you also know how you can help. All you have to do is phone the principal and describe Ankit's tendencies and also that, having interviewed me, you have nothing against me.'

'Of course,' says the man. 'That is what I am here for. To help people.'

Alif give him the numbers, thanks him profusely. Miss Moloy gets up to leave, she too acknowledging the man's kindness.

'The cost is only five hundred rupees,' says Chaturvedi.

Alif hesitates. What is this? A sophist shamelessly insisting on a bribe or a sage demanding his rightful due for the superior knowledge he's handed out? The man is looking at him without a trace of compunction.

Smiling wryly, Alif hands over the money. He is thinking of what he and Miss Moloy were discussing in the taxi. In the

Hegelian view we are moving ahead all the time; in the Hindu view things operate in cycles, they tend to get worse, the gods have to intervene, and then perhaps, if we're very lucky, they might get better.

*

'Oye Sardarji, mujhe gun dilwa de,' says Ganesh and he has been mouthing this line, between intervals of moaning, for a good half hour, while Sardarji plies him with double whiskeys and assures him he has no truck with those who deal in guns and 'voilence'. He cannot get him a gun but he can give him his honest opinion, which is that everything in this country sucks and if Ganesh should happen to want to emigrate to Canada he knows just the agent for the job.

'Na, na, na,' says Ganesh pressing back tears with the heels of his palms. 'Mujhe gun dilwa de.'

What does this look like – Ganesh crying – handsome Ganesh with never a hair out of place, his clothes impeccable, his arguments always at the ready, his mind ever alert to the workings of the world economy? He understands money and so, more or less, he understands everything. But today he has been thwarted. Alif is trying to drink slowly, seeing as this will be a long evening.

'I told you,' he says to his friend, his voice trembling with enraged pity, but this too has been repeated.

All the same, Ganesh stops massaging his swollen eyes and shouts at Alif. 'So what if you told me? Did it make a difference? Did I listen? Tell me what to do *now*.'

'Let her go,' says Alif wearily. He cannot understand human bondage – why this love that is no different from hate, why this hate for something you were supposed to love? Ganesh's long-estranged wife has just resurfaced and wants out. She is remarrying – a divorcee with two children.

Ganesh wants to kill him and then kill her and then perhaps kill himself. This last bit is somewhat unclear still – Alif is not yet able to tell how much remorse he is feeling for neglecting his wife and how much is just hurt pride.

Ganesh puts Alif's suggestion to Sardarji. 'Saali ko jaane doon? Just like that? You screwed me and you insulted my parents and thank you very much and goodbye.'

Sardarji politely suggests he have a talk with her, try to sort out matters. He is sitting down with them in view of the gravity of the situation but not drinking; he has never been seen drinking with his customers. Maybe if he did he would lose his barkeeper equanimity, that ability he has to appear acutely sympathetic and yet never partisan.

'If Canada doesn't interest you, what about America? Do you know who produces most of the peaches, the almonds, the raisins in California? Thousands of tonnes of fruit? Jat Sikh farmers. I have relatives there – one brother, actually a cousin, and his two cousins – and they're doing better business on farms of their own than they would in Punjab. I know you can't run a farm, bhai sahib, you are a professional, but what I'm saying is: you might be one thing here but going over there can make you into something else altogether. Have you ever thought of starting your own company?'

Ganesh bangs his drink down forcefully but not so hard that any of it spills. 'I will challenge this in court. I will drag her to court along with that dirty, devious divorcee of hers.'

'They're not letting in Indians in droves any more,' says Alif to Sardarji. 'This dream that you're talking of, it's over. But did you never consider going abroad yourself, then?'

Ganesh answers for him. 'He'll never emigrate. Don't you know how many things he runs? From behind the scenes? Underhand? Which is why I'm saying, he's the only man who can get me a gun.'

Alif recalls the hotel-cum-brothel that Ahmad used to work in and feels a moment of unease. He does not want to be let into any sordid secrets or hear about nefarious shit. He likes the man and believed him to be wholly dedicated to Bright & Blue. On the basis of all their passing conversations over the years that he and Ganesh have patronised this dive, Alif had formed an impression of a regular guy just tending to the place, even if it was via the wanton destruction of people's livers. He came across to Alif as a businessman through and through. *But why did I assume this means transparency*, he wonders. Isn't it the rule of business to make money no matter what? Businessmen are not Kantians. They use not just people but all things on heaven and earth as a means. And he sees the brisk-mannered yet unfailingly polite Sardarji in a new light, even though the light is the same as always – a pulsing, dim, electric blue. *Nothing is straight in this city*, laments Alif silently. Everyone has another face. Each is busy manipulating the system. When he runs out of generalisations, he tries to consider things in the singular but in the singular it is only her he can think of – Prerna. She has not replied to his third message and his fingers are itching to send her a fourth.

Sardarji is denying Ganesh's charge, reiterating that he has nothing to do with 'voilence', that he spent the long years of the Punjab insurgency in the 1980s lying low in Lucknow, running a humble neighbourhood restaurant before he came out to Delhi and started this place. Then he gets a waiter to bring them a complimentary platter of the restaurant's famously indigestible bhuna gosht and slips away to attend to another customer even though Ganesh hasn't given up trying to get him to procure that gun.

'Do you even know what to do with one?' asks Alif.

'Abey, I can shoot...' slurs Ganesh. He is never drunk. Five drinks down, he will still be enunciating clearly his contempt for the world while Alif is enlivened by two, made sloppy by three and has never tried more than that number in a row. But today it is Ganesh who is a liquid mess, while Alif is turning to ice – freezing over the trouble to do with his job, freezing over his father's mysterious grief, freezing over his friend's despair. The only thing that can melt him is the face of that woman. He had resolved to spend the evening coming clean, recounting to Ganesh that strange – because it was so compelling – meeting in the cafe and the stranger one in her apartment. But when he got to the bar, Ganesh was already drunk on his wrath and there was no question of bringing up Prerna. She is probably no longer even a subject for him. And whose problem is she, then, what

193

am I to do with her? He tears at his hair, but only inwardly, and tries to apply himself to the issue at hand.

'I hope you haven't told your parents yet?'

'How can I keep it from them? I was screaming at her on the phone last night when she called just like that out of nowhere and that too at dinner time. Not even a polite question about them – are they alive? Are you alive? Nothing. Just business. I want you to sign some papers. I'll be sending them across next week. That's all. I can't believe she's the same woman. Alif woh bahut badal gayi hai.'

He is going to start cry again. Or he already is crying.

'What are they saying?'

'He's not saying a thing. She is saying too much – good riddance, now you can marry again, now you can have a child, now everything will be all right.'

'You don't have any ground to stand on – in a court of law or outside it,' says Alif. 'You haven't lived together for almost a decade. What are you after?'

'Peace.'

'You want peace?'

'The kind of peace one feels after all one's scores have been settled.

'And you think your parents will survive this, this settling of scores?'

'Papa heard everything but he's just sitting there quietly saying nothing. What am I supposed to do if he doesn't talk to me?'

'I've told you so many times, he needs to see a doctor. He doesn't talk to you but have you ever tried sitting down and talking to him? You're the one to blame here.'

'Alif Mohammad tu kaun hota hai…? Who are you to tell me…?'

But he doesn't even have the will – or the conviction – to complete the sentence, to whole-heartedly tick off Alif, and Alif thinks of that incomplete question Ganesh sometimes put to him. *Who are you, Mohammad?*

How many times over the course of his adult life the Prophet must have been asked that and how many times he insisted that all he is is merely human. *Ye bhi durust hai ki payambar nahin hoon main/ hai ye bhi sach ki mera kaha hone vaala hai.* He smiles despite the mood and thanks, as always, Mir's genius of a memory, sublet to his own patchy one. Those lines by Zafar Iqbal sum it up. You're right I am no prophet/ and just as true that what I say will come to pass.

Ganesh is still going on about the wretched gun so Alif pays for their drinks and pushes him out of the bar. The man insists on driving. He is in a particular frame of mind and wouldn't mind running over a pedestrian or throttling a traffic policeman. He drives desperately and swerves dangerously all the short way from Chelmsford Road to Daryaganj, while Alif, realising that to restrain him is useless, thinks of how death has increasingly become something that happens to us while we are in motion – mid-sentence, *in situ.* In days of yore the brave rode out to their deaths and meeting one's end by accident, by drinking, by conspiratorial murder was never heroic. Today we are so sold on life that every death is received by its victims with an expression of surprise. So if they die now, the two of them, if they die like this, willing death on themselves, racing it to the finish line, it'd be fine. The city of Delhi would welcome it as entirely just – the drivers who yell at Ganesh for his mindless honking, the beggar children who shriek curses when he rolls down the window they're pawing at to smack them, the throng of tourists outside a restaurant on Asaf Ali Road who stare in disgusted disbelief as he lurches past the red light and into the zebra crossing.

But they do not die. They park on that road and stumble into the mouth of their neighbourhood – Ganesh, fiery-eyed and whimpering, wishing his life had turned out different, and Alif imagining his life *is* different, that it is not him but his funeral procession winding through the night lanes of the old town so that he sees everything he is used to seeing from the perspective of one now forever prostrate. His vision has been weirdly reconfigured by McDowell's No. 1 and like in some of those Mughal miniature paintings, he seems to see things from above as well as at eye-level: the impossibly convoluted bunches of electrical cables, the blurred black sky that no one writes love songs for any more, the open mouth of the man in office clothes standing on the broken pavement and eating a pastry at the little Al-Sikander bakery as if it were three in the afternoon rather than close on midnight. (And despite himself Allif recalls that Alexander the Great is, in some traditions, the Prophet Sikander).

On Bazar Chitli Qabar Road the restaurants are still doing business but the huge griddles of fried chicken legs that have simmered in gravy all day are now almost empty. It being Friday, groups of hungry men would have squatted outside the more generous of these establishments at lunch hour and each been handed a couple of warm rotis and a small plastic bowl of daal, with the owners watching from behind their meat-filled cooking pots – fat and dressed in white while the hungry are inevitably all colourless. Colourless faces, colourless clothes, colourless, knotted working bodies that even Friday charity does not unbend. This is it: the old heart of Delhi where rough men in the streets abuse in a rich vein and poor men peddling plastic trash speak with the modulated refinement of courtiers, where ageing men with kohl in their eyes might still paint calligraphy for a few rupees or incise a headstone, and where, just then, a woman rushes past, a green flag tied around her shoulders, shouting 'Babri Zindabad'. The owner of Arora Brothers 'Dry Cleaners Since 1948' is polishing his sign though it already looks new, and Alif can see the undersides of the breasts of the girl who walks very close past him, as well as the top her head, as she teases him with her pert eyes, aware he can make no moves on her because he is dead. If he were animate he could tell the old man in a filthy kurta-pyjama sitting patiently with his stacks of chinaware at the giant peepul tree in the intersection that there will be no more customers tonight. He sees the new pink and green paint on the spindly columns of the little mosque whose calls to prayer he hears morning and night, and then he is no longer dead. He is trying to stand up as straight as possible for they have run into the imam going home on a beaten-up bicycle, the same personage Alif succeeded in dodging the other day at Jama Masjid. But now he is upon them and there is nowhere to hide.

'Alif mian,' he says. 'Aap dikhai nahi diye aaj jumma ki namaz pe.'

This is his preferred style. Alif hasn't darkened the mosque's doorway for years and yet the imam when he meets him will only ask with maddening politeness why he didn't drop in that Friday, taking away the burden of Alif's guilt and then increasing it manifold with this insistent discreetness.

'I was teaching,' says Alif. 'Fridays are busy.'

'But mian, maybe you can explain to them why you need some time out one day of the week. Teach harder on other days.'

'Of course, of course,' says Alif, trying to step back from the imam though he probably already knows about his vices – if not from the smell of his breath then from the unsteadiness of his gait. Perhaps in some Muslim land at some point in the past, the man of history and the man of God might have had a spirited colloquy. But here and now is not the time. The imam asks after his parents, enquires into the sort of education he is giving his son, curses the government, and ends where he always ends – with an elegy in pointlessly elaborate Urdu on the sad decline of Muslimdom. Ganesh he roundly ignores.

Alif feels a muted fear whenever he thinks of the imam and, certainly, face to face with him. A common zealot and there are a thousand such elsewhere – in all likelihood the one Ahmad was going on about is worse. Alif's man is, at least, civil. History has entrusted him with this task and he is too powerless and insipid to resist it: harry his congregation, read the Urdu papers which on occasion preach jihadism, try to sniff out ambivalence in the soul of every man he meets. Alif's soul is all ambivalence and the camouflage so tatty. And yet he could never challenge the man or dismiss him. He must stand there mumbling answers to his routine questions.

Imam sahib hands Alif a pamphlet which he extends into the orangey light of the street lamp to read. It concerns the right way to sit and the right way to stand, the correct hand to eat with and the best foot to put forward when leaving the house, which fingernail to start with when clipping and which angle to hold the comb at when making a parting. And in all of this to follow the example of the great apostle – if there is anything he did not prescribe then it is by implication proscribed. Alif looks at the man; it is possible he would find fault with just the way Alif is raising his eyebrows. The man says, 'The umma are forgetting.'

'I'm quite sure they are.'

'So you will join us, then, next Friday?'

'Of course, of course.' And he rereads the injunctions, finding it hard to believe that he's reached this ripe and useless age without once having come across them.

Imam finally wheels his bicycle away and Ganesh mutters, 'Bairam Khan come to life in the middle of the night!'

Alif snorts and agrees, 'Yes, that's what the great Khan has come to.' For this neighbourhood around the three-way junction, tiraha – where bags of garbage lie heaped in wheelbarrows and the bustle of commerce never ceases – is named after a great man, greatness being, in his time, one career option among others. Bairam Khan, prominent footnote in the story of the first three Mughals: teenage general in Babur's army, friend to Emperor Humayun, regent to the young Akbar after Humayun died. And his son, one of the nine jewels of Akbar's court – poet and teacher to Salim who went on to become the emperor Jahangir.

Alif is not, as the fairy tales put it, of noble birth. His paternal grandfather was a clerk in a mofussil post office and his older ancestors were probably scraping a living off the land in the hinterland of Delhi, or they could have been sailing boats on the Yamuna, or grooming horses and taming elephants; maybe they were hereditary cooks in the outhouses of the rich or had been for generations weaving fabrics for the high-born to wear. Something humble at any rate, something workmanlike. So in mourning the extinction of the likes of Bairam Khan there is no personal lament but there is lament all the same – that inevitable nostalgia for a time when well-laid gardens were as important as well-designed homes, when loyalty counted for more than profit, when poetry was a serious art and a time-taking one. Ganesh, had he lived then, could have gone and pulled on the golden chain at Jahangir's fort in Agra and sought justice, his wife might have done the same, and someone deemed wise and impartial and above all divinely touched would have issued a decree. Now their case will be decided by some dour judge. Alif is unspeakably sorry for his friend, even sorrier knowing he's wronged Sahana.

After he has left him, still inconsolable, outside his door on the ground floor and climbed the stained stairway to his own home, after he has lain beside his dreaming wife in the small room, which apart from the bed has little else but books – spilling out of a cheap-looking wood veneer rack and forming small silos on the floor – Alif sleeps, as he has done for decades, cushioned by the clamour of the crossroads. At some point in the small hours, the old man selling crockery under the tree will transform into a young one selling the day's vegetables, and the cakes in Al-Sikander will be replaced by fresh ones, and Arora Brothers will open to business again. But that transition will always remain elusive to Alif. He goes to sleep in noisiness and wakes into noisiness and he can never tell when the previous day passes its baton to the next.

It is a late Saturday morning when he rises reluctantly, rueful about the night's sentimentalising over the Mughals. Golden chains and godly emperors indeed! He knows the history's student primary lesson: quell all nostalgia. And especially over that lot who forgot to modernise, and then let the Europeans in to do the job. Groaning at his habitual follies, he goes into the living room. Wife and son have long seized the day. Salim is explaining to his mother how a wind turbine works and how renewable energy is the answer to the world's problems; she is on the internet looking for jobs and reading out descriptions of the city's new showrooms and the unheard-of things they sell. Alif, too bleary to talk, hoping to ease his headache with scalding instant coffee, tries to put a date to it – that point in history when a giant, killer wave of consumables leapt out of the ocean and killed the poetry in us. And now we can't go back. We don't know what to do with ourselves except long for more things. And how is that not a fate more wretched than nostalgia? He thinks of the mullah of the previous night, trying to bring the errant to heel, ringing the warning bell of his bicycle up and down the half-lit lanes of Daryaganj.

Salim eventually gives up on his turbines and asks if they might install a closed circuit camera just to keep an eye on who comes and goes.

'But our neighbours are so close they can keep an eye on our dreams, forget who comes and goes,' points out Tahira. She is out and out an old Delhi girl. She can wander about late at night in her hijab, throw a loud 'marjani' at any woman who messes with her, spit a vicious 'randi ki aulad' at any man who tries to feel her up. She gossips like a crone with the neighbours about the other neighbours, and yet more and more feels the greatest restlessness where she is most at home.

Alif is thinking of the sunny green vales and wonderfully solitary chalets in the pictures that tend to illustrate mottoes at dentists and barbershops, or appear, combined with cheering Urdu verse, in the children's books sold in gullies around the great mosque. He never feels a longing for these idylls, not because he is a selfless renunciate. He just doesn't deserve them. A simple inference from the law of karma. But legitimatised greed has thwarted that particular law. Everything is within the reach of everyone – it's just a question of adjusting the monthly instalments.

'What do you want to eat?' Salim asks his father, informing him that the aloo parathas Khanna Aunty sent over early that morning have long been dispensed with.

'Nothing, my child,' says Alif but Salim insists that he can cook. And so he goes into their mucky kitchen to attempt French toast for his father while Tahira continues trawling the job sites and talking to herself. She has been anxious following that iftar conversation with Ganesh and cannot bear the thought of another MBA – not just the cost but also the idea of continuing to study, of studying without being sure if it will immediately improve her chances. He's mistaken, she says. He's not in this line. He's just a computer mechanic, what does he know about sales and marketing?

The doorbell rings and Farouk bustles in with far too much energy for a weekend morning. He makes his salaams, gives them belated Eid greetings, apologises for being able to get away only today, demands to know what career moves Tahira is planning, and hands over a profligately large boxful of Eid sweets. Then he settles down with a cup of tea and proceeds to give them news of sundry distant relatives whom Tahira barely even knows but is anyway curious about. She is always interested in everything Farouk says and in agreement with every opinion he proffers. Maybe she should have married him instead, thinks Alif perversely and lets the thought linger as he tries to eat the only slightly burnt breakfast his son has lovingly made him.

He watches his wife and his cousin guffaw over trivialities, and while their fondness for each other usually makes him glad in an avuncular sort of way, today, egged on by his migraine, he imagines them meeting much before he arrived on the scene, he imagines them recognising in each other an uncommonly common spirit, and he imagines them holding hands, falling into an embrace and he goes on, much further than he should, all through the prolonged panting and heaving to the fascinatingly sickening end. He is unable to even be angry with them for their horridness, he just sits there in the grip of a headache now grown to the size of Satan, feeling stupid, hating the clingy humidity of the day and wishing it would rain. And then there is a lull, they are looking at him; they have a question he hasn't caught. 'Of course,' he says. 'Why not?'

So they take turns to bathe and dress, then pile into Farouk's car to see his new property. And Tahira is glad now, she is murmuring some filmi tune in the back seat, Salim trying, with the awkward croaking of a child straining for manhood, to join his voice to hers. The men sit in front and discuss the rumours to do with wealth. Farouk knows all about it – what counted for opulence a mere decade ago won't pass muster now. Today a rich Delhiwallah seeking to buy a luxury home insists on a personal pool and jacuzzi, a golf course on the premises, centralised air purifier, terrace garden, state of the art security... Anything is possible in Delhi. Farouk loves it: the limitlessness and the savageness in this *anything*; he gets off on stories about how much money government officials stole building shoddy public housing or half-baked infrastructure; he relishes the fact that class and connections override every rule in the book; he loves driving in circles around the roundabouts of Lutyens's Delhi, as he is doing now, and then racing down the radial roads, marvelling at the leafiness, the quiet, the expanse.

The day's unsparing glare worsens Alif's suffering and he is thinking of that very man, Lutyens, the architect who a century ago designed the British capital, the core of which became New Delhi, rendering the town where Alif lives Old Delhi; Lutyens who, when he came out to India, remarked on the 'violence of the light'. It is in this daggered light that Alif must heed his cousin going on about the perverted excesses of their fellow citizens. They have too much money but what bothers Alif is not the usual objection – that were some *deus ex machina* to intervene and flatten their riches no one in this city would ever need to go hungry again. He is taken more with how all the crores in tens and hundreds and thousands do not seem to have gifted their owners with half an original idea. He realises, listening to Farouk, that these folk consider their filthy lucre well spent if they live this in country believing they are not in this country. They want their homes done up by award-winning international firms, they want their palaces to evoke the atmosphere of an alpine ski lodge or a Moroccan courtyard house, they want the marble to be Italian and the lifts to be made in Germany and the in-house spa to be run by Thais. We're all in trouble, this whole society's sunk, muses Alif, if all God's chosen ones can come up with are these expensive sleights-of-hand so as to escape themselves.

Farouk's new flat across the river from where Alif's parents live, when they finally get to it, is unremarkable by contrast. The just-completed paintwork is rough around the edges, the switchboards all affixed askew, the foot-wide balconies look out into the ghost-white cement dust of the construction site next door, the living room is nice but the bedrooms minuscule, the kitchen passable – and the rent considerable. Alif tries to get his head around the fact that his brother, the man he grew up with, is now pitching to be his landlord with whom he'd be obliged to bargain on rent.

'But of course if you want to buy, as I suggest you do,' says Farouk smoothly, noticing Alif's expression, 'that would be even better. Mortgage is adjustable, unlike rent. And rents rise, unlike mortgage. Hain na, Abba?' he says, turning to his father for confirmation. Farouk's parents live with him, and the old man, it appears, has been roped in to try and sell the virtues of the flat. He was already there when they arrived but just embraced Alif and made his salaams to Tahira and let Farouk, obviously the more persuasive salesman, take over. Alif remembers his uncle's workshop from childhood, a busy, unassuming man always seen through a haze of sawdust. He didn't have much time for children then but seems to enjoy now Salim's persistent questions to him about his former life as a carpenter.

'Janab,' says Alif addressing his uncle with some formality; he's never been able to call him by the more familiar kinship tag of Khalu. 'How do you spend your time these days?'

The old man nods and smiles and Farouk says he's starting to disappear, goes and sits in a corner of the mosque by himself every evening. Alif promptly thinks of his grandfather and that extraordinarily straight-backed bearing. So here is another one of them, the quiet ones, the contented souls, the men who would have been just as fine in the heyday of Akbar, in the grey days of Zafar, in the British rise and the British fall, the Hindu past, the Hindu present. He remembers a snatch of a story – a man goes into the mosque and leaves his shoes out, another takes his shoes in, and people watching approve of the piety of both but debate which one was right in the matter of the shoes. Meanwhile, a Sufi slips in unnoticed, says his prayers, and goes away, everything between him and his God.

Tahira asks Alif what he thinks of the dimensions and what he thinks of the style and what he thinks of the finish, and Alif says Tahira must decide and retreats to the balcony. For all the great historical hash that fills his head and even his heart, he sometimes hungers for a wide empty space, the sort his uncle seems to have found. Where is it to be had now, in this city in which, as Farouk said in the car, all the excitement is over building exteriors and fitting interiors and the suburbs are all gigantic construction sites, the largest in the world. He wishes he and Farouk were children again, not because things were better then, but because he misses the predominant colour of those years, a washed-out yellow. He doesn't know where it comes from, that pale cast of his memory – maybe the old pages of the *Illustrated Weekly of India* or the walls of his first school or the colour of the pista kulfi he loved or even the neat piles of planed planks his uncle traded in… faded yellow years. The 90s changed all that. Colour blasted into their lives, advertised in a thousand different shades, and now there's no escaping from it. And no getting away either from this great charade – the playacting about being affluent they are all involved in – he, his wife, his cousin. Only his son is really free, only he does this honestly because he knows nothing else.

Alif watches Salim chatting with his uncle who is seated on a stool by the open door of the blanched cube of the living room, composed as if for a portrait. That harsh light is fast clouding up now but for a few moments both exist – rain shadow and sun ray, and a broken beam lights up half the old man's face. A character study in chiaroscuro, thinks Alif. So different from the miniature paintings he had inserted himself into last night. There all jewel hues and fulsome detail, here all white light and deepening shade. He can see Tahira from where he is; she's peeking out at him from one of the bedroom windows as he stands there massaging his temples. What do you think, he asks her, without needing to spell it out. She gives him a quick look whose meaning too is not hard to get. She is the consumer and the consumer calls the shots. Farouk is trying to sell her something that doesn't cut ice but she will humour him a little while longer to see how far he can stretch the fast talk.

Tahira. As the skies give in and it finally starts to rain, he can see in her eyes that she is back to being the long-married wife who gets her man perfectly, even if this understanding is keenest in the area of the beloved's defects.

★

Tahira comes from a family a notch above Alif's – financially at least – and she grew up in one segment of a mid-sized haveli, a family home from four generations ago. It had been divided up over the years without architectural modification or even necessary repairs, as if the inhabitants liked the house to reflect their own increasing decrepitude. And while once six people may have lived in its ten rooms, by the time of her childhood, that number had grown threefold. Tahira emerged, as it were, from a background of sagging eaves, hollowed mortar, creaking rafters, as well as the crowding and interference inevitable in a joint family, and as soon as she could she fled.

The ancestor behind the mansion had been a minor figure of landed gentry – he owned a farm outside Delhi and in Dariba a large workshop for the making of gold alloy beaten into thread and wrapped around silk skeins, used for that high glitter art of the Mughal era, zardozi. Later generations sold off both land and enterprise and set up semi-successful ventures of their own.

Alif always seizes on the opportunity to accompany his wife on her not too frequent visits to see her now-widowed mother, her two brothers and their families. They also run into other relatives whose names and designations Alif tends to forget, having only been introduced to them once – at his wedding. The place torments him; the smallest floral detail in a lintel, the tiniest leaf moulded into the wrought iron of a balcony balustrade, mock at him who grew up in the most functionally prosaic of homes. The haveli has been built in the manner of the day, with a walled-in courtyard off the street, large enough for a tamarind tree, an outhouse, a couple of toilets, a parking space for scooters. On the far side of this elongated rectangle is the double-storeyed house, the rooms side by side facing out and likewise on the upper floor, fronted with a veranda. Above, a flat roof terrace to escape to, to sun pickles on, to house the water tanks, and from where one looks out at the other high and low terraces of the old city.

It seems to Alif that everyone in this city is clued in to the slow, century-long decline of these mansions, the picturesque crumbling, column by fluted column, one graceful archway after another, one carved corbel after another, one wooden double door with recessed panels after another – everyone except his wife. It is aluminium-and-glass tower blocks and landscaped leisure areas that excite her and so here they are now, a week after their visit to Jamia Nagar, nervously sizing up a house-owner in Noida's sector something or other who wants to rent. Tahira's research has revealed that this is the sector with the best facilities at the price they can afford. Alif wonders what it would be like to live in a neighbourhood named not after kings or generals or even architects, in fact not named at all, just coldly and bureaucratically numbered. And what sort of name is Noida? Not a name at all but likewise a cold and bureaucratic thing – an acronym. They sit drying out in powerful air conditioning in a high-ceilinged living room decked with chandeliers and fitted with glossy wooden floors, neatly plastered cornices and French windows, on luxuriously leathery sofas, before them tea served in tinkly china.

Alif cannot shake off the feeling that there is some misunderstanding. The rent this man, Jitender Singh, had mentioned to the broker seemed somewhat high to Alif but now, looking at this deluxe setting, it seems unbelievably low. Have he and his family really lived here for the past decade, as he's just explained? There is something untouched, impersonal about the apartment. Like it was the product of black money. Or white lies. Alif tries to listen for the voice of a wife or find some evidence of teenage clutter but there is nothing – just a man called Atul Pandey looking them up and down with gleaming eyes, whom Singh has introduced as his friend and neighbour, and Singh himself, who is offering them small talk about the advances made in this neck of the woods. ('We have European bistros here now! And speciality clinics!') He has not yet come around to the matter at hand.

Over the course of her house-hunting, Tahira has accumulated a stock of the usual responses. Some people, on hearing her name, say they will get back but never do; others inform her that they prefer vegetarians; still others state, more forthrightly, no Mohammadans please. Some are kind – you will feel out of place here, it's better you look elsewhere; others unkind – we cannot guarantee your safety if there is trouble. Alif is unsurprised and Tahira undeterred. She knows that somewhere in town is a place for her, a religiously neutral home, a flat that she has chosen because she likes it and not because it is refuge to people humped together in suffocating anthills of Hindu or Muslim, Jain or Bohra, Parsee or Catholic.

Singh cross-questions them about their professions and then says, 'Bahut accha laga tumse mil ke, to meet a modern couple like you.'

Tahira smiles. 'It's we who got lucky. May we have a look at the other rooms now?' she asks, rising from her seat.

Alif can see that she feels her persistence might just be starting to pay off.

'Have tea, what's the hurry?' Singh shoots back, and then barks, 'Priya, aur chai lao.'

'You must have fasted recently, during Ramzan. You must be hungry,' says Atul Pandey smiling.

'Ramzan was more than a month ago actually,' says Alif.

'Of course not,' says Singh. 'These are modern people, bhai.'

'I do fast ...' begins Tahira.

'Where are you planning to move, yourself?' asks Alif quickly.

'Of course, I have another place in Gurgaon. All these years we were here because of my daughter's schooling but she's gone to US for further studies now.'

The offhand tone in which this is stated, that misplaced 'of course', that dropped article before the name of the country, all imply Mr Singh is a rich man. If Alif happened to ask him about his line of work, he would probably say, I am in business, suggesting that the nature of this business is irrelevant; all that matters is having made a success of the moneymaking. Alif thinks of Sardarji at Bright & Blue and how he's moulded his personality and his person to his establishment, of the despondent Khanna Uncle in his unvisited shop who can find no new purpose, and Farouk for whom business is a means to rub elbows, counsel, exhort. But it's still all a mystery to Alif – he has never understood how money can be used to make more money but he is sure that to hold it this close is to be soiled by it, noticing the many rings on Pandey's fingers – coral and emerald and diamond.

'What sort of people live in the building?' asks Tahira.

'Mostly in business. No service people here. Of course, very respectable people,' says Singh.

'How was your Eid celebration? I have many Muslim friends. They invite me to their homes. But one thing I wanted to ask. For Eid ul Zoha are you bringing a lot of meat to the house? The full dead goat?' asks Pandey, and again Singh answers before they can.

'Kaise sawal kar rahe ho, bhai? These are not kasais with knives in hand you're talking to. He is only asking because mostly vegetarians on this floor,' he explains to Alif and Tahira. 'Arya Samajis. Holy people. Of course.'

*Oh no*, thinks Alif tiredly. Here we go again.

'We don't kill any goats ourselves,' says Tahira stiffly but politely. She wants the place no matter what.

Pandey looks satisfied.

'You have very nice shoes,' Singh says to Alif, switching to Hindi, having made his point and established his credentials in English. Alif is elated and sticks out his feet to improve the display. He wants to shake the man's hand. He has taste. He has feelings. Alif did not make much of this replacement pair, afraid to tempt fate and bring on new wounds, but they have so far stood him, literally, in good stead.

Priya, barefooted, bright-eyed, comes in with a second pot of tea that they don't really want but drink anyway. Pandey takes no tea, just fiddles with his rings as he flicks glances at them.

'I know many Muslims,' he suddenly states. 'I grew up in Jogiwara and what is there in Jogiwara but Muslims?'

'So what?' snaps Singh. And then offers the stunningly original view that the country can only prosper if Hindus and Muslims bury their differences.

Alif says nothing; he is aware of the dangers. Admit to differences and you are practically saying: Muslims are butcher-like and bigoted, Hindus superior and insecure.

Pandey asks him, 'Do you know how many Muslims there are in this city only? Millions. And in India? Millions.'

Alif wonders if he should apologise. Singh is laughing in words like a comic book character – ha, ha, ha. Tahira reddens and asks again if they could see the rest of the house.

'So what subject did you say you teach at school, bhai sahib?' asks Singh.

Alif wishes he could say geometry, it would be less contentious, but Singh is still smiling so he confesses to history and Singh says he likes history.

'Which bits of it do you like?' Alif asks him.

'The riches. Rama, Rama, the riches. One thousand years ago Indian ships would go loaded with Gujarat cotton to Southeast Asia, they'd pick up spices from Indonesia and Malaysia and trade them for the cotton, then they'd go to West Asia and sell spices for gold, and bring all the gold back to India. We had high exports, little imports and too much gold. These days people go to West Asia to work as coolies and cleaners. In those days Indian merchants went there to supervise business. Of course we were bosses then.'

Alif was teaching his children just the other month about how all that gold started to attract the invaders but he couldn't bring that up here because the invaders were Muslims.

Tahira says, 'We can't stay for much longer, it's a long drive back.'

'Madam, I wanted to ask you one thing if you do not mind?'

'Yes, yes.'

'Do you at home also put on this thing?'

Tahira tightens her hijab.

'Ha, ha, ha,' says Singh. 'They are good, decent people. She is store manager. He is history teacher.'

'I was just asking, that's all. People sometimes behave outside the house different from inside,' says Pandey.

'Not us,' says Tahira. 'You can take us at face value.'

Singh dismisses his friend with a click of his tongue and says, 'Accha, tell me something, History Sir. What about the Gupta golden age? You like that?'

Alif admits that there is much to admire in that chapter of the history book. Those couple of centuries fifteen hundred years ago couldn't have all been a golden dream but there is something both golden and dreamlike about that fecund time.

'Yes, take Aryabhatta,' says Alif, referring to the mathematician and astronomer who discovered in this period that the earth was spherical and the heavens seemed to rotate because our planet was spinning on its axis.

'Kalidasa,' replies Mr Singh.

Alif nods. The playwright whose work is the great archetype of Sanskrit language and literary imagination. 'Nalanda,' he says, the remarkable Buddhist university that housed several thousand students and teachers from all over Asia.

'Kamasutra,' responds Singh, that famous manual of lovemaking for the urban aesthete, also written in this period.

'The zero,' says Alif of the Indian invention which was introduced in the late fifteenth century.

'Not just zero. All numerals. One to ten. And decimal system.'

'True, true. We gave them to the Arabs,' says Alif.

'And from there Europeans took them,' says Singh, gloatingly stroking his moustache, but then his face falls. 'After that the Muslims came over here.'

'They brought the biryani, bhai sahib,' says Pandey.

'I know, I know. But in our culture there was deterioration. As soon as people come from outside this happens. People' – he breaks off to tell Tahira that as soon as they have finished with the Guptas he will take her on a tour of the house – 'people from outside have always wanted to destroy Mother India but in the golden age we had strong borders, you see, we had strong willpower, we had strong weapons, we had strong-muscled men, the Kshatriyas, and we had strong-minded men, the Brahmins. Then the Muslims came...'

'Umm,' says Alif, with his usual circumspection. What he wants to say is: It's not quite as straightforward as that. We were invaded during the golden age too. Think of the White Huns from China who attacked in the fifth and sixth centuries. They ruled north India for a short time and were then pushed back. Another branch of them ravaged Europe under Atilla. But it's unlikely that Mr Jitender Singh of Noida has heard of this influential barbarian. Alif mulls over the lines of connection that the Maharishi had long ago sketched for the class. The Muslims were only links in a chain, he'd said – one among a long procession of invaders and settlers who came over the north-western passes into the northern plains, starting with the Aryans, and then, among others, the Greeks under Alexander, the Bactrians, the Shakas or Scythians who some say are the ancestors of the Rajputs, the Kushans, a nomadic tribe from China, founders of a ruling dynasty whose most well-known emperor, Kanishka, was famous for being a prose-lytiser of Buddhism, and much later the Turks who set up the first sultanates, followed by the Mughals or Turco-Mongols. This is our history, he thinks. This is who we are – nothing if not mixed up.

But all he ventures to tell Singh is, 'Take Aryabhatta. He discovered the zero and he calculated the solar year right down to 365 days but he didn't live in a vacuum called India, you know. He was aware of the Roman theories of astronomy.'

Singh looks put off at Alif's attempt to bring complexity into the straightforward biryani-versus-brahminism view of history.

'Just as earlier Pythagoras, that Greek chap who invented the tuning system in music, remember? He was influenced by Indian philosophy,' adds Alif.

Atul Pandey says, 'There is only one problem. Plenty of mosques in Greater Noida but there is no mosque nearby to this apartment. And no madrasa nearby either.'

Tahira puts down her teacup. 'Okay, fine. I understand you have no interest in the matter we came for. We're leaving. Before you can insult us further, we'll go.'

'Insult?' asks Pandey in what seems to be real surprise.

Singh just chuckles. 'Calm down, madam. You don't listen to this man. He is just my friend. I am house-owner. Mohammad ji please explain to your wife.'

'We are renting Hindu property to Muslims and asking a few questions. How is that an insult?'

'Stop it,' says Tahira in a trembly voice. 'I know your sort. We're taking over every street of India with our namaz. Want a house on rent and we are doing land jihad. Move into a Hindu area and the azaan will be blasting day and night and the drains always running with the blood of slaughtered animals!'

'Did I say all that, bhai?' asks Pandey, turning to Singh.

'And you haven't brought up terrorism but that is the next question. You think I've not had such things thrown at me before? Just like our religion is Hinduism, their religion is terrorism.'

Singh says, 'Madam, the real issue is that the rent is excessive for you. On the phone you said you're managing a supermarket so I thought you are in business but after meeting you I realise –'

'You will never give us your property,' Tahira scolds Singh who continues to sit there, looking complacent. 'You believe we whip out our Korans as soon as you look away. We hide biryani-eating terrorists under our burqas. Everywhere we go, Islamic problems.'

Singh laughs out loud again and Alif too has a wild urge to giggle. He snorts into his teacup, hoping Tahira is too angry to notice.

She has risen and is glaring at her husband.

'We should be going...' he says lamely.

'One last question I have for you, History Professor Sir,' says Singh. 'When the Muslims came they destroyed all our temples and took all our gold. Of course, that is fine. Once and for all, that is fine. You see the problem is that they stayed for so long. Do you understand? They should not have stayed.'

He says it with so much genuine regret, Alif is almost sorry.

'Thank you for the tea and the ... um ...'

'Please, please, please ji. You are a reasonable man and you know so much history. Just accept this one thing and I am ready to give you my house. They should not have stayed.'

'But they stayed, na,' says Pandey. 'Go and look in Jogiwara, go and look at Chandni Chowk.'

'You agree?' Singh says to Alif.

'It is, of course, always interesting to consider alternatives,' begins Alif, avoiding Tahira's eye. He can hold himself back no longer. 'What might this country have turned out like if – one – those Arab conquerors and their Turkish slaves had not taken over North India; or if – two – once these conquerors were installed, the Mongol hordes, who were then at the gate, remember, had succeeded in ousting them; or if – three – the Rajputs in the sixteenth century, Rana Sanga, say, had overthrown the

Lodhis; or if – four – Babur had lost the battle of Panipat and the Mughals had never got a foothold in India; or if – five –'

'I'm out of here,' says Tahira and pulls open the door.

'But you agree?' asks Singh, and he's almost pleading now. 'They broke down our temples and with those stones, exactly those stones, built mosques. *Why?*'

Alif follows his wife out; she's in the corridor, jabbing at the elevator button. Pandey and Singh both come after them.

'Mister History Professor Sir. Mohammad Sir. Is this the history you are teaching your children? That it was a good thing they stayed. You stayed?' His voice is hardening, and it is Pandey who laughs now at Singh's ridiculous appeals – ha, ha, ha.

The madness of the centuries, thinks Alif with despair. Nietzsche again. *Not only the wisdom of centuries – also their madness breaketh out in us. Dangerous is it to be an heir.* He so wishes he could somehow comfort the man but cannot think of anything that would make for an antidote to this dangerous inheritance of wounded pride, this modern madness.

Finally, the elevator heaves to a stop; just as Tahira is making to throw herself in, Pandey waves his fat, gem-encrusted fingers centimetres from her face, insisting she has misconstrued, then hums an old tune about someone dying to set fire to the veil behind which someone's hidden their visage. *Jee chaahata hai aag laga du naqaab mein . . .*

'Mohammad ji . . .' Singh is still clamouring as the doors slide shut.

Tahira slumps against the polished steel wall. 'What if they decide to follow us home?'

'And do what?'

'He set it up.'

'What?'

'How can you not see, Alif? He pulled you into stories about how much gold we had in ancient India and how we ruled the universe, all that nonsense, so you thought he was a serious man? It was all arranged. He had no intention of giving us his flat. He just called us here to teach us a lesson. Show us our place.'

She gets into the car, then sits in the driver's seat nodding her head in disbelief, the keys clenched in her hand. Alif is silent, going over the strange encounter, realising she's probably right but reluctant to admit it.

'They had planned the whole thing beforehand. I will be the nice one, Singh must have said to Pandey, and you poke at them as much as you like.'

She starts up and zooms violently out of the car park, her face reflecting as violent a struggle, between wanting to forget these men and all they represent, maintaining her hijab-covered honour, carrying on her search for a dream house, and giving up, allowing herself to be crushed by the animus that surrounds them.

'He may have put something in the tea. How he was forcing us to drink his tea while they didn't touch it,' says Tahira.

'You can't do this any more. Stop making these trips. *I'll* go with the brokers. If it seems like a half decent place, or rather if the owners are okay, then you take over.'

'You'll never manage on your own. You won't ask the right questions. Or give the right answers. You won't even blink if you're told that all Muslims hide bombs under their burqas and breed terrorists in their wombs.'

'Not all, just some,' says Alif, trying, now that the danger has for the moment passed, to return to light-heartedness.

Tahira steps on the accelerator as they hit the gigantic, tarred, metalled river of the dual carriageway that soars over a real river, the Yamuna.

'Why are people like this?' says Tahira.

*Why*, he wonders. Did we know once and have forgotten? Was there a time when the individual did not have to invent or justify his identity, when the social order was so fastidiously fine-tuned that it left no room for personal angst. Is this, ultimately, what golden ages are about?

'We should all just die,' he says quietly. 'That's what we really want. To go on screaming about how we differ from each other and then proceed to kill each other. War. War is human nature, said Napoleon.'

'And Napoleon will turn up here to help? Just no point bringing all such information into every situation. If they were not interested, we should have left in ten minutes. Now they got a chance to beat us down…'

'It doesn't matter, Tahi. They think they have the upper hand but it doesn't matter. We're doing all right. Think of our ancestors. Your grandfather lived in a small portion of that crumbling place, trying and usually failing to make ends meet, my grandfathers both only managed because they cut corners all the time. That's where we come from.'

'But we can't go on living the way we do,' says Tahira. 'When I have a new job, when Salim is married, when…We need space. We need air. Why can't we have just a few of the things that everyone else has?'

She is crying; she probably can't see very well through this cataract of tears and she is driving unnecessarily fast. He feels a subdued tenderness for his wife, for her uprightness and her endurance. He is much too listless to yield, the way she does, to the world's provocations, so he tries to make up by caressing her shoulder.

Mathura Road and the other drivers seem concerned with them only to the extent of wanting to edge them out of the way or mow them down. The many circles of hell that are Delhi's roads. *Gar firdaus rue zamin ast, hamin ast, hamin ast, hamin ast.* That famous couplet of Amir Khusrau's about how if there is any paradise on earth, this is darned well it, which one of the Mughals later took up and inscribed in a corner of the Red Fort, and which people believe describes Kashmir though scholars say it's probably about Delhi because when did Khusrau go to Kashmir? He loved Delhi. Alif too loves it, after a fashion, even if his only basis for loving it is that he cannot imagine himself as anything other than a Dilliwallah. If the city is defiled, he is defiled – if the air pollution is bad beyond any synonym for bad he smokes a cigarette to subject his lungs to worse, if his colleagues are conniving he tries to edge away, and if his wife has been insulted he cannot find in himself either the courage or the fury to punch the bastard in the face. Instead all he does is to mention: *Don't forget the eternal give and take.*

He looks at his wife's profile and sees in the tilt of that wet chin, in the slapdash confidence of her driving, that she has become something over the last few years which she was not when they married – obtuse. Alif has not undertaken that journey with her, he does not know what it is to become both more steadfast in one's pieties and hungrier for the world, and to believe that these developments are not incompatible, that they sustain each other. For regarding his religion too he feels an affection not very different from the one he feels for his wife – something once lovely, now crumpled and shadowed yet still firmly lodged in his heart.

'We should put in a police complaint,' says Tahira, holding to her tears the neatly folded handkerchief Alif has found in his pocket and offered her.

'And say what? A man was rude to us? He refused to show us all the rooms of his flat? No one's obliged to rent to us.'

'The things that Pandey said!'

'But all in the guise of polite enquiries.'

'If we'd stood there a minute longer, he'd have stripped me down. He asked me if I bring dead animals to the house. He asked me why I wear what I wear. Weren't you listening?'

I was listening, thinks Alif. I was listening to the madness of the centuries.

'And what about us?' he asks.

'What about us? We have nothing against vegetarians and temples. We have nothing against anyone.'

'Take a look at the Muslim kingdoms to our right and to our left. How exactly do they behave there? Are they letting the other person live, even, let alone take up occupancy in *their* houses?'

He wants to say that despite his doubts about nations they can form character and maybe we Muslims here have been somewhat softened by the Indic. And now if house-owners are out to reduce us to headscarf-wearing, goat-eating dorks, then the proper retort would be: we're far from just that. But all this she already knows.

Tahira switches lanes. 'I'm worried about Sallu. That day when you both walked away from the iftar. What did you want to talk about? Were you able to put any good ideas in his head?'

'He's putting things in *my* head. He's downright smarter than me. I am, as you know, a believer in sitting together in a classroom in order to learn but this child, God knows from where, has got the idea that school doesn't matter. He is done with school. He is already ready for the world.'

Delhi Gate. That familiar old stony solitary, that high-arched gatehouse now holding nothing in, keeping nothing out. They are almost home. 'We haven't been able to teach him one surah. And as for daily namaz...'

She stops short of saying Alif is to blame.

'He never showed any interest,' he says. 'All I can tell him is to make up his own mind and that I have done more than once.'

'His own mind? Who is he – Aflatoon of old? – that he has a mind of his own?'

'He's not a child any more.'

'That's why I worry. Because he's not a child any more and he knows nothing. He's completely without direction. His mother's faith is not a serious thing to him but his father's might have gone some way...'

Alif compares Tahira's hidden plaint – *why are you not a Muslim?* – to Ankit's public one – *you dirty Muslim!* He has never been able to convince his wife that, however meagre and battered, he has a faith too. He can still be drawn to the image of those desert Sufis who loved so much they dissolved themselves in loving. Waking up sometimes at dawn, not to heed the fajr azaan but nevertheless listen to it, he is struck by the possibility of such love. But in the fullness of the morning light he always returns to being a storm-tossed, minor figure in history, not a soul straining to achieve timelessness. So all he can think of to rescue himself from Tahira's now dry-eyed, sober charge is yet again the same old snatch of a prayer. *Ya Allah raham farma. Ya rasool Allah raham farma.*

Salim is at the table, chatting with a friend – or rather both are addressing his laptop, their attention wholly absorbed by it even as they direct remarks to each other.

'Got the place?' Salim breaks off to ask his parents and, looking at them, he knows the answer. He continues with the game they are on but Alif can see he also wants to come to them, get their news, comfort them in his clumsy teenage way by making them tea too strong to drink or telling them as he did the other day, inspired by something he'd seen online, that the coolest thing would be to make a home from a container and live on top of their existing house with a view of the Jama Masjid. My son, thinks Alif. And he is many sons, and even daughters, for Alif had wanted a brood but Tahira was quite clear about the limit of one. The burden of the past remains heavy as ever but the burden of the day lightens for him, looking at Salim's face, and he thanks God for answering his call so swiftly.

# SIX

He is here at last. The square pool of olive-green water in the centre, under open sky, inverts the white and mint-green arched arcade running on all four sides and he sits on the parapet looking at that blurred reflection, finding himself alone for the first time in months. The vertigo of a momentary solitude in a life lived in relentless company.

He searches in his mind for God and finds two. Ya Khuda, the Persian, and Ya Allah, the Arabic. Both conjoined in him and in the currents that created this mosque, this town, this city. When did one get the better of the other? It started some two hundred years ago, that graceful, eclectic, courtly Mughal Persian culture declining and individualised, Protestant, reformist, hard-nosed Arabic mores taking over.

Pray, he tells himself, and tries to recover that long-ago feeling called God. When he closes his eyes all he sees is colour – the two greens here and outside a third, close cousin, the turquoise of the large stone blocks of which the thick walls and circular bastions are made. A bright, new turquoise that brings to mind the name of the sultan in whose reign it was erected – Firoz. Why a fortified mosque? Long before the Persian stamp and long before the renewed Arabic influence there was this: the always embattled Turkish kings of the Middle Ages.

*Please pray*. Instead he is thinking of the lanes he just walked up, narrow as the eye of a needle, dark as the pits of hell, through the open doorways men hunched on floors, soldering flimsy-looking trinkets. And unfazed by people, fighting over scraps in those garbage-strewn alleys, rodents the size of small cats. As he dodged them he was thinking of a story-poem he might tell his children. In the land of the Blue-Green Sultan lived the Bandicoot Boss of the underworld... This is why he is here, to appeal to God to restore them to him. He chose a house of prayer some distance away, not wanting to run into anyone he knew. Looking at the painted water, he thinks: either you can see the intent behind each heartbeat and I needn't say a word or...

Every sound so lucid as if the stilled enclosure of the mosque had distilled it: from an inner room young boys reciting the Koran, the susurration of paper kites in the dusk sky, tearing against the wind, and now on the roof of the mosque two men flying a dozen pigeons, sending them off with one set of notes and calling them swooping back with another. It's too late to pray. Just as he is getting up to leave, a stocky muezzin with – Alif is startled to see that colour again – eyes of greyish-green, sidles up to him. For some moments they watch the pigeons.

'Dustoor hai,' says Alif, invoking tradition.

'Shauq hai,' says the muezzin, invoking pleasure.

Alif smiles – another echo – and takes his leave.

'Masjid ka khayal rakhiye.' Even now, this: etiquette. No chance he will make a demand outright, like that poor Brahmin did the other day, for money. Just a polite request to keep the mosque in mind. Alif slips him a note and right then the boys come tumbling out, six or seven years old, small, scrubbed, sweetly round faces. 'Do you go to school as well?' he asks them. Yes, yes, they nod eagerly but in passing, chasing each other down the high stone steps.

Alif goes home to polish his shoes.

Be humble, he says to himself as he brushes and buffs. Accept that you are wrong even if you believe you are right. He tests that dictum a few times and realises that it practically sums up his life. All the same, he is not prepared to buy the argument that his whole approach to education is wrong and his very existence an affront. Be humble, he repeats and realises that he needs to keep his most offensive aspect, the history-loving side, in check – there is no point trying to educate the benighted given their misplaced pride about their benightedness.

When he gets to school the next morning, he is the first to take his place at the table. Previous principals of the school have all sat in the modest office from where the illustrious founder once directed operations but Rawat found that space too narrow, poorly lit, simply furnished, old-world for her tastes so she took over one of the students' common rooms and had that refitted. The new get-up only serves to highlight the somewhat run-down character of the rest of the school. It's of an extravagantly ugly sort in Alif's view – furniture so full of baroque protuberances and embellishments that it has almost lost its purpose as furniture, oppressively heavy drapes, and those posters with their false optimism, their uncalled-for zealotry. Alif is particularly resentful of the posters. He studies each in turn, simulating interest in them as he tries to think of pleasant things to say, solicitous remarks that will mean nothing but pacify everyone.

The committee that joins Alif consists of Rawat, Sports Sir, Jha busy with some papers, a lady Alif has never seen before, and that geriatric gent, Shukla ji. Alif bumps into Shukla ji at school events off and on and he'd been on that other committee two decades ago which gave him the job. Alif wishes, naturally, that Miss Moloy were there but she's gone, finished with the minor goings-on within these four walls and passed on into dignified retirement.

The meeting starts with Jha reporting that Ankit is to be withdrawn from the school once the academic year is over.

'I trust his grandfather explained the reasons. It has nothing to do with me,' says Alif.

'Yes he did say there were deeper causes,' says Rawat. 'He did say he wishes to bring up the child himself.'

Alif pitches in with an account of the child's congenital lying.

'But how is it that *we* have never noticed?' asks Rawat. '*I* have been asking my teachers to keep close eyes on the students' personalities and no one reported anything about the boy to me.'

'That just goes to show what a good liar he is,' says Alif. 'He knows well how to cover his tracks.'

'Are you saying you didn't touch him, you didn't threaten him?' she asks.

'No, no. He is not denying that he did,' jumps in Parvez, the sports sir, trying to soothe the boss.

'It can happen,' says the mysterious lady whom no one has thought to introduce to Alif. 'Who doesn't lose their temper with children? You need to take into account his record as a teacher. It's the first time I'm hearing of a complaint against him.'

In response Jha reads out a list of grievances. Alif always fails to take a second teacher along on his field trips. He has been bunking school assembly for years. He is far too cosy with Miss Moloy and spends hours talking with her about non-academic matters such as holidays in Kerala. He is known to criticise many of the principal madam's new ventures – complaining to Miss Moloy about the biometric machine, the proposed closed-circuit cameras in the classrooms, the costly office refurbishing, the time-consuming rehearsals for school plays. He teaches poetry when he is meant to be teaching history and history when he is meant to be teaching civics.

'If there's one thing I can't stand, it's civics,' breaks in Alif. 'Yes, one ought to know the preamble to the Constitution but that is memorised in five minutes.'

No one seems to quite know what to say to this though Sports Sir nods in what could be construed as agreement. His role, self-appointed no doubt, is to keep everyone happy, a task which only the most suicidal would undertake. Alif decides not to bother defending himself against the other charges. Any fool can see through them though it is also fools who have drawn them up and it's hard to tell, looking around the table, how to distinguish faint fools from ferocious ones.

'Alif Mohammad,' says the old man in a booming voice. 'You please tell me one thing. How are the children gaining from all this? Ultimately we are all here, this school is here, for the children's benefit.'

His tone is kindly; Maharishi's friendly chat with him about the unfair suspension has probably had the intended effect. Alif points to the picture hanging behind the old man's head – the one featuring *his* old man and Nehru.

'That sahib,' he says, 'was enchanted by history. I am enchanted by history. Is it such a crime to hope that the children might be distracted for an hour a day from computer science and environmental damage so as to be able to think of where and what we have come out of?'

'Very good,' says Shukla ji. 'Most appreciated. But exams also have to be passed.'

'My students usually do well in exams even though I believe they're of secondary importance.'

'Then it is fine,' he says, suddenly sounding very decided. 'Mrs Rawat, should we consider this an apology and end the matter?'

'But it is not just this one thing. What about all those other problems?' she whines.

Jha starts reading them out again from his paper scroll like a good courtier, one who can anticipate the despotic sultan's every demand.

'My daughter has been your student since she was nine,' says the anonymous lady. 'She likes your classes even though she always fails in history. She has a logical mind, a problem-solving mind. So maths and science suit her but she can never remember dates and facts. Those dates and facts don't lead to anything, she says. So they don't stick in her head.'

She is the obligatory parent. Alif recalls that such committees must always feature one.

'What's your daughter's name?'

'Ayesha Siddiqui.'

'Let me point out, Mrs Siddiqui, that all the well-meaning leaders of this country believed there was no point in reflecting on the past for its own sake; it should spur us to action. Sir Syed Ahmad Khan said this, so did Iqbal, so did Nehru, Tagore, Gandhi, Ambedkar... So I am not retailing dates and facts for children to unthinkingly imbibe. The question always is – what is one going to do? In other words, how is one going to live? It is better to live, even if only for the sake of one's own sanity, with some perspective, a little awareness of how other people once lived. Maths and science do not provide this service.'

'I used to have a wonderful teacher of history in my time, back in boarding school,' starts Shukla ji. 'An Englishman called

Arnold. He held everything in his head. Not once do I recall him opening a book in class. Not once. He would just stride up and down, thundering at us. I remember he was especially taken with the Mughals. *You chaps, consider what Babur was like in Ferghana, barely out of his teens, swearing he would take back Samarkand. Take a leaf out of that.'*

He looks dreamily wistful; Rawat butts in and declares, 'We are having the same problem here. This man is bringing too much Muslim history into this school.'

'Too much Muslim history,' repeats Jha and makes a note, adding this to his fault-finding list.

Alif loses his voice. He is truly stumped and for the first time, looking squarely at Rawat, wonders if she really is one of those defenders of the faith, the sword-bearers, the blood-letters, the fearsome fanatics.

'Just stick to the syllabus,' says Sports Sir with great cordiality, and Alif realises this man is worried too. Mrs Siddiqui has received a well-timed phone call and left the room. Alif glances at Shukla ji who looks bored and is saying nothing. *Defend me, old man*, he thinks and then realises he is not even defending himself. But if Rawat is a holy warrior and the others are all scrambling to fall into line, then the only sort of person who could vanquish her would be someone exactly like her but from the other side of this divide. And that Alif is not.

'What syllabus?' says Rawat sarcastically. 'Sports Sir, you know nothing of the liberties our friend has been taking.' She dispatches Jha to get a copy of the Class Eight textbook. 'I will give you just one example with just one class,' she tells Shukla ji, who is fast losing interest and says he has another meeting to attend in half an hour.

Ramu comes in just then with the trembling tea tray and he greets Alif with his usual comically exaggerated deference, that bowing and scraping that is his way of saying – nothing is funnier than you high and mighty. To him this meeting is no different from any other meeting, and in his eyes Alif the reduced and ridiculed is no different from Alif the proud and persevering. This everyday vision of the unflappable Ramu cheers Alif somewhat and he thinks – no, this is no genuine battle, and I am no Tiger Babur fighting the Uzbeks over Samarkand. It's a frivolous charade and I've got to just play along.

Jha returns with the book and Rawat starts to explain to Shukla ji that the text mostly features modern Indian history while Alif is always going on about the older one, and that only one chapter is devoted to a Muslim, namely the emperor Akbar, while Alif insists on wasting the students' time on other worthless Muslims.

'Adil Shah the second,' chips in Jha. 'Amir Khusrau, Alauddin Khilji...'

'Alauddin Khilji,' says Alif, holding up his hand. 'Now I know he's mostly remembered today for the bad things he did. He was not a gentleman but it was difficult, in the thirteenth century, with the Mongols always threatening, and the Rajputs always revolting, and the nobles of the court always conspiring, to be a gentleman. None of these early Turks who gradually took over North India were. Their ancestors were hardy nomads from the steppes, they became slaves and mercenaries and then rose to be kings, and they were the strongest military power in the Eastern world.'

'Arnold used to say no one destroyed as much as Khilji. I can't now remember the names of all the Hindu kingdoms...' says Shukla ji.

Alif lists them – the temple towns of the north and south that were laid to waste by Khilji and his equally go-getting general Malik Kafur.

Shukla ji shakes his head in mild regret.

'It's part of folklore, the terribleness of Khilji. And for that very reason it must be studied carefully, the facts separated from the inevitable fictions.'

'And no one could stand up to him?' asks Shukla ji.

'They tried. The Kakatiyas of Warangal, the Ranas of Mewar...'

'They tried to defend Hindu dharma,' says Sports Sir happily.

'I don't know,' says Alif. 'I'm not sure whether it was religious feeling or military ambition or both. Just as we don't really know what combination of the two things spurred on Khilji.'

'Religion, military ambition, all nonsense! The bastard came here to loot us,' spits out Jha. 'And what should I call you, who is teaching all this to our tender minds, what should I call you except a worse name than I am calling Khilji.'

'Oh don't be an idiot,' says Alif.

Jha immediately makes a note.

'Arre bhai, Khilji is dead and gone,' says Sports Sir. 'Why are we fighting over him?'

Mrs Siddiqui has returned to her seat and agrees.

Alif says, 'Look I'm not here to defend any of the conquerors through the ages. Khilji destroyed, Khilji caused pain across the land.'

'Didn't he kill his uncle?' asks Shukla ji.

Alif nods. 'He killed his uncle and then everyone else who might have challenged him and he clipped the wings of his nobles. He deposed the king of Gujarat and married the man's wife and had their daughter seized and married to his son. Was he a saint? The Chiragh of Delhi thought so but we now know that's probably a stretch. But how can we throw him out of the history books?'

'Throw him out of the history books?' asks Rawat in surprise. 'But he's not there in the first place.'

'We have to understand what made him so successful. Some would say superior tactics and superior horses. We've never had good horses here, the best have always been imported.'

'Accha?' says Shukla ji. 'Must be the weather. Or is it the diet? These things play a part, I know. Old Arnold used to say – never forget the camels. The Muslims were able to expand so fast in the first decades after the Prophet's death because their camels could handle everything. Except cold weather and uneven terrain.'

'Yes, and when they took over the provinces of the Byzantine empire in the eighth century they replaced those straight wide Roman roads with narrow winding ones – for their camels.'

Shukla ji is delighted but Rawat declares again, 'Too much Muslim history.'

'Madam,' says Alif and finds he is breaking into a sweat despite the newly installed air conditioning, 'there is *no* such thing as a Muslim history of India. You try separating Muslims from Hindus in this way when you go into the past of this country and all you find are entanglements.'

'Very right,' says Shukla ji and looks at his watch.

Alif doesn't pause for fear of being interrupted.

'Those who see things in these terms will say a Hindu, Prithviraj Chauhan, was defeated by a Muslim, Mohammad Ghuri and that victory inaugurated Muslim rule in India. But an Afghan tribe, the Lodis, fought both in the Ghuriyid army and in Prithviraj's. In those days, madam, there were none of our contemporary ideas about what rights the majority should enjoy and how the minority should behave. In the fifteenth century... in the sixteenth century...'

Having long forgotten his resolve to go easy with the history lectures, Alif feels instead like he is starting on what could be the most long-drawn out one of his life. Rawat is far from convinced and Jha looks annoyed, perhaps because he is on the side of the Chauhans or, more likely, because Shukla ji, and even Mrs Siddiqui, show some interest in these twists and turns of history and have been distracted from the main point – which is the upbraiding of Alif.

'There is no such thing as a Muslim history of India,' says Shukla ji with all the aplomb of having reached a definitive conclusion and then he rises and shuffles out of the room even as Alif is thinking of a way to return to the Khiljis whom he is greatly interested in. The Khiljis alone require half an hour. Then come the Tughlaks and there are things about them worth considering. Was, for instance, Mohammad bin Tughlak mad or merely ahead of his time? He has come out looking like one of the great fools of history for his hare-brained schemes such as shifting the capital of the country from Delhi to Daulatabad, twelve hundred kilometres away. But he was interested in philosophy, hung out with yogis and Jains, celebrated Holi and wanted, like a statesman and not merely a ruler, to establish political contacts abroad.

Rawat, however, has had enough and flinging the textbook aside tells Jha angrily that he is careless to have brought her the

Class Eight one when it was the Class Ten one she wanted. Jha, in response, calls the meeting to a close. Sports Sir slinks out before the principal's ire can find a target in him. Mrs Siddiqui politely thanks Alif for his insights. Everyone leaves and Rawat too makes to go, but Alif is still standing there, facing her, awaiting a decision.

'When can I come back?' he asks her, trying not to whimper.

'Give us time, give us time. I must call a meeting of the school board and discuss —'

'But it's been three months,' he breaks in.

'Give me just another week.'

Without her sidekicks in supporting roles she appears somewhat defenceless.

'Wonderful,' says Alif and means it. 'One week, then. Next Monday I will be here at 8.30 to talk to Class Ten about Mohammad bin Tughlak. It is time they learnt about this great eccentric.'

He pauses, impressed at his own daring, waiting for her to ask if Mohammad bin Tughlak is actually in the syllabus or another one of his whims, but she doesn't. She just sits there eyeing him warily.

'Okay, okay,' she mumbles. 'Before Monday I will let you know.'

Alif wanders away exhausted but pleased. Shukla ji is clearly on his side, Sports Sir is a neutralising force, Mrs Siddiqui was sympathetic and Rawat is outnumbered. He stands in the empty lobby listening to the garbled kindergarten rendering of a rhyme coming from a nearby classroom. *Little Miss Muppet sat on her puppet, eating her cud and wait.* Then the bell rings and a group of Class Four students rush out, on their way to the computer labs on the first floor. They might have yawned their way through geography or English but are uniformly enthusiastic about computers, already at home with the simple binaries of digital language, which is maybe why all the many ambiguities of history will never compel them.

He steps back and waits for them to be swallowed by the future but they have spotted him.

*Sir, why you're not coming to class and Rawat Miss is teaching us history? Sir, when are we going to go and see the Mughal empire? Sir, why you're looking sad like the Rani of Jhansi when the British were chasing her?*

He lets them pile on the questions just to be able to continue gazing at their lit faces and curious eyes, feel close to him again that native spontaneity, that flurried guilelessness. *I know nothing as well as I know them.* I must return, he thinks, not because of all the history lessons that need imparting but simply because I have nowhere else go. And then he sees Ankit, hanging back, saying nothing, but, as always, provocation in his eyes.

'How are you?' he asks and waits for some fascinating lie in response.

But Ankit keeps mum. He knows that Alif knows.

'Are you able now to tell your Humayun from your Hanuman?'

The other children snicker.

Ankit looks away and then turning back to Alif declares, 'My grandfather will take care of you.'

Alif considers the steeliness of his expression, the deliberate antagonism. Is this the only choice left? That I kill him or he kills me? *No, no, no.* Why has it come to this? We've lived with these mutually inflicted wounds for so long, why not a little longer?

*

'Consider the great Arab historian of the fourteenth century, Ibn Khaldun. Part of the reason why he wrote that universal history is to understand his own situation. Why was it that his stints serving rulers in Islamic Spain and north-western Africa had always ended in disaster? So he looks to his society, theorises about the rise and decline of states, understands his own life story in relation to that.'

Professor Maharishi Jain sits at his desk, a fraying woollen muffler wrapped around his thin neck against the mild post-Diwali chill, and discusses with Alif how people in different epochs have zeroed in on a sense of their time.

'And then there are the men of the European Renaissance who believed they belonged to a new, highly progressive time.

That's what inspired those scholars and artists to reach the heights they did.'

'Always, always. You become what you believe you are. In the nineteenth century the Victorians saw themselves as pioneering. In the twentieth century Nehru felt we were in decline out here,' Alif replies.

'Ah,' says Maharishi, smiling as he quotes the former prime minister on the subject, that sentiment Alif is already all too familiar with. *Have we had our day and are we now living in the late afternoon or evening of our existence, just carrying on after the manner of the aged, quiescent, devitalized, uncreative, desiring peace and sleep above all else?*

'But that is just what we don't want to buy any more.'

'Hmm, perhaps we are tired of one too many late afternoons and evenings and wish to usher in a new dawn.'

'Can one muscle one's way into a new dawn?' muses Alif.

The Maharishi looks grave. 'The ancient religious energies of the people are being exploited for a political cause. But the monster that's being created could well turn on itself, that they don't realise.'

There has been trouble on campus. A couple of days ago, two men barged into the office of one of Maharishi's colleagues who specialises in ancient history, announced that he was a traitor to the nation for his views on the composite origins of Hindu civilisation, slapped him, socked him, knocked him down to the floor, then left threatening worse might follow. The professor's students had insisted he go to the police; the police listened with apparent interest but were reluctant to file a case. The students accused them of being in cahoots with the slappers; a constable had in turn roughed up a couple of the more outspoken ones, and now more students had joined the cause and were agitating outside the vice chancellor's office, demanding his intervention.

'He is beaten but not broken,' says Maharishi of the man and Alif nods uneasily, recalling the boy who had threatened him too: *Your time is up.* It terrifies him, this anarchy. And with the fear something else: a quick degradation, an easy slide to becoming one who creates inner Siberias so as to avoid being deported to the ghastly one out there. He has not given too much thought to his wife's recent trauma, but hearing now about this attack, the memory of what that blackguard Pandey insinuated to his wife redoubles back on him and he tries to hold fast to Ibn Khaldun.

'And you?' his teacher asks him. 'Just peace and sleep or have you seized the day?'

Alif has told him about the previous day's proceedings of the What-Shall-We-Do-With-Alif committee, thanked him for his help, said he's likely to be back at school soon. Even though it'll be a battle hereon for him to keep the flag of history flying.

The Maharishi rues, not for the first time, Alif's disinterest in a PhD and a university career. 'You would have made a fine scholar.'

Alif disagrees. 'I can hardly start on one book before I'm pulled in by another and then I must look up a third and so on. I only feel confident about presenting my conclusions to children under seventeen.'

'But you were one of my best students.' Maharishi looks dejected for a moment. 'It's important to remember certain things and forget others in order to move forward in time.'

Perhaps he is hinting at something he has hinted at before: that one can't be too taken with the romance of history if it's rigorous scholarship one is aiming for.

'Do you remember that old distinction between shruti and smriti?'

Alif nods. 'Revelation and interpretation.'

'The beauty of the system is that the Vedas, the Upanishads and so on may be considered of divine origin – only to be heard, shruti, or to be seen, drishti – but they have always been open to logical examination. They'd be dead without that. You interpret, later generations remember what you said, smriti, and then they add views of their own. A constant dialogue. And you must join it too. Read all you want but add your voice to the great river.'

Alif feels tremendous love for this man and sick fear about what might become of him if he continues to sit there unprotected from the Frankensteins, nothing to defend himself except quotations from Khaldun and Nehru, Sankara and Ramanuja. Maharishi Jain, the man who taught Alif not just history but, in his own words, or rather, the words of some European writer he admired, the historical dimension of human existence. How that had transformed Alif's outlook! Not just the facts but the outlook – everything human is historical and the present is not merely a progression from or sequence to the past, it is also brilliantly illuminated by it.

His name is not really Maharishi; Alif and a classmate of his, a sincere girl with a passion for the bhakti revivals of medieval India, who went on to become a college professor somewhere in the American Midwest, had given him that moniker because it seemed to go well with 'Jain' and because he is nothing if not sage-like.

'The historical dimension of human existence ...' Alif murmurs.

'Yes, but it's relatively new, you see. The Vedas and their interpretations may be ancient but it was only in the late eighteenth century that history became central to education and that we started looking to it – rather than to religion or philosophy or poetry – to give us an understanding of human life as a whole. You don't seem convinced.'

'My big problem has been how to counteract one's personal shortcomings. For the flesh always ends up too weak to sustain the exaltations of the imagination. To be a historian is to adopt a certain kind of attitude, hold oneself in a particular way, as it were, and that I am not able to do.'

'Ah, you don't have to be Napoleon to understand Napoleon ...'

'I know, but all the same that which you are informs the history you write. Nirad Chaudhuri imagined himself writing a grand Monumenta, one volume every year. Because he believed in self-assertion, his dream project would have to have something of the same grandeur. Abul Fazl got his head cut off for his influence with the emperor Akbar and his loyalty to him. So that's another model of a historian – one who was both living history and writing it for he was also a military commander and a theologian. Herodotus of ancient Greece was, as you told us, the first to write history as narrative, create the figure of the historian as storyteller, the teller of tales who has wandered far and wide to collect them.'

'Which one are you, then?' asks the Maharishi, amused.

'If only I knew...'

'You know all too well. The angel of history.'

They smile worriedly over that strange figure with his face turned towards the past and his wings blowing him towards the future, the great philosopher's unforgettable image. The past has been shattered forever by the storms of progress blowing in from paradise and the angel would like to turn back and make it whole again. But the storm cannot be resisted; it's propelling him forward.

'The future,' whispers Alif. Then he thinks of Salim, of Salim's grandchildren, his great-grandchildren, and can't help feeling soothed. Will those distant men and women care about the fact that their ancestors once believed themselves to have fallen very far back in the race of the nations?

His phone rings; it's his mother. Ahmad appears to have lost his mind or at least crossed some more lines in pursuit of his religious ambitions.

'Wherever you are son, you need to get here at once.'

His mother is rarely distressed and rarely calls him so he must take leave of the Maharishi who says he will check in once again with Shukla ji to make sure all is well.

In the taxi, leaving the campus, he looks out for those dishes of bread and milk for hungry animals he had noticed last time but they're gone. The pavements are empty and the walls are plastered with white handbills printed in large black type, calling for the vice chancellor to step down, the police to back off, the fascists to give in, the righteous to lead.

He wonders, as Ibn Khaldun once did, about what defines our times and can only come up with one word: mediocre. He is a mediocre man in a mediocre age. Mediocre, this country: its paltry culture, its petty hatreds, its inequalities preserved from five thousand years ago, its chest-thumping stickmen leaders, its morally empty and self-serving upper classes, its ignorant and reviled lower classes – all mediocre. And this city as well, mediocre – its bitter air and dirty water and blemished light, the thirty million savage hopes of its inhabitants, each cancelled out by the other, and its crumbs of history ground down into so much dust and so many wisps of cobwebbed memories. His own life is no doubt a monument to mediocrity – that small-time school principal he has just tried convincing, those disappointed parents whom he cannot console, that upset wife. And yet, amazingly even to himself, he can laugh off all that, the whole heaving subcontinent of second-rateness, only because of three transformative words recently received from Prerna. *Yes, of course.* To his offer of showing her around Purana Qila. She had been quiet lately but now, again, this opening of a door, this invitation once more to cross over the dehleez.

As soon as he presses on the bell of his parents' flat, his father leaps out at him, in his right hand the biggest of the green-handled knives from the set of four that Alif had presented to his mother some months ago. The knife is not loosely clasped in the attitude of one who's been interrupted in his onion-chopping, though it's another matter that Mahtab never chops onions. It's held up aggressively high and he lowers it slowly as he steps back from the doorway to let Alif in.

There is silence in the room. Shagufta is on the sofa looking spent and bandaging a weeping Ahmad's right elbow.

'What...?' asks Alif.

'You ask him,' says Mahtab.

Alif cannot remember the emergency number nor what sort of first aid to offer to victims in shock from knife wounds.

'Abba, first you sit down,' he says, trying to keep the agitation out of his voice and sitting down himself.

'I want this person out of my house,' says Mahtab.

'He could have killed me,' sobs Ahmad.

'Our man was going on as usual about needing some quick money and your father,' says Shagufta, without looking at Mahtab, 'said he's had enough.'

She finishes tying the gauze and pats Ahmad on the back. 'Not too bad, it should stop bleeding soon.'

Alif is not sure who the greater lunatic is here. He tries to pacify Ahmad. 'We were hoping little Aftab's fees would be more important to you but if you really think the umrah is crucial...'

'It's not just the umrah,' say Shagufta. 'That's to start with. From there, the gentleman says he wants to proceed to UP and take up a course in theology. His family can fend for themselves here.' She sounds sardonic as usual; she seems to have lost now the momentary panic he heard in her voice on the phone. 'I've been telling him all morning to control himself. And then your father just went to the kitchen and...'

Ahmad gets up and retreats to a corner, away from Mahtab who still clasps the knife though he's no longer holding it aloft. Ahmad wipes his teary face on one edge of his stained kurta and cradles his injured arm.

'Do you want to see a doctor?' asks Alif.

'If they don't have that kind of money then you can give it to me,' he says.

No longer the polite 'bhai'.

Alif again asks his father to please sit down.

Ahmad says, 'You have many years of work left, you'll earn it again. It's time for me to start my education. I must go. And if I can't go, I may as well die. Kill me,' he shouts, suddenly advancing towards Mahtab.

'Give me that knife, Abba,' pleads Shagufta. But the man seems to have turned to stone. Finding Mahtab unresponsive to his melodrama, Ahmad turns to Alif. 'You know what I have done for you all these years.'

'What you have done for *me*?' asks Alif. 'Who taught you to read and write, who sat with you for weeks before every exam and took you through history and English and maths... Okay, not maths, that you were good at and I wasn't... But for God's sake, who's been your support?'

'You've had and have only one friend, that drinker,' says Ahmad bitterly. 'You may have helped me now and then because I was your parents' servant, you took me out with you during the times Ganesh wasn't around, but I never mattered. He's been the only influence on you; I could rant on about my faith day and night and you'd pretend to listen but it would make no difference. Whereas with him and for him you'd do anything. It's not as if I've forgotten that girl whom you both…'

'Will you shut up?' says Alif, raising his voice for the first time. *Prerna*. He has absolutely no recollection of having told Ahmad about her but Ahmad clearly knows and he's holding it over him now as obviously as Mahtab just held that knife over *him*.

Alif clears his throat and tries to take on the tone of the just. 'Once there was a poor boy begging on the streets. A family took him in and made a man of him. And the man now repays this by pointing fingers at them all the time. Grow up!'

'You grow up. You think I cannot see what's going on in this family? Ammi doesn't even cover her head when she steps out. Abba goes to the mosque only on Fridays. Their son, Alif Mohammad, doesn't go to the mosque even on Fridays.' He grows calmer reciting this litany. Finding that no one interrupts, he continues, using that word that the holier-than-thou have lately adopted to damn the apparently blasphemous with. 'Shirk, shirk, shirk. In this family, though it is banned in the Koran, there are pictures of human faces on the wall. The men don't grow their beards, the women go out to work, the children have never strayed near a madrasa. In this family, people cry at the feet of the so-called saints, even though they have been told over and over again there is no one worth worshipping except the one God. Tawhid, tawhid, tawhid. In this family there is great wickedness afoot…'

Mahtab lunges at Ahmad, the knife now aimed at his chest. Barely aware of what he is doing, Alif leaps up and hits side-ways with all his might at his father's raised hand. The knife is suddenly flying and, completing a graceful arc, lands near Shagufta's feet which she hastily pulls away. Mahtab moves fast; he has got Ahmad's throat in a wrench in the crook of his arm. He roughly pushes him down so he's on his knees and then flat on the floor. Alif is sure his father is going to break the man's neck. He can see it right before him, the tensed strength in the muscles of Mahtab's bare forearms, the flailing of Ahmad's skinny limbs and the spluttering from his mouth.

'Abba,' pleads Alif. Mahtab tightens his hold on Ahmad. And then just lets him go. Ahmad collapses, yelling the name of Allah. Alif picks up the knife and runs to the kitchen; he looks for a place to hide it and then, feeling silly, lays it on the counter alongside the abandoned preparations for lunch.

Shagufta has pushed her shaking husband out onto the balcony and shuts the door to it; she then gets on the phone to Ahmad's wife, Zainab. Ahmad is curled into a ball on the floor. Alif looks at his hands, flexes his fingers and thinks, *we have become them*. The citizens of Delhi who day in and day out do similar and even worse things to themselves and others – this is what saturates so many fevered brains and twisted hearts: the knives and guns, the fists and the kicks, the nooses and poisons.

Ahmad won't respond to their entreaties but when the petite and shy Zainab arrives hand in hand with their five-year-old son, he gets up groaning. The child is goggle-eyed and grave, then breaks into gap-toothed giggles when Shagufta tries to present him with a bowl of creamy ras malai from the fridge.

'Abba lost his temper ...' says Alif to Zainab. 'They had a quarrel.'

Ahmad staggers out without saying a word; the girl and the child speedily follow. Mother and son look at each other in shared pain and then Shagufta asks, 'Have you eaten?'

Alif nods. 'I'm worried about what he might do. If he does something stupid now ...'

'You mean he'll complain to the police? Or kill himself? Let him do what he likes. I can't watch out for him any more.'

'Kill himself? He ought to know his scriptures better.'

'It's learning the scriptures he's going on about all the time. But let him become a maulana if he wants to,' says Shagufta. 'Let him became the biggest maulana in the world and at some point in his life he'll realise that you don't step on others to fulfil your ideals.'

As always her framework is ethical – what is the right thing to do? – as against Alif's which is a diehard bookish one – which chapter of history to reach for?

Shagufta says she will heat up leftovers, setting out three plates on the table and through that simple action restoring some balance to the off-kilter afternoon. Alif goes in to wash and carefully hangs up his shirt, locating an old T-shirt in the small pile of clothes his mother retains for him. He feels better but, going to the balcony, finds everything out of joint again, for his father's eyes, as he focuses them on the narrow alley four floors below where a man is trundling a pushcart with heaps of custard apples, are wet. It is not the hoarse shouts of the fruit vendor that are making him cry, even though the word for custard apple, sharifa, echoes the word for a decent man or a noble one, sharif. What could it be? Alif ducks, mortified at seeing the father who has just tackled a man less than half his age now crying softly like a penitent.

'Lunch,' says Alif, but he keeps his head down, his eyes on the T-shirt that bears the legend 'History Repeats Itself – See the Back of this T-shirt'. The back says 'History Repeats Itself – See the Front of this T-shirt'. Alif does not know how the esteemed clothes dealers of Urdu Bazaar, usually with just rip-offs on offer, once had this among the jumble on sale. Had some drone in a sweatshop taken a break from embroidering misspelt logos of giant global casualwear corporations to make a philosophical statement via a T-shirt?

Salim would have done better for he too had once espied Mahtab crying and promptly demanded an explanation; he felt nothing of Alif's shame, nothing of the dumb despair that can strike a grown man when faced with a father's grief.

*

Alif – despite his admiration for that long line of paternalistic statesmen who thought of history as a mode of doing rather than just being – has really just hedged about all the challenges in his own life with such self-devised rhetoric as, *why bother with something when you can manage with nothing?* So he does not understand, in fact can on occasion feel alienated by, the zeal that led his father to become a policeman, a committed one at that. Mahtab rarely spoke about his work. When he came home every few months, on visits from the towns outside Delhi where he was posted, it was never with accounts of his adventures, just interrogations for Alif and Samara about their studies, their disciplines, their daily habits. The stories about him came from their grandparents, stories which were, perhaps, just that. Mahtab became, in the child Alif's mind, a comic book hero, sprinting smartly after robbers with black eye-masks and bags of valuables, powering a jeep through midnight streets to come to the rescue of old ladies held down by kidnappers, or twirling his baton in march-pasts on police grounds. As he grew older, Alif realised from what his mother would let slip that Mahtab was pretty low down on the scale, that he was not up to heroics but just doing his humdrum duty and trying to stay out of trouble with his superiors.

But today, as father confides in son for the first time, Alif notices that, like his mother did a few minutes ago, he is holding on to a clear distinction between right and wrong.

'There was a riot...' he begins hoarsely, and Alif remembers again, from all those years ago, the dark room and the defeated mother.

'Imagine this. A small town in UP. A pig strays into a mosque during an Eid namaz. The men are enraged and appeal to the police at a nearby chowki. A couple of constables turn up but do nothing to get the pig out or find out who let it in. It's just a pig after all.'

'Where were you?'

'Posted in the same town. So the men forget their prayer, some start stoning the policemen. I'm at the station and called out by the deputy superintendent. Me and a bunch of other SIs and ASIs. There must have been six or seven of us in all.'

'So you get there?'

Mahtab nods. 'We know what's expected of us. This is not the first time we've had to control a mob.'

'A mob? But they were there to pray.'

'Some are loosening bricks from the half-built wall of the eidgah and hurling them at the police, some are being lathi-charged, some are running. We know the rulebook. Minimal force in other circumstances but in a communal riot the obligation to use force to effect.'

'But how is it even a riot yet?' Alif must keep prompting his father, afraid he will lapse into silence and tears again.

'It could become one. The deputy SP is harrying us, there is no time to think. Fire, he says. It's time to teach these bastards a lesson. *Fire*. And we all do.'

'And then?'

'What then? People die. Don't ask me how many. People die and things get worse.'

'What could you have done?' Alif asks, aware that having just disarmed and deterred his father – who is still very much the cop, however morose – and thus saved Ahmad from death or at least further injury, his voice has a certain, entirely new firmness to it. All the same, he's not sure he wants to know any more. Just the thought of his father's bullets tearing into that bathed and perfumed flesh dressed in festive white...

'The obligation to use force to effect. But even so firing is the last resort. On such a large crowd – several hundred and of course many were children – on an unarmed crowd of families and friends on Eid day – no rules would justify that. But in my mind at that split moment I did not waver. A big crowd, mayhem, screaming, the boss saying, fire, and all of us did.'

'And you think the others also had second thoughts later?'

'I don't know anything about the others. It's me. Why did I not stop to say to the deputy SP: Sir, that seems excessive. Sir, should we get in more constables and round up these boys who are stoning us? Sir, there are old men here, and little girls and boys. Why didn't I *ask*?'

'You didn't have a choice,' Alif assures him without feeling a jot of assurance himself.

'I must have believed that. For years together I must have believed that. But what would they have done? Abused me. Shoved me out of the way. Killed me, even?'

'You could have lost your job? You could have missed your promotion.'

'It's not that easy for a cop to be thrown out. Simpler to do away with him. And so what? If it came down to that. My life against all those lives.'

Alif wants to somehow get across to his father that he is tinier than tiny, that history renders him about as effective as a mote. How many times has this played out? The pig in the wrong place, the cow slaughtered when it shouldn't have been, the Koran messed up and the Muslim seen to be making too much noise about it, the Muslim man in love with the Hindu girl, the Muharram procession passing too near Brahmin homes. All this in the years after Independence. In the years before that it went both ways, he realises, thinking of the many riots of the 1920s, thinking, too, of Gandhi's remark about cowards and bullies.

'No one has a clear idea of how many people died in all,' Mahtab is saying. 'It started with this firing that summer and continued till the end of the year and even spread to other towns. A whole six months of murder – killing, retaliation, killing again. Was it five hundred who lost their lives, was it a thousand? Does anyone even remember that riot any more?'

'I remember,' says Shagufta who has been sitting quietly all along, darning an old velvet quilt, darning over the darns her mother once made. 'My Abba would try calling and could never get across. We thought you were dead.' She doesn't add that she collapsed, took to her bed. 'When you finally called you said nothing. When you came back to Delhi at the end of that time, you said nothing.'

'What matters is what I did. Or didn't do.'

'Was anyone brought to book?' asks Alif.

Mahtab says theories have abounded. Some believed the then prime minister set the policemen on the Muslims because they hadn't voted for her in the previous election. The prime minister said it was the foreign hand. One of her union ministers blamed the Hindu right wing. The leader of the Hindu right wing said it was the Muslim right wing. A prominent newspaper editor, sitting in Delhi, agreed. The chief minister of Uttar Pradesh said nothing. The judge who authored the report on the affair blamed the chief minister. Nobody resigned, no one was fired, no one felt culpable and, ultimately, no one took responsibility.

'All those poor Muslims…' starts Shagufta but Mahtab turns on her at once.

'Stop that. They were people. Human. You think that was the first time I used my pistol? You think one doesn't fire in the line of duty and how does it matter Hindu or Muslim when someone has been knifed, when someone is running away with the goods, when one's own life is in danger? But this was different. These were common people. I couldn't have saved them all but maybe... at least... a handful less would have died if I...' He's openly crying again.

A quite unnatural calm fills the house. No reports from Ahmad working at something noisily, crankily. No TV dispensing its clangourous entertainment. No Shagufta urging food or common sense on her family. Even the usual hollering of the passing vendors is missing. Alif starts to feel a shiver coming on; someone's got to speak.

Then the lilt of the muezzin's call.

How would stabbing poor, demented Ahmad have helped, he thinks. Is this what the thwarting of a man of action leads to – murderous intent? He feels again a strange tingling in his hands and a searing in his chest. If he hadn't intervened, if he hadn't rushed across when his mother phoned...

That evening he comes down with a raging fever and crouches under covers on the divan, looking at the sketches on the living room wall, the work of his niece and nephew when they were four or five – a couple of childish renderings of their grandparents that are all rounded eyes and crazy hair and yet somehow manage to look like them. Shirk, he hears Ahmad saying, and wonders what sort of religion it is that would want to beat down so innocent a practice: a pre-schooler's doodling. Again the painted art produced under the enthusiastic aegis of Mughal emperors marches through his burning brain as he lies there, a farrago of images which eventually comes to an end, strangely, in the emperor Akbar's toenail.

It's a highly naturalistic ink sketch of the ageing Mughal that's been buried in Alif's memory. No courtly fanfare, no jam-packed miniature depicting war or suggestive one showing amorous ambushes. In smudged lines, the emperor sitting cross-legged, gazing fondly at a falcon perched on one raised hand, a bolster tucked under the other arm and one foot peeking out from under one folded knee. To the prevalent view that the artist should not presume to create when there is only one Creator, Akbar is believed to have said that the artist when he creates cannot but help think of the Creator for so little does his art resemble life. And thus does he, and likewise the viewer of his art, draw closer to God. And perhaps this is proof: Alif recalls that small toenail and somehow feels himself blessed. Not only were they great champions of art, they are best met there too, Akbar and his ilk, he realises.

A worried Shagufta feeds the sick man the same poppy paste blended into warm milk that she'd once been fed. The sick man tries to clear his mind and relive his father's suffering. He lacks the courage to go all the way there – to that particular blood-soaked Karbala. Instead he thinks of what Mahtab said about having had occasion more than once to bring out his pistol. And Alif understands. He is a policeman; he doesn't believe in histrionics and he has never had the time for activism on behalf of this religion or that. The struggle has been this forced re-examining of something done in good faith. It had seemed right to him, that command to fire. And then it started to seem wholly wrong to him. It's his own misjudgement he is flayed by, not the affinities of those who happen to have died.

When Alif is better he goes out and buys his parents a humongous TV set, instructing the shop assistant to deliver it to their flat. Then he takes off to see Miss Moloy. He has in all these years of their friendship never visited her at home, a certain delicacy on his part preventing him from taking up her invitation to drop in whenever he likes. And now he finds her there, in Greater Kailash of all places. Who would have thought the noble legacy of the Bengal Renaissance would end up in a gated colony of bureaucrats and businessmen along with their long, sullen retinues of servants – maids, cooks, nannies, drivers, housekeepers, gatekeepers.

It turns out Miss Moloy has a posh address but a small rooftop house, a barsati, stuffed with books, shelves of CDs, comfortable sofas, and the padding about and excited panting of not one but two well-groomed dogs – not the superior breed she had wanted but strays she has adopted. The dogs grudgingly settle down once Alif does and he eyes the neat rows of books – science and history and philosophy on the lower shelves, fiction and poetry in the higher reaches – as Miss Moloy finishes her cooking. Perhaps she has no secrets after all, he thinks; she certainly draws on no sugar daddy if this small refuge is all she has. It could be that her formula has just been to lie low and read. When they sit down to lunch, he comments on how several of her book titles feature the words 'West' or 'Western civilisation'.

'There is no such thing in the absolute sense,' he says earnestly, 'not in the way it's usually imagined – a straight line from the Greeks to the Romans to the Renaissance, with an interlude for the Middle Ages. No, no, no. The progression has been more winding.'

'But Tagore spoke of this all the time, uniting East and West. It was his big thing. And you won't go on about it unless you believe first that there's a fundamental difference between them.'

'There is a way in which the East is implicit in the West. Just as today the West is implicit in the East. You know, I'm sure, that if a thousand years ago the Arabs had not engaged with the Greek classics of poetry and science, these texts would not have found their way into Latin and become so foundational to your great European civilisation. And your maths and science too. Advanced by the Indian and the Chinese, taken up and developed by the Arab, and then seeding what came to be called the European Renaissance.'

'You've mentioned it before,' says Miss Moloy.

'Al-Biruni calculated the earth's circumference and was almost accurate, Avicenna wrote the hugely influential Canon on Medicine, Averroes produced those famous commentaries on Aristotle. And those are just three examples. Also, it was from this culture that the West took the tools to conquer the world – the navigational aids, the triangular sail – without which there would be no Columbus and no Vasco da Gama and no East India Company.'

'I know, I know. But why didn't they go further and become the intellectual powerhouse the West later became?'

Alif is about to reply but Miss Moloy answers her own question. 'Because Islam doesn't subscribe to the humanism that was the cornerstone of the European Renaissance. Man as the measure of all things.'

'True but where has that led us finally – man as the measure of all things? To the imminent collapse of the planet. Ask Mother Rawat, she is an expert on Mother Earth.'

Miss Moloy serves him more khichdi, apologising for the plainness of the meal. Alif goes on eating even though he is not sure if it is food or something else altogether that he is hungry for. He makes no protest; he is used to women feeding him – his grandmother, his mother, his sister, his aunt, his wife, even if she has forsworn cooking, his landlady, his friends. There has never been any need for him to even reach out and fill his own plate and all his life he has taken for granted this female affection that expresses itself through overfeeding, as if every hole in the universe could be plugged with chicken pulao and aloo poori, as if every bitterness needs only as much sugar to obliterate as goes into ladoo and jalebi.

'But why not be a migratory bird with spiritual homes in both east and west as Tagore said?' asks Miss Moloy. 'Why don't we learn from both cultures and create a new vision of man – and of woman – who combines the best of both?'

Alif thinks for a while, then says, 'I don't know if at any point in the modern period any culture has achieved that combination. In older times perhaps the Byzantine empire did. The Byzantines offer lessons worth revisiting. Their empire was a melting pot. And they did not see themselves as either Eastern or Western in today's sense. They were proud peoples, the Byzantines, they believed theirs was the only civilised kingdom, and yet the barbarians could become Byzantine provided they accepted God and King.'

'So what must I do now, throw out my books?' says Miss Moloy in mock despair.

'Look at those women,' says Alif, gesturing at the TV he can see across the room. A girl in a white headscarf is raising slogans to revolution and the camera pans over a large crowd of women of all ages, dressed in all black or variegated colour, chanting back the slogans to her.

*Chappa chappa jhoom uthe ga inquilaab ke naaro se.*

'I've been doing nothing but look at them the last few days,' says Miss Moloy. 'All they're asking for is an honouring of what's been promised them by the Constitution.'

The slogans get more portentous and shriller.

*Ham leh ke rahenge, azadi.*

*Awaaz do, ham ek hain.*

*Ham kaagaz nahi dikhayenge.*

*Hindu Muslim, bhai bhai.*

He recalls Mir saying, you don't know the inside story. But these women seem to. They have risen as one body to declare: *Jaan se pyari, azadi.* Freedom dearer than life. They wave the national flag as they say it. They have wrested it from the other side. That single image from the past that can stir us to action. Yet try as he might, it does not stir him. He smiles. 'The Constitution.'

'What else do we have?'

'Most of us are borderline cases. The parade of equal citizens marching shoulder to shoulder that you're dreaming of – it doesn't exist except within the covers of that book and maybe not even there. Thinks of all the clauses, the sub-clauses, the caveats, the exceptions that disprove the rules, the messy politics. There is nothing new here really. We've never been that – homogeneous. But now these rifts are taking on the contours of battle and the opponents are starting to see themselves as enemies.'

'Would you have any ideas? What are we to do?'

'What can one do except write fretful editorials that few read? Or sing "We Shall Overcome".'

'People have overcome so many times before by doing just that,' insists Miss Moloy.

'Populist leaders claim to represent the people. So they're not going to allow *you* to speak on their behalf. They're going to paint you as the saboteurs, the trouble-makers, the intellectual riff-raff, the seditious fringe.'

'But we were the ones who freed this country from the British once.'

'True, true,' he says, then thanks her for the meal and goes across to the bookshelf. 'Because that is the direction in which the leaders channelled our passions then.'

'Things are bad,' says Miss Moloy and urges Alif to pause in his historical researches and instead give some thought to the contemporary situation, but he explains that he's unwell. Or has been recently. He pulls out a volume on Muslim Spain and asks if he can borrow it.

'So you think it's all right to stay put?' She's really perturbed. 'That one shouldn't *do* something?'

Alif sees again the knife flying; he thinks of the pain in his balled hands as they crunched down on the bones of his father's wrist. But he cannot share that still not quite digested horror with this refined woman who lives with dogs and books and the swooping and soaring of trumpets playing a jazz tune on her stereo speakers.

'To do something one must be squarely committed to some vision of a happy future and that I am not,' he declares. 'Future's overrated. The present is all I have.'

He goes back yet again to the Byzantines, shares with her a poetic observation once made about those medieval creators of sad-faced Christs and complex, colourful mosaics. At its peak, theirs was so advanced a civilisation that we cannot quite grasp it yet because ours, more than a thousand years on, is so retrograde. It is entirely possible for much older cultures to be ahead of present ones, just as people across the ages can be contemporary to each other which is why the expression on his face the other day reminded the children of Rani of Jhansi, and which is why while Rawat in all her shallowness belongs squarely to the twenty-first century, Miss Moloy would be at home in the high-minded rationalism of the eighteenth.

Miss Moloy lets him be, tells him instead about a trip she is planning, this time to the north-east of the country. She has been there before but enthuses about all she is going to see, eat and do as if there is no approach to the north-east except one of discovery and conquest, despite the place having been discovered and conquered ad nauseam since at least the thirteenth century of the common era. Alif thinks vaguely of a quick lecture on the Ahoms who migrated from further east to Assam and not only gave the state its name but also an empire that lasted for centuries. But he suddenly finds himself lacking the inspiration.

Miss Moloy notices his silence and asks him what malady it is he's suffering from.

'It's a woman,' he blurts out, unable to hold it down any longer. And he has the satisfaction of seeing Miss Moloy taken aback; for a moment she is out of words. But then he wonders if he's blown it and lost her respect forever. She recovers and says gaily, 'Cherchez la femme. Tell me, tell me all.'

Alif's private life before Prerna resurfaced was a small domestic patch of common blooms and overgrown weeds, and even if a damp rosebud sprang forth now and again, even if sometimes a sleeping bird dreamt itself into flight, there was nothing about this home-grown quarter that ever needed much attention. And now? Where to start? Certainly not with once upon a time because this story is upside down. First, the corrupting of innocence. And then the attempted recovery, still underway, of honourableness.

He looks at Miss Moloy as she clears the table. 'Am all ears, I'll just be back with some coffee.'

He opens the book in his hands and sees her name on the flyleaf. *Amita Deb*. He has all but forgotten that Moloy is her preferred nickname and she has long let go of Amita Deb. And yet there must have been people, maybe there still are, who call her Amita. For some reason, the sight of her name embarrasses him, as if something's been brought uncomfortably up close. There is just no way he can tell her about Prerna. He doesn't want to make demands on her sympathy or upset the balance between them, and that passing look of shock on her face gave her away.

And so, sipping coffee, he apologises, says it's some trivial old thing he will share with her some other time, and he is sure, despite her clucking, that she's relieved. And so he is able to leave Greater Kailash with his self-esteem undamaged and his image of Miss Moloy intact, that diehard believer in the Cunning of Reason. He's not sure he's with her. Can the flag-waving women, just through hollering those slogans, fulfil a higher historical purpose, or are they already on the other side: the fallen victims, those upon whom the rulers have always trampled?

The husky- and poodle-walking servants of the neighbourhood pass him by without a glance and the security man at the gate to the colony is trying to outdo the Bhojpuri disco hit playing on his phone, and despite this afternoon of civilised chat, this book in his hands warm with nostalgia's sunset glowing on the remains of Alhambra, Alif is compelled to be in Delhi again, a city made so insistently, so noisily of now.

# SEVEN

A nimble-fingered electrician snaps open cartons and tests lengths of cables as he installs the new, wall-obscuring TV screen in the living room.

Mahtab stares guardedly, seeming to anticipate some fault with it though there is none unless the compelling lustre of the colours, the lifelike sharpness of the images, the resounding voices of newscasters and film actors is too much of a good thing. The wordless, busy-mannered man sweeps out of the house and Mahtab, now appearing moderately satisfied at least, if not outright joyous, sits down to watch a famous British food writer munch on freshly fried kachoris in the gullies of old Delhi. Alif, standing around, hoping to hear some words of warmth or even just acknowledgement from his father, eventually wanders off to chat with his mother.

She tells him about Ahmad; Zainab reports that he is recovering from his injury and mooning about in the house, not saying much.

'And as for your father, you can see the results for yourself?'

'What results?'

'You haven't noticed the new state of the house? He's been clearing up. Thrown out those files of papers. And his cracked old boots. Called in the kabbadi wallah for the mountains of magazines he collects.'

'Nice,' says Alif.

'I told Phuphi and she was glad. She said she'd gone to the Khwaja herself for the first time in five years. Bano had to hold her every step of the way but she did it. So of course the Khwaja took note of my appeal, she said.'

Then his mother moves on to what Samara is up to – nothing much as usual – and what her children are up to – moving heaven and earth with their naughtiness. Alif can't be bothered. What's flattening him at the moment is no heavier than the single page of a typed letter folded into the pocket of his jeans. He received it the previous day via registered post and had hastily hidden it away as soon as he'd scanned it, though all through the morning he'd had to pull it out again and again to reread in sickened disbelief. The letter has the general's usual lack of finesse and usual sinister trumpery.

Shri Alif Mohammad,
You are hereby dismissed from your post for insubordination to the authorities and for mistreatment of the children. We have on file written complaint from your student you abused. We have on file written complaint from your colleague you abused. The committee has taken an unanimous decision in this regard. We would be grateful if you do not visit the school premises henceforth. Your pending salary will be transferred to your bank account.

Alif called Maharishi who was astounded on hearing the news – and then resigned. Either my word does not carry much weight with old Shukla ji, he mused sadly, or Shukla ji's word does not carry any weight with Mrs Rawat. Let me know if there is any other way I can help, he says. Alif thinks he ought to call Shukla ji and demand an explanation but twenty-four hours have passed and he's been unable to do a thing. He has not shared the news with wife or son; he cannot imagine telling his father and tries telling his mother.

But instead of coming out with a heart-wrenching confession of failure he finds himself asking her casually about Imtiaz, the pregnant woman whose survival she'd been worrying about.

'Oh, she's all right,' says Shagufta as if nothing had ever been the matter with her, Imtiaz, thinks Alif, whose functional, frightened, unlettered, malnourished existence he had once scorned. And now his own existence is missing the necessary buoy of a job; without a job he will be at sea. Work to do, he tells his mother and says goodbye to his father who with a rapt expression is pushing buttons on the new remote control and he too almost smiles at his departing son. Theek hai, he says.

Back home Alif takes the letter out of his pocket, then puts it back into his pocket and goes downstairs to knock on Ganesh's door; he hasn't seen or heard from him since that night of bitter whiskeys, that night of broken epiphanies. Ganesh, who is always *in medias res*, deep in some disaster of his own imagining or gripped by some parvenu desire too extravagant to realise.

'Just watching something,' he says. 'A behenchod love story of course.' Alif follows him into his bedroom.

'What's with you? Have you been avoiding me?'

'Of course not,' says Alif as he considers the semantics of this description – how can a love story be sister-fucking? – then recalls all that drunken talk about guns and revenge and is suddenly suspicious of this relatively sedate Ganesh. He notices his friend has been drinking alcohol from the steel glass in which his mother usually serves him bedtime milk.

It's hard to sit. Ganesh's obsessive care with his appearance, even on weekends, does not extend to his living quarters. He is wearing chinos no wrinkle has ever dared disturb, a dress shirt of probably Egyptian cotton in muted checks, shoes which he keeps on in the house and which are shinier and pointier and no doubt made from a better-fed cow than Alif's, but he is unconcerned about the empty liquor bottles secreted into corners of the unkempt room, the distinctly grubby sheets on the unmade bed, the uncombed tangle of wires on the table at which he sits on a creaking chair borrowed from the dining-table set.

Alif finally settles on a corner of the bed and watches with Ganesh some schmaltzy film with sham music – now qawwali choruses, now hip-hop riffs – and watches also Ganesh's expression, alternating between leering and longing.

He waits for the man to let loose but the man is drinking whiskey like milk and acting like all his troubles are over. So

Alif tells him about some of his own. He pulls out the letter and hands it over. He asks him half-fearfully if he has any advice about finding a lawyer, going to court, getting justice. Ganesh laughs out loud.

'All fuckers,' he says. 'Women.'

Alif tries to explain about Rawat's ignorance of history and history of ignorance, about Rawat's self-serving fabrications and fabricated self-serving, about Rawat's Hindu versus Muslim and Muslim versus Hindu world view but Ganesh waves it away like he has heard it all before, which he has. He pours some water into what's left at the bottom of the McDowell's No. 1 bottle, sloshes it about and hands it to Alif who cannot recall ever having had a drink before 6 p.m., the idea of afternoon drinking being associated in his mind with a slide to alcoholism, whereas drinks imbibed in the night are business as usual – just a man's way of being a man.

'Women,' repeats Ganesh, his one-word diagnosis of both his problem and Alif's. 'Women.' He slams down the screen of his laptop on the heroine at her most endearing, dancing in a streetscape amalgamation of Old Delhi and New York.

'What's happening with Sahana?'

'It's over,' he says. He's not crying or shouting for a gun, is in fact full of brutish calm. 'I have finished with her.'

Over half an hour of diluted drinking the story behind his laying down of arms emerges – Ganesh has been paid a visit from the husband-to-be and the husband-to-be is, to begin with, a good half a foot taller than him.

'He came with the divorce papers. Yes, he. Not my wife, she is obviously too scared to face me after what she's done.'

But for once he doesn't sound convinced about it himself – his superiority, his suffering. The husband-to-be not only has two children from a previous marriage but is also CEO of his own company which employs two dozen people. Fintech, says Ganesh jealously, which sounds good even if it means nothing to Alif. Ganesh earns well as systems administrator at that American behemoth but this man is in a different league, he says. He is minting money or at least that's the impression he gave. And just as Alif always notes how much nattier Ganesh's get-up is than his, Ganesh admits sourly that the man who has cuckolded him was dressed like a prince.

'He was wearing a watch exactly of the kind I need. He beat me to it. We know it from the advertisements, we know it from the films, but to actually see that amazing chronograph on a man's wrist in front of my eyes, in my own living room, that was such a chutiya thing.'

'That's all? A watch?' says Alif.

'You should know that wristwatches are no longer in. It's a Swiss-made chronograph one is after. I wanted to kill the bastard but first asked about chai. I didn't want him to drink my tea, I didn't want him to even exist but one has to say something to a visitor, no? Then Mummy starts feeding him dahi bhalla — as if it's her son's wedding she's celebrating and not this son's being trampled underfoot by a monster in size nine penny loafers. So completely unnecessary. And even my father, yes Papa who never says a word, do you know what he did?'

Alif is breathing easy now that he knows there was nothing dark involved. It is a simple evolutionary matter, the stronger, sharper, richer man gets the girl.

'Papa came and sat with us as we were talking. He asks this man about the nature of the financial services he offers, he asks him how his children are doing, he wants to know what sort of car he drives. Which car! He can sit for hours like a stone while I try to fend off Mummy, and now, suddenly, he wants to find out the make of his lordship's chariot. Which is an Audi, if you must know.'

'So he can speak when he wants to!' exclaims Alif.

Ganesh nods, irritated.

'They must be so relieved that it's over now, this neither here nor there condition of yours,' says Alif.

'Wait, and then there are the charioteers.'

'Who?'

'You think he'd come alone? A man like that, a thug. There were two other thugs with him who sat sprawled on the sofa like they owned the damn place. He didn't even bother to introduce them and they themselves didn't say a word, just stared at me the whole time.'

And there is it again, the shadow of violence. It still sticks in his mind: the stain of blood seeping through the hasty bandage Shagufta was tying on Ahmad, the damp of the knife handle as he rushed away with it...

'So *that's* why all of you were so nervous...'

'I wasn't nervous, I could have ignored them, I could have walked out of the room.'

'Anyway, did you sign the papers?'

'You think I had a choice?' Ganesh says without any apparent awareness of contradicting himself. 'It's over.' He looks so sorry, so diminished, that Alif doesn't know what to say.

'What about you?' asks Ganesh, giving Alif's termination letter, which is still lying on the table, a closer look.

'Salim says I pass as a teacher.'

Ganesh says Salim has great potential, that twelve-year-olds are making apps these days and eight-year-olds taking courses in coding and robotics, that he'll likely soon come up with a killing idea for a start-up.

'Yet I failed with him,' says Alif.

He tells Ganesh how the child had agreed to be tutored and how Alif narrated to him, by way of an inaugural history lesson, a story from prehistory: the Upanishadic one about the spiritually precocious child Nachiketa and his three requests to the God of Death, Yama.

'Yama tried to evade the boy's final question, I told Salim, *is there life after death?* Yama said, I'll give you all the gold and horses and elephants you want, I'll give you as many pretty women as you want, I'll give you as many sons and grandsons as you want and they'll all live for a hundred years. But the boy held fast. He dismissed all these goodies as blandishments. He just wanted his answer. And do you know what Salim said?'

Ganesh is laughing already.

'No awe at this boy who resists all the world's riches. No curiosity at all about what Yama's answer finally was. All he wants to know is: so there was socialism even in the olden days? This is the child to whom I've promised a chunk of my savings.'

Ganesh narrows his eyes.

'What for?'

'Something he wants to try, I don't know... I don't like the sound of these start-ups. Seems like too much of a good thing to me that any kid can get rich off one. I won't say it outright to him but I would prefer for him to dirty his hands: learn a real trade.'

'Plumbing?' snorts Ganesh. 'Carpentry? Look, bhai, you don't understand cash. It's got to move. We are obsessed with making money for the sake of making money and then sitting tight on it, or buying bits of jewellery or bits of property with it. That's not what money is for.'

'I'm without a job. I want to keep the child happy but I don't know how I can fund his fancies at the moment.'

'There are a dozen schools in Daryaganj,' says Ganesh. 'You'll get another job tomorrow with your experience. Start scouting around for vacancies.'

This hasn't even occurred to Alif – that he is, after all, just a worker. And if he can work in one school, why not another? No matter that his heart is with his children, those he is teaching now, and those he has loved over the decades in five-year batches, from the ages of nine to fourteen, passing through his hands and benefiting from his enlightened ramblings. And then there is the peon he is friends with, the corridors he has paced, the beaten-up furniture in the staffroom, and that old portrait of the founder with Nehru...

'I'm attached to this school,' he says.

'And now you're not. You've been fired.'

Alif sighs. 'So bonds of feeling count for nothing?'

'Beta, you're living a lie,' says Ganesh, pointing his forefinger at him.

Alif looks at him steadily and then Ganesh turns the finger, now the barrel of a pistol, on himself, pressing hard against his temple, index finger squeezing the trigger. A cold and uncharacteristic silence.

'Listen, are you still harassing her?'

Alif stares, baffled. He tries to work out the meaning of this sentence – Still? Harassing? Her? Each word boggles the mind. He has not even breathed the name 'Prerna' to his friend since that first meeting.

'Who?' he asks stupidly.

'What's on your mind, man?' asks Ganesh, then, noticing the suddenly stricken expression on Alif's face, pulls up his chair to where his friend is sitting and says, 'Look, she's always liked you, you know that. She would show you her art and request your opinion. And her poems. Or her father's poems. Anyway, she respects you.'

He puts a cloying emphasis on the word 'respect', which Alif finds so hateful he wants to shout but instead slowly takes a swig. *Respect*. He knows what's being suggested – she thinks of you like a sister would a brother, she treats you like she treats those who wouldn't dare lay a finger on her.

'So, you know, don't mess it up by stalking her and sending her messages all the time.'

'I wasn't...'

'You're too old for that sort of thing. And Tahira wouldn't like it.'

Alif empties the bottle, considers smashing it into a wall but instead puts it down carefully with the other empties.

'What is she after? And you, what are you after?' he asks in a thick voice.

Ganesh smiles cryptically and nods. 'Women,' is all he says.

Alif has just comforted himself with the thought that the better man gets the girl. Now, as he stands up to go, he's forced to ask himself who that might be. In the living room he finds Mrs Khanna working her slow, arthritic way towards her son. Alif has to pause and ask how her day is going. She wants to know if he has heard the marvellous news about the exit of that witch and he must listen then to her plangent complaints about how Ganesh has been unreasonably downcast, dressed up but gone nowhere. Her angel face, her fairy-queen demeanour are no hindrance to her heartily cursing her soon to be former daughter-in-law for all the trauma she has wrought.

'You tell him,' she whispers. 'You're the only one he listens to. He must marry again.'

'Of course,' says Alif. 'Haan ji.'

She pronounces her wahe gurus and Alif thinks here is living proof. All she has now, all she has had for some time, are her gurus, all ten of them, from Nanak to Gobind Singh, and they are enough. Nothing to lighten her days, friends and relatives infrequent visitors, pain a constant companion, and yet she is always busy and animated with this – the conversation with the holy ones which is really a conversation with herself. All these years, I've learnt nothing from you, he thinks. I wasted time with your dreadful son. He wants to tell her that he'll do anything for her. But she already looks so happy that he instead concedes, because he has always been susceptible to her great charm, that perhaps in this happiness there is for him too some small intimation of joy.

★

'How am I to know it was a secret?' says Prerna. 'What was the secret? That we had a cup of tea together? That you visited and we talked about... what did we talk about? History? Politics? Religion?'

Alif hasn't even used that disreputable word 'secret'. All he's asked her is why Ganesh has been keeping tabs on them. Her matter-of-fact style is confusing him greatly. He cannot tell if it is a ruse to cover up the admission she made – *you are from back then* – or if he was misled by that meeting, one that he, with his limited understanding of sentimental matters, had designated as undoubtedly tender, but which might have been, he is now starting to see, just an expression of mild friendliness.

'He didn't turn up at the cafe and he didn't call afterwards. So I tried putting it out of my head. He reaches out after all these years and then he just ignores me?'

And now the voice is no longer so cool and the face is turned away. Alif looks at the mosque before them, a sixteenth-century beauty concealed in one of Delhi's old walled gardens. Ya Allah, it's him, he realises with a dull shock. *It's him, it's him, it's him. What on God's earth made me believe even for a moment that it was me?*

'I put it out of my mind,' repeats Prerna. 'And then last week he calls and says he has nothing left. His wife is leaving him. So we chat after he's done with his moaning and groaning, and I happen to mention that you'd come over. That you have been eagerly in touch.'

'Why?' cries Alif.

She looks surprised.

'Aren't you friends?'

And now it is Alif who feels the blood in his face. He wishes he had never set eyes on this woman and he is damned if he cares whether there is a ghazal or not that can measure up to his mortification. Five bays double-arched, he thinks, trying to calm his breathing. A central dome. Eaves supported by carved brackets. Octagonal turrets. Lotus rosettes on the spandrels. Those little projecting windows with their little cantilevered supports. Slabs of yellow sandstone. Slabs of red sandstone. So much geometrical, abstract and floral detailing one could spend a week going over just the exterior of this small mosque. And if we go inside what will strike us at once is the elegance of the mihrab, he instructs himself.

They go inside to where perhaps men once prayed on rough rugs of camel skin and where boys and girls in cheap goggles take photos of each other on their cheap mobiles. Did they, in the past, live with more awareness of the past than do these excited youths who pay not a moment's attention to what Alif is dying to show them – all this painstakingly created beauty right under their noses, all these arches within arches, this exquisite symmetry, the carved calligraphic verses, the perfection of the stone and marble inlay work. If you don't get down on your knees right now in wonderment, then it's likely nothing built on earth by human hands will ever move you.

And so, once again, medieval glory. Alif does not have to try very hard to humble himself before it. He can't bear to look at her but senses that she's not seeing what he is. She wanders away, back to the gravelled walkways between the lush and sloping swards, the bastions, the pavilions and mosque and bathhouse of this old fort, Purana Qila.

When Alif finally finds her on a bench, facing the ruins of one of the three gates, he can't help telling her, 'Bombastic gates. Like mansions. Look, this one's two storeys, the lower must have been connected to the moat. But that's not the most important thing. Do you know what that is?'

She nods, her expression faintly sad in the weak winter sun.

'That in 1947 thousands of Muslims camped on these grounds to escape the rioting that had taken over Delhi. So did my grand-uncle; he was on his way to Pakistan but they had to wait for permits from the government of that new country. This was a refugee camp after Partition. And I doubt he or his wife or his children were looking at the tilework on that gate or appreciating the merlons between the crenellations on top of that wall. Maybe they were praying. Or fighting every day for a piece of roti. Or trying to avert their eyes from the squalor, the illness, the injuries, the daily deaths around them. Nana said there was no way he was leaving Mehrauli where his ancestors had lived since I don't know when. He would rather risk being killed at home than face the uncertainty and travails of setting up abroad. But his brother took the opposite view.'

'And did he make it?'

'Yes but he never spoke about the hard passage. He would call Nana sometimes but they seemed to have decided to leave alone his horrifying time in this camp. I learnt about it later, at university, through books.'

'I never knew,' says Prerna. 'We used to come here and picnic as children. I remember my father saying this is sacred ground going back to the time of the Mahabharata: the Indraprastha of the Pandavas.'

'Perhaps. But the thing is we aren't usually interested in any history that doesn't concern us directly,' says Alif. 'Look around you. Is there a single stone to commemorate the people, especially the many children, who lived here in those months, who died of cholera and typhoid or of their wounds from the riots, who are buried here?'

'It's anger,' says Prerna. 'Anger and shame that buries things.'

'Which is why I say to my students, the best thing is to dig. Archaeology. Look under your feet. There is no better place than this in all of Delhi to bury the past.'

He presents to her a representative gallery of what excavations into Purana Qila have uncovered: from the Mauryan period, depiction of a horse rider in armour; from the Sunga period, a miniature bowl with an incurved rim; from the Saka-Kushan period, dice made from bones; from the Gupta period, a seal showing a Sassanian fire altar; from the Rajput period, ghungroos made of copper; from the Sultanate period, a shard of glazed ware; from the Mughal period, Chinese porcelain of the Ming era.

At the end of his recitation, Prerna hands back to Alif the book on Delhi he had given her; perhaps she's saying history is delightful but not her thing.

'Ganesh told me about his father. There too a buried past. Do you think it's too late to ...'

'They don't talk much in that family. Can they start now? I don't know,' says Alif, thinking to himself of the silences in his own family.

She nods. 'He told me everything.'

'It was always him, wasn't it?' asks Alif, no longer able to take cover behind history. She seemed to have pulled away from life, ask nothing of it. But today he sees her in a different light. She's been in mourning. She is still willing to stake a great deal. She was happy to see Alif only because it was like seeing something of *him*.

'Why?' he can't help crying out loud. 'Why were you never angry?'

'It seems like a failing to you,' says Prerna. 'But I've accepted it now. I can only live by failing.'

But you don't have to fail so desperately, pleads Alif silently. You don't have to fall so far down. And he recalls what she told him the last time — *we are all fools in our own ways.*

They walk past Sher Mandal, the pavilion that Humayun used as a library; down its stairs he tumbled one evening, dying three days later, thus elevating the teenage Akbar to emperor of all of India. For the first few years it was that canny general Bairam Khan who kept an eye on him, the man after whom Alif's neighbourhood is named. And then he lost the emperor's trust, and Akbar had Bairam Khan killed. Always he sees things through the great mist of these connections, that dense vapour that swirls around his head wherever he goes. He remembers how, when this wise, adult Prerna had appeared before him, he was certain she was part of history too, that she had emerged from some profound work of art. But now she's aloof, withdrawing not just from Alif but also from his fantasies, effacing any and all images he might have created of her.

'Ganesh told me,' she says. 'About your troubles. I can't help, I know, but if you ever need to talk...'

'When are you seeing him?' Alif asks quickly, finding it unbearable, this token offering of friendship, this polite regard.

'Soon, I hope.'

They are at the gate, the grand western gate through which Humayun must have entered, and he touches her lightly on the elbow in farewell and she recoils as if stung but then looks sorry and says she will be in touch.

Alif thinks as he walks away that he was wrong, he does need a line or two to hang himself with. And for once he has no need to ask Cousin Mir for a couplet. For all the thousands of still glittering gems that have been recited in the language, there is only one that every inhabitant of Old Delhi will call up when trying to take the measure of their grief, there is only one that has echoed in these lanes for more than the hundred and fifty years since it was written, or so the belief goes, by the heartbroken last Mughal while he was dying in the faraway exile to which the perfidious British had sent him, and this ghazal says nothing of exile or politics or history – all it says is *Na kisi ki aankh ka noor hoon/ na kisi ke dil ka qaraar hoon/ jo kisi ke kaam na aa sake/ main wo ek musht-e-gubaar hoon*. I'm the light that lights no one's eyes/ and I'm the calm that stills no one's heart/ I'm as good as a handful of dust/ that's how much use I am to anyone.

He is still repeating these lines to himself when he gets home and can't help saying them out loud to Tahira, who is sitting by herself with a book, looking unusually pensive.

'It's just the beginning, things will get worse,' she says.

Alif is so startled he has to leave the room. Then the loudness of the television draws him back to her – she's tuned in to the news but the badness, whatever it is, has now passed, for the moment it's just the weather – and he turns the thing off. Of course it's not Prerna his wife is talking about for she does not and cannot and will not know of her existence.

'I've been trying to call you,' says Tahira.

'Oh,' says Alif, who is not always sufficiently attentive to his phone, who is, all these years later, still unable to treat his phone as an extension of himself. 'It's school, there was some meeting...'

Which is true. There is school and there was a meeting but that was last month. *I am lying to my wife*, thinks Alif. And he's impressed for a moment at how often he's been doing this till he realises he's no good at it and he doesn't enjoy it. She pays little attention to his vacillations in any case.

She gestures at the TV's blank screen. 'What will save us?'

She is tearful now so Alif has to sit down with her and try to find some words of comfort. He takes her hand and looks at the book in her lap. To fortify herself against such a world as this, she is reading *Ikhlaqi Kahaniyan*, stories of good deeds by good guys – usually historical figures like the sultans of various Muslim kingdoms in times gone by. So-and-so Sultan realised one night that he could not sleep in the room where the Koran lay, it would be grave disrespect, so he put it out of the room. But then he felt bad about putting it out because that would be further insult to it. So he didn't sleep at all, thus proving his piety. Or a certain virtuous king did not touch the state coffers for his personal expenses which he covered by stitching caps and writing out verses from the Koran. When his equally virtuous wife burnt her hand one day making him rotis, she asked if they could hire a maid. Impossible, said the king, the treasury belongs to the people. And so on.

Alif's grandmother would tell him and Farouk these tales with their blindingly obvious morals. Why are the upright ones in these tiny, page-long parables – the ones at whom God smiles through some symbolic means – usually kings, or heads of tribes or noblemen? Maybe they were higher-ups because of their virtues and these tests of character in turn proved the rightness of their rule. Alif has long outgrown the little homiletics but Tahira still clings to them with a child's constancy.

'What's happened to you, you're never this quiet?' she asks, feeling his forehead. 'Are you falling ill again?'

He mumbles that he's all right, afraid that if she showed even a touch more solicitude he might break down. But she tells him instead about a job offer she has: inventory supervisor in some big-name make-up and perfume store.

'Should I take it?' she asks.

Alif nods a neither yes nor no nod, thinking of how to broach the subject of his unemployment. He tells her instead about the fiasco with Ahmad.

'He's gone mad and so did my father that day.'

'Why didn't you tell me? All you said is you're sick and staying back.'

Alif tries to hide his own feeling of complicity in the man's having fallen to pieces. He finds it easy to cover it up by dropping him from his life.

'It's over with Ahmad,' he tells Tahira. 'We can't let him into the house. I don't want him anywhere near Abba and Ammi.'

'So who'll look after them?'

'We have to move closer,' he says.

Alif prepares to take on her usual arguments and her old objections, then notices as she ruffles the thin pages of her book, that she is still scared. She hasn't been able to put Greater Noida out of her mind and she has made no mention of house-hunting the past few weeks. Is it slipping from her grasp, that particular sort of modern person she wants to be – someone who lives in a mixed neighbourhood and follows her religion; wears a hijab and drives a car; reads both moral lessons and marketing texts?

Her silence seems to be grudging acquiescence.

'I'll talk to Farouk,' says Alif eagerly. 'He was showing off but he'll bring down the rent, I'm sure.'

She shrugs grumpily, then says, 'I don't know if Ahmad's son when he grows up will gives thanks to your parents. They say they want to save their money for him but what if he one day turns around and says "you should have helped my father instead"?'

Alif suppresses a sigh. She may have accepted that she has nowhere to go and live except among the brethren, but this doesn't mean she's giving up the fight altogether. There is a life-time yet of Tahira versus his parents, his parents versus Tahira.

'Let it be,' he says. And then, though it's the last thing he imagined resorting to. 'Read me a story instead.'

She looks at his features, more miserable than her own, and relents, takes up the book and reads in her clear Urdu diction about a prince who, out hunting, injures a fawn and carries it back home. The fawn's mother turns up at his door and begs for her child to be released, so the prince takes pity on her and lets it go. The Prophet appears to him in a dream to laud him for his kindness and promise him a reward. And then she goes on, reading story after story while Alif is slumped on the settee beside her, wondering at that simpler world in which such men and such ideals held sway, and asking himself if such a world really did once exist.

★

Alif wakes early the following day and calls Farouk who is already busy with his shoe selling but cheerful as ever.

'Subhan Allah, subhan Allah,' he says when Alif informs him of their decision. There is something complacent in his congrat-ulatory tone; he seems to have been expecting it. It puts Alif off and he does not bring up the matter of the rent; Tahira can handle it, Tahira knows Farouk better than he does.

Wife leaves for work, son heads unwillingly to school, and Alif has the house to himself again. He returns to bed and looks through all the messages he has sent Prerna over the months.

If Delhi were ever excavated in the far future they will not be preserved – they are worth less than a piece of broken, carved bangle or a coin from which time has erased the emperor's face. Yet he is loath to delete them or her occasional replies, all civil, all amounting to nothing. How is it possible that a great roaring fire to one can be, to the other, the vaguest suggestion of a breeze? It is possible.

Blinking hard, he gets up to search through the mess of his books and finally finds the one he had borrowed from Miss Moloy. The Maharishi's mention of Ibn Khaldun had drawn him to it, a book he has read before but enjoys returning to: Washington Irving's *Alhambra*, a nineteenth-century account of wandering among the ruins of Moorish Spain. What could be more comforting than an old telling of an even older history? He reads all morning, deaf to the pandemonium outside his window, there with Irving in Granada as he reflects on the golden age of Andalusia. Do they go together, golden ages and ruins, romanticised golden ages and then centuries' worth of ruins?

Just before lunch Farouk calls and Alif decides not to answer, then answers half-heartedly, upset already at the intrusion, unprepared to have to deal so soon with real estate nitty-gritty. Then he sits up and the book falls away from his hand. Farouk is almost whispering; there's been trouble. His father was on his way to Mehrauli to visit a relative and attacked on the metro. Someone objected to his beard, or his language, or his being on the train.

'They've been after us since the protests started.'

'After us?'

'You'll have to leave your classes, I need you in the shop.'

'I'm at home.'

'Turn on the news, for God's sake.'

Alif does and it's all fire and brimstone under the studio lights. Farouk doesn't know where the man is. Some good Samaritan called from his father's phone to tell him what happened: that he was lying bleeding on the platform, that the police were on their way.

'Can you come at once? I need to find him and I can't leave the place unsupervised.'

Alif messages Tahira and then, changing hastily, goes out into the acrid grey of the smoggy day. Farouk ought to have just shut down the store, he thinks, but the businessman in him is practical even in an emergency. On the other hand, coming to his cousin's aid gives Alif something to do; it's better than sitting at home and trying to make sense of this. When he gets there Farouk is on two phones, trying to calm his mother on one, contacting various police stations on the other. Then he rushes out, handing Alif the keys to the cash register and declaring it's all in God's hands.

Alif doesn't know where he should sit. He is not a customer so can't settle down on the low benches meant for them but taking his cousin's place behind the counter feels presumptuous. Thankfully, there are no shoe-buyers around. The two shop assistants are watching him silently from across the low-ceilinged, windowless store with its gleaming parquet floor, while spotlights pick out details in all those rows of single shoes. He looks around, thinking of the shop fixture jargon Farouk had proudly spouted last time. No big deal about this place, he realises. It is like any good-looking shoe shop anywhere in the global world and the leather-scented excitement that had infected him on previous visits seems childish now. He wishes he had brought his book along; the voice of Irving as he makes his way over the imposing and lonely sierras of Granada is still echoing in his ear, and he pretends to busy himself with his phone, certain he will not last very long.

Finally, one of the assistants comes over and pours him some tea from a flask. Another one switches on the small TV above the counter. Alif slides self-consciously into Farouk's chair and watches those tightly knotted huddles of Muslim women again, demanding that the government take them seriously, see them for the staunch patriots and good citizens they are, stop calling them anti-national because here they are, waving flags and holding up banners, reclaiming the nation. There follows a debate and the same thing all over again: *Muslims should, Muslims can, Muslims need to, Muslims are...*

*Muslims.* Something clutches at his heart and then he knows. Those men his father could not save. Cut down on an Eid morning. He must talk to his Mahtab, tell him what would help is seeking out their widows and children. It doesn't matter if they don't believe him or have no use for him. Someone needs to hear the man's crushing dilemma spoken out, soft and clear. That's all. What other attempted salvation can there be?

Two customers walk in whose loud, assertive chat identifies them as young mothers on their way to pick up their children from playschool, stopping by the mall for a spot of late morning shopping. The assistant with the remote promptly turns down the volume on the TV. Alif tries to ignore them, which is how he imagines shop owners are supposed to behave – not too eager for customers who should in turn feel slightly humbled by their indifference. But he cannot help sneaking glances; their way of going over the shoes, trying them on, comparing rates, without breaking the flow of their conversation, as if everything they experience fits effortlessly into the narrative of their lives, or as if they only choose to see and hear that which ruffles nothing. They certainly look like the kind of people who would've missed the news even if it was in their faces; they are those to whom the news, whatever it is, never makes any difference. The men are adept at dealing with them, bowing before them, approving of their choices and yet always having a better choice to present with a flourish, expertly handling their shod feet, unshoeing them, shoeing them again...

Alif sees that there is a minor art in this and he forgets he was meant to be unconcerned and look away till it's time for the payments. In the event, the women, having tried everything from the highest heels to the flattest sandals, buy nothing. They walk out as cheerfully as they came in, still talking of their toddlers' cute habits, without a backward glance at Alif.

'Unbelievable,' Alif says to the men putting away the shoes, their expressions having reverted to their normal neutrality and their movements back to their usual slowness.

'That's how it is,' says one of the assistants, whose name is Latif, and who is moderately chatty unlike the other guy. 'Every second customer makes us run in circles for no good. They come to the mall to have a look around, have pizza, have shakes. Things were different in Farouk bhai's shoe shop in Sarojini Nagar. Only serious customers stepped in. They didn't have time to waste, like these people.'

Alif reflects on how Farouk moved out here to improve his business and up his status but perhaps one is only possible at the expense of the other. Just then he calls and his voice is, as before, low and quavering. His father is dead.

'No!' blurts Alif.

Some misunderstanding, he thinks. Some other dead Muslim. And then for some reason, shame. And then, only then, the first stab of pain.

*Inna lillahi wa inna ilahe rajiuun*, Farouk is murmuring. Alif asks, fearfully, for the details. The police picked him up from the metro stop where he was lying injured and they didn't have too many questions about his attackers even though the cameras in the carriage would have shown them up. The old man was alive – struck down, bashed up, but alive. The boy who had first called Farouk said his father was talking, could sit up, though he was spitting blood and his arm seemed to have been broken. But the police, instead of getting him to hospital, hauled him off to the station. No one knows what happened there but the man is dead; they phoned the family to come and get the body. Had they murdered him? Why? Nothing personal. Just the wrong man in the wrong place, just something anti-national about that look.

Alif, who knows about strife in every land, whole populations, entire civilisations, wiped out by conflict or calamity, finds he does not know what to say. He remembers seeing the old man in that empty flat just a couple of months ago, how the sun and shadows divided his face and rendered it a Rubens or a Rembrandt. And now that he is dead that mild manner seems like a tragedy, his skullcap seems like a tragedy, the weakened old-man knees that didn't support him, the elastic human skin that bloodies at the very first lash, the ribs that are liable to shatter if worked on with a metal-tipped baton, the easily smashable head holding in that easily spillable precious matter, the kidneys that erupt when pierced, the heart whose ticking a violent hand can still – all tragic.

On the TV, the camera zooms in again on the bright-eyed chants of the women, and he winces at the nearness of those faces, he begs them silently to go home. Like Kannagi in that old story, like Antigone in that other one, Alif wants to appeal for justice but there is no one to appeal to, not even reason, not even God. And so how can it be a tragedy – if there is no completion and no catharsis? How can it be a tragedy if there is no knowledge possible to draw from it? No knowledge, only disgrace. It is not a tragedy, it is something else for which he does not have a name even though he's here, right in the middle of it, and his uncle has been killed by it. He asks Farouk if he should come over.

'No, no, you just manage things there for a few days,' he answers in that same muted tone. Alif assures him he will.

He falls back in his seat and phones Tahira to tell her, listens to her shocked silence and then listens to her weeping as she rues over and over again, through grief-distorted words, the suffering of Muslims.

A customer comes in and knows what he wants, makes his purchase in five minutes and pays. Alif unlocks the drawer with the keys Farouk gave him, looks at the loose notes and bowls of coins arranged there. He hands the man his change as Latif prints out the bill.

'It's very easy,' he says and shows him the ins and out of the billing software.

Alif must call his mother but doesn't have the heart to. He sits there listening to the imposing sounds of the world out there: the piped piano music and the satisfied laughter of shoppers, the pinging of elevators and the sales and special offers announcements, and he starts to doubt that, should the wave crash over his head, should the knives fall upon him, he will be able to resist. And why should he? Let my end be what it's always meant to be. It is this thought that, finally, slowly, calms him. He calls Ahmad.

'Have you stopped beating your wife?'

'I'll beat my wife if I have to,' replies Ahmad promptly. And Alif knows this misled creature is wholly lost to him.

'Then you can't have it,' he tells him.

'What?'

'What you want so badly, my money, that's what, you fool.'

And Ahmad immediately drops to his knees, or at least his voice becomes the voice of a grovelling man's. 'Alhamdulillah,' he shouts, praising God before praising his brother. 'Alif bhai, Alif bhai, Alif bhai. I always knew you had a good heart. Despite all your weaknesses. And I only scold Zainab when she speaks too much but you can ask her yourself how many times we've quarrelled in the last one month. Not more than four or five times. In any case I'm going away, Alif bhai. Thanks to your kindness, I will be able to go away.'

'Ammi is going to keep an eye on Zainab. If you lay a finger on her...'

'Of course, of course, Alif bhai. Your family has been my provider and can I ever and would I ever go against what Ammi says?'

'Come over to Farouk's shoe shop in a few days, after the murderers have gone home, and I'll give you a cheque.'

He cuts into Ahmad's effusive thanks and his praises of Allah, telling him to stay away from his parents.

Another customer arrives and asks Alif if they have shoes of a particular brand, one Alif has never heard of. Latif says they do and takes over. When it's time for this chap to pay it comes more easily to Alif – handing over the payment terminal, printing out a receipt.

So is this it, he wonders. Farouk will return in a few days but he might now want, more than ever, to flee the country, take that chance in Dubai. And if he puts the question again to Alif, he won't have a decent excuse – he has no job, is obliged to help his shattered cousin, and must fork out the higher rent for the apartment they're to move into. No good reason to say no. So is this it? A shoe seller. But how will he, as a shoe seller, present himself to Miss Moloy? And the Maharishi, will he laugh? And

Prerna, does she talk to shoe sellers? But there is no Prerna. She is as mythical as a figment of the imagination.

Alif's face is turned away from the news, now on top volume again. He seems to be looking though the open door at the many excitements beyond but what he's seeing as always is the debris of the past, the glintings and gleanings there that forever attract him. Those powerful winds are coming in now – bringing with them not just the cheerful commotion of the mall but also Farouk's broken voice and his wife's keening, and his uncle's last gasps, and his phone ringing with a call from his father. Resist as he will, this remorseless force will propel him into the future.

And then it comes to him, the memorable line of that Mir Taqi Mir poem whose conclusion he had murmured to himself walking in Jamia Nagar with Ahmad that burning afternoon, that well-known lament on Delhi, that Delhi the once chosen, that Delhi the universe's former crowning glory.

*Dilli jo ek shehar tha alam mein inthikaab...*

# Acknowledgements

Many thanks to all the kind folk who have helped me with this novel over the years:

Zac, whose feeling for history and knowledge of the facts are more robust than mine and whose abiding curiosity about the past, as much as his instinct for fiction, spurs me on;

R. Sivapriya, Siddharth Chowdhury, M. Asaduddin, Vineet Gill, Saikat Majumdar and Nafis Hasan for pointed and generous remarks on the manuscript;

Neyaz Farooquee, Anisur Rahman, Harish Trivedi, Taran Khan, Chiki Sarkar, Gautam Chakravarty, Himanshi Sharma, Mohammad Afzal and Fayyaz Ali for talks on Delhi and walks in Delhi;

Eshwar Sundaresan for valuable inputs on corporate life, Ram Guha for books and conversation, Usha Rao for sage advice and sympathetic ear;

I. Allan Sealy who knows what it takes to keep angels going;

Jayapriya Vasudevan for being a trouper, Nigel Newton and Allegra Le Fanu of Bloomsbury for backing this, Charlotte Norman for painstakingly tidying the text.

A lifetime's worth of chats with my mother on her Delhi are one of the sources for this novel. And I'll always be curious about what my father would have made of it.

## About the Author

ANJUM HASAN is the author of three novels and two short story collections, which have been shortlisted for the Indian Academy of Letters Prize, the Sahiya Akademi Award, the Hindu Best Fiction Award and the Crossword Fiction Award, as well as being longlisted for the Man Asia Literary Prize and the DSC Prize for South Asian Literature. Her short fiction and essays have appeared in Granta, Paris Review, Los Angeles Review of Books, among many others.

## A Note on the Type

The text of this book is set in Bembo, which was first used in 1495 by the Venetian printer Aldus Manutius for Cardinal Bembo's *De Aetna*. The original types were cut for Manutius by Francesco Griffo. Bembo was one of the types used by Claude Garamond (1480–1561) as a model for his Romain de l'Université, and so it was a forerunner of what became the standard European type for the following two centuries. Its modern form follows the original types and was designed for Monotype in 1929.